FOOL'S

GOLD

I0634077

PDMAC

Fool's Gold is a work of fiction. Though actual locations may be mentioned, they are used in a fictitious manner and the events and occurrences were created/invented in the mind and imagination of the author, except for the inclusion of actual historical fact. Similarities of characters or names used within for any person – past, present, or future – are coincidental except where actual historical characters are purposely interwoven. The actions, thoughts, and dialogue of the historical characters featured in this story are fictional and not meant to reflect actual personalities and behavior.

Copyright © 2015 by pdmac

All rights reserved
Printed in the United States of America

No part of this book may be reproduced, stored in a retrieval system, or transmitted in any form or by any means, electronic, mechanical, photocopying, recording, or otherwise, without express permission of the author or publisher.

Published by Trimble Hollow Press, Acworth, Georgia

ISBN: 978-0-9861523-0-6

eISBN:978-0-9861523-1-3

Cover design by Trimble Hollow Concepts
Cover art by Gulliver Vianei

for Terri Lynn
my Soulmate and Best Friend

& for gjc
a harmony of unmatched being

A very big *Thank You* to Patricia Moreno, Council Woman and Steampunk aficionado of Tombstone, Arizona for so willingly answering my questions and taking the time to help me in my research.

And another big *Thank You* to fellow Sci Fi author, T. D. Raufsen for his time and efforts in editing this improved version.

Contents

Chapter 1

A shot of whiskey in hand, U.S. Marshal Mason Sadler leaned back against the bar, watching the finale of the stage performer, an attractive woman vocalist singing comic opera. The audience, mostly miners and cowboys, some professional gamblers, and even a few soldiers from Fort Huachuca, knocked back their whiskey and beer, and peered through the fog of tobacco smoke as she pranced and sang in the glare of kerosene lamp footlights. She had a good voice and her overt naughty innuendos had them whistling and cheering. They were there for a good time and raucously applauded for one more encore. As she happily complied, Mason felt a gentle nudge at his side. Looking to his right, he smiled when he saw the very attractive woman, dressed in the latest Parisian fashion.

"*Bonsoir*, Monsieur Mason. *Comment ça va?*" She smiled flirtatiously at him.

"Good evening, Miss Dubois," he said, giving the Bird Cage Theater's Madam a pleasant nod of acknowledgement. Belle Dubois, a buxom blond with piercing blue eyes, was the immediate desire of every miner and cowboy as far away as Tucson when word had spread that a French woman was working at the Bird Cage Theater. They were soon letdown when they discovered she was the madam and not one of the working girls. However, their disappointment was quickly vanquished in the whirling pleasures and enticements of the other girls, gaming tables, dances, and performances.

"She's very good," Mason added, ticking his head at the performer.

"*Oui*, she is. She's here for another two weeks," Belle replied. Catching the attention of one of the crisply dressed bartenders in white aprons, an older man with broad moustache, she said, "Monsieur Jack, a sangaree, please, the way I like it."

"Right away, Miss Dubois," he answered, giving her a respectful nod.

Noticing Mason's look of curiosity, she explained, "I prefer it with squeezed fruit juice instead of water."

"A little too sweet for my tastes," he said, holding up the shot glass as evidence.

"And a little too strong for mine," she smiled in reply.

The performance ended and the girls from the Theater, in colorful tights and extremely short dresses, lined up on stage, linking arms. Casting mischievous eyes at the audience, they waited their cue from the band. Delaying just long enough to create anticipation, the band broke out into a raucous Can-Can. The girls performed with a savage vigor that elicited joyous hoots and cat-calls.

"See anyone you like?" Belle impishly asked.

"Not up there," he bluntly answered, not realizing the implication.

Smiling at his lack of guile, she sipped her drink, pleased with his answer.

The dance number finished, the men wasted little time quickly pushing the benches to the side to make room for dancing. The band began a rousing rendition of 'Turkey in the Straw' and men lined up to pay their quarter to dance with one of the girls. Soon the walls shook with the loud music and foot stomping.

"Don't look," Belle leaned in and warned Mason, "but the man in the black Gus Stetson over by the wall pretending to be waiting in line to dance is a bounty hunter."

Mason casually scanned the dance hall, lingering only for a moment on a man who wore his importance like a scarf around his neck. "Don't recognize him. Probably here for Frank. He still upstairs?"

"He's with Stella in number three," she replied, looking up at the seven upstairs cribs on the opposite second floor that overlooked the dance floor. All of them had the curtains drawn. "He's probably carrying."

"Not my jurisdiction," Mason shrugged. "No weapons is a city ordinance, not a federal one. If Dave Neagle's awake,

I can let him know. If not, I can tell one of the Officers when I take Frank in."

Belle smiled prettily as though flirting with him. "How much is the reward?"

"Five hundred," he casually answered, smiling back. Nodding in the direction of the bounty hunter, he said, "Might as well settle this before our friend over there has a chance."

"I'll send one of the girls up to warn Frank," she said, leaning in towards him and giggling coquettishly as though sharing a humorous anecdote. "He'll come out the back, like usual."

"I'll be there." He inhaled the delicate lilac scent of her perfume, immediately reveling in the fragrance and the closeness of her flawless face, the pert nose and full lips glossed in ruby red lipstick. The way she looked at him, her eyes locked on his as though daring him to kiss her, made him awkwardly stand to full height. Clearing his throat, he downed the rest of his whiskey in one gulp. Pinching the tip of his Stetson in acknowledgement, he nodded politely to her. "See you in a little bit."

Belle's gaze followed him with more than admiration as he nonchalantly ambled towards the door. Mason was a tall, broad-shouldered and ruggedly handsome man who had one glaring defect; he was married. Still, that little fact didn't seem to bother any of the working girls from attempting to get him upstairs, or anywhere else for that matter. Having a wife waiting at home didn't seem to bother far too many other married men, regardless of social stature. Some of her best customers were respected citizens, town leaders, and even lawmen. So why should Marshal Mason Sadler be any different? Yet all their attention and efforts were politely, though with great charm, rebuffed as Mason was an unusual man – he was faithful to his wife, even if his marriage was doomed. Belle had once met the unfortunate man's wife, and even from the brief encounter she could tell the lady enjoyed the bliss of laudanum a bit too much.

Catching the eye of one of the girls, she beckoned her. "Caroline, Stella's in number three," she said to the young doe-eyed girl. "Her customer has a man down here looking for him, a bounty hunter. Tell Stella to take him out the back. Be discreet," she cautioned.

"Yes Miss Belle," Caroline respectfully replied. A few moments later, she was upstairs navigating the narrow hallway between the cribs and the exterior wall. Gently knocking on the door to the crib, she quietly called out, "Stella?" When no response came, she knocked again and called out a little louder. "Stella?" She heard a scraping of a chair across the floor then Stella answered.

"Gimme just a minute," came the muted response.

Caroline patiently waited until finally the door opened slightly and Stella popped her head out. "What?"

"Miss Belle said to tell your gentleman that there's a man downstairs looking for him, a bounty hunter. She said to take him out the back."

Stella opened the door further and Caroline could see Frank rapidly buttoning up his trousers. "Didja hear that?" Stella said over her shoulder at him.

"Yup," he briskly nodded. "Tell Miss Belle I'm mighty obliged." Giving Stella a quick peck on the cheek, he grinned. "Thank you, darlin'. Be seein' you later. I know the way out." Slipping between the two women, he hustled down the hallway and down the stairs to the stage that thankfully had the curtains drawn. He quickly descended down the stairs to the basement, where the non-stop faro game was in full progress, each man intensely focused on the game and his hand, impervious to all else. Hangers-on and those waiting their chance to play mutely surrounded the table. Pushing through the tobacco smoke laden air, he turned the corner and paused before the door that led to the outside.

Inhaling deeply, he gingerly opened the door and took a brisk step out into the night. Giving a rapid scan to his surroundings, he grinned to himself that he had escaped another bounty man. That lasted only a moment when he heard the click of a pistol hammer drawn back, and the cold steel of a barrel from a Colt .45 pressed to the base of his neck.

"Frank Blackwood," the voice spoke. "I'm arresting you for the murder of rancher Johnny Smallwood in Dos Cabezas, Arizona Territory. I suggest you think long and hard about resisting arrest as the warrant says either dead or alive. And I doubt that bounty hunter inside will be as accommodating as I am."

"That you, Marshal?" Frank chuckled. "Thought I recognized the voice. I ain't goin' nowhere, not with that gun o' yours stuck in my neck. 'Sides, I ain't got a gun."

"Fortunately, we don't have far to walk," he said as he nudged his prisoner forward. Making their way behind the livery stable towards 6th street, Mason added, "You be real good. I'd hate to have to shoot you."

"Now Marshal, I know you," Frank calmly said. "You wouldn't shoot a feller in the back."

"Not unless I have to," came the quiet reply.

Just as they stepped onto the boardwalk and turned right, a voice rang out. "You two! Hold it right there."

The two men jerked to a halt. Mason placed a hand on Frank's shoulder and slowly turned him around, putting the outlaw slightly ahead of him, his right hand still gripped his pistol. Standing ten paces away, the bounty hunter stood, his feet spread wide, a gun in each hand.

"Where d'ya think yer goin'?"

"I'm Federal Marshal Mason Sadler," Mason calmly, though firmly stated, "and this gentleman is my prisoner." He pulled his coat open with his left hand to show the star on his chest.

"Wish I had a nickel for every time I heard that one," the bounty hunter sneered. "You think that tin star means anythin'. I've seen that game played out dozens of times, pretendin' to be the law. Don't know who you are mister, but he's worth five hundred. You got five seconds to make up yer mind. Drop the gun. The warrant says dead or alive, and truth is, dead's a heap easier than alive."

Instead of dropping his gun, Mason's hand shot up to point his Colt directly at the man's forehead. "Mister, you're beginning to irritate me. Now the truth is that you might get a shot off… before I plug you right through the eyes. How about I give *you* five seconds to clear out of here?"

The bounty hunter paused momentarily before slowly dropping his hands to his sides. "Sure, sure," he calmly replied. "Don't get excited. I can see I made a mistake. All right then. Have it your way." Taking two steps backwards, he feinted as though turning to leave. When he saw Mason drop his pistol, he whirled around, guns high.

Anticipating the move, Mason shot once, hitting the man square in the right shoulder beneath the collar bone, jerking him spasmodically to the right. The man's surprise abruptly turned to anger, and he twisted back to shoot with his left hand when he felt the jarring impact of the .45 bullet in his left shoulder, along with the retort from Mason's second shot. Standing there slumped against the post holding up the awning that spread over the sidewalk, bleeding from the armpits beneath both shoulders, guns in his hands hanging limply at his sides, he glared at Mason whose pistol pointed again at the man's head.

"You're a damn fool, mister, and you're lucky, this time. I didn't hit a bone, so you'll heal right fine." By now, a crowd had quickly assembled, curious to know what happened. Seeing someone he recognized, a miner who was a regular at the Bird Cage, Mason said, "Hey there Walt. How about taking him over to see Doc Matthews, or whoever's on call tonight. I'll be along in a little bit."

"Sure, Marshal," Walt answered matter-of-factly, regarding the bounty hunter as though he was quite a few bricks shy of a load. "C'mon, mister. Let's get you patched up."

"OK folks," Mason announced to the crowd. "Show's over. Go about your business." With nothing to see, the crowd rapidly evaporated and Mason was left standing with Frank. Walt and the bounty hunter were at the end of the boardwalk, when he heard Walt chiding the man.

"You seriously stupid fella? That's Mason Sadler. Not only is he a federal Marshal, he's faster'n Johnny Ringo. You're dang lucky to be alive."

When they turned the corner, Frank said in a subdued voice, "Much obliged, Marshal. He's the kind that woulda shot me in the back."

"I don't particularly like bounty hunters," he said, slipping his pistol into the holster.

Frank noticed it. "You sure you want to put that away? I'm supposed to be a mean killer. Suppose I try and make a run fer it?"

"Now why would you do a fool thing like that for?" Mason sniffed. "First, I'm likely to beat the stuffings out of you before you got two paces away. Second, if you did happen to escape my reach, you can't outrun a bullet. Now I wouldn't kill you, but you wouldn't be able to walk right for quite a while. Either way, you'd go before the judge looking a lot worse than you are now. Is that what you really want?"

Frank sized up his captor, immediately recognizing the Marshal would make good on his threat. Not only was he half-a-head taller and stronger, what he just witnessed in the man's shooting was enough to convince him. "I suppose not."

"Anyway, I intend to see you get a fair trial," Mason said. "C'mon."

"It was self-defense," Frank self-righteously pointed out as they continued down the boardwalk.

"Just like the other two you shot?" he retorted.

"Exactly," he smugly replied. They turned the corner at Tough Nut Street and headed towards the jail. "How'd you know I was here?"

"Heard there was a bounty hunter in town," Mason lied. "I followed him to the Bird Cage. I wasn't sure where you were in there, but I knew someone would tip you off. Was it one of the girls?"

"I don't know what you mean?" Frank innocently said, not wanting to expose Miss Belle for warning him.

"I'm sure you don't," he said, his voice dripping sarcasm. He was about to reach for the door to the jail when it opened and Deputy Harry Solen, a lithe muscular man, nearly bumped into them.

"Hullo Mason.   Who's this?" Harry asked, quickly recovering.

"Frank Blackwood.   I have a warrant for his arrest. Those gunshots you heard were mine," he explained, pushing Frank to follow Harry back into the jail room.   "There's a bounty hunter over at the docs with a hole in each shoulder. Didn't know you allowed folks like him to carry in town."

"We don't," Harry frowned in indignation.   Retrieving the key ring from the hook on the wall, he cast a cold glance at Frank.   "C'mon you."

"See ya later Marshal," Frank cheerfully said, following the deputy through the door to the cells.

A few moments later, Harry was back, hanging up the keys.   "Mind telling me what this is all about?"

Mason reached into his shirt pocket and withdrew a folded piece of paper.   Unfolding it, he handed it to the Deputy.   "Blackwood's wanted for three murders.   There's a five hundred dollar reward for bringing him in, dead or alive."   He went on to describe the events and the involvement with the bounty hunter.   "The man's a menace," he said, referring to the bounty hunter.   "If I were you, I'd hustle him right on out of town."

Though listening, Harry briefly studied the paper then rummaged through a stack of 'Wanted' papers on the desk, finally settling on one that bore the same caricature.   Sitting down, he pulled out a receipt book.   "I'll take care of both him and Frank," he curtly said.   "Take this to the bank in the morning and you can get your reward."

"Which one?"

"Hudson's.   The one on 5th."

"Thank you," Mason smiled, accepting the receipt.   "You here guarding the fort by yourself?"

"Yeah, pretty much.   I got the night shift this week along with Jimmy Coyle.   He's over sorting out a problem at Dutch Annie's cribs.   Looks to be a miner beat up one of the girls. Jimmy ought to be along any minute."

Mason's lips tightened at the news of the woman's abuse.   Half of him wanted to intercede and teach the miner a lesson he would remember until the day he died, which, if

Mason had his way, would happen sooner than later. Part of him wondered how old the woman was, and how long it had taken her to go from working in a respected brothel to hustling for coins from the dregs of society in a wretched crib.

Harry looked up at him. "You do realize that you've made an enemy of that bounty hunter."

"Won't be the first time," he casually replied. Giving the Deputy a respectful nod, he folded the receipt and stuffed it into his shirt pocket. "You have a good and quiet night." Once outside, he stood for a moment listening to the sounds of the town. It had to be close to two o'clock in the morning, yet the town pulsed with activity. He chuckled wondering how long a town could last that never slept.

An odd noise caught his attention and he twisted his head side to side only to realize the sound was coming from high up above. Craning his neck backwards, he stared up into the moonlit night. The sound increased as an oddly shaped airship came across the sky not more than 200 feet above him. He could hear the thrumming of the engines.

At first, he worried that if he could hear the engines here, the airship was far too low and most likely going to crash. He had heard and read the horrific stories of air envelopes tearing and the weight of the engines speeding the descent. Yet there was something puzzling about this ship until he realized it was actually two very small airships side-by-side.

Then he heard someone above shout, "That's Tombstone down there," followed by "We'll come back here in a couple of days." Another voice shouted back, "Sounds good."

Mason's gaze followed the two ships until they disappeared over the edge of town. Shaking his head in bemusement, he figured they were a couple of crazy machinists out for a joy ride. He knew they were headed towards Bisbee because there were no docking stations in Tombstone.

Deciding he'd have one more drink before heading home, he strolled on back to the Bird Cage Theater. As he languidly walked along Tough Nut Street towards 6th Street, his thoughts turned to his wife waiting at home. Well, 'waiting' wasn't exactly right. Most likely she was passed out on the bed, the bottle of laudanum on the nightstand. Once he got home, she might waken momentarily to berate him for bringing her 'to this god-forsaken hell hole.' Then in the morning, if she was awake, they might have breakfast together, her morosely picking at her food. His once curvaceous wife had become painfully thin. If he complained that she wasn't eating enough, her bleary eyes would then stare at him, barely concealing her anger. Without a word, she'd throw the fork on the plate and go back to bed.

Despite his repeated entreaties to get help, she refused to listen saying she already had all the help she needed. He knew it was only a matter of time before she would be hospitalized... again. He had tried that option once, and once she had improved enough to come home, it took little time for her to return to her former state. With a sigh, Mason turned the corner onto Allen Street, joining the throng of late-night revelers.

As he opened the door to the Bird Cage, dance music and tobacco smoke poured out. It seemed an odd contrast to his ruminations. Here, life was exploding with frivolity and sensual pleasures. Casting a glance around the bar area, he found Belle holding court with several customers. Catching her eye, he gave her a subtle nod before walking up to the bar.

"The same, Marshal?" Jack the bartender smiled at him as he wiped a shot glass clean.

"Thanks, Jack," he smiled back. Through the cacophony of dance music, the stomping feet of whirling dancers, loud chatter, and tobacco filled air, Mason felt relaxed, content with this part of his life. Accepting the glass of whiskey filled to the brim, he took a quick gulp then looked at the half-filled glass. Deciding to treat himself, he waved a finger to get the bartender's attention. "Jack, I'll take some Tennessee whiskey, if you have it."

"Right away," he replied giving him the nod and glance that said Mason knew his drinks.

As he reached into his pocket for coins to pay for the drinks, he inhaled a faint bouquet of lilac and knew Belle had walked up behind to him.

"Your money's no good here tonight, Mason," she announced as she sidled up close to him. "Give him what he wants, Jack, and place it on my tab. I'll take another sangaree."

"You don't have to do that," Mason said.

"I know," she smiled at him, "but I want to. Besides, I don't expect it to cost me much as you don't look like a man who drinks a lot."

Chuckling in reply, Mason lifted his glass in a toast of thanks.

"I heard there's a bounty hunter who won't be 'swinging his partner round and round' for quite a while," she innocently said. Taking her drink, she turned around to lean against the bar and watch the dancing.

"The man's a fool," he replied, shaking his head. Turning around, he mimicked Belle's pose. "One of these days someone won't be so accommodating as I was and will kill him."

"Probably," she nonchalantly answered.

They watched in silence for a while before Mason said, "Things are a bit quieter since the Earps left. I imagine Johnny Behan's glad they're gone."

"I wouldn't bring them up if I were you," she offered. "He's still a bit touchy about what all happened."

Accepting the advice, he said, "I'll get the bounty tomorrow when the bank opens. Do you want your share here or do you want me to come round to the house, like last time."

"I think here would be best. Don't want tongues to wag with you coming to the house too often." She grinned knowingly at him.

"Tongues will wag no matter where we are," he matter-of-factly said.

Belle abstractedly watched the dancing, lost in thought. Then turning to Mason, she asked, "Do you believe someone can come back from the dead?"

"Pardon?" he replied, staring quizzically at her.

"Do you believe someone can come back from the dead?" she repeated.

Blinking as he tried to comprehend the question, he frowned. "What are you talking about?"

"What?" Then she realized what she had asked and giggled. "I guess that was rather a strange question."

"I would say so," he smiled back at her. "You having problems with someone who's dead?" he asked, feigning innocent inquiry.

"No," she answered, giving him a light playful tap on the arm. Directing his attention to a tall, curvaceous red-head enthusiastically dancing with two miners, she said, "You know High Step Annie. She's a local girl. You might remember her father got lynched a couple years back for cattle rustling."

"I wasn't here then," he said, studying the young woman. She looked to be about twenty years old. From the way she danced, he understood why they called her High Step Annie.

"I wasn't either," Belle reminded him, "but I make it a point to know my girls."

"She the one having problems with the dead?" he wryly asked.

"In a way," she coyly answered. "She came to me a day or so ago and said her father appeared to her a few days back."

"You mean like a ghost?"

'Well," she paused. "That's what I thought. But she swore he wasn't a ghost. Said he looked like someone who'd been in the grave for a while."

"And what does someone who's been in the grave for a while look like?" he asked, cocking an eyebrow.

"I don't know," she smirked. "Probably mostly skeleton."

"How'd she know it was him?"

Belle shrugged. "I suppose a daughter knows her own father."

"Sounds to me like someone might be taking too much laudanum." He involuntarily flinched when he said it, for he immediately thought of Elizabeth passed out on the bed in their room.

"A reasonable thought," Belle replied, noticing the reaction and guessing the cause. "But Annie doesn't do that. She doesn't even drink."

"Doesn't drink?" he repeated, surprised. "Maybe that's the problem. So what did her father want?"

"That's just it. She didn't know what he wanted. He just kept waving his finger at her and shaking his head like he was telling her not to do something."

'Maybe he doesn't want her working here," he suggested.

"I said the same thing to her, but she said he used to enjoy the Bird Cage before he was lynched."

"Enjoying it is one thing," Mason counseled. "Having your daughter work here is another."

One of the girls walked up, frowning. "Miss Belle. Sadie's customer is being a bit on the ornery side and wants more than he paid for."

Rolling her eyes, Belle placed her drink on the bar. "Get Billy."

"Need some help?" Mason offered.

"I can manage," she sweetly replied, gently placing a hand on his arm. "I've done this before."

Mason watched her as she gracefully swept away. She was an extraordinarily handsome woman adorned with a pert nose, flawless cheeks, dazzling and captivating blue eyes, and wavy blond hair that was swept up to the top of her head with tight Josephine curls on her forehead. Tonight, she wore a sleeveless and low-necked, tight-fitting dress of mistletoe green that showed enticing cleavage. The dress hugged her body until it reached her narrow waist then flared briefly at her hips before descending in drapes and folds to the floor. Mason watched the numerous men follow her with their eyes then heads as she passed. Far too frequently, he had felt his heart flutter when he was with her, and he had to remind himself that he was married. Still, he couldn't help but be attracted. She was everything his wife wasn't. Lithe and elegant, she was a woman a man could get lost in, even if she was a Pinkerton agent.

Leaving Mason at the bar, Belle gracefully made her way past the cavorting dancers then up the stage steps and turned left to go up the narrow stairs to the individual cribs above the dance floor. Halfway down the hallway, Sally, a slender blonde, angrily stood outside her crib, arms folded.

"He wants it for free," she fumed.

Belle grimly nodded and entered the crib. The miner sat on the folding bench, his arms stiffly crossed. He looked up when she entered. "Is there a problem?" she charmingly asked.

"I paid good money fer this crib and expects to get my money's worth," he said, his chin jutting forward. "I ain't payin' jest to sit here and watch them folks down there dance their fool heads off."

"And how much did you pay?"

"I paid twenty-five whole dollars fer this crib, an' I expects to get what I paid for."

"What you paid for was the use of this crib for the evening," she patiently explained. "Favors and drinks are extra."

"Like hell they are," he sneered. "Tell that whore to fetch me a drink and get back here an' take care of me." Leering at her, he snorted, "Or you can take her place little lady. You look right fine to me. Go ahead an' close them curtains."

Giving him a patronizing smile, she moved forward as if to draw the curtains. Instead, she flicked out a hand and twisted his ear as she jerked him to standing. "First," she firmly said, twisting his ear harder. "She is not a whore. Second, neither am I." Ramming her hand between his legs, she squeezed hard causing him to double over. She then followed with a knife-handed rabbit punch to the neck that sent him crashing to the floor.

Billy, one of the basement bartenders, arrived just as the miner flattened onto the floor. "You OK, Miss Belle?" he asked, half in amusement.

"Toss this crude man out, please," she said, smiling pleasantly at him. "See that he never comes back here." Delicately brushing her hands as if dusting off something unsavory, she brightened. "Now I can go finish my drink with that handsome Marshal."

Chapter 2

Remembering all the people who called him a fool, Caleb sniffed in smug satisfaction when they finally discovered he had outsmarted them all. They had downright laughed at him when he laid claim to a cave not far from the Champion Mines, a cave no one wanted. That was because there was nothing there, they had told him. The cave was nothing more than a fornicating spot for lovers who didn't want their spouses to find out, that he was a fool to be working a claim by himself, that even if he did find something it wouldn't assay out to anything worth the effort. Told him that there was not a damned thing in that cave and instead of wasting his time, he might as well hire out with one of the bigger mining companies.

But Caleb refused to listen to their jabber. Why would he want to work digging in someone else's mine, ten hours a day, six days a week for a measly $4.00 a day? Instead, he had scoured the surrounding hills for nigh three months before settling on this spot, making sure no one else had a right to the claim. When he had found the cave, something told him this was the right place. He had doubts at first because it was obvious the cave had seen plenty of use, at least near the mouth, for there was a small fire pit containing the crumbled remains of charred mesquite, circled with blackened rocks. There were even some food tins, most likely from the soldiers at Fort Huachuca.

The entrance to the cave was large enough for a man to stand and went back a good twenty paces before rapidly shrinking to a gaping hole just tall enough for a man to hunch over to enter. Holding his lantern high, he had carefully made his way farther and farther back, until he was on hands and knees, placing the lantern ahead and scooting up to it as he moved along. Just as the tunnel made a turn to the right, he had noticed it, a slender glimmer in the wall to the left.

17

Pulling out his hand pick, he had chipped out a few small pieces and scooted back the way he came. Examining his find in the sunlight, he knew he had made the right choice.

That was three months ago.

Then two days ago, his luck had dramatically improved.

Placing a toughened hand on the warm rock wall at the mouth of the cave, Caleb squinted in the afternoon's aching bright sunlight. Shading his eyes with his other hand, he slowly took in the wide vista that stretched all the way past Charleston to the southwest. The loud noise of a steam engine starting up caused him to look across the draw to a cave on the opposite hill where just outside the entrance, Henry Mitchell leaned close to an odd contraption that looked like a shrunken locomotive. Instead of the normal train engine wheels, the thing had something like metal conveyor belts that went around cog wheels. Henry listened and studied the machine for a moment, scribbled some notes in a small notebook, then hustled over to sit behind a magnificent mahogany field table under the shade of a well-constructed canopy up the hill. Surrounded by his odd machines, tools, and far too numerous small packing crates, he held a magnifying glass in one hand while furiously scribbling notes with the other.

Caleb studied him for a moment then returned to his scanning once he recognized the man was engrossed in whatever he was doing. Caleb's stomach grumbled and he thought it would be nice to have a real meal again instead of the same old hardtack, beans, and biscuits he had as his staples.

But Caleb didn't have time for lunch right now. He had to think. Turning, he studied the hidden trip wire linked to the tin cans containing loose pebbles that would make enough noise should someone trip the wire. The problem was that he was working too far into the cave to hear anything, especially when he was slinging that pickaxe. There had to be a better way of warning.

Yet, hard as he tried to focus on his self-preservation, his mind kept drifting to his discovery. It had been only two days ago that he had found it, right here in the main cave, right in the open, behind a pile of stacked stones off to the right side of the hole he had been crawling in and out of for these past six months. At first, he had ignored the stones, assuming they had merely tumbled from the cave walls, or maybe someone else had already been here and merely tossed the stones out of the way.

For these past six months, he had worked the claim, slowly and methodically exposing the thin vein, collecting small amounts of very high-grade silver ore and transporting the nuggets to the Corbin stamping mill in Millville. Once smelted to bars, he exchanged these for cash in Charleston right across the river. Yet instead of depositing his earnings in a Charleston bank, he would instead take his money and head out to Tombstone to make his deposits, because Charleston was just too dang close to the rail line, even if the rail line itself was up in Fairbank. Tombstone just seemed to be safer. He was especially careful with the amount he carried, purposely depositing smaller amounts than so many others. He endured their ridicule when they saw what he had. Though he always had enough to meet his daily needs, it couldn't compare to what others plopped down to deposit, especially the larger mines like the Contention or Grand Central.

That was fine with him. All those others who mocked him spent what they made in saloons or whorehouses. Why he knew one miner who spent more time at the Bird Cage Theater than he did at his claim. But not Caleb... he was too smart to squander what he made. If he worked steady and saved, he could be a rich man in a couple of years. That was until two days ago. Two days ago, he had been carefully prying more nuggets from the vein, mentally calculating how much he had in the bank, wondering if he should actually buy a mule for transporting his meager amounts of silver, quickly deciding against the increased cost of maintaining an animal. He would continue to walk the eight miles between Millville and Tombstone to exchange his nuggets and make his deposits.

Henry had asked him several times why he was willing to transport his cash all the way from Charleston to

19

Tombstone, especially as dangerous as it was to carry cash, and besides, Charleston had a good bank as Tombstone. But Caleb was too smart for that. He knew robbery was far too common all along the San Pedro, especially with the trains running the silver ingots up to Benson. Besides, he always made the journey during the day, making sure he used the same route the mule teams used hauling the ore out from Tombstone. And anyway, he was too smart to carry large amounts of cash.

Henry had then offered use of what he called his Motorized All Terrain Engine, or, as he called it, his 'MATE.' It was that strange contraption he was fiddling with this morning, the one with iron conveyor belts running around the iron wheels. Once fired-up, its top speed was about as fast as a horse at trot. Henry controlled it using two levers that allowed him to slow the left or right conveyor belt whenever he wanted. Why he could even make the thing spin in a circle. Henry could even hitch up a metal wagon with large metal wheels to the back of the MATE and carry as heavy a load as eight or more mules, providing the wagon itself could hold the load. But Caleb had no use for such new-fangled things, and besides, he didn't want to be indebted to anyone. Anyway, he liked the walk. It gave him a chance to stretch his legs and be outside for a change.

Two days ago, he had made the walk to Charleston and returned to his camp, thinking he might have enough to make the walk into Tombstone. The thought of a good home cooked meal added justification to the journey. Besides, it'd been almost eight days since his last trip, and Marshal Mason Sadler would be expecting him for lunch. Caleb smiled at the thought. The Marshal was a good man. Why the lawman had taken a shine to him was a wonder, but he liked it. Folks treated him nicer, and those who might not left him alone.

Turning around, his eyes immediately settled on the small canvas bag that lay next to his clothes. The bag held his precious livelihood, and he kept it with him whether he slept or worked in the tunnel. As he walked over to retrieve the bag, he casually glanced at the pile of stones he had seen every day for the past three months. Two days ago, there was something about them that made them look different. He noticed something odd that he hadn't noticed before. They were all uniformly the same size. This caused him to pause, tilt his head slightly to the right, and stare at the orderly pile of stones. As it was too late to make the walk into Tombstone, and curiosity getting the better of him, he tucked the bag under some clothes and walked over to begin prying stones away from the pile.

The pile itself was about waist high and beginning at the top, he pulled a stone down and placed it to the side, repeating the process until he had reduced the top of the pile to about mid-thigh high. When he removed another stone, he noticed it, a thin layer of mud mortar filling a space between the cave rock and a stone below. Quickly moving more stones away, he began to reveal what looked like a walled-up entrance to probably another cave. Feverously removing the remaining stones, he sat back to study the wall before him.

The wall was about as high as it was wide. Taking his small pickax in hand, he carefully chipped away the mortar. When he pried the top stone away, a foul and musty smell gushed through the opening causing him to back away and clear his nose. The offensive odor soon vanished, and he continued removing stones and layers until he had removed all the stones of the small wall. Lighting a lantern, he slithered through the opening. The tunnel's height was about two palms width above his head. He didn't have far to crawl before the tunnel's ceiling gave way and opened up to expose another taller cave.

Standing up, he held the lantern high aloft, sweeping to his right to see what it held. The cave puzzled him at first as there seemed something different with this cave, especially with the uniformity of the walls until he realized it was probably manmade. The walls were cleanly vertical and smooth. Someone had obviously taken a lot of time to make this cave. It was when he swept his light to the left that he stutter-stepped backwards.

The skeletons lay at full length, head to head, breasts pressed against the earth, with the finger bones of the long stretched out arms reaching forward. In between them, just

21

beyond their touch lay a large pile of golden objects, almost mid-thigh high – necklaces, earrings, pendants, cups, plates, and bowls glimmering in the lantern's light. One skull lay on its side, the empty sockets staring at the once walled up tunnel. The other was firmly embedded on its base in the dirt, the dark hallow eye sockets trained upon the pile of gold as though in some macabre taunt.

The men had been dead for some time as the desiccated and mummified bodies revealed. Their clothing, though surprisingly whole and covered in a layer of dust, was nothing he had ever seen before. One man's torso was covered in a thick padded jacket, with bits of tiny metal chain link showing around the edges. The other wore a similar padded jacket, but with slices and tears on the outside. On the dirt floor next to one of the man's splayed legs was a metal helmet with a brim pointed at both ends.

Caleb quickly swept the lantern around in a circle, determined to see if anyone else might be there. His first pass revealed only the dead men and the gold. Gingerly approaching, he held the lantern higher and stared down at the pile of gold. Quickly forgetting the men, he cautiously approached, dropping to his knees to take in the size of the stack. Placing the lantern on the dirt floor, he forcibly suppressed his overwhelming elation as he gingerly reached out to lift up a golden bowl, feeling the heft of the finely crafted workmanship. Barely containing his jubilation, he slowly dug his hands into the loose pile, luxuriating in the touch of wealth. His first inclination was to leap up and dance around the room, but the feel and vision of the gold in his hands kept him rooted to the ground, as did the dead men beside him.

Licking dry lips, he withdrew his hands and lifted up a delicate necklace to better examine it. It was heavier than he realized, and he let the necklace rest on his lap while he selected a pendant decorated with deep blue turquoise stones. Lovingly caressing the pendant, his mind raced at the endless possibilities. He was now rich beyond all his expectations.

It was then he felt the nape hairs rise and goose bumps erupt, as though someone was looking over his shoulder.

Grabbing the lantern and jerking it aloft, he swept it in an arc behind him, twisting his body to catch whoever was lurking in the shadows. But no one was there. It was just he and the dead men, but instead of the feeling going away, it grew stronger.

Carefully placing the items back on the stack, he stood up, turned up the light a bit more and slowly walked the confines of the room, carefully skirting around the corpses. When he was satisfied nothing else was there, he again sat before the gold, the feeling of being watched lessening.

Staring at the neatly arranged pile of gold, he felt giddy and dizzy at the same time. His heart racing near panic levels, he inhaled deeply to calm himself. His mind ached and raced with the possibilities. He was far richer than even he had expected. The reality hit him that he could now do whatever he wanted, buy whatever he wanted, and go wherever he wanted. He was rich! But his elation was suddenly tempered.

There was one obvious problem. How could he remove the gold without arousing suspicion? There was far too much here to take out at once, and he couldn't do it piecemeal like with the silver, for once the word got out that he had found gold, his little claim would be crawling with jumpers. His life wouldn't be worth a damn.

Then again, what about taking it out all at once? Do it once and get it over with and simply walk away from the claim. Whoever wanted it could have it. Looking at the amount of gold, he reasoned he'd probably need at least two or three mules to carry all that weight into Tombstone. Three mules... They'd have to be fed and cared for, for several days at least. Then the obvious hit him – he didn't have enough in the bank for one mule let alone three mules. And besides, even if he could afford three mules, once he passed the other claims and ore trains along the way into town, word would spread faster than he could move and he'd get jumped.

Uttering a soft, "Damn," Caleb rubbed his bearded face, pondering his dilemma. He'd have to give this more thought. There had to be a way to get the gold out without arousing suspicion. He needed to think, but he couldn't do it here.

Staring at his gold was causing him to get distracted, daydream instead of being practical. And if Caleb was anything, he was a practical man.

It was then he noticed something by one man's left side. Reaching down, he picked up a small leather-bound book. Blowing the dust off the dry leather, he decided to take it outside to see what it contained. Holding onto the book as he stood up, Caleb held the lantern high and cast one happy, yet wistful look at his treasure before quietly plodding to the narrow tunnel leading to the main cave. Crawling back the way he came, he slowly emerged into the dim light of the cave. Quickly scrutinizing his surroundings, he saw nothing out of place. Likewise, the weird feeling that someone was watching him had evaporated.

Frowning at the strange feeling, he stood with his back to the opening and contemplated his future actions. Admitting he could do nothing more at the moment, Caleb set the book down with his gear and set to work, carefully replacing each stone, ensuring the hole was completely covered. Grabbing handfuls of dirt, he spread it on the stones doing his best to make it look just like before. He then went to the main cave entrance and sat down, more to clear his head than anything else.

Remembering the book, he hustled back to retrieve it from among his gear. Settling back down near the mouth of the cave, he studied it for a moment. The leather itself was simple, without decoration. The corners were protected by small silver edgings, though the top front one was missing. Gingerly opening it, he carefully turned the first dry page. The writing began at the top of the second page. The script was graceful and fluid. But that mattered little to Caleb, for he as hard as he could, he could make little sense of a single word. Slowly flipping to more pages, he saw the occasional drawing. Towards the end of the book, the writing became less fluid, as though the writer was in a hurry.

Sighing, he slowly closed the book, his frustration mounting as he recognized the little book was another problem he would have to deal with. He would have to keep it hidden lest someone find it and his secret revealed.

That was two days ago.

Here, now, standing in the entrance to his cave, the pile of stones covering his wealth seemed to taunt him. His frustration had grown with each day as he could find no good solution to get the gold out, undetected. The sheer amount of objects would require too many mules, which would draw immediate attention, especially since he had had no use for the dang creatures up 'til now.

A large shadow passed behind him, and he turned around, stepping outside. Shading his eyes, he gazed up at the airship as it slowly passed overhead, its shadow undulating on the hills below as it headed towards Bisbee. Mooring lines dangled from the nose. He could hear the high pitch of the twin motors at the back as the propellers spun furiously, pushing the ship forward. Billowing steam, escaping in short trails behind the engines, quickly dissipated in the dry desert air. From the size and numerous windows on the gondola, Caleb figured it was another passenger ship, sourly thinking it was probably loaded with more miners.

In that instant, he was glad Tombstone decided against setting up a docking field and tower. There were so many claims around the city that there was no space for it. Besides, he didn't need any more unwanted folks traipsing around his claim. Even Bisbee was still too close, but at least some of the new arrivals would get waylaid there and decide prospecting was too much work. The rest would spread out only to realize that just about every inch of desert for more than a hundred miles around had already been claimed.

Distractedly watching the ship disappear, Caleb remained rooted in indecision. He needed to get to town; he was running out of supplies. But that meant leaving his treasure – unguarded. He looked over across the wash to where Henry sat in his tent, the side flaps rolled up to roof level. He couldn't tell exactly what the man was doing, but Henry sat behind his field desk hunched over, his attention focused on an opened book while scribbling on a writing pad. He would pause read a page or two, then scribble some more. Surrounding the tent were the MATE, an empty metal trailer, another metal trailer containing a large machine with a metal lattice framework on top and a metal cone attached to the end, and a few other contraptions he didn't understand.

The man was downright pleasant enough. A fine good-looking man, though peculiar, Henry had his routines. Every Saturday, about mid- morning, he would dress like he was going to church, fire up that driving machine and head into town. He wouldn't return until well after sun-up the next day, looking quite pleased with himself, but worn out. Caleb could always hear that contraption of his and he would wander out to watch Henry come back and head straight to bed and sleep until almost supper time. Then he'd rouse himself up, fix some coffee and fiddle around his desk for a while.

Henry seemed harmless enough and they even had meals together. Several times he shared and cooked a rabbit he had shot. The man certainly liked to talk. When Caleb had asked him why he wasn't spending more time mining, Henry had answered that he wasn't interested in mining.

"Then why in tarnation are you here?" Caleb had responded, dumbfounded at the reply.

"I'm not a miner, my good man," Henry smiled. "I'm an archaeologist."

"A what?"

"Archaeologist."

"What's that?"

"Someone who studies past civilizations," he confidently stated.

"What for?" Caleb asked, not sure he really wanted to hear the answer.

"Why, to learn about the past, my good man," he cheerfully answered. "Our past teaches us about who we were and what happened to cause us to be where we are now. As an archaeologist, I scour the terrain looking for clues of ancient civilizations. When I discover a clue or a shard or evidence of past human activity, I collect it and study it, put it with other discoveries to make sense of what was there before we arrived on the scene."

Caleb stared at him as though the poor man had a severe case of heatstroke. "You took out a claim here, but you ain't diggin' 'cause yer lookin' for somethin' that's gonna tell you somethin' about someone who's been long dead thinkin' he's gonna tell you somethin' about what we're doin' now?

"Exactly."

Caleb studied for a moment wondering if he was about to say it was just a joke, but Henry's chipper demeanor told him the man was serious.   "So, what's here that so dang interestin'?"

Leaning forward, Henry conspiratorially whispered, "Indians." He sat back triumphantly.

"Indians?" Caleb sputtered.   The only Indians Caleb knew were the Chiricahua Machinists whose tribe operated and maintained every machine south of Phoenix. Even the airships that came out of Tucson heading to Bisbee were maintained by the Chiricahua. "What's so dang fascinatin' about them?"

"Why everything," he expansively answered. "Just think – they were here before us, ancient civilizations thousands of years old, some as old or older than the ancient Greeks. Why I've found numerous pieces of pottery in my cave here from the Hohokam civilization.   Would you like to see them?" Caleb's look caused him to laugh. "Perhaps another time, my good man, another time."

"What makes them any different from the ones here now, them Chiricahua?" Caleb asked, frowning.

"Ah yes, the Chiricahua," Henry pontificated, "a most resilient and genius people. Even before Cochise's demise in 1874, they were already well advanced in the intricacies of the modern machine. It was a logical step for them to assume control of the machinist's guild for the southeast part of the territory. But that's not quite the same as the Hohokam, now is it? Why anyone can see the essential, and I might point out, glaring differences." Henry then proceeded to expound on the Hohokam way of life

Despite the pleasure of initial conversation, Caleb grew quickly bored, all the while thinking he wasn't too sure Henry was in his right mind. Thanking him for the meal, he made his way back to the sanity and security of his own claim. After that, Caleb held Henry at arm's length, keeping his distance, but still polite and amiable. That lasted until he discovered that Henry had an ample supply of good Kentucky Bourbon. From that time on, Caleb forgave Henry all his peculiarities.

It became a regular thing at the end of the day. Caleb would emerge from his cave, collect what he was going to eat and mosey over to Henry's. He had refused Henry's repeated offers of sharing his meal as he had his own food. But when it came to Bourbon, he wanted to do right. He had tried paying Henry some of his mined silver for the drinks, but Henry had adamantly refused. He said having Caleb there was far better than drinking alone. Caleb came to eventually enjoy the man's company, even if he did seem a bit too obsessed with dead Indians.

A day or two later, an incessant thrumming noise caused Caleb to rapidly emerge from the cave, only to see Henry tinkering with the large rectangular machine resting on one of his metal trailers. Protruding from the top of the machine was a tall lattice type tower that rose almost fifty feet into the air. Perched at the very top was the cone with a rod sticking out of it. Down below, steam escaped from several vents on top of the iron casing.

Puzzled, Caleb shook his head wondering what Henry was up to now. Brushing his hands on his pants, he ambled down the slope, skipped across the dry stream bed and made his way up to where Henry was preoccupied with his device, his hands gripping a small wheel attached to the side of the machine. Staring up at the cone and tower, he turned the wheel left and right, effectively raising and lowering the tower. Noticing movement from the corner of his eyes, he paused to smile at Caleb.

"Did I wake you?" he called out above the noise, grinning at his own joke.

"What is this?" Caleb shouted back.

Holding his finger up telling Caleb to hold on, Henry carefully twisted the wheel to the left, lowering the tower, until it was about ten feet above them. He then flipped the power switch, and the machine's thrumming dwindled to silence.

"Caleb, my good man," Henry theatrically said. "You are witness to the very first intruder alert system."

"A what?"

"An intruder alert system, or I-A-S. What this little beauty does is tell you when someone is out there." He pointed out over the scrub brush filled landscape towards the direction of Charleston.

Caleb's ears perked up. "How's it do that?"

"The rod inside the cone up there," he pointed, "sends out an invisible electronic signal that bounces off an object and it returns and is collected by the cone. If the object is stationary, like a rock, nothing happens. But if the object is moving, say like a man on horseback, the machine picks up the difference and emits a loud noise telling us an intruder is coming. It can pick up something moving up to almost an eighth of a mile away." He folded his arms, proud of his creation. "Of course, one has to remember it is line of sight, so that anyone slipping in under the signal won't be seen, but that's a small concern considering the sheer brilliance of the concept."

His face a study in concentration, Caleb silently stared at him. He thought he understood, except for one small detail, to which he gave voice. "How can ya hear the warnin' if the infernal thing's so dang loud?"

"I'm working on that," Henry smiled, though not without concern. "In another day or so, this little beauty will hum with the quiet of a humming bee."

Caleb continued staring at the man, wondering how a man could afford to be so frivolous. Shaking his head, he gave Henry a humorless smile. "I got work to do."

A few days later, Caleb saw him out prowling around the mouth of the cave on his claim. In one hand Henry held a large canvass bag with two long wires coming out of it. One ended in a stick-type thing that he held in his other hand. The other wire led to the back of his head, apparently attached to the goggles he was wearing. Henry waved the stick around various parts of the Cave opening, pausing on occasion to kneel down pull whatever it was out of the bag, fiddle with it and then continue on.

Curiosity getting the better of him, he wandered over to see what Henry was doing. As he approached, he could hear clicking noises. Unnoticed he continued watching the man's odd movements. Henry waved the stick, which Caleb now recognized as a long metal wand, near some parts near the mouth of the cave, the clicking increased in tempo. The tempo decreased when he moved the wand away. At the points when the clicking increased, Henry would pause and focus his attention, fiddling with something on his goggles. Turning at one point, he noticed Caleb watching him.

"Morning," he cheerfully grinned, waving the wand at him. Placing the bag on the ground, he pushed down the canvass sides to reveal a device of spinning gears and arcing electric current, all enclosed in a glass case, edged in brass. Twisting one of several knobs on top, he shut off the machine. Sliding his goggles up on his forehead, he stood up, his contentment obvious.

"Now what're you doin?" Caleb cocked an eyebrow at him. "What is that thing?"

"This, my good man," Henry replied, pleased to show off his invention, "is my Residual Cell Emanation Detector, or R-C-E-D." He held up the wand as evidence.

"What's it for?"

"Why detecting cells, naturally."

Caleb stared blankly at him for a few moments. The only cells he knew about were those in the Sheriff's office in Tombstone, and bad folks or drunks were usually locked up in them.

"Cells," Henry explained, seeing Caleb's vacant look, "those little things that make up life. We grow and lose cells every day. The very dirt in your cave has some of your cells in it."

"It does?" Caleb skeptically replied, struggling to think what he might have left inside the cave. Except for the cooking fire, he did everything else outside, to include eating meals and his relieving spot downwind from there.

"Relax, my good man," Henry jovially said. "You can't see them. But I can," he winked, "with this little invention of mine. Here," he announced. "Let me show you." Holding up the wand, he explained, "The wand acts as a receiver. When I point it at a specific location, it collects cellular information on all the life forms that have been there over the years. Now I know what you're thinking. If it collects the cellular information on all the life forms that have been there over hundreds of years, how can I tell what from what?"

Though that wasn't what Caleb was thinking, he gave Henry a lame shrug. "OK?"

"That's where this little amazing device comes in," he proudly said, kneeling down and pulling the glass case completely out of the canvass bag. "This is the residual cell analyzer. It takes the information from the wand and lets me know what is what. See these dials here?" He pointed to the top. "The small one here controls the power. This larger one next to it sorts the type of cells, whether animal or plant or human. I simply set it on the type of cells I want to find, and it eliminates everything but the kind I want. This final dial here is calibrated in intervals of decades. I just select a specific decade, and the analyzer does the rest."

Caleb couldn't decide whether he was impressed or not. The machine seemed wonderful, but frivolous. What was the point of wasting so much time on dead folks? "Do the machinists know about this?"

Henry stiffened. "This is a private, copyrighted invention, the only one of its kind."

"No offense," Caleb reassured him. "Just wonderin', with them all as machinists and all."

Relaxing, Henry nodded. "I understand. While the Chiricahua are certainly a worthy and interesting tribe, the Indians I am interested in predate the Chiricahua. And this device is none of their concern. I don't need some machinist poking his head into my affairs. The last thing I want is to garner unwanted attention here."

"Won't get no argument from me," he readily agreed, his own paranoia evident. He was about to make his excuses to leave when he noticed the odd goggles on Henry's head. Attached to both eyepieces were several smaller lenses that twisted in front of the eyepiece. Pointing, he asked, "What're them for?"

"Ah! These little beauties work with the Analyzer," he answered, taking the goggles off. "The Analyzer tells me where to look. These," he held up the goggles, "show me what I'm looking at. They give form to the data. These little lenses make what I'm looking at appear larger, sort of like a magnifying glass."

Caleb smiled with only his lips. "Guess I better get back," he said, thumbing over his shoulder to his own claim.

"Certainly," Henry smiled warmly at him. "Thanks for coming by."

As Caleb had worked his way down the side of the hill towards the wash, he frowned. What he couldn't make sense of was that Henry was a good-looking man, tall and well built, a man who could have his pick of the ladies. Why he chose to spend his time out here alone poking around looking for dead things was not only foolish, it was unnatural. Caleb wondered if he wasn't maybe hiding from someone, a cuckolded husband perhaps. Still, all this stuff about dead Indians was beyond him. What a waste of time.

Now standing at the mouth of his cave, Caleb was glad he had gotten to know Henry. The man was strange, but harmless, far too preoccupied with his silly research. Still, the man appeared to be one he could count on. Looking back at the pile of stones hiding his future, he decided he had no choice but to go to town in the morning. He was down to his last bit of grub.

When he got into town, he knew he would have to appear as though nothing was different. That meant making his deposits, taking lunch with the Marshal, and a bath this time. It'd been at least a month since the last one. Then he'd collect his supplies and head on back, no one the wiser. Ruefully wishing he had more supplies at hand, Caleb ruminated about his problem. He was rich but was stuck here until he could come up with a sound way of transporting and figuring out how to exchange his gold. He had even thought of enlisting Henry's help. But asking him to look after his claim while Caleb went to Tombstone was one thing; entrusting him with his secret was quite another.

Chapter 3

Sitting behind his field table inside the cool shade provided by the tent, Henry uncorked the leather bota bag and took a satisfying swig of water. Stretching his legs out in front, he recorked the bag and nestled in comfort against the padded leather of the foldable chair. A warm breeze filled the wash causing the tent to flap a bit. Lifting his notebook, he reread his recent entries. He knew he was close; all the readings indicated activity, but he needed Caleb to make his trip into town so Henry could see what lay on the old man's side of the wash.

Lifting his eyes to look across the divide, Henry chuckled. The man was an odd old coot, though probably not that much older than Henry. Yet Caleb looked like he had been 'rode hard and put up wet,' as the saying went. 'Grizzled' was the word that came to mind. 'Paranoid' was the second word that seemed to fit, especially these past few days, for anytime Caleb emerged from his cave, he had this ritual of first halfway hiding behind the pile of rocks that he had carefully placed at the mouth of the cave. From behind the protective barrier, he would slowly scan the entire area until he was satisfied there was no evil lurking close by. Then he would skip around one side as though catching someone about to jump out. Only when he was satisfied no one was around, would he calmly go about his business.

Looking back at his notes, Henry rubbed his stubbled chin. After so many years of painstaking research, he knew he had to be in the right area. Flipping halfway back in his notebook, he opened it wide to gaze at a meticulous hand drawing of the Arizona and New Mexico territories that spread across both pages. Of particular interest was a thin line that began at the bottom left page and snaked its way across both pages. At the bottom of the right-hand page was a note: *Route of march of Francisco Vazquez de Coronado in search for the Seven Cities of Cibola.* He flipped the page to another drawing that concentrated on the southeast portion of the Arizona territory. The line of march passed very close to Tombstone.

Flipping several pages, Henry read the entry at the top of the left page. *Captain's log of the San Cristobal, September 4, 1542, Can no longer wait for Diaco de la Fuente. Will sail on the prevailing winds.* Henry inhaled a deep breath. Such a simple entry was so misleading. Who was Diaco de la Fuente, and why was he so important to warrant an entry into the captain's log? Such a simple entry that could so easily be overlooked. What the entry did not say was that Diaco de la Fuente was one of Coronado's lieutenants who had crossed the Southwest territories looking for those seven cities filled with gold, silver, and precious jewels.

Below that entry was another lengthy entry that went for quite a few pages of tightly handwritten script. It was titled *An account of the expedition to Cibola which took place in the year 1540, in which all those settlements, their ceremonies & customs, are described. Written by Pedro de Castaneda, of Najara.* Though the original had been lost, Henry had discovered a copy written in 1596 in the Lenox library in New York City. He had painstakingly copied the entire account. What was most significant was de Castaneda wrote in the second chapter about three Spaniards named Cabeza de Vaca, Dorantes, and Castillo Maldonado, and a black man named Esteban, who all had become lost on the expedition that Panfilo de Narvaez had led into Florida. These four eventually reached Mexico. They came out through Culiacan, having supposedly crossed the country from sea to sea. They related in significant detail about some powerful villages, rich in gold, silver, and precious jewels, with houses four and five stories high, of which they had heard a great deal from the Indians.

With the excitement stirred from their accounts, a second expedition was mounted, led by Marcos de Niza, a Spanish priest. Esteban went with de Niza, eventually forging ahead and leaving the expedition behind in the hopes of being the first to discover the fabled cities. Esteban was treated royally along the way and by the time he reached Cibola he was carrying a large quantity of turquoise the various tribes had given him, along with some beautiful Indian women who followed him and carried his things. Unfortunately, Esteban met his death at the hands of the Indians from the town of Hawikuh, one of the seven cities.

When de Niza reached Cibola, he was not allowed into the cities and forced to return. However, once safely home, he claimed that he saw Hawikuh from a distance and said the village appeared large and very wealthy. His report led to an expedition headed by Francisco Vasquez de Coronado in 1540 to find the cities and claim their wealth for Spain. Frustrated in his search, Coronado captured six villages in the area he believed de Niza visited and called them Cibola. He found nothing more after that and returned to Mexico in 1542.

Sighing, Henry settled into his cushioned chair and gazed at his surroundings. Scattered across the hills, the tall and spindly ocotillo cactus was in bloom with bright orange flowers. For some reason, the color reminded him of gold. Then again, everything these days reminded him of gold, and with Caleb's odd behavior these past few days, he was sure the old codger had stumbled onto something. Inhaling the clean morning air, he wondered what he could do or say to get Caleb to leave for long enough to get over into the cave and see what was there.

Unable at the moment to think of a reasonable idea, Henry returned to his notebook. Though pretending to read, his mind was elsewhere. From his studies, he knew that the Aztecs had a legendary homeland called Atzlan where they believed the first people had emerged from caves – seven caves to be exact… the seven cities of Cibola. It was a revered place that held immense riches.

An entry in his journal caught his attention.

1542 – Coronado's journal - Diaco de la Fuente is missing, along with at least four other conquistadors. Coronado sends back several men to look for them. De la Fuente and men never found. Not until Coronado is home does he discover de la Fuente and others have set out on their own to find Cibola.

Sighing, Henry closed the book. When he had lost track of de la Fuente from the Spanish sources, he pursued the Indian traditions and stories, especially those of the Tohono O'odham. The stories of conquistadors abounded, but they all had one underlying theme – white men in strange costumes laden with gold, silver, and dazzling jewels. Finally, after all the years of research and wandering and studying had led him here. How ironic that after all the time spent in Spain and Mexico that he should find the end of his quest in the United States.

Looking back up, he saw Caleb going through his routine. Softly chuckling, he watched the antics with enjoyment. Yet for all his humor, there was a growing impatience. It had been over a week since Caleb's last visit to Tombstone. The last time, Henry had waited an hour before gathering up his Residual Cell Emanation Detector only to discover that once inside Caleb's cave, the damned thing had a disconnect somewhere and wouldn't start. Lugging the device bag to his camp, he had spent the rest of the day taking it apart and fixing it. To his dismay, by the time he had it fixed, it was late afternoon and Caleb was already walking back along the path next to the small wash between the claims.

Fortunately, Caleb was a creature of habit. Every eight days, the miner would rise early, shoulder his pack and trudge across the wash. Standing outside Henry's tent, he would perfunctorily ask, "You awake Henry?"

"Yes, Caleb," Henry would reply from the comfort of his cot.

"I'm fixin' to go to Tombstone. Get you anything?"

"No thanks, Caleb. I'm good."

"Mind lookin' after my things while I'm gone?"

"I'd be happy to. Have a good time."

"Much obliged."

Caleb would then amble off while Henry tossed off the covers and got up to fix some coffee. But the eighth day had come and gone, and Caleb was still here. In fact, it was day ten and Caleb was still here. Henry knew Caleb's supplies had to be running low. Something had happened that made him suddenly skittish about leaving. Henry had an idea, but he needed Caleb gone to find out.

Movement off to his right caught his attention. Up the wash a distance away, a rider was approaching, his pace unhurried. As the man got closer, Henry recognized Marshal Mason Sadler riding a beautiful chestnut Morgan. Waiting until he was about a hundred yards away, Henry gave him a friendly wave, which was returned in kind. Mason tugged on the reins and led the horse across the wash, splashing in the small stream courtesy of the Grand Central pumping plant.

"Afternoon, Marshal," Henry cheerfully greeted him.

"Afternoon, Mister Mitchell. How're things?" Mason remained in the saddle, leaning forward, his cobalt blue eyes looking at Henry, but scanning the area at the same time.

"Just fine, my good man," he replied. "I've found some very interesting artifacts." Henry inwardly chuckled at Mason's affected lack of interest, all the while taking in the various machines and gear.

Mason then looked at the packing crates neatly arranged in uniform stacks at the mouth of Henry's cave. A number of them on top were open with the straw stuffing visible. "Seem a might small to be of any use."

"That's because they're for smaller items," Henry obligingly explained. "Here, let me show you." He popped up, went to one of the crates and tenderly lifted a small clay vessel with red geometric designs surrounding the sides. "I found this just the other day. Because it's so rare to find intact larger pieces, this is about the largest I get. On the occasion that I find a larger piece, I simply make a larger crate." He held it up for the Marshal to see. "Isn't she a beauty?"

"How old?"

"Probably five to six hundred years old," he proudly announced.

Mason nodded in admiration. "All those crates have something in them?"

"Only about half," Henry replied, "though not all of it found here. Some are from Benson, others from up near Tucson. Once I've finished here, these all get shipped back to the university."

"University," the Marshal mused, impressed. "And which university would that be?"

"Why Brown University, my good man," he boasted. "Best archaeological department in the world."

"Didn't realize you were from back East."

"Actually, I'm an Ohio boy. Born and raised in Bellefontaine. Moved east when the digging bug hit me hard."

Giving the man a congenial smile, he asked, "Caleb around?"

"He's around," he smiled back. "I last saw him just a few minutes ago. I believe he's probably still in the cave."

"Appreciate it." Mason took a glance at Henry's MATE. "Interesting machine."

"Thank you."

"What do you use it for?"

"Just about anything," Henry expansively said. "It can go anywhere a horse can, and I don't have to clean up after it." He smirked at his own joke. Mason gave him an obligatory smile in return. "By attaching a trailer to it, I can haul heavier loads than ten mules can carry. If I need to get some place in a hurry, I simply crank her up and off I go. I even take it to town on occasion when I need supplies.

"I know. I've seen you. Creates quite a stir each time you're in town."

"I hope that's not a problem, Marshal," he amiably said.

"Not at all. Seems like something new is coming into town all the time."

They both paused and looked up when they heard the noise. Another airship was headed towards Bisbee.

"That's the second one today," Henry said, watching the airship with a mixture of curiosity and admiration.

"Looks like a cargo ship," Mason opined. "Only windows on the gondola are in the front."

"Ah, to be able to fly like the birds of the sky," Henry wistfully admitted. "I've been down on terra firma too long. I must return to the skies."

Mason turned to look at him. "You've flown in one of those?"

"Across the Atlantic and back," he triumphantly replied.

"You'll have to tell me about it some time," he amiably said.

"With pleasure, Marshal. Perhaps when I'm in town next, we can sit and enjoy a drink or two."

"I'd enjoy that." He cast a quick glance over his shoulder at Caleb's cave. "Guess I'd better check up on him. You have a good day." Mason turned his horse around and headed back across the wash.

Henry watched the man ride away, smiling at the man's easy nature. Little seemed to bother him. Even in some of the reputed gunfights he had heard about, Mason was always the cool, calm lawman, saving lives and settling scores. Broad shouldered and handsome in an unaffected way, it was said that Mason was always polite to the ladies, but he had an interest in one special – Belle, the French Madam of the Birdcage. Henry chuckled to himself, knowing Mason was married.

Watching Mason still atop his horse, chatting with Caleb, Henry grinned in admiration. Belle was a stunner. Oh, he knew she wasn't really French. He had been to France and could tell a native from what she pretended to be. Sure, she knew enough French to carry on an elementary conversation, but nothing more intricate than small talk. He had tried the first time he met her, and nearly exposed her secret. Quickly realizing her limitations, he had suavely changed the tone and direction when he complimented her on her excellent command of English. Quickly recognizing that he not only knew, but would keep her secret, she returned the compliment concerning his French. From that point on, he was careful to play her game and in reward, she gave him very good deals on the girls.

That was enough for him. He wasn't going to spoil her hustle. Besides, unlike her, he wasn't planning on staying in this god-forsaken dump of America called the West. Once he found what he came for, he was going back East, back to civilization and culture.

Henry drifted into reverie as Mason gave Caleb a friendly nod, turned his horse and lazily headed back to Tombstone. Caleb didn't wait long for Mason to leave before heading over to see Henry.

"The Marshal said he was just checkin' up on me, seein' as how I ain't been into town like usual. So I'll be leavin' first thing in the mornin'. You mind lookin' after my things while I'm gone?"

"Be happy to," Henry reassured him. "I'll even hoist up the old IAS to make sure. Be sure to stop by tonight for a nightcap."

Satisfied, Caleb nodded his thanks and said he'd see Henry later. Returning to his claim, Caleb scanned the arrangement of his possessions. All were neatly organized according to function, with cooking utensils close by the fire pit, digging tools and implements near the mouth of the opening at the back of the cave, and his clothing over by his sleeping area. He had hidden the book in one of the haversacks containing extra clothes.

Though he was making ends meet with his claim, the thought of how to dispose of all that gold still eluded him. Perhaps he should talk to Mason about it? Mason was honorable and trustworthy. The more he thought about it, the better he liked the idea. He liked the Marshal. Every time Caleb went into town, the Marshal was always friendly and even bought him a lunch now and then. And didn't the Marshal come all the way out here just to check and make sure nothing had happened to him?

Making up his mind to tell the Marshal, Caleb relaxed for the first time since he found the gold. He knew Henry would be leaving later on today for his weekly Saturday night visit to Tombstone and he wouldn't be back until tomorrow morning, that infernal machine of his making enough noise to wake up the dead for miles around. Hopefully he wouldn't be too sauced to watch over Caleb's claim. The man was harmless enough and it was highly unlikely he'd stay awake once that people-finding thing was turned on. Caleb remembered the sound the IAS emitted and knew it was probably enough to scare off most folks.

Rubbing his hands together in uncontained glee, Caleb danced a silly jig and hooted.

Belle Dubois stood in the teller line at what once was the Pima County Bank and now known as the Cochise County Bank. The building housing the bank was just six months old, the original having been destroyed in the fire not quite a year ago. They had spared little expense in rebuilding it. The front double doors were twelve feet tall and set obliquely across the northeast corner of the building. Inside, the desks and counters were black walnut and mahogany, and beautifully finished to a glistening sheen. Even the attitude of the tellers seemed to improve with the enhanced furnishings.

Yet what Belle appreciated most was the vault. Steel lined with iron netting, it was said to be both fire and burglar proof. Access was controlled by two combination locks and a time lock. As her accounts grew, so did her appreciation for her financial security.

When the Agency first sent her here, she thought she had been exiled to the remotest part of the world to live among the dregs of mankind. That thought had quickly evaporated in the milieu of the wealth that flowed in and out of Tombstone. Charged with thwarting criminal activities in the border region between the US and Mexico, it had been her idea to go undercover as a Madam knowing that liquor and women make even the most reticent man a talker. What better place to gather information than a brothel? As Tombstone was the beehive of activity, she had settled on the town as her center of operations.

A quick survey told her that the Bird Cage seemed to do the most business. She approached the owner, Billy Hutchinson, and took him into her confidence. He had been more than willing to assist, and more than a little pleased to have someone else deal with the girls. Assuming her persona, Belle thrived in the role, as did the business at the Bird Cage. Belle not only took the Madam's cut from the girl's earnings, the Agency paid her monthly Madam tax.

It was only a month after she began her role as Belle Dubois that she met Mason, recently appointed US Marshal in the Arizona Territory. That first meeting had been memorable as he was accompanied by his wife who referred to herself as 'Missus Sadler,' not 'Elizabeth' or 'Beth' or some other friendly moniker, but 'Missus Sadler.' Belle's first inclination was to tell her to get off her high horse and come down where the real people live, but instead she smiled sweetly and pretended no affront. She chatted amiably with them both, giving flirtatious attention to the handsome Mason, much to 'Missus Sadler's' irritation. The interaction did much to add to her persona as a woman of low repute.

Even now she felt the condemning glances and sibilant whispers of many who likewise stood in line, mostly the few gentrified ladies whose airs of superiority would be crushed if they knew how many of their husbands were frequent visitors to the Bird Cage Theater or one of the cribs on the other side of 6th Street. Then a voice spoke, just loud enough to ensure she was heard.

"You'd think they'd have a care about their reputation."

Turning, she caught the haughty eye of the one who had given voice to her thoughts, a plump woman known for her devout church work. She was the kind of person who ensured all knew of her piety. Belle choked back a laugh for the woman's husband was not unknown at the Theater. The woman and another lady, an obvious friend, gazed upon her with overt loftiness.

"Ah, Madame," Belle smiled at her, her eyes brimming with feigned admiration. "You are so right, *n'est pas*? If only more women were like yourself, so full of love and charity. Had I such a mother like yourself, I would not be here today. I never knew my father. Because my mother was so poor, she could not afford to keep me. So she sold me –"

"Sold you?" the woman said, aghast.

42

"*Mais oui*," Belle shrugged. "She needed the money. Who can afford to feed twelve children when one is poor?"

"Your mother had twelve children?" the other woman interjected, blinking in shock.

"*Oui*," she nonchalantly replied. "But after selling the rest of us, she was able to find a nice place with a garden just outside Chaumont. She so loved that garden."

"Your mother sold her children?" the first woman gasped.

"*Oui*," Belle replied, as though the act was an everyday occurrence. "How else could she afford the nice place with the garden?"

"But, but…" she sputtered.

"Oh, I know," Belle commiserated. "One has to be careful when one sells children. If the price is too high, no one will buy. And of course, if the child is sick, one must wait until it returns to health for no one wants a sick child. It's far better to sell a healthy child, the plumper the better. Sometimes though, it is better to get rid of a sickly child, otherwise it is too much of a strain for the medicine, *n'est pas*? A simple pinch of the cheeks," she grinned knowingly, squeezing her thumb and forefinger in demonstration, "will give color to the cheeks."

A stunned silence enveloped the listeners until one ventured to ask, "What happened to you then?"

"Ah," she sighed in regretful memory. "I was sold to a fabric merchant, an old man with garlic breath. He was an evil man who beat me, for I did not like sleeping in his bed."

"You, you… He made you sleep in his bed?" the woman asked, her disgust mixed with a pale queasiness.

"*Oui*. He liked me to keep him warm. But his breath, and he made the gas too much…" she waved her hand in front of her nose. "It was too much for me so I run away. But I cannot run far enough, for the gendarmes, they find me and bring me back. So I run away again. I say to myself, 'He is a pig. I will find a job and find a place to live of my own. After all, I am ten years old. I am old enough for work.' But the gendarmes find me again. This time he locks

43

me in the basement and waits until they are gone. The next day I am sold as a slave."

"A slave?" the woman sputtered.

"*Oui*," she simply said, "to an Arab prince in Beirut who like my blond hair. He keep me locked away in his harem, until I was old enough to, um… how do you say," she flicked her eyebrows up and down several times accompanied by a forward thrust of her hips.

Instead of speaking, the woman's mouth slacked open.

"I stay in the harem for a while, but the others did not like me because I am young and beautiful. I was sixteen when I run away. The prince, he goes to Paris and takes me with him for I speak the French, *n'est pas*? On the second day, I run away, as fast I can, for I know Paris. At first, I was not missed. Surely, it is sometimes hard to keep track when one has fifty wives."

"He had fifty wives?"

"Those were just the one he brought with him. The rest, they were back in Beirut."

"He had more?"

"*Mais oui*," she smiled innocently. "He was a prince. Ah, but once I was discovered missing, he sent his spies throughout all of Paris and France, and I was caught on a train to Lisbon. Brought back to the harem, he had me chained and whipped. I vowed then that I would escape. Fortunately for me, the ship we sailed on out from Marseilles was attacked by pirates and in the fighting, I jump overboard. But I was not a strong swimmer and the pirates, they caught me. The captain, he liked me and made me his wife."

"You were married?"

"Just pretend," Belle explained, "so the ship's crew would not use me. Well, except for that one time… there were six of them, all strong and handsome." Her eyes glistened with pleasure at the memory. Seeing the woman's reaction, Belle quickly turned away, pulling out a silk hankie pretending to dab her eyes as she struggled to contain her laughter. Fortunately, she was saved by the teller.

"Afternoon, Miss Dubois. Can I help you?"

"*Mais oui*," she cheerfully said, opening her purse and handing him a banker's check. "Deposit this into my account, *s'il vous plaît*."

Belle waited patiently while the teller verified the check with his supervisor whose awkward demeanor said he hoped Belle would be discrete enough not publicly announce his frequent patronage at the Theater. Flourishing his pen, he quickly approved the check, and then hurried off to find something to do in the office, closing the door behind him. The clerk carefully wrote out the deposit on the summary sheet then wrote out a deposit receipt for Belle, listing the amount deposited and the total in the account.

"*Merci*," she smiled as she read the growing amount in her account. If the future continued like the present, she could retire in style while she was still young enough to enjoy it. Being a Madam was turning out to be far more fun than she expected.

Turning to leave, she smiled graciously at the woman, "*Au revoir*, Madame." Leaving the woman to absorb the wild tale, she waited until she was outside before snorting a laugh. She could only wonder what the yarn would be like in the retelling. At the same time, she heard the approach of the archaeologist's traveling machine. Looking up Allen Street towards the Theater, she saw Henry's MATE chugging in the distance, the clanking of the metal belts loud as they spun around the cogged wheels. Steam poured from the engine spout. Turning onto 6th Street to park his machine behind in the empty lot by the miners' cabins, Henry shut down the machine and leaped down from the platform. He was in the Bird Cage before Belle was halfway down the boardwalk.

Belle nodded appreciatively. Henry was a good-looking man with close-cropped auburn hair and deep brown eyes. He was refined and carried himself as one who had a privileged upbringing, which was also evidenced by his university education. In fact, he was educated enough to know that she wasn't French. Initially caught off guard, she had quickly recovered when he had gallantly covered her secret with a compliment of her command of English. He had given her a wink, effectively saying 'I know you're not French, but it's a great hustle.'

They came to an immediate arrangement. Henry wisely kept his knowledge to himself, and in return, he was treated like royalty. His sophisticated attitude, extroverted personality, and elegant clothing made him a welcomed guest. Though he stayed away from the Faro tables, he was known to wager on the horses. Word had it that he was quite successful.

Belle liked the man and the fact that he was single only added to his attraction. Had she not been undercover, she might have yielded to his attentions. Yet there was something about him that made her wary. Perhaps it was his confidence, or rather his over-confidence. Over-confident men were usually in love with themselves too much.

Still, he was an excellent customer. She could count on him spending at least $100 every Saturday night. He treated the girls especially well, finding some small trinket to give them after a session. As he had expressed no preference to a particular girl, Belle spread the wealth and ensured all the girls had the opportunity and benefit of his attention. More often than not, he simply wanted their company as they enjoyed the performances and dancing. He was such a good and consistent customer that she reserved Russian Bill's upstairs crib for him.

Poor Russian Bill had got himself hanged last November over in Shakespeare, New Mexico territory for stealing a horse. It had been a great disappointment for the Theater as the man had reserved the same crib every night for the longest time. At $25 a night, it was a nice steady income. And the fact that he was a good-looking man didn't hurt. Still, he was a strange one, pretending to be such a rough and tough desperado. That the man had a quality education was evident when he would occasionally lapse into quoting Shelley or Keats. And his manners bespoke one raised in a cultured environment. Pity he got himself hanged. Seemed such a waste of all that education and training.

With a shrug and a sigh, and while ignoring the indignant looks of the proper ladies of the town, Belle gracefully made her way towards the Theater, wondering if Mason would stop by tonight.

It was late and Belle had resigned herself that the good-looking Marshal was too preoccupied with his home life when he strode in through the doors. Though he attempted to appear indifferent, she recognized the look of someone unhappy with a part of his life. The fact that he was here at this hour meant he and Elizabeth had another "disagreement." The woman was a damn fool, she silently mused. A part of her wished Elizabeth would do everyone a favor and take enough of her laudanum to finally push her over the edge. Realizing what she had just thought, she silently chastised herself for being uncharitable. Then again, she grinned, she was a madam and didn't have to worry about being charitable.

"Hello Mason," she said, smiling at him. "I was wondering if I was going to see you tonight."

"Not much going on," he replied with a shrug, "Thought I'd come to my favorite place and have a drink." Jack placed a whiskey in front of him and moved off to serve another customer. Lifting the shot glass, Mason stared at his reflection in the mirror behind the bar, frowned and drank the contents in one gulp.

Belle let him brood a bit before gently asking, "Do you want to talk about it?"

"Not much to talk about," he said, lifting the shot glass for another for another round. Twisting around, he took in the raucous joy of those dancing, drinking, flirting with the girls, and gambling. "Seems to be a good crowd tonight," he observed, changing the subject.

His attention was diverted when he saw Henry descending the narrow stairs from the cribs above. He was dressed elegantly in a cutaway morning suit with a dress shirt and ascot tie. Several girls followed him to the bottom of the stairs, giving him a kiss on the cheek. His eyes brightened upon seeing Mason.

"Marshal Sadler," he grinned as he made his way across the room. "Fancy seeing you here. What a pleasant surprise."

"Evening, Mister Mitchell," he politely replied.

He waited momentarily while the bartender loaded several bottles of beer onto the dumb waiter then yanked on the rope. While the girl upstairs hauled up the drinks, Henry held up a gloved hand to get the bartender's attention. "Bourbon, if you please, my good man." Turning his attention to Belle, he suavely said, *"Bonsoir, ma jolie hôtesse. Vous êtes très belle ce soir."*

"Merci, monsieur," she nodded with coy acceptance.

"Isn't she beautiful, Marshal," he grandly said, still looking at Belle.

"Yes she is," Mason replied, suddenly feeling awkward as though intruding. Quickly downing his drink, he placed it on the counter with firm clink of the glass. "You folks have a good night."

He was about to move away from the bar when Belle chirped, "Leaving already? You just got here."

"Yes Marshal," Henry said, turning his head to smile at him, his countenance exuding the confidence of one in control. "Why not stay a while longer. We can have that chat I promised you about my trip across the ocean in the airship."

"You went to Europe in an airship?" Belle marveled.

"That I did, my ravishing hostess," he gallantly replied.

"What was it like?" she asked, her blue eyes blinking with fascination.

Henry inwardly smiled when he saw the Marshal's lips purse in response to Belle's rapt interest. The lawman was out of his element and Henry was enjoying putting him in his place. "It was, how shall I say... uneventful. We left the airfield just outside of Boston and flew along the coast to Nova Scotia then up to New Foundland and then out over the waters of the vast Atlantic. I must say that the views of the coast were majestic. Four days later I was dining in Paris."

"And the airship?" she said. "What was it like?"

"Ah, the airship," he smiled in reverie. "It was called the Chalais Versailles, accommodating almost 200 passengers and crew. All the passenger cabins had large windows to look out over the vast scenery. And the cuisine! Ah! *Il était magnifique!*" He kissed his fingertips before spreading his fingers in a burst. Casting an amorous glance at Belle, he urbanely said, "Imagine what an experience it is to be standing in the prow of this great airship, miles high in the air, a glass of the finest champagne in hand, and watch the sunrise. And then, when the sun has filled the sky, toast to another glorious day and then sit to a breakfast of caviar and eggs benedict."

"Sounds exciting," Belle enthused.

Mason watched the change with growing annoyance. That Henry captivated Belle with his story only added to the annoyance. "You'll both have to excuse me, but I have to go."

"But I've only just begun my tale," Henry protested, pleased he had skillfully maneuvered the Marshal out of the way.

"Another time," Mason flatly said.

"Why not stay and have another drink?" Belle encouraged, not wanting him to go, yet enjoying the attention of the sophisticated Henry. With a daily diet of dirty miners, grubby cowboys and tobacco-stained gamblers, the archaeologist was a breath of clean air, someone who could actually talk about more than digging, cards, or running cattle. She then realized she looked forward to his Saturday night visits, for it afforded her intelligent conversation. And besides, he was a very attractive man. This wasn't the first time she had thought of spending more than just a conversation with him, but she knew she had to be careful. If word got out, and it probably would, it would undermine her authority with the girls, for how would it look if the madam was sharing the customers with the working girls, impacting their income. Still, a woman had needs and what she needed was someone steady, a one-woman man... like the Marshal.

"Another time. I really need to get back."

"I understand you are married," Henry affably said, subtly making a point. "Is she a local girl?"

"No," he replied, wanting to be on his way, but not wanting to appear boorish or impolite. "She's from San Francisco."

"San Francisco," Henry expansively said, "a city of charm and refinement. Do not misunderstand me," he solicitously added. "Tombstone certainly has its charms, especially with the fair Belle DuBois holding sway over so many men's hearts. Yet the desert cannot hold its own against the lush beauty of San Francisco. Were it not for the presence of this epitome of pulchritude," he bowed at Belle, "I should be quite ready to move on. I say, has it been difficult for your wife to make the adjustment, coming from the Eden called San Francisco to the vast desert of Tombstone?"

Mason bristled slightly then touched the brim of his hat in respect to Belle. "You both have a good night." Without waiting for their reply, he spun around and strode out the door.

With smug satisfaction, Henry watched him leave. It was obvious he had hit a nerve. "I say, I do hope I've not offended the good Marshal," he said to Belle. "I was attempting to get him engaged in the conversation. Seems to be a rather taciturn sort, don't you think?"

"That's a sore subject with him," she said, disappointed he had left.

"San Francisco?" he asked, knowing the answer.

"No, his wife."

"His wife?" he innocently inquired.

"Yes."

"She is unhappy here, then?" he said, the audible tone of concern belying his desire to know more.

"That's putting it mildly," she smiled at him.

"Ah," he nodded thoughtfully. "Still, Tombstone is not without its culture. The Nellie Boyd Dramatic Company puts on as fine a show as to be found in San Francisco. And there are musicals, dances, and social events. Why, there's even this new sporting event called 'baseball.' Surely she must participate in some of the finer aspects of Tombstone's artistic diversity."

"Actually," Belle replied, lowering her voice as though sharing a bit of gossip, "she spends all her time in her room."

"My word," he said, an eyebrow raised in shock. "Whatever for?"

Belle tightened her lips for a moment, debating whether to tell him what pretty much everyone in town already knew. "She takes laudanum," she finally admitted.

"My goodness," he startled, though pleased with the tidbit of gossip. "I didn't know. I should have been more sensitive to the man's pain. Perhaps I should express my regrets for my callous behavior." He looked up at the door, his face flushed with great dramatic effect as though ready to rush after Mason and beg forgiveness.

"It would be best to leave it alone," she counseled, impressed with his concern.

"Yes, you are right, I'm sure," he soberly agreed. 'There are some things best left alone, things that must be dealt with alone." Pausing only a moment, his countenance changed, and he cheerfully said, "Perhaps I can entice you to take a spin on my machine." Belle gave him a half-lidded smirk until he realized what he had said. "O my goodness," he laughed. "That's not what I meant. And I will not be so crude as to suggest it be interpreted in any other way."

"That's quite alright," she smiled suggestively, patting his arm. "I would enjoy a ride on your... what do you call it?"

"I call it a MATE," he impishly grinned, "which stands for Motorized All Terrain Engine."

"I would like that," she said, then mischievously added, "perhaps the next time you come into town, you can take me for a spin."

Smiling broadly at the innuendo, he said, "I'll do better than that. I'll come back into town the day after tomorrow and we can take a spin down by the San Pedro. I can order a lunch for us to take along."

Smitten with the idea of a picnic along the river with a handsome man, despite his status as a customer, she readily agreed then asked, "Why the day after tomorrow?"

"The gentleman whose claim lies across the wash from me, a prospector who goes by the name of Caleb has a ritual where every eight days, he packs up his ore, takes it to be stamped in Millville then trudges the distance to deposit his precious earnings in a bank in Tombstone."

"He walks from Milleville to Tombstone? Why not use the bank in Charleston?

"I asked the same question," he said, rolling his eyes. "He is a creature of peculiar habits and will not be dissuaded from them. Thus, every eight days, while he is making his rounds, I stay behind and guard the fort, so to speak."

Belle looked at him with new respect. "That's very thoughtful of you."

"It's really no bother," he shrugged. "Though peculiar, he's a good man."

The music from the dance hall stopped as the musicians took a short break before striking up another session of dancing. Though there was still plenty of noise from the low humming chatter of the men, the Theater felt empty, as though a great presence had just vanished.

Pulling an ornately designed silver pocket watch from his vest pocket, Henry clicked it open. "And I see it is time I headed back home. Caleb will want to be leaving early. But first, one last bit of music before I go."

He walked over to the Polyphon Music Box against the opposite wall. The Polyphon stood taller than most men. Made of richly carved walnut, it had a glass front that displayed the metal music disc being played. Henry pulled open the base selecting one of the music discs. Opening the glass front, he removed the large disc, replacing it with his selection. Closing the base, he reached into his pocket and pulled out a silver dollar, which he inserted into the slot on the side of the Polyphon. Soon the sound of *Kathleen Mavourneen* filled the Theater, to the hoots and cheers of the Irish workers present. Not long after, not a few voices added their harmony to the song. It was an odd sight, for those who

52

not more than a few moments ago were raucously dancing to a polka were now somber, giving heartfelt emotion to the song.

Smiling, Henry gave Belle a gentlemanly bow. "Day after tomorrow then."

"I look forward to it," she smiled back.

With a dapper wave of the hand, Henry opened the doors and walked out into the night, a happy man. Things were working out better than he expected. The Marshal's weakness might prove beneficial. The question was, how to use it to the best advantage?

Though quite tired, Henry was out setting up the IAS when Caleb came out of his cave, his six-shooter strapped to his side, a small bag with his earnings in one hand, and an empty haversack in the other. Henry chuckled to himself. For some reason the man had been antsy to get to town, and Henry's late-night carousing at the Bird Cage and subsequent later waking time had interfered with Caleb's plans. The man was impatient to leave and a bit more cross than usual.

Yet Henry needed to keep up appearances and changing his routine at the Bird Cage would have raised suspicions. Truth was, he wanted the old man gone as much as Caleb wanted to be away. Hopefully Caleb would stick to *his* routine and give Henry sufficient time to do his investigation.

Giving Henry a perfunctory wave, Caleb headed out on the familiar path to begin his walk to Tombstone, a little over two hours away. Henry continued leveraging up the tower until it was in place. Flicking the power switch, the machine came alive in a low dull resonant hum. Above, the cone began its arcing motion, sweeping side to side towards the direction Caleb walked.

Satisfied the machine was working correctly, Henry diverted his attention to make some coffee. Slowly savoring the strong brew, he patiently waited until enough time had passed for Caleb to be far enough away before pulling out the Cell Detector. While the IAS continued scanning, Henry finished his coffee and headed over to Caleb's claim. He had been in there several times before, all very briefly, feigning a polite interest in the man's claim. But today was different. He knew Caleb had found something just by the way the man's demeanor had so recently changed, no matter how hard he tried to hide it.

Flicking on the power to the Cell detector, he was rewarded with the sound of immediate clicking. Slowly waving the wand in front of him, he calmly worked from left to right. As he approached Caleb's sleeping area, the intensity and frequency of the clicking increased. Pausing by the clothing haversacks, he knew by the sound of his Cell Detector that there was something there.

Placing the Detector on the floor, Henry began rummaging through Caleb's clothing. It wasn't long before he found the book. His heart racing, he strode briskly to the cave entrance for more light.

His hands luxuriated in the sensation of the ancient leather. Carefully opening the tome, he nearly dropped it when he read the opening line – *Me llamo Diaco de la Fuente*. After all these years, he had finally found the diary of Diaco de la Fuente. Or rather, Caleb had found it, but that was mere niggling. He abruptly realized the diary was in Spanish and he knew that Caleb was not learned enough to either read or speak Spanish. What was it about the book that had him so spooked? There had to be something else that had sparked his recent paranoia.

Sitting down, Henry quickly, though carefully and reverently, flipped through a number of the pages, pausing at those with etchings and maps, lingering as he studied the drawings. Returning to the start, he began reading and page turning, immersing himself in the man's tale. It took better part of the morning before he came to the end.

It was a fascinating tale of intrigue, murder, and wealth. In the end, only two conquistadors remained of de la Fuente's group. The others had been either killed by other conquistadors or by pursuing Indians. The two who remained were de la Fuente and Alonso Ortiz, his cousin. With the others dead, all the gold was theirs.

But their luck had run out.

Henry read the last entries. *We are held captive in a cave and they play a game with us now. They will not attack, but they will not let us leave. We have tried several times to fight through, but there are too many of them, each time forcing us back into the cave. We have injured or killed a number of them but have sustained no wounds ourselves. It is a cruel game they play. There is no food and water left. I would say they are slowly starving us to death, but death will come much sooner than we know. I write these last words should anyone ever read this journal. Alonso and I found Cibola, but not where we were told to look.*

Closing the journal, Henry mulled what he had read. The sun was now overhead, and he knew it was past lunchtime and it wouldn't be long before Caleb was trudging back. Yet something puzzled him. Where had Caleb discovered the book? Knowing the man couldn't possibly read Spanish, what was causing him to act to oddly. There had to be something more in the cave. Once he thought 'cave,' the epiphany hit him. This had to be the cave where de la Fuente and Ortiz were held captive.

Jumping up, he quickly scanned the Cave's interior. His frustration mounted. He needed more time. Staring at the book in his hands, he knew he had only scanned the contents, that he would need to spend hours to sift and sort all the details de la Fuente provided. He needed the damned book… but not yet.

Reluctantly putting the book back where he found it and arranging the bags to look undisturbed, Henry reminded himself that the book would be his in due course. Lifting the Cell Detector once again, he began systematic probing. He was about to enter the enlarged tunnel to Caleb's silver vein when he held his hand out for balance, abruptly noticing the clicking increased. Pulling himself back out, he swept his hand to the right. The clicking dramatically increased and continued to increase the closer he moved towards the pile of stones against the wall.

By the time he stood before the stones, the clicking of the Cell Detector was loud and fast. Puzzled, Henry frowned, wondering what was behind the pile of stones.

Pulling out his pocket watch, he flipped open the top. If he kept to his usual schedule, Caleb was most likely already on his way back.

Letting out a sigh of frustration, he turned off the machine and slowly walked to the entrance, making note of where things were. What frustrated him most was that he would be forced to wait another eight days before Caleb returned to Tombstone. Consoling himself that he had waited years to get here, he could wait another eight days.

Henry was back at his field table, fastidiously studying his accumulated notes when the IAS began its loud beeping. Looking up, he saw Caleb striding forcefully along the path, his sense of urgency revealing his desperation to get back to his claim. Henry grinned at the man's lack of guile. Giving him a friendly wave, he scooted back from the table and switched off the IAS.

Caleb went straight to his claim, scrambling up to the cave. Pausing, he quickly examined the inside, reassuring himself everything was in place, particularly the stones. Crossing over to stand by the orderly pile, he wasn't sure, but he felt something wasn't right. Brushing his hand across the top of several stones, he felt the light layer of dirt that he had used to dust the stones. Relaxing, he told himself not to be so obviously suspicious. Dropping his pack, he methodically unloaded his gear, placing each item where it belonged.

Despite his initial misgivings, he felt good. His talk with the Marshal went better than expected. They had sat down to lunch together at Walsh's Restaurant, where the food was good and the portions large. Caleb had ordered his usual steak, eggs, and biscuits with plenty of gravy. It was when he was sopping up some gravy that Mason, leaning back sipping his coffee, smiled at him.

"You got something on your mind?" Mason asked. "You look like you've been about to bust ever since we got here."

Momentarily startled, Caleb quickly collected himself and leaned forward, whispering his secret. The Marshal didn't even seem the least bit fazed about the discovery.

"Looks like all those stories might be true after all," he said, placing a hand over the coffee cup, feeling the warmth from the steam.

"What am I gonna do?"

"Keep it very quiet for now," he had wisely answered. "We can't afford for word to get out. This town is crazy enough as it is. Just imagine the hell that would break loose if word ever got out. We'd need an army down here to restore order." Mason then offered some sound advice. "If you can afford to wait a while, I suggest you do so, but keep it quiet. Folks'll leave you alone if they think you don't have much. And keep to your routine," he cautioned. "You'd be surprised how many folks set their watches to when you come to town."

That surprised Caleb because he didn't think anyone ever noticed him, except for the Marshal who always had a kind word for him. "What do you think I should do then?"

"Like I said, nothing, for the moment," he shrugged, holding up his mug for more coffee. "Look at it this way. How many folks come out there now to bother you?"

Caleb thought for a moment before answering, "None."

"Then why change that?" he asked. "What about that fellow across the wash, Henry? Seems friendly enough. What do you know about him?"

"Spends all his time lookin' for dead folks," he said, shaking his head disdainfully. "Though he's a smart one with all them new-fangled gadgets and machines, he ain't got the sense to see what's under his feet."

"He's an archaeologist," Mason patiently explained. "That's his job, looking for ancient civilizations."

"He gets money for doin' that?" Caleb skeptically asked.

"Yes. He works for a university back east."

"Seems damned silly," he sniffed. "Man oughta work doin' somethin' useful."

"I suppose," Mason smiled. "Do you trust him?"

"Ain't got no cause not to," he said. "Treats me right decent."

"Seems to do that with everyone," Mason replied, thinking of the man's suave approach to Belle the previous evening. The thought irritated him. Sighing to himself, he realized he had no right to be irritated. The man was single, as was Belle. Pushing the thought from his mind, he returned his attention to the prospector. "And what would you propose to do with your newfound wealth?"

"I ain't rightly thought about it."

"But you're not going to become an archaeologist."

Caleb frowned at him then shook his head when he saw the sly smile. "Aw, now you're funnin' me."

"Just getting you to think about your future. You're going to have to eventually move it somewhere, and Henry *is* an archaeologist. He might know how to dispose of your finds. With his machines and things, he might be in a position to help you, perhaps for a portion of your find." Seeing Caleb stiffen, he quickly soothed, "I'm not saying that's the best solution. I'm just saying it's a possible solution. Just something to think about."

The waitress, an attractive young girl in her late teens came up to the table. "You boys want anything else?" she prettily asked, looking at Mason the entire time.

"I'll take a little more coffee, Mary Beth," Mason answered, holding up his cup.

"Right away, Marshal," she warmly replied and was about to move off before she remembered his table mate. "And you?"

"I'm fine."

As Mary Beth pranced off the get the coffee pot, Caleb studied the Marshal for a few moments before asking what was lurking around the edges of his mind. "How come you ain't out prospectin' or minin'?"

"I prefer to have steady work, and I like what I'm doing," he casually answered. "I have the respect of the citizens, I get to shoot people when they break the law, and I don't have to worry about whether I'll have enough for my next meal." He leaned back as Mary Beth approached. "Isn't that right, Mary Beth?"

"Isn't what right Marshal?" she asked, pouring the steaming black coffee into his mug.

"Being a Marshal is more fun than mining."

"Of course it is," she readily agreed. Another patron caught her attention, and she reluctantly moved away from the table.

"That's not what I meant," Caleb said. "What I meant was that you don't seem too... uh,"

"Too obsessed with striking it rich?" Mason offered. "Plotting to jump claims or steal someone else's silver? Or spend ten hours every day down in the mines digging silver for someone else for four dollars a day, only to spend it all in one of the whorehouses here in Tombstone? Or have my own claim and pray that I could be one of the few lucky ones who barely make enough to cover expenses, all the while dreaming of hitting the mother lode?' He leaned forward, crossing his arms on the table, the coffee mug in his right hand. "I'm a lawman. That's what I like doing. It's what I do best."

And they had left it at that. Caleb purchased the rest of his supplies and had just about decided against the bath when Mason's words reminded him to keep to his routine. Despite the overpowering urge to head home, he went by the public bath. Though he did on occasion use the stream in the wash below the claim to occasionally bathe when it had water, it was nice to have hot water once in a while.

When finished, he had collected his belongings, paid his quarter and headed out of town. He was pleased when he was close to home and heard the beeping of Henry's machine, warning that he was coming. He saw Henry look up and wave.

After stowing away all his gear, he carried a bucket down creek. Studying the small trickle, he was thankful they were pumping water out of the mines. It saved him a lot of time having to find water. Dipping the bucket in, he sloshed it around a bit, emptied the contents then refilled it. Looking up, he saw Henry stirring something in a pot over the fire. Knowing he'd find out what it was in a couple of minutes, he lugged the bucket back to the cave and set it next to the water barrel. By the time he made his way across the wash, Henry had cleared his desk and was setting out plates for the evening meal. "Have a good trip into town?" he cheerily asked.

"Fair enough," Caleb answered, scooting out a chair and setting his own food down.

"And lunch with the good Marshal?"

"Fine." He waited for Henry to sit before continuing the conversation. He stared in awe at the plate piled with spaghetti and tomatoes.

"Walsh's restaurant again?" he smiled. "One of these days I need to try that fine establishment." Henry sat down then saw Caleb staring at his plate. "I've plenty. Would you like some?"

For once, Caleb agreed. "How'd you make that?"

"Quite easily, my good man. Both the pasta and olive oil store well, especially out here. I got the tomatoes the last time I was in Hoptown. Just throw the pasta in some boiling water, add the tomatoes and olive oil when finished, and voila! A meal fit for kings." He fixed his guest a plate.

Caleb dug in with gusto, slurping up the noodles. "This is right good," he said while chewing. "Good as they make in town."

"I take that as a high compliment," he grandly said, "especially from one with your culinary tastes." He smiled to himself as he watched Caleb's simple mind work out the compliment. "I know I've asked this before," he casually said, "but in your digging, have you come across anything unusual, something out of the ordinary?"

"Whaddaya mean?" He stopped chewing, his guard up.

Henry noticed the change. "Oh, you know, pieces of pottery, maybe a piece of wood shaped like you could use it to eat with or stir a pot."

"Nope," he briskly replied, "just ore." He resumed eating.

"Ah," he shrugged, pretending to be disappointed. "If you do, would you let me know?"

"Sure."

Henry watched him scarf his food, at once fascinated and repulsed. Nevertheless, he was ready for his guest to leave so he could get back to his research. He wanted to compare what he had in his notes with what he remembered from de la Fuente's account. But he would have to continue the routine, sharing the post-dinner ritual of bourbon. Part of him wondered if he could get the old prospector drunk enough to loosen his lips.

Yet when the time came for the after-dinner libation, Caleb announced, "Just one fer me, thanks. Been a long day."

"Of course," Henry affably smiled. Lifting his glass in toast, he said, "Here's to wealth. May we find it sooner than later." Clinking his glass with Caleb's, he grinned in satisfaction knowing it was just a matter of time and whatever Caleb had found would be his.

Sitting at the vanity table, brushing her long blond hair, Belle raised an eyebrow in surprise when she heard the abrupt knocking at her door. Frowning, she wrapped a shawl around her shoulders and glanced at the wall clock. It was almost noon on a Sunday, a day that she normally would still be asleep.

Crossing to the door, she unlatched the lock and opened the door slightly and peered out. Standing just outside were several waiters from the Cosmopolitan holding covered dishes.

"Good morning, Miss Belle," the head waiter politely smiled. "Mister Henry Mitchell sends his compliments and hopes you will enjoy this excellent meal provided by the Cosmopolitan Hotel. May we come in?"

Her eyes momentarily fluttered in awkward comprehension before she stood back and fully opened the door. The waiters breezed past her and, with great flourish, deposited three plates of steaming food on the small table by the lounge chair – eggs benedict, braised veal and buttered toast along with a pot of freshly brewed coffee.

Inhaling the delicious bouquet of the cuisine, Belle looked up at the head waiter. "Mister Mitchell sent this?"

"Yes, ma'am. With his compliments."

"Well," she smiled as she scooted out a chair. "I certainly don't want to disappoint Mister Mitchell." Seating herself, she gazed up at the head waiter. "This is very kind of him and of you. Thank you."

"You're very welcome, Miss Belle. When you're finished, you can simply leave the plates outside your door. We'll come collect them later. Please enjoy this fine meal prepared by the kitchen staff of the Cosmopolitan Hotel." With that, he snapped his fingers at the other two waiters and in only a few seconds, the door was closed behind them, and she was left to enjoy her meal.

Belle stared at the food, marveling at the gesture. No one had ever done something like this for her before. It was an act of a man who had breading, culture, and refinement. He was wooing her and was conducting himself as a gentleman.

Chapter 4

The MATE chugged steadily along the road towards Charleston. Sitting close to the well-dressed archaeologist and inventor, their shoulders touching, Belle regaled in the experience. The views were wide all the way to the Huachuca Mountains in the distance. Cresting a low hill, she could see the lush and verdant ribbon of the San Pedro River just ahead. Well before they came into Charleston, Henry turned off the main road and headed southeast around Brunckow Hill towards Lewis Springs.

"I know a nice spot far enough away from the noise of the mills," he said. "The river runs clear and cool and there's plenty of shade underneath the trees."

"Sounds inviting," she smiled. Belle had eschewed her normal wardrobe as a madam and had dressed comfortably in long skirt and blouse. Her long blond hair, normally pinned up, billowed in the wind.

Casting a side glance at her, Henry thought she looked quite alluring, more like the beautiful girl-next-door than the French madam she pretended to be.

"What a marvelous machine," she complimented him. Pointing to two long brass tubes that ran from the front of the boiler near the crest and along both sides, ending just below where they sat, she remarked, "Who would have thought to have the smoke come out the back of the engine." She looked back to see the steady puffs of smoke trailing behind them.

"It makes it easier to see what's in front," he explained.

"I know. How does it work?"

Pleased to share his creative genius, he said, "The tubes are essentially just empty containers. The front of the tube is open to the air coming from the front of the machine. In each tube is a fan that sucks the smoke up and pushes it out the back. The fans don't require any energy because they're like whirligigs. Us going forward causes them to spin, which pushes the smoke out the back."

"What a brilliant idea. I'm surprised the machinists haven't taken note of this."

"I rather they didn't," he warned. "When I get all the kinks worked out, I plan on selling this to the military."

"I'm sure they'd love to have this. But what do the machinists have to do with it?"

"If the machinists get involved, I have to pay them to represent me, and I don't need or want their representation. It costs too much, especially when they had nothing to do with the work that went into the invention."

Belle nodded in understanding. "Do you have other inventions?"

"Yes," he confidently replied. He then explained about the IAS. "It's another invention I plan on selling to the military."

"Does the university mind you doing this?"

"The university?" he frowned.

"Yes, the university where you work," she said, puzzled by his reaction.

"Oh, them," he grinned. "I try to tell them as little as possible. They can sometimes be worse than the machinists' guild."

"And they don't mind you being gone for so long, digging up things?" She brushed some hair out of her face.

The simple movement was unaffected, yet graceful. Henry felt himself quite captivated by her seemingly innocent charm. Part of him wondered if she was the settling down type, but then her choice of profession argued against that. Then again, it wasn't like he was the settling down type either. For him, the fun was in the chase. The girls at the Bird Cage were obviously no challenge. They were mere diversions, a form of entertainment while he was here. While they knew what they were doing, they lacked passion and fire. For them, it was a job, a profession. Had he the inclination, he would have pursued one of the more genteel ladies in town, perhaps a fair wife of one of the town's more stellar citizens. That would have been an amusing game.

But that would have taken time away from his purpose here. Courting a lady requires time and effort, neither of which he was willing to devote. The lovely Belle, on the other hand, was an unknown entity. Though a madam, her manner and conduct bespoke a woman educated, perhaps raised in an upscale home somewhere. Though, in truth, no one knew her past for she had immersed herself in the persona of a French woman. Further, no one could lay claim to have tasted her charms, though many had tried. Thus, a woman like Belle was a challenge, and he would bed this temptress sooner or later.

"They like the things I bring back," he said, returning to the question. "It adds prestige to the department and the university. But tell me, how is it you determined to make Tombstone your choice of location?"

"I go where the money is," she blithely said, "and there's plenty of it in Tombstone."

"That there is," he agreed. Turning the MATE onto an overgrown path, he slowed it down as they approached the tree line, stopping just under the spreading arms of several cottonwoods. Close by, the San Pedro curved around a wide sandbar.

"Here we are," he announced, hopping down to come around to assist Belle. Holding her by her narrow waist, he lifted her down. For a moment, their eyes locked and lingered.

"Shall I get the lunch, or will you?" she said, holding his gaze with hers.

Despite the overwhelming urge to kiss her, he gallantly smiled. "I'll get it."

While he retrieved the basket with the food and wine, Belle looked around. The lushness of the spot both surprised and pleased her. Inhaling deeply, she savored the fragrance of things growing. "This is pretty," she said. "I spend so much time at the Theater, I forget this is here. It reminds me of home."

"And where would home be?" he asked, spreading out a blanket on the ground.

"Why Paris, France of course," she grinned at him.

Looking at her with bemused skepticism, he said, "Tell me truth now. Have you ever actually been to Paris?"

Looking casually around to ensure they were alone, she gave him a bewitching smile. "Actually, I have. Quite a few times, in fact. Next to Berlin, it was mother's favorite city."

"Ah, a world traveler," he nodded is appreciation, quietly pleased with her growing trust. "So you also speak German?"

"*Ja, Ich kann auch Deutsch sprechen.*"

"I'm afraid my German isn't all that good," he shrugged with a smile.

"Neither is mine," she laughed. "It's been too long, and I've forgotten so much. Fortunately, there's not a big demand for German madams."

Placing the basket on the blanket, he opened the top and pulled out the wine bottle, walking over and wedging it into a spot in the river. "So where is home then?"

"Actually, not far from your university," she answered, settling herself onto the blanket. "I grew up in Newport, Rhode Island."

Henry stiffened but made sure she didn't see the concern flash across his face. "You are familiar with Brown University then?" he ventured.

"Not really," she replied. "I've been on the campus a few times, but that's it. That was more Father's interest. Mother sent me to Ipswich, assuming I was going to be a teacher. I thought so too," she chuckled. "I created a bit of a stir there before Mother sent me packing to Oberlin. Last I heard, Ipswich has since closed its doors. I do hope I'm not to blame." She grinned impishly at him.

"Now you have me curious," he said, sitting next to her. "How did you go from Ipswich to madam?"

"Economics," she simply said. "I looked about for where a woman could make the most money without having to marry into it."

For the next two hours, Henry probed and prodded, seeking to learn more about this fascinating woman. Belle was careful with her answers, likewise probing Henry's past. By the end, each was convinced the other was hiding something. Yet it seemed not to matter as each understood and accepted the other's privacy.

Whatever game she was playing was acceptable to Henry, and he liked her brazenness, her confidence. It bespoke someone who could take care of herself, someone who could .handle any situation. He had the passing thought of bringing her into his confidence, making her a partner as such. She could be a strong asset. But he needed to know more about her. More importantly, he needed to know the truth about her.

Belle was enjoying herself, and the company. She found herself attracted to him. He was suave and gallant, and he had manners. Whether or not she bedded him was another matter. She needed to know more about him, especially why he was so bothered when she mentioned Newport. She had noticed his very subtle tensing. What was it about Newport that had him guarded? She had been careful in her questioning, but he was just as careful to reveal nothing of his concerns.

It was after he had packed up the leftovers, placing the basket back to its place on the MATE that he reached over to help her up to her seat. However, his hand lingered and instead he slowly pulled her to him. Delighted she did not resist, he held her eyes before leaning down and kissing her. He felt her lips return the kiss, seemingly holding in check a wild passion. It excited him and he knew she would be a marvelous lover.

"Thank you for a wonderful afternoon," she said, giving him an intimate smile.

"The pleasure is all mine," he charmingly replied, helping her up.

The trip back to town was all too quick, and he found himself delivering her to her door outside the Brown Hotel just down the street from the Theater.

"*Bonsoir, ma belle petite*," he bowed. "Until the next time."

"*Merci, mon ami*," she demurely answered. "I will see you Saturday?"

"*Mais oui, madame.* I would not miss the chance of your exquisite company. I would consider it a great kindness if you would allow me to enjoy your company once again."

"With pleasure, Monsieur."

"This week perhaps?" he asked with hope.

"Ah, I am sorry, Monsieur. The Theater requires my attention. Perhaps early next week?"

"I would like that." He then took her hand, bowed, and kissed it. "Until then."

He watched her move gracefully through the door before climbing back aboard the MATE and heading up the street towards Hoptown. In only a few moments, he was parked outside Wuhan Mei's Shop.

Standing up on the pilot's platform, he removed the seat cushion revealing a locked compartment. Unlocking the keyed lock, he lifted the top and pulled out a small satchel. Glancing casually around before he hopped down, his mind was momentarily distracted with the memory of Belle's lips. His smile revealed his confidence that she would be his. Leaping down, he opened the door to be greeted by a plump woman wearing a purple brocaded silk dress and adorned with a rather large amount of Asian jade jewelry.

"Good afternoon, Miss Mei," he gallantly hailed her.

"Ah," she smiled brightly in reply. "Good afternoon, Mister Mitchell. How are you today?"

"I am well, thank you. I see you are looking as trim as ever." He bowed his head slightly in amused respect.

"Ah, Mister Mitchell," she jovially grinned at him. "You are the flatterer, no?" Glancing quickly around, she continued smiling and said, "There is no news for you today."

"Excellent," he replied, thankful for her ability to know all that went on in Tombstone. No news meant he was still nothing more than an oddity.

Both Henry and Wuhan Mei turned to look when the door to the shop opened, and a woman walked in. She was a white woman, elegantly dressed, yet Henry observed that beauty was seeping away from her. It was much too obvious that addiction had affected her allure, for she had that wan

68

look of dependence. Giving him a polite but distant nod, she walked up to where Wuhan Mei had positioned herself behind the counter.

Henry looked at Wuhan Mei whose hardened eyes belied the smile.

"Miss Mei," the woman began. "I... I know you've been very patient with me. I... I don't know when I can pay you."

"I can't give you any more," Wuhan Mei firmly stated. "You need to pay."

"But I can't," she replied, her voice almost a whine. "I don't have the money."

"You get your husband to pay," she curtly answered.

The woman's eyes widened in agitated shock. "I can't. He'll refuse," she brusquely said, her tone edged with resentment.

"You find some other way to pay then, Missus Sadler," she said. "Until you pay, no more for you."

"Missus Sadler?" Henry's ears perked up. "Is the Marshal your husband?"

The woman turned to him as if stung. She seemed about to suddenly flee, but remained rooted like a cornered animal, her eyes wild and accusing.

"I know your husband," he soothingly said, recognizing the look. He had seen it often enough in the wharves and back alleys of port cities when he descended to the lowest levels of humanity, looking for information. "He's a very busy man. Perhaps I can help you."

"I... I don't need your help," she unconvincingly said.

"I'm sure you don't," he suavely replied. "But I would like to offer it, as a friend. We could keep it as our little secret." Turning to Wuhan Mei, he asked, "How much does she owe you?"

Wuhan Mei reached beneath the counter and withdrew a wide book. Placing it on the counter, she pulled it open, flipping several pages and scrutinizing the entries. "She owes me $64."

Opening his satchel, Henry pulled out a large envelope. Withdrawing a stack of large ornately designed bills, he counted out sixty-four dollars in National Bank Notes, neatly arranged the edges and placed them before her. "That should cover her present obligation." Turning to Elizabeth, he gallantly said, "I would consider it a favor if I might be allowed to offer some assistance." Counting out another $64, he slid the Notes to Wuhan Mei. "Please let me know when this runs out."

"Of course, Mister Mitchell," she happily replied, only too willing to receive the settlement of a debt plus a bonus. Reaching again beneath the counter, she lifted up a bottle of laudanum, placing it on the counter near Elizabeth.

Her eyes moistened in mixture of gratitude and relief, Elizabeth gushed a soft, "Thank you. I'll pay you back." In one jittery motion, she spun around and hurried out.

Waiting until she was through the door, Henry said, "Is laudanum all that she uses?"

"No," she nonchalantly replied, counting the Notes and sequestering them beneath the counter. "She also likes the opium very much too."

Henry counted out another $100 in Notes. "Will this cover it for a while?"

"Yes," she smiled ingratiatingly. "Will do fine, for a while."

Chuckling, he looked at her. "You haven't asked why I'm doing this."

Holding her hands up in benign defense, she said, "Not my problem why one man wants to help another man's wife."

"That's what I like about you, Miss Mei," he smiled appreciatively. "You know how to mind your own business." Closing the satchel, he said, "You will ensure she gets home safely after her visits here?"

"Of course, Mister Mitchell," she smiled the same ingratiating smile as when he first walked in.

Pausing for a moment, he asked, "By the way, do you have anything a little, shall we say, 'stronger' than the bottle she just took with her?

Wuhan Mei carefully regarded him before saying, "Yes. I have something a little stronger."

"Would you see that she gets a bottle?"

"Yes, Mister Mitchell."

"Excellent. Well then," he grinned. "I leave you in good health and long life."

Once he was out the door and sound of the MATE's engines diminished, she safely locked away the money before pulling out a bottle of laudanum from behind the counter. Calling one of her workers, she said, "Wait until it's dark and take this to the woman in the Pascholy Boarding House. Use the tunnels."

"Yes, Ah Lum," he deferentially replied.

Already motoring his way back to his claim, Henry couldn't help but grin. Elizabeth's stumbling in while he was at Wuhan Mei's was a stroke of luck. Done right, Elizabeth's drug addiction would keep the Marshal occupied and out of his hair. So far, things were going perfectly.

"Hey Marshal," a man said, hurrying up to Mason. "I was just in Tom Moses' Capital Saloon and looks like there's some trouble." He pointed behind him to the saloon up towards Fremont Street. "Couple of Machinists are in there and the bartender is fixin' to give 'em some trouble."

"All right then," Mason calmly replied. "Get a deputy while I take a look." As the man ran off, he strode purposely down the middle of the street then turned the corner at Fremont. Pushing through the swinging doors, he quickly took in the standoff. Behind the bar, the barkeep had his shotgun ready, his face scrunched in an angry scowl. The bar was empty except for the two young machinists, their arms crossed, who stood seething in indignation near the front doors. They appeared to be about the same age, impeccably dressed in slacks and button-down shirts. Both also wore the tanned leather jacket of the Machinists.

"What's going on?" Mason calmly asked.

"He refuses to serve us," one machinist answered. He was a lithe man, with coal-black hair cut to his shoulders.

"Is that true?" the Marshal asked.

"You blind man?" the barkeep snapped. "I don't serve their kind here. They can get their firewater somewhere else."

There was a pause as Mason and the two machinists digested the statement, before smirks replaced the machinists' anger.

"Firewater?" the other machinist repeated. He was half a head taller, with long black hair neatly tied behind his head. He looked at his friend and said, "I believe we may have gone about this all wrong." Walking casually up to the bar, he straightened, thumped his chest and dramatically said, "Me wantum firewater." Pointing to his friend, he theatrically repeated, "Him wantum firewater too." Despite his effort to maintain composure, he broke out into in broad grin.

"You get back," the barkeep threatened, waving the shotgun at him.

"Just hold on a minute," Mason interrupted as the machinist held up his hands and retreated to stand next to his friend. "Why won't you serve them?"

"I don't serve their kind here," he sneered.

"And what exactly is 'their kind?'" Mason asked, knowing the answer and direction of the standoff.

"I don't serve Injuns here."

"We are not 'Injuns,'" the one machinist corrected. "We are Chiricahua."

"Same damn thing."

"They're machinists," Mason said, pointing out the obvious. "You can see that by their clothes." He pointed to the cog-wheel and wrench brand on the left sleeve of the jackets.

"I don't give a hoot in hell who they are; they ain't drinkin' in here."

"Does Tom know about this?"

"He ain't here and it's my way that sez what goes on."

Sighing at the man's ignorance, Mason turned to the two machinists. "Unfortunately, he can refuse to serve anyone he sees fit, and there's nothing legal I can do about it, at least until I can get Tom Moses to fix it. This one here," he said, thumbing over his shoulder, "is new to town and doesn't know how things are done here. He'll soon learn. In the meantime, there are other, far better establishments in town who will be more than happy to oblige you. I'd be happy to point you in the right direction."

"Thank you, Marshal," the taller machinist politely replied. Stepping quickly towards the bar, he stopped in the middle of the room. Staring evilly at the barkeep, he said, "Me no likum you." Erratically waving his hands, he added, "Me curse this place. Twelve moons pass and you will be no more." Spinning around, he haughtily made his way to the doors, yet unable to hide his mirth. Once outside, the two friends burst into laughter, with Mason ginning as well.

"Me no likum you," the shorter machinist snorted. "That was hilarious. I love the curse you put on him." He mimicked the waving of hands.

"I'm glad you boys can see the humor of it all," Mason smiled with respect. "Fortunately, not everyone is like him. You're new in town."

"Yes, Marshal," the taller one answered. "Nantan and I are down in Bisbee working on one of the airships. This is the first time we've been down this way. A friend said we needed to come to Tombstone for some fun. I'm Teboca," the Machinist said by way of introduction, "and this, as you already know, is Nantan."

"Glad to have you boys in town." Mason tilted his Stetson back and looked to his left. "Not sure how you ended up here, but there aren't a lot of saloons on the side streets. This is Fremont Street here," he said, nodding to the road in front. "You need to head that way," he explained pointing to the busy road to their right, "to Allen Street. You'll find plenty of saloons there. The two best are the Crystal Palace up towards 5th Street and the Bird Cage on the corner at 6th Street."

"Which do you suggest, Marshal?" Teboca asked.

"Well, as it's getting towards dinner time, the Crystal Palace has better food. But if you want excitement, the Bird Cage is the best. If you decide on the Bird Cage, tell Miss DuBois that I sent you. She'll treat you right."

The two machinists shared a knowing grin, expressed their thanks, and headed down the boardwalk towards Allen Street. Mason chuckled knowing where they were headed.

Sooner or later, almost everyone experienced the Bird Cage Theater. Striding down the boardwalk along the same direction, Mason paused when he arrived at the corner. Directly across on 4th Street, business was still brisk at Hafford's Saloon. On the opposite corner, the bank manager was locking the doors to the bank. Casting quick glances up and down Allen Street, Mason nodded with satisfaction. All was quiet. The good citizens of Tombstone went about their daily business. Pulling his pocket watch out, he checked the time, deciding he ought to head back to the Courthouse one last time before getting a bite to eat. After all, the town would truly come alive, once the sun went down.

As the evening's skies began to settle to darkness, Mason stood in the bedroom staring at his wife who had recently stumbled in from a visit to Hoptown and was now stretched ignominiously across the bed. On the nightstand next to the bed was another bottle of laudanum. Mason sighed with slow resignation for he had heard she was now mixing opium with her laudanum. How she managed to stumble back here was anyone's guess.

He had purposely taken the rooms at Pascholy's Boarding House on Safford Street at the end of town hoping they would be far enough away from the pulse of activity so that her fall from respectability would not be so evident. Yet he knew the wagging of tongues was already prevalent. He could feel it in shadows behind the rustling of curtains as he passed by the homes of respected citizens.

Gazing at the sunken shell of the woman he had married six years earlier, he searched his heart for an ember of affection, but finally admitted he felt nothing for her anymore. He wondered why he stayed with her. Perhaps it was the fool's hope that she would emerge from the depths of her melancholy and return to the vivacious, charming, and beautiful woman she had once been when she had captivated him.

But his head told him it was too late for that. Still, he stayed with her, and remained faithful. Why? Part of him believed her downfall and his pain were retribution for bringing her here. Another part said this would have happened regardless of where they were. Where she was happiest, back in San Francisco, was where he was the most miserable. The city choked him, and her balls and galas and high society suffocated him. He needed space to breathe, and he found it in the San Pedro Valley of the Arizona Territory where he had been appointed U.S. Marshal almost a year ago.

Her audible breathing interrupted his thoughts. Duty took over, and he undressed her, lugging up the limp body to slip off the petticoats and unbutton the dress. Pulling back the covers, he slid her legs in and pulled up the covers just under her arms, lifting her head to tuck a pillow beneath.

Standing back, he studied her for a moment. He had tried sending her back, but she refused to leave. He knew why; she knew she had lost the freshness of her youth, and San Francisco would never accept her the way she was now... and the drug-induced euphoria here was too cheap and too hard to leave. He pondered the thought of divorcing her but felt that would only add insult to her pain. Lurking in the recesses of his mind was the idea that he wouldn't have to divorce her as she would probably die of an overdose, saving him the ignominy of a failed marriage.

The thought irritated him as he berated himself for thinking the solution to his own happiness was for his wife to die. Gazing at the somnolent woman, impervious to the vagaries and challenges of life, he again searched for an emotional connection, something to salvage from the wreckage of their marriage.

But the truth was that he felt he was staring at a stranger. Shaking his head, he took down his pistol belt from the wall hook and strapped it around his waist. Turning down the kerosene lamp, he left the room in darkness, opened the door and entered into the hallway.

Languidly striding down the hallway, past the doors of other boarders, he shifted his thoughts to his growing bank account. The arrangement with Belle was working out quite well. A few moments later he was standing outside the boarding house, inhaling the clean freshness of the vast land.

The sounds of the town mixed with the noise of the mines. It was a gratifying sound, the melody of people living, working hard and playing hard.

Deciding to enjoy the solitude a bit more before heading to the Bird Cage, he walked along Safford Street, past St Paul's Episcopal Church still under construction though quiet now, past numerous vacant lots, then past Turnverein Hall, so recently the site of Tombstone's fledgling school with almost 200 students who were now packed into two small classrooms behind Patton's Saddle Shop on Allen Street.

Turning right on 5th Street so he wouldn't have to get propositioned by the whores working along 6th Street, he was soon through the doors and into the smoke-filled air of the Bird Cage. On stage, a man was holding the audience spell bound with magic tricks. Belle was by the bar in the front, holding the fascination of a number of men with coquettish flirtation. She brightened when she caught his eye. Excusing herself, she sidled up next to him as he approached the bar.

"Hello Mason," she sweetly said.

"Evening, Miss DuBois." He politely touched the brim of his hat.

"Can I buy you a drink?" she smiled.

"No need to do that," he smiled back at her. "I can pay for my own."

"Of course you can," she chuckled. Leaning in, she said, "There's no one here tonight."

"I just came for a drink," he amiably replied.

"Mind if I join you?"

"Of course not," he said, pleased with her attention.

"Jack," she said to the bartender. "You know what I like, and even though he can pay for it, give Mason whatever he wants." Turning back, she gave Mason a wink. "There's still some of that Tennessee Whiskey you like."

"That will do quite nicely," he chuckled.

With the drinks served, Belle held hers up in toast. "To love and happiness."

"Happiness at least," he answered, clinking her glass.

She was about to comment on his limits of love when her face hardened as Johnny Ringo pushed through the doors and stood defiantly surveying the crowd. His liquored eyes lit favorably on her then a scowl filled his face when he saw Mason. With a snarl curling up a corner of his lips, he stalked over to where Mason still stood leaning on the bar.

Turning to face him, Mason sipped his whiskey. "Evening Ringo," he calmly said.

Ringo stared at him for a moment before reaching into the chest pocket of his coat and pulling out a handkerchief. "I hear you're the gamest man in town," he taunted. Flicking a corner of it towards the Mason, he said, "I don't need but three feet to do my fighting. Go ahead and take hold."

Mason smiled benevolently at him. "You're drunk, Ringo. Why don't you go home and sleep it off." He turned his back on him, only to feel Ringo grab his arm and twist him around.

"Wyatt Earp did that once to me before," he fiercely said. "I challenged him, and the coward walked away. I'm not letting you get out of it that easily."

Mason stared calmly at him, slowly extracting his arm from Ringo's grip. "I believe it was Doc Holliday once said, 'I'm your huckleberry, Ringo.' I like those words enough to say them again. I'll be your huckleberry tonight, Ringo. Are you sure that's what you want?"

"Grab ahold," he barked.

"Not in here," Belle snapped, her irritation with both of them obvious. "Take it outside if you can't be civilized."

Without a word, Ringo marched to the door and spun around. "Well Marshal? You coming?"

"Don't do this," Belle quietly pleaded to Mason who seemed quite unperturbed.

"Don't worry. It'll all be fine." Placing his drink on the countertop, he told Jack, "I'll be back."

Belle stood in indecision as those who witnessed the altercation poured out the doors to watch, while those either impervious or too engrossed to care continued to drink, dance, gamble and partake of the ladies. Part of her wanted to remain by the bar, aloof, indifferent to this wanton display of male daring. Were it someone other than Mason, her choice would be easy. Instead, she found herself following the crowd outside and onto the boardwalk.

Mason had followed Ringo out onto the street while a crowd gathered at the edges, watching with macabre fascination.

"You sure you want to do this, Ringo?" Mason asked, standing a few paces in front of him. Instead of answering, Ringo flicked out the handkerchief for him to hold. Firmly taking one end, he felt the pressure of an opposite tug from his opponent.

As both tensed and shifted positions before settling, Mason said, "You let me know when you're ready."

"I'm ready," Ringo retorted. Before the sound of his reply had finished, he felt himself jerked forward and the barrel of Mason's .45 was jabbed into his throat, just below his chin, followed by the click of a hammer pulled back. It happened so quickly that he hadn't even had the chance to grab hold of the smooth ivory of his pistol's grip, let alone draw.

Exhaling a sigh of resigned fate, Ringo said, "Go ahead, Marshal. You'd be doing me a favor." Then he heard the hammer being gently released.

"Now why would I do that?" Mason replied. "I hear you're an educated man. It would be a shame to waste all that education. How about we call this match even?"

"Even? You bested me fair and square."

"I can recognize when a man's drunk, Johnny." Releasing the handkerchief, he pulled his gun away and slid it back into the holster. "Deputy Billy Breakenridge tells me you're a good man, sometimes misguided, but an honorable man. He says that when you give your word, a man can take it to the bank. Billy's a good man and I trust him. I'd like your word that you and me are good."

Ringo blinked at the request then nodded. "We're good, Marshal."

"Good. Now why don't you go on home and get some sleep." With that, he calmly turned around and headed back to the Bird Cage.

"Careful Marshal," a voice called out. "He's likely to shoot you in the back."

Mason abruptly stopped and glared in the direction of the voice. "Who said that? Who said that?" When no one answered, he said, "Johnny Ringo may be some things, but the man is not a coward. You saw that when he stood toe-to-toe with me and didn't back down. He's no coward to go slinking in the dark and shoot a man in the back, or to throw out damnable accusations in the dark. He and I are good. You hear that? You all leave him alone and go back about your business."

Before he stepped onto the boardwalk in front of the Bird Cage, he turned to see Ringo still standing in the middle of the street. "Good night, Ringo."

"G'night Marshal," he sighed then slowly turned to trudge his way home.

Belle slipped a hand around Mason's arm. "That was very gallant, very chivalrous. You saved the man's honor."

"He has his own demons to deal with. I saw no sense in adding to them," he matter-of-factly replied.

Squeezing his arm, she said, "This calls for a drink, my treat."

His smile vanished when he looked up and saw a scarecrow of a barefoot woman in nightshirt standing just off the boardwalk, the moon-glow giving her a spectral aura. Her furrowed brow hung heavily on an angry glare. Her arms stiffly at her sides, she snorted a haughty laugh before turning her attention to Belle.

"You think some cheap two-bit whore is going change him. Don't fool yourself. He'll drag you off to some god-forsaken hell hole just like this dump."

"Go home, Elizabeth," Mason said, his lips tight.

"I'm leaving, Mason," she said, her voice dull, empty. "I can't take it here anymore. I'll be gone in the morning." Without waiting for a response, she turned away and shuffled up the street, her feet scraping a thin pattern in the dry dirt.

"You should go to her," Belle counseled, hiding her disappointment.

"No reason to," he answered, watching his wife lumber down the street. "That's not the first time she's said that. By the time I get home, she'll be passed out and quite forgotten she'd ever been here."

"Why do you stay married to her?" Belle asked, suddenly horrified she gave voice to her thoughts. "I'm sorry. That was impolite. It's really none of my business."

"Though it is a question others have asked," he lamented. "And my answer is always the same. I married her 'for better or for worse.'"

"And you've never been tempted to stray?"

"Don't see the sense to it," he honestly replied. "The pleasure is temporary while the problem remains. Then there's also that part about being faithful."

"Even if you don't love her?" Belle softly said.

Mason pursed his lips before answering. "I did once. At least I thought I did."

"But not anymore?" she asked, less curious than hopeful.

"No," he quietly responded. "One of these days I'll figure out what to do."

Belle looked up at him, content to be outside for the moment, though every time the door to the Theater opened, noise poured out with the invading light and billows of tobacco smoke. "Why did you bring her here, to Tombstone?"

"I was suffocating in San Francisco. You see how she is here? That would be me, if I was still in San Francisco. I was meant to be a lawman. I like it here. A man can breathe."

"Why not send her back?"

"Already tried that," he said. "As you can see, she likes the laudanum too much to be far away from it."

"She could get it easily enough in San Francisco," Belle pointed out.

Mason slowly nodded. "That she could. I think she stays here to be a thorn in my side, a stubborn reminder of what I did to her bringing her here."

"You didn't do this to her," Belle objected. "She did."

"Not everyone sees it like that," he quietly answered.

Silence settled between them before Belle softly said, "I'm sorry."

"You have nothing to be sorry about," he said, adding a weak shrug.

Giving him a warm smile, she said, "You're an unusual man, Mason."

"So I've been told."

"How about another drink?"

"Thanks. I can use one right about now."

Slipping an arm around his, she led him back into the Theater.

Chapter 5

Sitting behind his field desk, his notes and drawings spread before him, Henry looked up to see Caleb emerge from the cave, go through his latest paranoiac ritual of checking behind rocks and scrub-brush before heading off to relieve himself. As his gaze followed the prospector, Henry wondered how he could get Caleb away from the cave long enough to explore. He knew the man well enough to know Caleb would reveal nothing, even if threatened with death. It had only been two days since his last visit to Tombstone. That meant another six days of waiting. To be so close frustrated the archaeologist. He had gone over his notes enough times that he was no longer paying attention.

Then an idea surfaced. Waiting until Caleb was trudging back, he got up from the desk and walked down towards the wash.

"I say, Caleb, my good man," he called out. "Might I have a word with you?"

Startled, Caleb jerked to a halt. Realizing it was Henry, he relaxed and came down to the wash. "Howdy."

"Howdy, yourself," Henry smiled good-naturedly. "I was wondering if you might be so kind as to assist me."

"How's that?"

"I seem to have exhausted the capital on my lowly claim here and I was wondering if I might try my luck on your side of the wash."

"You wanna do what?" he frowned.

"I was wondering if you would allow me to explore, to look for artifacts on your claim."

Caleb blinked at the request, his mind racing as to the right answer. To say 'no' would likely give Henry the idea he was hiding something. Likewise, the man might not be so free with his bourbon. To say 'yes' meant he'd have to keep an eye on the varmint. Settling on a compromise, he gruffly said, "S'long as you sit outside my cave. Not that I don't trust you, mind you. Hell, you been here while I was away. Just don't like anyone messin' with my personals while I'm workin'."

"Of course not. I'd be only too pleased to abide by your requirements. I am indebted to you, my friend." He placed a hand over his heart and bowed. *"Muchas gracias, señor."*

"What?"

"I said 'Thank you,' in Spanish," he said.

"Don't speak Spanish," he sourly replied.

"What? After all these years prospecting? Surely you've picked up some of the language."

"Haven't been down here that long," he defensively answered. "Spent most of my time in Colorado."

"Ah yes," Henry expansively said. "The recent addition to the Union. A lovely place. Well, my good man, I know you have work you wish to resume. I again thank you for your generosity."

Caleb gave him a nod and watched him happily return to his holding. He decided to wait and watch what the man would do. A short while later, Henry made his way down toward the wash. He carried a canvass bag strapped to his back. Protruding out the top of the bag were two wires, one leading to the metal wand he held in his hand, the other to the goggles he was wearing.

Sighing with impatience, Caleb turned around to continue his mining. From the corner of his eyes, Henry watched him leave. Chuckling to himself, he knew the man could never be a poker player. Yet the revelation that the old prospector did not speak Spanish revealed that de la Fuente's journal was not the cause of the man's recent paranoia. Something else was in that cave, and Henry had a good idea what it was. Yet he would have to wait until the next time Caleb went into Tombstone to find out. In the meantime, he would pretend to hunt for artifacts.

Unslinging the cell detector, he sat down on the ground to adjust the settings. He had made some significant alterations to the device and now was as good a time as any to see if they worked. On top of the detector were a series of switches in two orderly rows. The first switch of the top row separated the readings based upon Ernst Haeckel's three kingdom system of unicellular organisms, plants, and animals. Subsequent switches in row one further divided the animal kingdom using Charles Darwin's evolutionary taxonomy.

The first five switches in the second row further refined the data by time sequence. Each switch had an additional knob switch linked to it to allow finer adjustments. The final five switches controlled the wand detector and the sensor goggles.

Flipping the numerous switches to the desired settings, Henry flicked the machine on. Pausing a moment to watch the arcing electric current rise up among the numerous electrodes, he shouldered the canvass bag, adjusted his goggles and set out.

Starting at the bottom of the wash, Henry moved in deliberate elongated loops to the right then left, slowly working his way up towards the mouth of the cave. At first, the jump in readings surprised him, but as the clicking increased each time he got closer to the cave, the more assured he became that he was at the right spot, or rather Caleb was at the right spot.

For the next two hours, Henry focused his attention on the volume of readings as he walked. Each time the clicking significantly decreased, he took note of the location. By the time he was finished, he had a clear idea that a group of Indians had approached the cave from the west and southwest. This appeared consistent with what he remembered reading in de la Fuente's journal. If only he could get his hands on the journal, he could assure himself of the findings. But one thing was clear… de la Fuente had been here… and Caleb had found something else far more important than de le Fuente's journal

It was as he was working his way back to his side that he saw them, two machinists riding bareback. His shoulders slumping in frustration, he ambled back up to his tent, unloaded the CED by the field desk, and pulled open the top drawer to retrieve a folder with official looking papers.

Placing the folder on the desk, he assumed a persona of cheerfulness. He studied them as they approached. They were similarly dressed in white shirts, tan slacks, and machinist jackets. One appeared a little taller than the other, with long black hair pulled back behind his head. The other likewise had coal black hair that was cut to shoulder length. They seemed young for machinists.

"Good morning, gentlemen," he affably greeted them. "May I fix you some coffee?"

"Mister Mitchell?" the taller one said.

"I am he."

"I'm Taboca and this is Nantan," he said by way of introduction. "We heard you had some interesting machines out here," he said casting an appreciative gaze at the MATE and IAS.

"Just so you know, I have authorization for them. Likewise, I also have sole proprietorship."

"We're not here to harass you Mister Mitchell," he smiled. "We've heard about your machines and wanted to come see for ourselves."

"Fine," he grinned back. "As long as we understand each other. Coffee?"

"That would be most appreciated," Nantan said, swinging down from his horse.

"What happened to your saddles?" Henry asked.

"Didn't want them," Taboca said, hopping down. "Every now and then it's nice to get back to our roots, to feel the horse beneath us, to be one with the magnificent creatures."

"Yeah," Nantan chimed in. "When you spend all day working on engines and fixing other people's stupid mistakes, it's nice to get out in the open again."

"Other than coming out to see my inventions, what brings you to my neck of the desert?" Henry filled up the coffee pot and placed it on the low coals, adding several pieces of dried mesquite to bring up the flame.

"We're actually in Bisbee working on two airships down from St. Joseph and Salt Lake City," Nantan explained.

"Doesn't Bisbee have machinists?"

"They do, but some are on vacation and they were short a few hands, so we were sent down from Phoenix."

"Interesting machine" Taboca observed looking at the MATE. "An unusual concept, but intriguing. I assume it works well?"

"I can go almost anywhere a horse can, and I don't have to clean up after it," he joked. "Further, when I attach a wagon to it, I can haul as big a load as ten mules could carry."

"And what is that?" Nantan pointed to the IAS.

"That, my good man, is the future of modern warfare," he grandly stated. "It is an intruder alert system."

"What does it do?"

"Why detect intruders, naturally," Henry replied.

"How?"

Henry spent the next fifteen minutes explaining and answering questions about both the IAS and the MATE. By then, the coffee was ready and he poured several cups.

"This is good," Taboca complimented.

"My own secret recipe," Henry smiled. "How long will you be in Tombstone?"

"We'll go back to Bisbee today," Taboca answered. "Might have to come back tonight to visit the Bird Cage Theater again."

"Ah ha!" Henry grinned. "I see you've been to the premier establishment in town."

"Marshal Sadler sent us there."

"The Marshal did, did he?" Henry wryly replied. "Did you have to good fortune to meet Miss Belle DuBois, the madam?"

The two machinists exchanged knowing looks. "She was very accommodating," Taboca grinned.

"I'm sure she was," Henry chuckled.

"What's that?" Nantan said, pointing to the CED by the desk.

"That is one of the tools of my trade," he said. "It's a cell detector."

"What's it –" Nantan caught himself. "It detects cells. Why?"

"In addition to being an inventor, I'm an archaeologist by trade. In this instance, I'm looking for ancient artifacts of the Hohokam civilization. What the machine does is analyze residual cell deposits within the context of layered time."

"And the Wand thing?" Nantan asked.

"That's the sensor."

"Reminds me a bit of your stun gun," Taboca said to Nantan.

"His what?" Henry perked up.

"Stun gun," Nantan answered, "though I'm still working on it."

"It's genius," Taboca proudly said. "Explain it to him. He's someone who can appreciate what you've done."

"I use a variant of the Leclanché battery cell as my power source," he expounded. "I mix the ammonium chloride with some paste so that the battery is solid, won't spill, and can be used in any orientation. I attach two wires to the external electrodes. The wires are then attached to projectile electrodes that I can fire into a person or animal. I'm using an altered coach gun right now with the barrels expanded to fit the projectile electrodes."

"Killed a bull with it," Taboca smirked.

"I'm still working on the voltage," Nantan sheepishly admitted.

"I'd love to see it," Henry said, genuinely impressed then added, "as long as you don't use me for target practice."

Grinning, Nantan said, "I didn't bring it with me. It's back in the shop in Phoenix."

Henry nodded as he pondered the device. "What paste did you say you used?"

"Plaster of Paris," he smiled.

"Brilliant."

"Thank you."

"Well," Taboca said, "we won't take up anymore of your time. And don't worry, your inventions are safe with us."

"I appreciate that," Henry said. "I'd like to return the favor. Miss Belle is also a friend of mine." Taking a piece of paper and writing on it with a graceful and fluid script, he handed it to Taboca. "Here. Give this to her and tell her that

I sent you and that I will take care of all your expenses for the evening."

"Wow!" Nantan burst, wide-eyed.

"That's very generous, but you don't have to do that," Taboca said.

"It would be my pleasure. Besides allowing you to have a pleasure-filled evening, it also helps support that fine establishment."

"If ever you need our help," Nantan gushed, "just let us know. It'll be off the record."

"Now *that* is very generous," Henry replied.

"We'd better go," Taboca said, "so we can get back to work."

Giving him a friendly wave goodbye, the two hopped up on their mounts and languidly rode away. Henry watched them until they crested a far ridge and disappeared. Smiling contentedly, he mused on his good fortune. These two machinists might prove useful. It never hurts to have allies in strange places.

The more he pondered, the more he wondered about how he could exploit this new friendship with the two machinists. Yet what intrigued him more was the young man's stun gun. Looking around at his various machines, he knew he didn't have the tools or equipment necessary to make one. He happened to look down at the CED and his meanderings took an abrupt turn. Perhaps… just perhaps, he might already have what he needed.

Looking over to Caleb's cave, his lips curved into a smile wondering if Caleb would like to assist him, volunteer to be the test subject.

Having finished another lunch eating by himself, Mason paid the tab, pushed through the door and stepped out into the street. Suddenly he felt the Stetson fly from his head at the same time two shots loudly reverberated. Jerking down and whirling around, his six-gun was already out by the time he saw the man slumped over the hitching post in front of the Alhambra Saloon, his six-shooter slowly slipping from his lifeless grip to tumble to the ground. Then he saw Johnny Ringo crossing the street, holstering his pistol as he walked over to inspect the dead man.

Standing back up, Mason slid his gun back into the holster and walked back to retrieve his Stetson, more than irritated at the hole in the crown. Turning around to head over to where a crowd had now gathered, he was passed by Deputy Jimmy Coyle who blew by him and ran up to where Ringo was casually examining the dead man.

"You've done it now, Ringo," Jimmy called out, pushing the crowd aside. "Someone go get the doc."

"He was going to gun down the Marshal," Ringo indignantly replied, pointing at the dead man.

"Sure he was. You can tell that to the judge. Give me your guns."

"I swear I was only protecting the Marshal," he shot back.

"Sure you were. Give me your guns." He held his hand out, staring at the outlaw.

"Now hold on a minute, Jimmy," Mason said, shouldering his way in. He looked down at the dead man and recognized the bounty hunter he had shot several days ago. "I know this one. He's a bounty hunter, the same one I had to persuade to leave Frank Blackwood with me. I take it he wasn't too happy about my methods."

"That may be, Mason," Jimmy coldly replied, "but this here's a police matter, and I'm taking him in." The crowd began to churn volatile, and the subtle murmur of lynching this murderer overlapped demands of getting rid of this trouble-maker once and for all. "You all go about your business," he snarled. "This man is my prisoner. Anyone who interferes with me will be in big trouble. Now move along."

"Let me through," Doc Goodfellow called out. Working his way through the dividing crowd, he stopped in front of the man molded to the hitching post. After only a moment's hesitation, he said, "You need the undertaker, not me. This man's obviously dead." Summarily dismissing the problem, he turned around and passed back through the throng.

Sensing a tipping point that always led to lynching, Mason stepped in between Ringo and the crowd. "C'mon now folks. Jimmy's got this under control. Let the law takes its course. Go on about your business." Lowering his voice, he said over his shoulder, "Give him your guns Johnny."

Up until now, Ringo had his hands lightly touching the pistol grips. Knowing he had no options left, he straightened to full height. Slowly and deliberately, he unbuckled his two guns and handed the belt to Jimmy.

Quickly extracting him through the simmering crowd, Jimmy pushed Ringo towards the jail, Mason in tow. It wasn't until they were safely the inside the jailhouse that Jimmy let out a sigh of relief. Placing Ringo's guns on his desk, he unlooped the ring of cells keys from the wall peg. "Let's go Ringo."

"Just a moment, Jimmy," Mason interrupted. "You know there's been too much bad blood passed about Ringo. I'm not saying he's a saint, but he deserves a fair trial. You heard them out there. They want a hanging."

"They'll calm down," Jimmy countered, though not without some hesitation.

"Give me my guns, and I promise to never come back to Tombstone," Ringo offered.

"Can't do that Ringo,' Jimmy sniffed in disdain. "You shot a man dead back there."

"I told you I was protecting the Marshal."

"So you said. We'll let the judge sort that all out."

The door opened and lawyer Alexander Goodrich hustled in, looking worried. "I just heard," he said to Ringo.

"Well?"

"Johnny," he lamely explained. "No bondsman going to cover you anymore."

"What's the bond?" Mason asked.

"Don't know. I got to get to the judge."

"Well don't stand here, man," Mason snapped. "The judge is probably still in session." Giving him a gentle shove towards the door, he said, "Get back here as quick as you can. You tell him that I, Marshall Mason Sadler, say this man is innocent and was trying to protect me."

Once the lawyer had hurried out, Jimmy turned to Mason. "Why are you so all fired up about this?"

"You heard me. I believe Ringo did just what he claimed he did," Mason soberly stated. "The man he shot deserved what he got. The man was a fool."

"We'll see," Jimmy replied, his skepticism obvious. Turning to Ringo, he opened the door to the cells and said, "Until then, let's get you safely tucked away inside."

It was several hours later before the lawyer returned. The two lawmen followed him into where Johnny Ringo lay distractedly staring at the ceiling. Hearing them enter, he got up.

"Well?" he demanded.

"It doesn't look good, Johnny," the lawyer apologetically began. "The judge said that because the Marshal is vouching for you, he set the bail at $500."

"Get it," Ringo said. "Get me out of here."

"It's like I said, Johnny," the lawyer equivocated. "No bondsman wants to take you on anymore."

"When's he go before the judge?" Mason asked.

"That's another problem," he simpered. "Judge said he wouldn't get to you until next week."

"Next week?" Ringo snapped.

"Might as well get comfortable, Ringo," Jimmy said. "Looks like you'll be here for a while."

"Not if they don't get to me first," he sourly replied, referring to the group who were hurling lynching threats only hours before.

"I'll post the bond," Mason calmly said.

Silence settled momentarily as the other's made sure they had heard correctly. Jimmy cocked an eyebrow. "You'll post bond?"

"Yes. Both you and Alexander are witnesses. I will post bond for him. Go ahead and release him."

"You sure you know what you're doing?" Jimmy said, frowning at him.

"Just do like I asked, Jimmy. It will be OK."

With a doubtful sigh, Jimmy went back to retrieve the keys. "This is damned stupid. It'll be on your head when he doesn't come back."

"I know."

The four men went back to the front office where Jimmy gave Ringo back his guns. Leaving Jimmy and the lawyer in the office, Mason and Ringo stepped outside, where Johnny inhaled a deep breath of freedom.

"Why'd you do this, Marshal?" he asked, his eyes a mixture of surprise and respect.

"You're innocent."

With a bemused smile, Johnny looked at him with a studious regard for a few moments. "I'll pay you back," he said, adjusting his pistol belt.

"I know you will."

"And I'll be in court when I'm supposed to be there."

"I have no doubt about that, Johnny. You and I are good, remember?"

Ringo nodded thoughtfully then looked up to the hole in Mason's Stetson. "You may want to find yourself another hat."

Mason took off the Stetson and fingered the hole. "I don't know," he mused. "I might just keep this as a reminder of how close one can come to leaving this world unexpectedly." Turning his attention back to Ringo, he said, "You get clear of here for a while. Stay out of trouble, for at least the next week."

"I'll do that, Marshal. You can count on me."

There was a momentary pause before Mason said, "Thank you Johnny. That bounty hunter was a coward. You saved my life back there. You're a good man."

Adjusting his hat, Ringo looked out past the miner's cabins and over the barren hills alive with men digging for wealth. "That's where you're wrong, Marshal. I'm not a good man. I did it because *you're* a good man. See you in a week." With a wave of his hand Ringo disappeared around the side of the building.

Watching Ringo vanish, Mason pondered the man, wondering what demons tormented him. The man was a paradox. Billy Breakenridge had told him about the time he served a warrant to Ringo in Galeyville for robbing a poker game in Evilsizer's Saloon the week before. For some reason Billy was in a hurry to get back to Tombstone and Ringo had other business to settle. Ringo gave Billy his word that he'd be there before Billy got to town. Good to his word, Ringo showed up, even though it meant getting tossed in jail. The man certainly was a paradox. Fast with a gun, willing to rob you for fun, but once he gave his word, you could take it to the bank.

Deciding he could use a drink, Mason headed up the street to the Theater. It was now just past dinner time, and the streets were crowded with the more respected citizens of Tombstone heading off to Schieffelin Hall to watch a performance by the Nellie Boyd Dramatic Company, while the common folks filled the saloons, dance halls and billiard rooms.

When Belle saw Mason come through the door, she coquettishly extracted herself from the group of men vying for her attention and breezed over to him, taking him by the arm, much to the irritation of the former suitors.

"I hear you had a close call today," she said, cocking an eyebrow as she looked up at the hole in his Stetson.

"I'd forgotten about that," he said, sheepishly taking off his hat to reexamine the hole. "Guess I'll need to get a new hat." Unconsciously pushing his fingers though his hair, he placed the Stetson on the counter.

Belle found herself gawking at him. His thick and wavy auburn hair fell to his shoulders, framing a chiseled and clean-shaven face that reminded her of a renaissance painting. Suddenly feeling foolish, she said, "Some say that Ringo shot him in cold blood."

"They don't know what they're talking about," he tersely said. "Johnny got to him just as he opened up on me."

"Some don't see it that way," she said. "There's talk of lynching."

"They'll have a long way to go to find him," he replied, nodding his thanks as Jack set a whiskey in front of him.

"What do you mean? He's in the jail, isn't he?"

94

"He was," he said, taking a sip and savoring the smooth fullness.

"What happened? I heard there was at least a $500 bond on him."

"I paid it." He took another sip.

Belle blinked at the revelation before raising an eyebrow. "Did I hear that right? You paid it?"

"You heard right."

"Why would you do that?" she asked, her voice revealing her obvious surprise.

"For two reasons," he calmly explained. "First, he's innocent, and I won't have some fools take the law into their own hands and lynch him for a crime he didn't commit." He drained the glass and held it up for another.

"The second reason?" she asked.

Holding her gaze with his, he said, "He saved my life."

Belle thought for a moment then said, "Sounds like good enough reasons to me."

"I'm glad you approve," he smiled at her.

"Well, now that you've disappointed the lynch mob, Jesse Two-Spades is downstairs at the Faro table and his luck is running south. I don't think it will be too long before he calls it quits."

"He's got some guts showing up here," Mason chuckled, "right across the street from the Palace. That was, what, only three months ago he shot up the place and killed the bartender? And he's back playing cards as if nothing ever happened." He shook his head. "I'll be ready." Downing the last of his whiskey, he put his hat back on and stepped outside. Just as he was heading towards the side of the Theater, a voice rang out.

"You there. You the man what killed my brother?"

Abruptly stopping, Mason slowly turned around looking for the man who spoke. The flickering light of the streetlamps gave image to a number of men clearing space across the street in front of Rafforty's Saloon.

"I don't rightly know. Who's your brother?" he said.

"Listen to him," the voice sneered before giving form to the sound as three men emerged from the shadows and stepped into the street. "I don't rightly know," the man in the middle mimicked. He was thick-bodied and wore an open-crease style hat jammed down to almost his eyebrows so that he had to tilt his head back to see clearly. He wore a gun on each hip, as did his two partners.

Mason calmly walked into the street, facing them, about ten paces away. "Mister," he said, his voice firm. "I suggest you think about what you're planning on doing."

"Oh, I thought about it long enough," he shot back, "all the way I was travellin' here. Funny how as soon as I gets here I find out he's been shot dead. And then I hear about who killed him and how Johnny Ringo's got loose and nowhere to be found, 'cause some Marshal sets him free. So the way I sees it, that makes you what they calls an accomplice." He spoke with the confidence of a man who knew little about the law but understood what some of the words meant. "You might not have pulled the trigger, but that don't mean you ain't the one actual responsible. I heard what you done to him afore the killin'."

Ah," Mason said in understanding. "You must be friends of the bounty hunter."

"I ain't his friend," the man huffed. "I'm his brother."

"Of course you are," he quietly smirked, though frustrated that his quarry might be escaping out the back door of the Theater. "I suppose you've come here to conduct an inquiry as to what happened to your brother."

"I ain't here to do nuthin' of the kind."

"I see," he calmly answered. "Pity. It would save a lot of trouble."

"You're the one that stated the trouble when you not only shot my brother but stole the bounty that was rightfully ours."

"And what do you propose to do about it?" Mason asked, seemingly unaffected by their overt threat.

"We aim to settle it, right here and right now," he arrogantly stated.

Heaving an audible sigh, Mason called out to the crowd keeping out of the way. "Someone go get the sheriff. Tell him it wasn't a fair fight. There were only three of them."

"Pretty brave for a dead man," the man in the middle snarled.

"You do realize the penalty for shooting a US Marshal," Mason pointed out.

"I'll take my chances," he cavalierly replied.

"Well then," he said. "You let me know where you're ready."

"Oh, we're ready."

Before the words had escaped his lips, two shots erupted and the men on either side of him crumpled to the ground, and he was facing the barrel of Mason's .45 leveled at his head.

"Hold on there," Sheriff John Behan called out running up, Police Office Harry Solen right behind him.

"Hello John, Harry," Mason said, his gun still pointed at the man's head. "Glad you're here. I'm charging these men with attempted murder of a US Marshall."

Brushing away a bead of sweat from his eyes, the man was suddenly not so sure of his future, though thankful he was still standing. "He killed my brother," he said in self-defense.

"No he didn't," Sheriff Behan sourly retorted. "Johnny Ringo did, and you're a damn fool to think you can take the law into your own hands. Now drop your guns to the ground."

Casting a quick look to the men on the ground, the man couldn't help but note that neither had moved since being shot. Their bodies lay in unnatural limp contortion, their guns still in the holsters. It didn't take a genius to see they were both dead, most likely shot through the heart. With the Marshal still pointing the gun at his head, his decision was not difficult. Slowly unbuckling his belt, he let it drop to the street.

Scooping up the belt and guns, Sheriff Behan bent down next to Harry to take a cursory look at the two men on the ground, knowing they were both dead.

"Sorry John," Mason said, holstering his six-shooter. "I couldn't take the chance of just winging them. They were too set on a shoot-out and too many innocent people might have gotten hurt."

By now, a small crowd had gathered a safe distance away. Sheriff Behan looked up and said, "Someone get the Undertaker." Standing up, he addressed the man. "You got a name?"

"Joe Haskell," he answered.

"Well Mister Haskell, looks like you're gonna come with me." He spoke with a tone that brooked no argument. "I've got a nice cot for you in a safe place where you won't get into any more trouble. You should have come to me first. Your friends might still be alive if you had."

"He started it by shootin' my brother."

"Your brother was a fool,' he snapped. Looking again at the crowd, he asked, "Any of you witnesses?" A few voices admitted to seeing what happened. "Give your names to Harry. Come by my office in the morning to write a statement." Giving Joe Haskell an evil stare, he said, "C'mon you," and marched him off to lock up.

Harry lingered behind waiting for the undertaker. "Nice shooting, Mason," he said, straight-faced.

"I'm getting better," he replied in kind.

Harry snorted a laugh. "See ya around."

Mason gave him a friendly wave and went back into the Bird Cage Theater. Seeing him, Belle gave him a quizzical look.

Sidling up next to him at the bar, she lowered her voice and said, "What are you doing back here?"

"I had a little trouble out front and figured he'd be long gone by now." He lifted the whiskey glass that Jack placed in front of him in a toast of appreciation that the bartender was always prompt in taking such good care of him.

"Trouble? What happened?"

"That bounty hunter had kin who didn't appreciate the finer points of law." He then related what had just happened and that thankfully Joe Haskell was now in jail.

"And the other two?"

"Dead," he succinctly answered, taking a sip.

"You can't keep doing this," she said, her voice edged with concern.

"It comes with the badge. You know that."

"Of course I do, but not everyone is out to shoot me," she countered.

"It's not like I have a lot of choices," he shrugged. "Is our boy still here?"

"Yes. His luck changed. Not sure how long he'll be."

"Then I think we'll just have to accelerate the process. I'm going in through the back. My guess is that he'll be up this way before long. See if you can hold him here 'til I get here," he said, swigging the rest of his drink.

"How?" she frowned.

"Use your imagination," he replied with half-a-smile. Placing a silver dollar on the counter, he walked out.

Frustrated, Belle turned her back to the bar so she could see out over the dance floor. "Give me a sangaree, Jack," she said over her shoulder. While Jack mixed the drink, she saw Jesse Two-Spades burst up the stairs from the basement Faro game, thrusting his way between dancers. "Quick Jack," she demanded.

Grabbing the drink, she smiled at a group of men across from the bar and stepped forward as if going over to greet them, causing Jesse Two-Spades to plow into her, knocking both of them down.

While the music blared loudly in the dance hall and men and women pranced and clopped around the floor, all conversations in the bar immediately stopped. Jack already had his Coach Gun out from behind the bar and had it pointed at Jesse who, half-dazed, had struggled to his feet ready to continue his flight.

"Hold it right there, Mister," Jack said, threatening Jesse with the Coach Gun.

While several men gallantly assisted Belle to her feet, Mason came striding into the bar. Rapidly assessing the scene, he walked over to confront Jesse. "Jesse Graham," he formally announced, his six-shooter drawn and pointed at the man. "I'm arresting you for the murder of Howard Leedy."

Turning to Belle who was brushing off her dress, he said, "Are you OK Miss DuBois?"

"I'm fine, Marshal" she said through pursed lips, then looked at the front of her dress wet with spilled sangaree, "though it looks like I'll need another dress for the evening." Turning to the four men who helped her up, she teased, "Now which one of you would be willing to help me get out of this and find a new dress?"

When the overwhelming response threatened to become physical, she coyly announced, "I simply can't decide, so I'll just have to do it myself." Looking over her shoulder to Jack, she gave him a wink of thanks. "Tell Billy I'll be back in little bit."

Placing a hand on Mason's arm, she solemnly looked up at him and said, "What a stroke of luck that you were here tonight. Who knows," she added, give Jesse a look of condemnation, "something might have happened here just like at the Palace."

"Are you sure you're all right, Miss DuBois?" Mason solicitously asked again.

"Yes, Marshal. Thank you. I'll have one or two of these gallant gentlemen here escort me back home. I'll be perfectly safe."

Mason chuckled to himself seeing the eager faces only too willing and ready to escort the very lovely madam. Yet his humor was tinged with the flicker of jealousy that they would have the privilege of having this special time with her, even if it was only going to her house and waiting for her to change clothing.

Pushing the thought aside, he turned to his prisoner. "Let's go, Jesse. And no funny stuff. It's been a trying night and I'm not in the mood for games. I've already killed two men today and I'd hate to have to add a third." Pushing him out the door, they headed to the jailhouse.

Watching him leave, Belle hoped he'd come back by the time she changed and returned. Yet something told her that he wouldn't be back tonight, that once he had settled Jesse into the jailhouse, he would most likely go home... to a woman he no longer loved.

Sighing with disappointment, she turned her attention to the surrounding admirers. Brightening, she smiled while pretending to choose. "Let's see. I only have two arms, so it will have to be you two gentlemen to escort me home, and you two to escort me back." Giving Jack a cheerful wave, she breezed out with her company of companions.

Mason opened the door to find Elizabeth sitting in bed, pretending to read. "You're awake," he said, unbuckling his pistol belt and hanging it on a wall peg. Taking off his Stetson, he placed it on the same hook

"Disappointed?" she coldly asked, not looking up.

"Why would I be disappointed?"

"I'm awake means you can't spend time with your girlfriend." She flipped a page of the book.

"She's not my girlfriend," he sighed, shaking his head in frustration.

"No, she's just a whore, which seems to be the level of existence you prefer these days."

"She's not a whore," he firmly replied.

"Oh, that's right," she sneered, looking up, her eyes flashing. "She's just a madam and that's *so* much better. She's not a common whore, one of those gutter girls who will spread her legs for a quarter. No, she's a madam. Yes, a refined pimp. It does sound so much better when one calls her 'madam' instead of 'slut,' don't you think?" She looked at him with feigned innocence.

Mason looked at her then at the half-empty bottle of laudanum on the dresser by the bed. "Maybe you should take some more of your medicine –"

"What? And miss out on this absolutely fascinating discussion?" she tartly interrupted. "Now where were we? Oh yes. We were discussing your girlfriend who's not a whore, but rather a madam, which is a polite term for 'slut.' I think that's correct, isn't it?"

His lips tightened as his first inclination was to put his holster belt back on and come back when she was asleep or unconscious. "What's got into you?"

"Into me?" she mocked. "Oh, that's rich. You spend your time with a whore and when you're not with her, you're running loose with outlaws." She glared at him. "It's not bad enough that you drag me here to this wasteland filled with humanity's dregs to live in this dump of a boarding house, you want to ruin what little reputation I have left by becoming a common criminal."

"What are you talking about?"

"You're such a bad liar," she said as though chiding a child. "You stand there pretending nothing happened, like I wouldn't find out."

"Find out what?"

She stared at him, her eyes boring into him. "You think I hadn't heard about you and that thug Johnny Ringo, about how you posted $1000 to bail him out of jail."

"It was $500, not $1000."

"Oh, that's much, much better," she scoffed. "Only half as much to let that killer free."

"He'll pay me back."

She tossed her head back and barked laughed filled with derision. "You are so pathetic. You honestly believe that thief will pay you back? You are either incredibly naïve or blatantly stupid. How did you ever become a marshal?"

Mason stood to full height, folding his arms. "I posted bail because he was innocent."

"That's what they all say," she ridiculed.

"He killed a man who was trying to kill me," he flatly responded, retrieving the Stetson to show her the hole in the crown.

Elizabeth glared hard at him for a few moments before saying, "Pity he missed."

Mason stiffened at the overt insult. Instead of getting angry, he walked over to the dresser. Placing the Stetson down, he picked up the bottle of laudanum. "Where are you getting this stuff?"

"What do you care," she retorted. "You blow $500 on a murderer and even more on that harlot and you worry about where I get my medicine?"

"Suppose I pour this down the drain?" he challenged.

"Go ahead," she spat, her eyes piercing him. "I'll get more."

Staring angrily at her, he abruptly realized all his outrage was worthless. There was nothing he could do, short of giving up his career as a lawman and going back to San Francisco, that would make her happy. Yet even then, they were doomed for they had long passed the point of saving the marriage. Why was he being so stubborn to think that he could save it?

Just as suddenly the image of Ringo came to mind and the fact that, despite the evil in the man, once he gave his word, he kept it, no matter what. Mason ruefully shook his head. If a man like Ringo could keep his word then so could he, even if it meant his bitter marriage was a failure.

Placing the bottle back on the dresser, he said, "Things will get better. You'll see. Once I save enough, we can find a nice house to live in."

"What?" she taunted, her voice full of scorn. "And give up all this?" She waved a hand at the single room that functioned as bedroom, living room, and sometimes dining room. "All this for a quaint bungalow in Tombstone... Tombstone, how appropriate. I gave up a life, a real life, with a mansion and servants and friends who can spell more than just their name. A life with culture and elegance, and real food... I gave up all that to follow a fool to a town called Tombstone." Looking up at him, she smirked, "It is ironic don't you think? We'll all die here, and these fools can't even spell 'ironic.'"

Heaving a sigh, Mason picked up his hat, turned and retrieved his pistol belt, calmly buckling it.

"Where are you going?" she tartly demanded.

"I'm going for a walk," he impassively answered.

"Sure you are," she said, curling a lip in disdain. Reaching for the bottle of laudanum, she said, "Tell that harlot girlfriend of yours that your wife says 'hello.'"

Without responding, Mason opened the door and stepped out into the hallway. Turning to close the door, he saw her feverishly uncork the bottle.

Chapter 6

It had been two days since the two machinists had visited him, and Henry was no closer to converting his CED into a stun gun. He knew he had all the pieces right there with him. It was just a matter of redirecting the electric current to the projectile electrodes which were simply pieces of highly conducive metal. The dilemma of projectile wire was easily solved when he had simply cut a section from the telegraph line going into Tombstone. That little escapade had actually been fun for he imagined the furor it would cause back in town.

It was when he was attempting to improvise the firing mechanism in his Coach Gun that he ran into problems. His frustration mounting, he decided now was a time to do something else. He knew his frustration was not from his unsuccessful experimentation with the CED, but rather knowing that there was something significant in Caleb's cave, and he was at the mercy of this ignorant prospector.

Even the evening meals had revealed nothing, despite his subtle attempts at dragging the information out of him. Whenever the topic edged closer to Caleb's cave, he suddenly became tight-lipped. Even feigned interest in the mining process was met with firm rebuff, despite the overflowing bourbon.

Deciding he could use some supplies, he informed Caleb that he was going into town asking the cursory, "Do you need anything?"

"Nope. Won't be just another three days 'til I get there myself." He brushed the sweat from his forehead with the back of his hand.

"Fine," Henry cheerfully acknowledged. "Guard the fort while I'm gone."

"Always do," he replied over his shoulder as he reentered the cave. Pausing just inside the shadows, he waited until he heard the MATE's engine starting up before he edged closer to peek around the side to see Henry mount the driver's seat, release the brakes, and motor off, the metal wagon attached to the back. Stepping outside to watch him as he dwindled in the distance, Caleb then turned around and walked over to the stone pile, methodically removing each stone and arranging it in neat symmetrical orderly lines as he opened up the entrance to the treasure cave.

Gathering up his lantern, he crawled the short distance to the other cave where de la Fuente and friend still lay, the glimmering treasure piled high between them.

"Afternoon," he greeted the two skeletons. "He's gone. Figured I'd come and check on things." Lowering himself to sit cross-legged in front of the treasure, he positioned the lamp to his side.

Looking at the size of the pile, he remarked, "Seems a lot for two men t'carry, even if they was strong ones, which you two ain't lookin' like, 'specially now." Selecting a golden bowl, he asked, "Mind if I take a look?"

Though it was a simple unadorned bowl, the heft and shine told him it was near as to solid gold as could be. Caleb knew enough about precious metals to know that the bowl had another alloy mixed in with it to make it sturdy, most likely silver that seemed to be plentiful in the area. Yet far from disappointing him, that thought pleased him as he knew whether silver or gold, he was rich beyond imagination.

"You boys got any ideas how I can get this all outta here?" Their presence no longer bothered Caleb, and the eerie feeling he had first experienced diminished with each time he came into the cave until now he felt nothing.

"Talked to the Marshal and he says to just leave well enough alone for the time bein'. Seemed a good idea at first, but I ain't takin' to it fer much longer. Fact is, I'm beginnin' to lose interest in prospectin'. Don't see the point to it no more. I was thinkin' I might talk to Henry. Feller seems to know somethin' about old things. Figured he might know somethin' about this here gold. Whaddaya think?"

Silence resumed its presence as he put the bowl back and selected a wide necklace of gold inlaid with turquoise stones.

Looking over at the man to his right, he said, "Oh, I know what yer thinkin'. It ain't like I've known him a while to trust him with all this. Once he sees it, he might want it for himself. Still, seems a harmless feller, even if he is a might touched in the head with what he does fer a livin'. But he's a smart one. You oughta take a look at them machines of his."

A thought came to him, and he frowned. "Say, where you boys from? That one book I found. Cain't read a word of it." Scratching his bearded face, he said, "Wonder if ol' Henry can make hide nor tail of it."

Placing the necklace back on the pile, he sat quietly and stared at the amassed wealth. While he gazed at his treasure, he ruminated on what to do. It was then he decided to test Henry to see how much he could be trusted. He'd start first with giving him the book. Anything beyond that depended on Henry.

With a sigh, he stood up. "See ya later." Scooting back out, he replaced the stones, dusting the pile with dirt when finished. Looking at the gaping opening to his silver vein, he sighed, knowing he'd have to keep up appearances, for a while at least.

While Caleb trudged back to work, Henry reveled in the open air and sun-filled day as he chugged along the main road into Tombstone. His mind drifted to the most recent dalliance with the lovely Belle. He figured time was running short if he was going to discover what was in Caleb's cave, bed Belle, and make off with what he hoped was a chest full of gold. He wouldn't be able to get back into Caleb's cave until the old coot came to town again. In between now and then was another visit to the Bird Cage. Perhaps this time he should spend more time giving his attention to Belle. He could forego the pleasures of the upstairs cribs for one night.

The Marshal came to mind, and he smiled. The man might be a good lawman, but he was out of his league in the affairs of the heart. His choice of spouse was testament to that. Yet Henry was no fool, for he saw how Belle reacted and looked at him. He wouldn't be surprised if there wasn't something going on between them. Still, the game was on and Henry would bed Belle while Mason dealt with his addict wife.

Henry smiled at the memory of Elizabeth's visit to Wuhan Mei. What a sad creature, pathetic really. A tall flowering ocotillo caught his eye and he thought of the dichotomy between the colorful cactus adapting and giving beauty to the arid landscape, and the used-up woman back at the Marshal's place, unable to appreciate the possibilities, unable to adapt and overcome. Instead, she chose the way of all cowards by slow suicide. Pity she was not the beauty she once was, for it would have been an enjoyable challenge to get into her bed.

Dismissing her as not his problem, he focused on the approaching town. In less than an hour, he had crossed the distance between his claim and Tombstone and was coming upon the city outskirts making quite an impression as he cruised his noisy machine up Fremont Street. Passing by the Chinese laundry, he waved at the young Chinese woman who stepped to the front of the store to see what the racket was.

Turning right on 1st Street, he followed it until he turned left onto Allen Street. Ensuring he was noticed by those sitting outside the numerous stores, saloons, restaurants, and other businesses, he motored his way to slow down opposite the Bird Cage Theater to finally stop in front of Callisher's General Store. Across the street, Belle emerged, and he doffed his hat in polite, yet intimate respect, receiving a pleasant smile and wave in return.

Locking the breaks, he released pressure to the boiler then hopped down and went in the store while a number of gawkers and children crowded around the MATE. A few moments later, Henry pushed through the door followed by Jesse Langley, the store owner, both carrying four small empty packing crates that they loaded into the trailer.

"I can have the rest by day after tomorrow," Jesse promised, glad for the business.

"I'll be back around the same time then," Henry replied.

"Hey mister," a young boy caught his attention. "How fast does this thing go?"

"Why I can get her up to almost ten miles an hour," he said with pride.

As the boy shook his head in wonder, a man pointed at the treads and asked, "How's it work?"

Henry proceeded to explain in the most scientific terms, wanting to impress, but the more he talked, the less interested they became and started drifting away to get on with their day. He was talking to one last interested fellow when Mason crossed the street and walked up.

"Afternoon Mister Mitchell, Billy," he affably greeted them.

"Good afternoon, Marshal," Henry grinned. "Come to see my machine?"

"Just checking to see what was going on," he smiled, looking at the crates in the back. "Looks like business is going well for you."

"Why all the crates?" Billy asked.

"Tools of the trade," Henry explained. "Each one will contain remnants of past civilizations."

"Kind of small, aren't they?"

"Not at all. In my trade, it's rare to find artifacts intact. They're usually broken into pieces, which we call shards. Here, let me show you." He pulled one of the crates over and pried open the lid. Reaching in, he carefully lifted out a small bowl. Though dirty, it was an intact specimen with a yellow tint to it. Inside the bowl was a geometric design in black.

"Whatchu got there?" a voice asked.

The three men looked up to see Ben Gilstrap, a part time miner who spent most of his days in a blind drunk, leaning unsteadily against an awning post just outside the door to Jesse's store.

"Hullo, Ben," Mason greeted him. "You're up early. What brings you here?"

"Come to see what all the ruckus was." He stared at the bowl in Henry's hands. "Whatchu got there?"

"It's an Apache bowl," Henry condescendingly lectured. "Most likely two to three hundred years old. I was just showing it to our friend, the Marshal."

109

"How d'ya know it's Apache?"

"I'm an archaeologist, my good man, a professor at Brown University. I've spent years of study to know these things." Ignoring the man, Henry turned his attention back to Mason. "I pack these in sifted dirt until I can get them back home to clean up and restore. Are you interested in Indian artifacts?" he asked Billy.

"Not really," he shrugged, bored. "Guess I'd better get back before Jacob comes lookin' for me." Casting an envious look at the MATE, he hustled diagonally across the street to Jacob Meyer's Clothing Store.

Placing the bowl back into the crate, Henry waited until Billy was across the street before turning to Mason. His demeanor changed as he lowered his voice so only the Deputy could hear. "I wish to apologize for my insensitive comments the other night."

"What comments" Mason frowned, trying to remember.

"Concerning your, um... spouse. It was callous of me. I did not know."

"Did not know what," he asked, his lips pursed.

Instead of answering, Henry said, "I know of some very reputable doctors who could help. I'd be happy to inquire of them if you wish."

Mason studied the man determining if he was genuine in his offer or simply being an ass. His look said he was genuinely concerned. "I appreciate that. I might take you up on that offer. Don't recall seeing you in town this often," he said, changing the subject.

"I was working on one of my machines," he said, rolling his eyes, "and needed a break. Thought I'd come into town and get some things."

"Then I won't keep you," Mason said.

"Remember about my offer," Henry said, climbing up to the pilot's seat.

"I'll keep it in mind." Giving him a friendly nod, he watched him as he made the turn on 6th street to head up towards Fremont then over to Hoptown. Mason stood distractedly staring after him, wondering if any doctor could help Elizabeth. In order to be helped, one had to want the help, and Elizabeth no longer wanted help. If only he could stop the flow of laudanum. He couldn't figure out how she was getting it, let alone paying for it. He was careful not to leave excess money lying about the room. He had learned all too quickly that it disappeared before he even had the chance to remember he had left it there.

The thought that someone was providing for her addiction bothered him as he could see no reason for it. Was it to get to him, to blackmail him, embarrass him? If that was the case, they were wasting their money. But what other reason could there be?

As the noise from the MATE diminished, Ben staggered down the steps to stand next to him watching Henry cheerily wave to folks.

"What's that feller say he does?" he asked.

"He's an archaeologist," Mason answered.

"Wull I reckon he cain't be much of one," Ben frowned. "Course he's got hisself a education and all, but I cain't see how he's any good at it."

"What do you mean?" Mason questioned.

"Why that there pottery he says is older'n the hills. Any dang fool worth a pennyweight o' salt can see it ain't old."

"How?" he asked, as they watched him disappear, the noise from the engine diminishing the farther away he went.

"'Cause I just know. That's how."

"You're not making any sense, Ben."

"Here, lemme show you," Ben said. "C'mon over to Jacob's store and I'll show ya." He began explaining as they crossed the street, using his hands. "The old Indian pots was made by rollin' out the clay so it'd look sorta like a snake. Then they'd coil it around into the shape they'd want and then they'd stick their hands in the insides and, usin' a scraper, they'd scrape and smooth it all out, doin' the same thing on the outside."

Stepping up onto the boardwalk, they pushed through the door, Ben leading. "Howdy, Jacob," Ben said, greeting the store owner, a well-dressed middle-aged man, in collarless shirt and ironed pants held up by suspenders. His bristling dark brown moustache made up for his short thinning hair.

"Hello Ben, Marshal. What can I do for you?"

"We come to look at the Indian pots."

"Over in the corner, Ben, same as always."

Ben led the way, and they stood in front of several shelves containing small, beautifully decorated jars and bowls. Lifting one, he held it up for Mason to look at. "See? This here's a real Apache pot." He stuck his hand inside it. "You can barely feel the bumps where they didn't get the coils smooth. Probably figured no one would notice on the inside. Here, see for yourself."

Mason gingerly placed his hand inside the bowl and felt the barely noticeable bumps and grooves. "So how is this different, from what Henry had?"

Grinning, his one front tooth missing, Ben held up a bowl. "See this one here? Go ahead and feel it."

"It feels smooth," Mason admitted.

"Course it does," he flatly stated. "That's 'cause it ain't been coiled. This one was wheel thrown or flattened out and put over a wood frame. See the color?"

Mason studied the golden-yellow color of the bowl. The geometric pattern was painted in black. "It's not quite the same as the first one you showed me."

"That's 'cause this one is made to look like Hopi, not Apache."

"How do you know that?" Mason asked, curious as to why this coarse man would know anything about the finer details of Indian pottery.

"Hell," he burst a laugh. "I make the Apache ones myself." He then dropped his head and looked rapidly around. "Don't let on though," he quickly warned. Pointing to a beautifully decorated and shaped small urn, he proudly said, "See that one there? That's one of mine."

"Really?" Mason said in admiration, taking the urn down. Studying the vessel, he quickly realized the man had exceptional talent. Pity he spent it all on drink. Placing it back on the shelf, he asked, "So how is this different from what Henry had?"

"Here," he replied, taking another bowl down, he handed it to the Marshal. "That one is Apache, 'cause the clay is redder and the design is plainer than the Hopi."

"I still don't see what this has to do with Henry," Mason said, looking doubtfully at the bowl.

"That's 'cause you don't know pots like I do," he winked at him, placing a dirty finger next to his nose. "What Henry says is Apache, ain't Apache. It's Hopi. And it ain't old, 'cause someone made it to look like Hopi, but they didn't coil it like they was supposed to."

"You mean..." Mason frowned with understanding and concern.

"Yup. Either that boy don't know nuthin' 'bout pots or he's humbuggin' somebody."

"Thank you, Ben," he thoughtfully said. "You've been very helpful."

"Yer welcome."

They were heading back out to the front when Ben put his hand on Mason's arm, quietly asking, "Say Marshal, think you could spot me two bits. I'll pay ya back."

Despite knowing what Ben would spend it on, he couldn't help but be grateful. "Tell you what, I've a better idea. How much does Jacob pay you for your Apache pots?"

"I get half, after it sells."

Turning around, he headed back to the shelves with the pottery, taking down the one Ben had made. Heading to the counter, he asked, "How much is this one, Jacob?"

Jacob looked at the urn then surreptitiously at Ben who, standing behind the Deputy, held up two fingers. "That would be three dollars," he said despite Ben's consternation and waving of hands.

"I'll take it," Mason pleasantly said, much to Ben's startled surprise, which quickly transitioned to glee.

While Jacob wrapped and tied the urn in a piece of cloth, Ben sidled up and whispered, "Much obliged, Marshal."

"You take care of yourself, Ben," he gently chided. "Save some of that and get cleaned up. You got real talent. Seems a shame not to use it." Clapping him on the back, he made his way out of the store and into the afternoon sun.

Standing on the boardwalk, he pondered Ben's revelation. Perhaps Henry was scamming someone back east. If he was, that was his problem. But what if Ben was wrong? It wouldn't be the first time the old coot had a whopper of a story. But then he quickly reminded himself that nine times out of ten, Ben's whoppers turned out to have some truth to them. Still, Henry's intellect was not so easily questioned, especially as the man had invented the MATE and his other machines. Yet the seed of distrust had been planted. Why would Henry not know his facts about Indian pots? What was his game? Was he really here looking for artifacts? Was he even an archaeologist?

Then the vision of Belle and Henry at the Bird Cage coalesced, especially her peaked interest in his stories. And then there was that little tidbit of the two of them on Henry's machine heading off for a picnic, most likely down at the San Pedro. Mason tried to push aside the twinge of jealousy, but it wouldn't let him go, no matter how hard he tried to rationalize it.

Walking back into the store, he saw Jacob arranging bolts of fabric. Jacob looked up when he entered.

"Hello again," he smiled at him.

"You know that archaeologist fellow?" Mason asked, getting directly to the point.

"The man with that loud contraption he frequently drives into town?"

"That's the one."

"Can't say that I know him. He comes into the store now and then for supplies and things."

Mason looked over at the Indian pots in the corner. "He ever buy any of your pots there?"

Jacob's eyes widened and he held his hands up as if pushing the Marshal away. "Now I can explain," he said. "I figured Ben told you that bowl you bought wasn't old."

"What are you talking about?" Mason frowned at him.

"That bowl in your hands," he said, nodding at the wrapped package Mason held.

114

"I know Ben made it," he said. "What I asked was whether that archaeologist fellow ever bought any of those Indian bowls or pots."

"You're not upset?" he asked, relieved.

"Jacob," Mason patiently explained. "A man has a right to waste his own money on whatever he wants, so long as he isn't lied to about what he's buying. But can we get back to my question? Did Mister Mitchell ever buy any of those Indian things?"

Jacob thought for a moment before answering. "No, not that I can recall. Admires them from time to time but can't say that I ever sold any to him."

"Thank you," he said, though disappointed with the answer. He had hoped it would be easy. Henry buying his artifacts here would have immediately exposed him. Furrowing his brow, Mason admonished himself thinking that the man wasn't that stupid.

Stepping back outside, he paused in the shade of the roof over the boardwalk. Maybe Henry really was an archaeologist. After all, he only had Ben's word to the contrary. Yet doubt nagged him. But what bothered him more was his response. Was it because he actually suspected Henry was not what he pretended to be, or was he jealous of Belle's interest in the man?

Frustrated that he was even wasting his time on the whole affair, he slowly walked along the boardwalk when an idea emerged, one that put his mind to rest. With a grunt of satisfaction, he turned around and headed off to the telegraph office.

Caleb paced the dirt floor of his cave, arguing with himself, second guessing his decision to give the book he found to Henry. Yet the more he paced, the more he realized that having the book was one thing, knowing what it said was another. The only person he knew that spoke another language was Henry. He supposed Mason might know some,

115

but Henry was a university professor, someone who could possibly make better sense of what was written.

With a sigh, Caleb collected his dinner items along with the journal and an unlit lantern, and headed over to where Henry was already seated, waiting for him.

"Good evening, my good man," Henry jovially greeted him. "What repast have you brought with you this fine evening?"

"Huh?" Caleb answered scooting out a chair.

"What do you have for dinner?"

"Usual beans and dried beef," he answered, sitting.

"At least let me share some fresh bread I picked up today," Henry offered, breaking off a chunk and handing it to him.

"Thank you." Then cocking an eyebrow, he looked at Henry's plate that had only greens and fresh vegetables. "What're you eatin'?"

"A salad, my good man," he answered. "Good for the digestive system."

"Looks like the stuff ya feeds ta hogs. Where'd ya get it?"

"Hoptown. Those industrious folks raise their own vegetables."

"Suit yerself."

The conversation dwindled as each devoted his attention to his meal. The evening skies spread across the wide expanse of the prairie and Henry lit two lamps placing them at the sides of the tabletop. Soon enough, the plates were pushed aside and Henry announced, "Now for some desert." He reached down to a crate by the table leg and brought up the bourbon bottle and two shot glasses.

While he poured, Caleb decided it was time. "Got somethin' I'd like fer you ta help me with." He placed the journal on the table oblivious to the momentary subtle yet visible shake in Henry's pouring. "A friend o' mine give me this a while back. Forgot I had it. Problem is, cain't read it. Thought you might make some sense of it." He slid it across the table toward Henry.

Handing Caleb the shot glass of bourbon, Henry took hold of the book. Lifting his glass in toast, he said, "Enjoy." Taking a satisfying sip, he set the glass down and pretended to study the outside of the book in the dim light of the lamp. "Looks old, though it appears to be in good condition. I'd say by the way it's bound, probably a hundred to two hundred years old, maybe more. It's hard to tell. Opening the book, he said, "Interesting. It's in Spanish. You say a friend gave this to you?"

"Yep?"

"Do you know where he got it?"

"Nope," Caleb replied, shifting his eyes to look down at his bourbon.

"Did you have it before you came here?"

"Uh... yep," he lied

"And you don't know where your friend found it."

"Uh uh," he replied.

"Pity," Henry mused aloud. "It would help with its provenance. Makes the connection of the writing and the purpose much easier if one knew where this was found." He read for a little bit, already knowing what it was, but wanting to appear only mildly interested. "It appears to be a journal or diary of someone named Diaco de la Fuente." Nonchalantly closing the book, he looked at Caleb's glass. "You've hardly touched your drink. Everything OK?"

"Sure, sure," he quickly answered, downing the smooth liquor in one gulp.

"That's one way to drink it, I suppose, but I don't recall you being in such a rush. You normally take your time, savoring it. Are you sure everything is OK? Something bothering you?"

Caleb quietly fussed at himself for doing such a lousy job at not being obvious. The Marshal's words came to mind *Folks'll leave you alone if they think you don't have much. And keep to your routine*, which meant act normal.

"Eh," he replied. "T'ain't nuthin'. Just tired I guess."

"We're all entitled to feel like that on occasion," Henry commiserated. "Here, let me refill your glass. This time you can slow down and relax."

"Much obliged."   He gave him half a smile of appreciation.

Refilling both glasses, Henry then held up the book. "Did you want me to read through this to find out what it is?"

"That's what I was figurin'. If'n ya don't mind."

"Be happy to," he smiled at him. Casually flipping the pages, he said, "It'll give me a pleasant distraction from my normal research. Give me a day or two and I can tell you what's in here. My initial impression is that it's probably someone's diary. Could be some interesting and juicy gossip about folks we don't even know," he chuckled.

Caleb relaxed as Henry placed the book at the edge of the table and took up his drink. For some reason, Henry's casual, almost disinterested view of the journal gave Caleb reassurance that he had made the right choice. If there was anything in there about the gold, Henry would want to know where he was when he got the book. Caleb was already rehearsing his story and 'Leadville, Colorado' seemed the easiest to work with.

With the meal finished and the last of the bourbon savored, Caleb said his 'good night', lit the lamp, and moseyed over to his side of the wash. Henry smugly watched him walk away, astounded by his good fortune. The fates had dropped a little bit of treasure right on his lap. Deciding now was as good a time as any, Henry turned up the lamp flame. Twisting his chair around so he could rest his feet on a crate, he leaned back in his chair, expecting Caleb to look out to see what he was doing. He wanted to give the impression that he was simply relaxing and reading a good book.

Sure enough, he saw the lamp in front of Caleb's cave pause as he turned around to check on Henry. Acting the part, Henry filled his shot glass one more time and settled down to read. A few minutes later, Caleb's lamp disappeared in the cave.

Though taking his time, Henry devoured the journal, paying particular attention to the drawings and details of the journey. De le Fuente's party was originally ten men, armed with guns and ambition. They had chosen to leave the main body because de la Fuente believed that Esteban was purposely misleading them. Choosing to keep this belief to himself, he gathered nine other trusted cohorts, including his cousin, and decided to venture out on their own. With the supposed blessings of Coronado, he organized his group as a scouting party. Once away from the main body, they veered off in a different direction.

Two weeks later, de la Fuente discovered the Seven Cities of Cibola. Thinking to use the methods of Cortez against the Aztecs, he applied shock tactics and gunpowder. Initially awed and overwhelmed, the Indians had been intimidated long enough for him and his small band of followers to collect a large quantity of gold. However, his luck abandoned him as he fled south as one-by-one, his little army of soldiers were either captured or killed. The last entries in the journal were hastily written as evidenced by the urgency of the script. The next to the last entry read: *Holed up in a cave. No way of escape. Mule's dead, out of powder. Only Miguel and I remain. Night approaches like the curtain of the final act. May God grant us rest eternal.* The final entry was a very brief statement: *We are finished.*

What followed immediately after his capture was anyone's guess. But, Henry chuckled with wry amusement, de la Fuente's loss was his gain, for somewhere in Caleb's cave was the gold from Cibola.

Though the night was late, he looked up and over to Caleb's cave. He knew the prospector was fast asleep. He then began analyzing his courses of action. Caleb obviously had the gold or knew where it was. In order for Henry to get to the gold, he would either have to get Caleb out of the way in order to search the cave or trick the old prospector into revealing where it was. There was virtually no likelihood of the second part happening, so he would have to search the cave the next time Caleb went into town. What happened after that would depend on what he found.

The morning was already halfway gone when Henry finally roused himself awake. Yawning and stretching, he remembered the journal, which lay on a small table next to his cot. Picking it up, he leafed through the pages knowing that Caleb would want it back, but that he needed time to really examine its contents.

He was going through his morning ritual of preparing coffee when he saw Caleb pop his head up just inside the cave. Seeing the archaeologist up and around, the prospector scampered out and across the wash.

"Was wonderin' when you'd finally get up," Caleb said, half in jest. Nodding at the journal now on the desk, he said, "Saw you readin' that book 'til the early hours."

"Yes," Henry pontificated. "It's the curse of those whose passion lie in things long past. Coffee?"

"Naw. Already had enough this morning." Looking expectantly at him he said, "Well?"

"Well what?" Henry replied, measuring the coffee grounds.

"Ya read long enough t'finish it. What's it say?"

"Now, now, my good man," he answered giving Caleb a patronizing smile. "I just skimmed the book, a sort of first read. I need more time to make any sense of it."

"Sense of it? What's in it?"

"As near as I can tell, and this is a based upon an initial reading, mind you, the book is a diary of sorts by a man named Diaco de la Fuente."

"Ya said that yesterday."

"Yes, yes, I know," he impatiently replied. "What I mean to say is that it's a bit confusing. It seems that de la Fuente was part of Coronado's conquistador army. At least that is what he claims. It seems far too impossible."

"Who?"

"Coronado. You know, the famous Francisco Vázquez de Coronado y Luján." He looked at Caleb awaiting recognition, knowing full well the man had no clue. Letting him stare blankly for a few moments, Henry added, "The man who led an expedition of conquistadors to what is now the state of Kansas."

"A what?"

"Coronado was a man who led an army of men from Mexico to Kansas and back," Henry slowly and patiently explained.

"Why?"

"Who knows," Henry shrugged. "Probably looking to claim more land for Spain, or perhaps looking for gold like they had found in Mexico."

Caleb blanched at the word 'gold,' but quickly recovered. The change of expression was not lost on Henry.

"Sad to say, not only did they not find any gold, poor Coronado went bankrupt and died in Mexico City, a mere forty-four years old when he shuffled off this mortal coil. What a pity."

Caleb frowned as he digested the information, vainly attempting to make sense of it.

"Where did you say you received this book?" Henry nonchalantly asked, pouring a cup of coffee.

"Uh, when I was prospectin' up in Leadville, Colorado," he answered, using his rehearsed response.

"Leadville, you say," Henry said, raising an eyebrow. "That makes it even more curious."

"What does?"

"Why this book, my good man. You state you received it in Leadville, Colorado. The diary is from a man who supposedly was with Coronado in his journey from Mexico to Kansas and back. Why and how would this book end up in Colorado? I'm thinking this may be a forgery, a hoax of some sort, made to look old. But that's just my first impression." He sipped his coffee carefully studying the man.

Caleb stood immobile, unsure of what to do. His first instinct was to take the book back, but the more he thought about it, the more he wondered why he even needed the book. He already had the gold and from what Henry said, what was in the book had nothing to do with the gold. Besides, what use was the book to him? He couldn't even read it. If ever he wanted to know what it said, he would have to get someone who spoke Spanish.

Henry let him mull a bit before saying, "Forgeries are a serious offense, not only in my profession but legally as well. Now I'm not saying this is a forgery, but it needs some closer scrutiny to determine whether it is real or not. On the other hand, if it is real, if it is the diary of Diaco de la Fuente, some university would probably pay quite handsomely for it."

Caleb was surprised at Henry's admission, that the book might have value. Giving voice to his thoughts, he said, "Why'd ya tell me that? Ya coulda kept that part to yerself."

"Now Caleb, my good man," he replied appearing to be affronted. "Why would I do that? The book is yours. I would be a thief to do such a thing. How could I call myself an honest archaeologist by cheating friends? Besides, I have more than ample income and have no need to swindle unsuspecting and trusting men such as yourself."

"Didn't mean no harm," Caleb apologized.

"Of course you didn't," he said, mollified. "Tell you what. This diary has me intrigued. Give me a bit more time to thoroughly read and analyze the diary. When I finish my analysis, I can submit my findings to some friends back east. Who knows, this diary might be genuine. If so, I'll help you find a buyer for it."

Surprised and pleased at the same time, Caleb brightened. "That'd be right nice of you. You go ahead and do like ya said. Guess I'd better get back," he said, thumbing over his shoulder towards his claim.

"So we're agreed?" he asked, holding out his hand.

"Done," Caleb grinned, shaking Henry's hand.

Henry smirked as he watched Caleb walk away, his step a bit lighter. That was much too easy, he grinned, something like 'candy from a baby.' Scooting out his chair, he settled down comfortably. With his own notebook in hand, he began comparing and studying, jotting down additional notes on a pad of paper.

By the time the dinner hour arrived, Henry had barely moved from his work. Caleb had wanted to come over a few times to see the progress, but each time he emerged from the cave, Henry was hunched over industriously reading, scribbling notes, and studying. Finally, as the afternoon skies were slowly drifting to evening, he packed up his meal and headed over to where Henry had cleared the table and was preparing his own meal.

"You been mighty busy," Caleb said, placing his food on the table.

"A very interesting tale so far," Henry replied, setting his plate down. "Is there anything more you can tell me about the man who gave this to you?"

Between mouthfuls of food, Caleb answered, unfolding the tale he had worked out. "Not much t'say. He was prospectin' just like me. Been workin' the mines fer a while then went out on his own. Got a claim a little ways south o' Leadville."

Nodding, Henry asked, "How did you meet him?"

"Got ta talkin' in one o' them tent saloons. Seemed a right decent fella."

"He have a name?"

"Went by the name of Charles. Hated bein' called Charlie."

"Last name?"

"Never asked."

"Why'd he give you the book?" Henry asked, marveling at the man's imaginative tale.

"He couldn't read it and figured I might know someone who could."

"And you've kept it for all this time?"

"Yup. Thought it a might strange him thinkin' like he was, but I figured I might find someone sometime."

"And he didn't mind you taking it with you?"

"Him and me parted ways, friendly like, him goin' north an me headin' south. Sorta forgot about it 'til I got here. I remembered it when you was talkin' that other language stuff and figured you might know how to read it, you bein' a what you call it an all."

"Archaeologist," he smiled indulgingly. Sensing Caleb might be coming to the end of his ability to fabricate, Henry said, "From what I can tell so far, it seems to be authentic. The man knows far too many details that would only be known by someone at the time." Leaning back, he let out a satisfied burp.   Glancing at Caleb's finished meal, he announced, "Time for the after dinner digestif."

"The what?"

"Digestif. It's French for digestive, something to aid in the enjoyment of a meal." Smiling at the man's still puzzled face, he pulled up the bottle of bourbon.

"That's bourbon," Caleb pointed out.

"That it is," he grandly agreed. "It is our digestif," he winked. Pouring two shots, he said, "Tomorrow's Saturday and as is my custom, I will be going into town, so I will leave this little treasure with you." He slid the book across the table to him. 'Guard it with your life." Smirking at Caleb's startled look, he added, "Well, maybe not that far. But this little treasure is worth protecting. Should this be genuine, you could be a very wealthy man."

"Really?" Caleb said, his doubt obvious.

"Well, perhaps not a Midas or a Vanderbilt, but you could give up prospecting for a little while."

"Just fer one little book?"

"If this is genuine, there will be a number of interested parties, some in Spain, some in Mexico, and many here in the US. Perhaps even a bidding war might erupt and drive the price up even higher."

Caleb continued frowning, though not without some satisfaction. Not only did he have the gold in the cave, this book would give him even more. "Just how does a body go about sellin' it?"

"That's where I come in," Henry expansively said. "For a fee of, say 10% of the sale price, I will do all the work for you."

"You'll do all the work fer only 10%? How come?"

"Why that's the normal seller's fee," he explained. "I certainly couldn't, in good conscience, charge more. That's just not honest business."

Caleb thought a moment, then looked around at the various possessions the archaeologist had. "Is that how you get to have all this stuff?" he said, waving a hand at the MATE.

"That, and other things. I act as a middleman for many wealthy investors seeking particular items. I also research and dig up the past, like I do here. What I don't bring back to my university, I sell to other universities around the world. And then," he proudly added, "I am also an inventor. These endeavors keep me fairly busy"

Caleb almost choked on his drink. Busy? For the past how many months, the man had spent all his time snooping around his claim or in town at the Bird Cage. You call that busy?

"Well then," Henry said. "Do we have a deal?"

"You get 10% when you sell the book and I gets the rest?"

"That's correct."

"An you do all the work sellin' it."

"Correct again."

"Deal." Spitting on the palm of his hand, he held it out.

Grinning widely, Henry likewise spit in his palm and they shook hands. Lifting his glass in toast, he said, "To your newfound wealth." Downing his drink in one gulp, he silently added 'which won't be yours much longer.'

Mason stood at the bar watching Belle talking with one of the girls. He couldn't help but admire the Bird Cage's madam. Not only was she a beauty, she had a captivating personality that drew men to her like moths to flames. As he stood there, a seed of guilt had settled in his gut when he admitted that he was no different from all the other men captivated by her. His guilt reminded him that he spent more time here at the Bird Cage with Belle than he did at home with Elizabeth. The rational part of him said that even being home with Elizabeth, he would still be alone. At least here, he had the noise and joy of people living. Living. Was that what he was doing? The rational side said 'look around. Look at the people. Now compare that to Elizabeth and her comatose state.'

His ruminations were interrupted when he heard a voice call out, "Hey Marshal." Turning, he smiled when he saw the two machinists approach. "Taboca, Nantan," he greeted them.

Belle had looked up when she heard Taboca. Sending the girl off to take care of business, she gracefully strolled over to them. "Three of my very favorite men," she flirted.

"Evening Miss Belle," Taboca said, giving her a warm and polite smile.

"Hi, Miss Belle," Nantan likewise greeted her.

"I'm pleased to see you two gentlemen back again," she said.

"Uh," Taboca hesitantly began, handing her a piece of paper. "Mister Mitchell, the one who's an archaeologist looking for ancient Indian things, said to give you this."

While Belle read the note, Nantan looked curiously at Mason. "Um, Marshal, you have a hole in your hat."

"That I do," Mason unaffectedly replied.

"Looks like a bullet hole," Taboca observed.

"That it is," Mason again answered.

"What happened?" Nantan asked, eyes blinking wide.

"Someone didn't like my taste in hats," he deadpanned.

Nantan grinned at the joke, waiting for him to elaborate. When the Marshal offered no further explanation, he asked, "What really happened?"

"He nearly got himself killed," Belle interjected, her voice barely betraying her worry. "It was a good thing Johnny Ringo was there –"

"Johnny Ringo?" Taboca repeated, apprehension evident. "He's supposed to be the fastest gun in the Territory."

"Second fastest," Belle calmly corrected.

"Second? Who's first?"

"You're drinking with him," she said with a hint of a proud smile.

"Marshal?" Nantan said, both amazed and impressed.

"That surprises you?" Mason said, an eyebrow raised in mock irritation.

"No," Nantan sputtered. "It's just that you seem so, uh, calm, relaxed."

"A man who can't control himself can't think straight," Mason said. "In my line of work, I can't afford to let emotions get in the way."

Looking at Belle, Taboca said, "You said it was a good thing Johnny Ringo was there. I thought he was a killer."

Instead of answering, she looked at Mason who said, "I doubt that Johnny ever killed a man who didn't in some way deserve it. Now he has a reputation that he's trying to live up to, and it's hard measuring a man's worth by someone else's standards. But Johnny Ringo's got some good in him, and that good is what saved my life." He then closed his mouth, having enough of the topic of conversation.

Sensing he'd had enough of the tale, Belle addressed the two machinists. "I'll tell you all about it later. According to this," she said holding up the paper, "looks like you two will have a very enjoyable evening." Folding the paper, she looked at Jack behind the bar. "Run a tab for these two gentlemen and charge it to Mister Mitchell. Give them whatever they want."

"Yes, mam," he answered, unaffected by the display of another's generosity.

Giving the two machinists a knowing look, Belle smiled and said, "I believe that also includes the other amenities."

"He's married," Nantan grinned, thumbing a finger at Taboca.

"And he needs to not take advantage of the man's gift," Taboca replied, looking sideways at his friend.

"I'm sure we can come to some agreement," Belle soothed. "Why not start with a drink first."

Taboca looked at Mason. "What are you drinking, Marshal?"

"Tennessee Whiskey," he answered, holding up the glass.

"I'll take what the Marshal's drinking," he told Jack.

"Me too," Nantan chimed in.

Jack served up the drinks along with a sangaree for Belle. Clinking glasses in toast, the four took a swallow followed by Nantan's coughing.

"A little strong?" Taboca joked.

"Just a little," he wheezed back. "But good."

"I'm glad you two are here," Belle said, looking at the two machinists. "You can settle a question for me. Do you believe someone can come back from the dead?"

"Not that again," Mason smirked.

"You mean like be alive again?" Taboca asked.

"Sort of, though I suppose one can't really be alive if one is already dead," she answered.

"Like ghosts?" Nantan asked.

"More than ghosts," she mused. "Ghosts are more spirit-like. I'm talking about a human form still prowling around after it's dead."

The two machinists exchanged bemused glances. Taking a sip of whiskey, Taboca said, "I suppose it could happen. The Chiricahua believe in life after death. And we also believe that there are supernatural powers associated with things that happen around us."

"What do you think?" Mason asked.

"I'm a machinist, a scientist," he answered. "While I suppose a supernatural could exist, I've never seen anything to say it does."

"That doesn't mean it doesn't exist," Nantan objected.

"The walking dead?" Taboca countered.

"It's possible," he stubbornly replied.

"When's the last time you saw one?"

"Just because I haven't seen one, doesn't mean they can't or don't exist. Besides, they only appear as a warning. At least that's what I've heard."

Taboca gave him a patronizing look and then turned to Mason, Taboca said, "We stopped by and visited Mister Mitchell a few days ago to look at his machines. They're wonderful," he gushed. "Very impressive."

"Did you see the one he calls the MATE?" Belle asked, eyes bright.

"Yes mam, we did."

"It's amazing, isn't it," she continued. "The thing doesn't need rails because of those, what does he call them?"

"Continuous traction mobility belts," Nantan said then sheepishly added, "I asked."

"Yes, those," she laughed merrily. "Did you see those two long brass tubes on top? They take the engine smoke and blow it out back behind the machine."

"How?" Taboca asked, curious that she would know so much.

"There's a fan in the front that acts like a whirligig and blows the smoke down the tube and out the back."

"How did you know that?" Nantan asked, impressed.

"I got to ride on it," she triumphantly said.

"How was it?" Taboca asked, impressed.

"Sort of like riding on a train with the conductor, except you're not confined to staring out a small window at what's on the side of the train. And because it doesn't go as fast as a train, you can enjoy the scenery and feel the wind in your hair. It was quite refreshing really." She smiled at the memory and took a sip of sangaree.

"Have you been on it, Marshal," Taboca asked.

"No," Mason curtly replied then caught himself, "haven't had the pleasure. So it's Mister Mitchell who is your benefactor tonight?"

"Yeah," Nantan happily answered. "The man must be loaded to be able to afford this." He felt a nudge from Taboca telling him to watch his manners.

Belle saw the warning sign and made light of the comment by lowering her voice and winking, "I agree. But I'm not one to complain."

Mason remained stoic while the other two laughed. He was beginning to not like Henry Mitchell, but he had little cause to... other than the man was rich, refined, and available. The fact that the archaeologist and Belle had shared a picnic irritated him, for he could easily conjure up all sorts of intimate scenarios between the two, all of which went beyond a simple kiss. Compounded with his own failed marriage, Mason felt no compelling urge to like the man.

And then there was that little tidbit about the ancient Indian artifacts. Had he heard it from anyone other than Ben, he might have given it greater credence. While Ben was a decent fellow, his overt fondness for the bottle often resulted in some outlandish tales. Still, if what Ben said was true,

Henry just might not be what he pretended to be. That thought alone gave Mason a glimmer of satisfaction.

Belle's attention was diverted when one of the girls came up behind her. Gently tapping her on the shoulder, she whispered in her ear. Belle gave her an understanding nod. Sending her back upstairs, she smiled benevolently at the two machinists. "Will you two pardon us for just a moment," she said, beckoning Mason to the side. As the Marshal and the Madam stepped away, Belle said, "Dan Lowry's upstairs in Black-eyed Susan's crib. She said he's spending money like he's got plenty."

Mason shook his head and cocked an eyebrow. "What is it with this place?" he marveled. "And what is it with these stupid outlaws who think that the last place anyone would look is at the Bird Cage?"

"What do you want to do?" she asked.

With a low sigh, he said, "Same as usual, but be careful. This one's not afraid to hurt someone." Rejoining Taboca and Nantan at the bar, Mason finished his drink. "Got something to do. Be back in a couple of minutes." He started to walk away then turned around and returned. "There's a man upstairs, an unsavory sort. I'd appreciate it if you'd look out for Miss Belle while I'm gone."

The two machinists straightened to full height. "You can count on us, Marshal," Taboca answered for them.

Touching his hat in salute, Mason slipped out the front door to position himself just outside the back door.

Not long after he left, a wiry man with fire burning in his eyes burst down the stairs by the stage, but instead of going down to the basement, he rapidly threaded his way towards the front of the Bird Cage. Belle realized too late his change of direction just as he blew past close to the bar.

Flustered, she called out, "Somebody stop him," as he closed in on the front door, his hands already up to thrust himself outside.

Snatching Mason's empty shot glass out of the bartender's hands, Nantan reared back and hurled it with all his might, hitting Dan Lowry at the base of the neck right behind his ear. Lowry dropped to the floor like a stone.

"Nice shot," Taboca complimented, sipping his whiskey.

While Belle sent one of the girls to fetch Mason, Jack came from around the bar, coach gun in hand, to stand over the dazed outlaw. A few moments later, Mason yanked open the front door and saw his quarry sitting on the floor, his legs splayed in front of him, holding the back of his head, Jack standing guard over him.

"Thanks Jack," he nodded appreciatively. "I can take it from here."

"Don't thank me," he wryly said, turning to look at Nantan. "I didn't do a thing. That machinist there's got quite an arm."

Mason looked quizzically at Nantan leaning against the bar. Lifting his whiskey glass is salute, he gave the Marshal a cheerful smile.

Though puzzled as to how the outlaw came to be on the floor, Mason looked down at him. "Let's go you," he gruffly said, grabbing him under the armpit and pulling him up to standing. Twisting him around, he escorted the still wobbly Dan Lowry out the door. A little while later, Mason was back at the bar listening to Belle's version of what happened.

"He ran by me and Nantan grabbed the shot glass out of Jack's hands and threw it at him, hitting him in the back of the head."

"He's got himself the beginnings of a nice bruise back there," Mason said. "That's quite a throw. Where'd you learn to do that?"

"He's a natural," Taboca said. "He's been like that since I can remember. He could knock a squirrel off a branch at fifty paces when he was only six years old."

"You two grew up together?"

"We're cousins," he proudly replied then added, "Nantan's the star pitcher on the baseball team we're putting together."

"We're going to call ourselves the Phoenix Machinists," Nantan said.

"I thought we were going to be called the Phoenix Indians," Taboca objected.

"Since when have we ever called ourselves Indians?" Nantan said as though the point was obvious. "We're Chiricahua, not Indians." Turning to Mason, he asked, "What did that man do to get himself locked up?"

"That's Dan Lowry, wanted for murder," Mason explained. When he saw Nantan's eyes widen in apprehension, he said, "You did a good thing and helped get a criminal off the streets."

"Suppose he escapes and comes looking for me?"

"Him?" Mason looked evenly at Nantan. "You're a machinist. You can take care of yourself. And besides, with that arm, I doubt he'll want to tangle with you again."

"Yeah," Taboca agreed, clapping him on the shoulder. "You could always use that stun gun of yours."

"Stun gun?" Mason's attention suddenly perked.

"I'm still working on it," he said, giving his cousin a look of annoyance.

"What does it do?" Belle asked, likewise interested.

"It's supposed to stun someone instead of killing them," Taboca interjected. With a grin, he added, "Although the results so far haven't been quite so successful."

"I'm getting better," Nantan defensively retorted. "Why'd you have to bring that up?"

"It's the truth," Taboca replied. Looking at Mason and Belle, he said, "It's really quite genius. He uses electricity to immobilize a creature. The challenge right now is modifying the strength of the jolt. It's just a matter of time. It'll be quite the marvel."

Mollified, Nantan said to Mason, "I can bring it with me the next time we come down from Phoenix, if you like."

"I would like that very much," he replied, impressed.

"Mister Mitchell seemed very impressed with the concept," Taboca said. "It wouldn't surprise me if he tried building one of his own."

Nantan's jaw dropped. "That's why he wanted to know how I mixed the ammonium chloride."

"You think that was why he was so nice to us?" Taboca wondered.

"I think you may be overreacting," Belle interjected. "I don't think Mister Mitchell would do something like that. My guess is that he's probably just curious, one inventor to another sort of thing."

"You're probably right," Taboca said. "Still, it might be nice to pay him another visit. Sort of look things over, see how some of his machines work."

"Mind if I come along?" Mason asked.

"That would great," Nantan readily agreed.

"You may want to wait until after tomorrow," Belle said. "He comes here every Saturday and stays late. And you might not get a warm welcome on Sunday," she laughed. "He's probably sleeping off his Saturday fun."

"How about sometime next week, Marshal? Monday?"

"That would be fine." Mason figured he could visit Caleb at the same time. Then he remembered Caleb came to town every eight days. The last time he came to town was almost a week ago. "Then again, you boys go on by yourselves. Seems I might have a visitor Monday."

Belle gave him a curious look then sidled closer to him, her delicate perfume surrounding her. Tucking a hand underneath his arm, she cooed, "You sound so mysterious. Should I be jealous?"

"Not unless you consider old grizzled Caleb someone to be jealous of," he replied.

"I do," she prettily answered. "He gets to have lunch with you every time he's in town."

"You can have lunch with me anytime you want," he responded before realizing what he said and how he said it. Feeling a warm flush, he tried to make light of his words. "I don't have a fancy vehicle though, like Henry Mitchell has." As soon as he said it, he regretted it for it made him sound jealous. Silently berating himself, he figured the best thing to do was keep his mouth shut.

Stepping up on her tiptoes, Belle whispered in his ear, "You don't need one."

Mason felt a pulse of passion burst through him as he suppressed the urge to forget his marriage vows. Locking his gaze with her intense blue eyes made it more difficult for him

133

to think clearly. She had often flirted with him, and he always brushed it off as her simply doing her job, performing her role as a madam. Though, in truth, he had taken great pleasure in her attention, wishing there was a way to make good on all the flirtation.

Yet this time there seemed to be something more, an offer should he choose to accept it. A large part of him wanted to find out if her offer was any good. Somehow he felt it was, and that made him cautious. Then he was reminded of the little fact that she had spent time with Henry Mitchell, had even gone on a picnic with him. Suddenly his ardor cooled, and he regained control of himself. Yet the debate still raged in his head. He was married. She was not. He had no right to expect or demand anything of her. She was free to associate with whomever she wanted, have lunch with whomever she wanted, even be intimate with whomever she wanted.

His thoughts were interrupted when two of the girls, one a pretty young brunette the other a svelte blond, swept up to tug on the machinist's arms to get him to dance. Nantan needed no urging while Taboca hesitated at first. Mason gave him a 'go on, it's OK' nod before he too joined his cousin. The two young men were soon cavorting around the dance floor.

The spell broken, Mason slowly turned to finish his drink. "Guess I'd better be getting back. I'll take care of business with the bank tomorrow. Where would you like to meet?"

"Is that offer of lunch still good?" she asked, noticing the subtle change in his behavior. For a brief moment she had felt his indecision and knew that he desired her. But that moment slipped away, and she knew why. Damn Elizabeth. "Or is being seen with a madam going to ruin your reputation?" Instead of her normal devil-may-care attitude there was a testiness to her question.

"My reputation was ruined long before you came along," he answered with a slump of his shoulders.

Belle's lips tightened, and she turned him around to face her. "Then why don't you just divorce her, Mason Sadler, US Marshal?"

He looked at her with tired eyes. "Because I gave my word." Suddenly Johnny Ringo came to mind, and it dawned on him that they were a lot alike. Perhaps the only difference was the side of the law one was on. And what good is a man if his word is no good?

Belle looked at him as though he were a simpleton. "You gave your word. What about her word? Does that account for anything?"

"I'm not responsible for what she does," he answered, "or her choices."

"Like following you here?" She didn't mean to say it like that, but it slipped out. When she saw the hurt fill his eyes, she tenderly reached out to him. "I'm sorry, Mason. That's not what I meant."

Setting his glass down on the countertop, he stood up straight. Looking out at the dancers, he let his eyes wander until he found Nantan and Taboca who both were thoroughly enjoying themselves. "Tell our friends I enjoyed chatting with them. I'll make arrangements for your share."

She grabbed his arm, gently. "I'm sorry, Mason. I didn't mean it like that."

Patting her hand, he gave her a sad smile. "I know." Reaching up to touch the brim of his hat, he gave her a polite nod.

"What a minute," she pleaded. "I have something for you." Going behind the bar, she pulled out a box with a lid on it. A single thin ribbon was wrapped around it. "Here," she said handing it to him. "Open it when you're alone." Again stepping up on her tiptoes, she gave him a kiss on the cheek.

Mason blinked at the demonstration of affection, submersing himself in her fragrance and touch. Momentarily dumbfounded, he mumbled his thanks and awkwardly pushed through the doors to stand outside in the night air. Inhaling a deep breath, he savored the clean night air, all the while touching his cheek where she kissed him.

He still had the box under his arm when he entered his room at the boarding house. Elizabeth was in bed, awake. She glared at him with filmy eyes. Then she noticed the box. "What's that?" Her voice was dry and gritty.

"I don't know," he honestly answered, setting it down on a table while he undid his gun belt, looping it over the wall peg. He placed his Stetson on the same peg.

"You don't know?" she sneered. "It's a damn box. That's what it is. Where'd you get it?"

Mason paused before answering, knowing nothing good would come from his response. Part of him thought about lying, but that would only make it worse. Looking at his shrill of a wife, it was small wonder he hated coming back here. It was as though she was sucking the life out of him. Every time he entered this room, he felt tired, drained. And then he realized it would be no different had he stayed in San Francisco. She would be different, more vibrant and alive, but he would be dying just the same.

"Well?"

"Belle gave it to me."

"So now the little bitch is giving you presents?" she mocked. "Well don't just stare at it, open it. I want to see what your little slut gave you."

With a resigned sigh, Mason undid the ribbon and lifted the lid. Inside was a new Stetson just like the one hanging on the wall. A handwritten note lay on the crown. Picking up the note, he read, *You have enough holes in you without one in your hat.* It was signed *Belle* with a heart next to her name. Feeling his own heart momentarily leap up at the thought of her, he lifted the hat out.

"Your little tart is now buying clothes for you?" Elizabeth snarled. "Isn't that sweet. Pretty soon you'll set up house together. What a picture that would be… You and your whore of a girlfriend living in some filthy run-down shack in some godforsaken cesspit. Why you might even get a room close to mine." Her eyes stared daggers into him.

Mason had enough. "What the hell are you talking about?" he exploded. "You think I like coming back here to you, seeing you looking like this, a drugged-out woman who

136

can't cope with real life.' Jerking the hat up to his side, he said, "At least she cares about what happens to me, enough to spend her own money to buy me a new hat. You? What do you care? All you think about is yourself. Any money you have is spent on drugs."

He stormed across the room towards the nightstand by the bed. At first, she thought he was coming to hit her and she stiffened in defiant resolve. But that quickly changed when she saw the object of his wrath. Her defiance turned to fear, and she was not quick enough to grab the bottle of laudanum before he snatched it up, brandishing it in her face.

"This," he sternly said, shaking the bottle at her. "This is your life. This is all you care about." He raised his arm to hurl the bottle against the wall when her pathetic voice cried out.

"No! Don't! Please," she pleaded, her bleary eyes wild with panic. "Please don't. I'm sorry, I'm sorry."

Mason paused mid-throw, his arm still in the air. Looking down as his wife groveled, her eyes filling with tears, he was momentarily filled with remorse. He had brought her to Tombstone knowing she would rather be sold into slavery than come here. But he brought her here anyway, taken her away from her life of plenty, a life of wealth and happiness. And now look what she had become, what he had driven her to.

She panted like an animal chased, eluding capture for the moment, but terrified of the predator. Seeing his hesitation, she begged and promised. "I'll do better. I'll get better, you'll see. It'll be OK. I'll like living here. All I need is just a little help now and again... 'til I get better."

Lowering his arm, he placed the bottle back on the nightstand. In one jittery swoop, she snatched it up and clutched it to her chest. Looking up at him with eyes full of child-like innocence, she spoke, her voice meek and helpless, "Please don't leave me."

Mason sat on the edge of the bed, gazing at his pathetic wife. There at that moment, he felt the need to take care of her. He had felt that way before, when they had first met. There was something about her, an almost innocent helplessness as though she needed someone to rescue her, to care for her, to give her an overt love that her father never gave her. It was a noble emotion, and he believed it was love. She had responded to his devotion and had thrown herself into his soul. Between her and her father, he soon began to feel the life draining out of him. To save his own life, he had escaped to Tombstone.

He watched her as she twisted the cork off the bottle, all the while holding his gaze with hers, as though waiting for him to tell her, 'No.' Staring at him, daring him to stop her, she lifted the bottle to her lips. What should have been a sip became a strong swallow before Mason reached up and stopped her.

"You've had enough." He took the bottle from her hands, recorked it and placed it on the table.

"Will you stay with me?" she asked, reaching for his hand.

"Yes." He squeezed her hand and placed it between his two strong hands. It seemed such a simple request, but he knew what she meant. He sat holding her hand until her eyes closed and she faded into her blissful oblivion.

Mason continued sitting and holding her hand until fatigue enveloped him. Getting up, he undressed and slid into bed next to her, knowing full well her promise to do better would all be forgotten by the morning, replaced by the hateful wife he had come to expect.

Chapter 7

Mason was in that moment of sleep just before one wakens, when the sounds and smells of the outside world begin to intrude and assault one's senses. This time, he smelled coffee… and eggs, and a steak. He heard a woman's voice say, 'Thank you,' and the door close. Blinking his eyes open, he turned his head to see Elizabeth sitting at the table, sipping a cup of coffee. When she saw him awake, she smiled warmly at him.

"Breakfast is ready."

Surprised, his initial thought was to wonder what recriminations were going to pour out once the pleasantries were over. Pushing himself to sitting on the edge of the bed, he felt his stomach growl. "Smells good."

"I had them prepare a nice steak for you, medium-rare, just the way you like it." She watched him stand up and go over to the wash basin. "Come and eat while the food's still hot. You can shave after breakfast."

Mason stared at his wife through the mirror. This was the longest stretch of civility and friendliness in quite a while, and though off balance, he liked it. Maybe she did remember what she said last night; maybe this time she meant it.

As he sat down, she got up and poured his coffee. Taking her knife and fork, she began cutting his steak into bite-sized pieces. "I think you're right. It'll be better when we have our own place, a place where I can have a garden."

"It shouldn't be too long," he said, warming up to the change in his wife. He cut a piece of egg and placed it on top of a slice of steak. Plopping both into his mouth, he savored the combined flavor. This was a man's breakfast. "I've almost enough money saved. I expect in perhaps another month or two we'll have enough."

"I don't know if I can wait that long," she said, attempting to be playful, yet there was a tone of urgency in her voice.

"But I, but we don't have enough. I don't want to be beholden to a bank, so we're not going to borrow."

She paused before demurely saying, "I could ask Daddy for the balance." She resumed her seat, staring hopefully at him.

"No," he stonily replied.

"Please Mason," she said reaching for his hand. "I don't want to spend another day in this room longer than I have to. I know you and Daddy haven't seen eye to eye, but I need to get out of this boarding house. I'll die here if I don't."

Mason knew she was right, yet his thoughts drifted to the acrimonious row he had with her father when he told him that he had accepted the position as US Marshal in the Arizona Territory and that he and Elizabeth were leaving for Tombstone.

"You're a damned fool, man," his father-in-law blustered when he comprehended Mason's plans. They were standing in the billiard room of the extravagant home up on the hillside overlooking the bay. Elizabeth had wisely excused herself and closed the doors, thus removing herself from her father's wrath, while hoping he would talk some sense to her husband. She stood outside listening.

"You've got a fine job with the company, a fine home, and a fine wife. You're on your way up in this world. Why in the blazes do you want to give that all away just to go to some godforsaken hell hole swarming with Indians and Mexicans, just to wear some fool lawman's badge?"

Mason had wanted to say, 'Because you're smothering me and my ambitions. Your only child, my wife, is used to having Papa give her everything she ever wanted. I can't do that. I'm not like you. In fact, I don't *want* to be like you. This city is choking me. Your so-called friends with their façade of refinement are all part of an obscene game. If you weren't so rich, they wouldn't even piss on you if you were on fire. Any time I do or say something your daughter doesn't like, she runs back to you and I'm called to stand here to listen to you lecture me.'

Instead, he resolutely replied, "It is what I want to do."

"What the hell for?" he snapped.

"Because," he calmly replied, liking the shift in power, "it is what I want to do. It is what I intend to do."

"Don't think you're taking her with you. I won't allow it," his father-in-law imperiously stated.

"You don't have a choice," Mason shot back, his bile rising. "She's my wife and I'll take her where I damn well please."

His father-in-law was startled to an abrupt silence, unused to anyone contradicting him, let alone raising his voice to him. "You leave now, I'll cut you off," he threatened. "I'll cut her off. You won't get a penny from me. And when you come crawling back here out of the cesspit of the Arizona territory, you'll have nothing. I won't be here to help you."

"I don't need your damned help and I don't *want* your damned help. We're leaving. And that's the end of it." With that, Mason had jerked the door open to a cold and resentful Elizabeth who turned her back on him and marched off to wait for him in the carriage outside.

When the time came for them to leave, he had agreed to take an airship, though he had wanted to go by train. However, he had adamantly refused to pay for it stating that he had fare for the train and an airship was far too expensive. If they wanted her to go by airship, they could pay for it. And her father did, more by way of insult than olive branch.

Though not as long as by train, the trip to Bisbee was painful. Elizabeth was more than petulant, she was hateful. By the time they arrived in Bisbee, he was half-tempted to send her back. But principle overruled his urges, and he did his best to make her life here enjoyable. But she refused all his well-intentioned efforts and cursed the day his mind left him to come here, as well as the day she consented to be his wife.

Not too long after their arrival, she discovered her emotional trauma could be alleviated with ample doses of laudanum, which the doctors here were only too willing to dispense. After repeated rejections of his warnings, Mason had gone so far as to tell the doctors to refuse to give her any more. But she always managed to find more.

And then she discovered the pleasures of Hoptown's opium. Once that Rubicon was crossed, she no longer cared where she was. But what he couldn't figure out was how she was getting it and how she was paying for it. He had already told all the doctors and everyone in Hoptown that he would not pay for anything they gave her. If they wanted to give her drugs, then they could pay for it.

But this morning something was different. Though still looking like she was spent and tired, there was a subtle change in her, a desperation for something better. He knew that if he wanted a marriage like before, he would have to fight for her.

"OK," he acquiesced. "Send your father a telegram. If he's willing, I'll accept. No strings, mind you. I'll not accept money if he thinks he can tell me what to do."

Clapping her hands, she smiled brightly. "Good. I'll do that today. How much do we need?"

"Another $250."

"I'm sure Daddy can afford a measly $250," she said. "And then we can buy our own home."

"Like I said, no strings." His voice was mild, but adamant.

"Of course, darling. You're the boss." Taking his coffee cup from him, she poured some more in. "Can I have some money?

His caution suddenly up, his first response was to tell her 'no' in no uncertain terms. Instead, he found himself saying, "How much do you need?"

"Well," she replied, smoothing the robe on her thin thighs. "I want to buy a new dress, something stylish. I haven't shopped for a new dress since we came here. And then I need to send the telegram to Daddy."

Mason relaxed. This was the Elizabeth he remembered, the one in San Francisco who was so preoccupied with the latest fashions and local gossip.

"That's fine," he smiled at her.

"And a hat," she added. "I need a hat."

"OK," he chuckled. "Anything else?"

"Will you be home for dinner?"

"I can be," he answered.

"Then you can take me to dinner some place nice tonight."

Mason paused mid-bite. This was so unlike the Elizabeth he had grown used to here that he was taken aback. But he liked the change. "I would enjoy that."

Elizabeth sat back and watched him eat. The conversation worked itself around to the hole in Mason's Stetson. "And here I thought Johnny Ringo was a vicious outlaw."

"He's misunderstood," Mason said, finishing up the last of the steak. "Deep down he's got some good in him."

"Well I'm glad he got that bounty hunter before he got you."

"Me too," he wryly observed. Pushing himself away from the table, he went back to the washstand to finish getting ready for the day. When he was ready, he stood by the door, wrapping his gun-belt on. Elizabeth stood before him and handed him his new hat.

Again surprised at her transformation, he was more than a little impressed that she so casually handed him the hat that Belle had given him. Reaching in his pocket, Mason withdrew a handful of silver dollars and handed them to her. "I'll be around and about town today if you need more."

"This should be enough," she said.

For one awkward moment they stood gazing at each other. Mason broke the spell by bending down to kiss her on the cheek. She turned her head so that his kiss was on her lips. Her kiss was tender, and she gently placed a hand on his face.

Her affection pushed him off balance. It had been easier to pull away from her, to withdraw his emotions when she was hateful. When she was like this, he felt guilty that he had entertained thoughts of another woman. The image of the vivacious Belle invaded his awareness, and he knew that if he was to help Elizabeth recover, he would have to forget Belle. That thought saddened him, but he pushed it aside. He would be what he told everyone he was – married.

Closing the door behind him, Elizabeth placed the coins on the table then picked up Mason's old Stetson and fingered the hole. She was no fool. If she wanted to keep her husband, she would have to make him forget that harlot at the Bird Cage Theater. She would begin by buying him a new Stetson to replace the one Belle bought him. Then she would send Daddy a telegram. $250 seemed such a paltry amount. She was sure he could send more, a lot more, enough for her to set up her own account, enough so that she wouldn't have to depend on Mason, maybe even enough to come back home if she chose to. But that depended on Mason.

Gazing at herself in the mirror, she frowned at her emaciated reflection. She would get herself back to the way she once was. She would make Mason desire her once again.

Seeing the laudanum bottle on the nightstand, she told herself that she could control her urgings. She didn't need anyone telling her what she could or couldn't do. To prove it, she twisted the cork out of the bottle and took a small sip. Recorking it, she bobbed her head with smug satisfaction and got dressed.

Henry was just about to walk into the Bird Cage Theater when he did a double take as he spied the Marshal and Elizabeth walking down Allen Street. Deciding to make the most of the opportunity, he changed direction and headed off to intercept them just as they were about to go into the Grand Hotel.

"I say," Henry called out as he walked up. "Good evening to you Marshal."

Elizabeth's eyed hardened, and she clutched Mason's arm.

"Good evening, Mister Mitchell," Mason affably replied, feeling Elizabeth's grip tighten. Thinking it had more to do with her disdain for strangers, he brushed it aside.

"And this must be your lovely wife," Henry gallantly said, touching the brim of his fedora and giving her a respectful bow.

Before Mason had a chance to respond, Elizabeth introduced herself, "Missus Sadler." Her voice was cold, barely hiding her contempt.

An awkward moment ensued as Henry waited for her to extend a hand. When none was proffered, he continued. "So good to see you both out and about."

"Mister Mitchell is an archaeologist," Mason said to her.

"Do you like archaeology, Missus Sadler?" Henry inquired with a smile.

"Not really," she bluntly answered.

"Pity," he replied, smiling knowingly at her. "You'd be surprised what one finds in unexpected places."

Elizabeth felt the message in the smile and hatred filled her eyes.

Ignoring her acid stare, Henry looked up at Mason's Stetson and pointed. "I see you've got yourself a new sombrero. Just when I was getting used to the one with the hole in it."

Mason chuckled somewhat sheepishly. "I suppose it was time for a change. Elizabeth bought this for me today." He took it off to admire the quality.

"How thoughtful," he complimented., "and from the looks, a bit pricey. A fine Stetson for a U.S. Marshal. Hopefully you won't see fit to fill it with another hole. It'd be a shame to ruin such a nice chapeau... or the man wearing it," he winked.

"I agree," Mason smiled.

"I'm hungry," Elizabeth cut in.

"And how impolite of me for I've kept you from your gastronomical delights," Henry said as though chastising himself. Giving the Hotel a quick glance, he added, "And you've come to one of the finest culinary establishments in all of Tombstone." Looking directly at Elizabeth he said, "Much better than the food in Hoptown, wouldn't you agree?"

"I would never dine in that horrid little part of town," she coldly replied.

"Of course you wouldn't." His smile said he was more amused than insulted by her rudeness. Touching his hat once again, he said, "You two enjoy the evening. Pleasure meeting you, Missus Sadler."

Waiting until he was out of earshot, Mason said, "You weren't very nice to him."

"I don't like him,' she tersely answered, her gaze following him as he strolled down the boardwalk.

"But you just met him," he said.

"Still don't like him. I don't trust him."

Mason thought the response odd, but then remembered her attitude towards those she felt below her station. The twinge of guilt again pulsed as he reminded himself that he was the one who dragged her away from a life of wealth to live amongst the common and less than common masses.

Up the street, Henry paused before the doors to the Bird Cage. Turning around, he saw Mason and Elizabeth in conversation as they entered the Grand. He grinned as he thought of her arrogance, her aristocratic superiority. She was fooling no one but herself. She had already fallen off that pedestal. Her legs were made of clay. Destroying her would be easy. Pity, he mused, for the Marshal seemed a decent fellow.

The middle doors to the Theater opened and a waft of smoke layered with boisterous music billowed out. Forgetting all about his plans for Elizabeth, Henry strolled in to the cheers and camaraderie of those waiting for the archaeologist to show up.

Belle stood just outside the doors to the Theater savoring the night and the cleaner air than the tobacco laden dance hall and card rooms of the Bird Cage. Normally three or four admirers would accompany her, and tonight was no different. Though she engaged in the banter of conversation, her thoughts were elsewhere. When Henry told her that he had seen Mason and Elizabeth going into the Grand Hotel, Belle's first reaction was a mixture of irritation and resentment. It was when he told her that he was wearing a new Stetson that her pride morphed to coldness when she discovered the one she had bought him wasn't the one he was wearing.

And then she felt foolish for spending money on another woman's husband. What was she expecting in return? It wasn't as though Mason was going to leave his wife. He had made that clear often enough. Yet deep within, that was what she wanted... wasn't it? But did she want him to leave his wife because it was a challenge, or did she really have feelings for him?

Truth was that she relished his presence. She looked forward to his evening visits, spending time with him. She liked their common bond of stomping out crime in the southeastern part of the Territory. She reveled in the game they had rigged for collecting bounty by using the Bird Cage as their mousetrap. They had both made a tidy sum over the past year.

Yet while she liked the game, she liked being with him even more. She had hoped that he would see the difference between her and his wife, that leaving the drugged-out woman was the best thing for everyone involved, especially him. She had hoped the comparison was so painfully obvious that he couldn't help but want to be with her. She had even secretly hoped the foolish woman would die of an overdose. That would be such an easy solution to the problem. But what she hoped for most was that he actually cared for her.

The fact that Elizabeth was out in public meant that the woman was, most likely, attempting to make a break from her past, or at least give the impression of such. It probably also meant that she was trying to make amends in her marriage, which meant there was a good chance that Mason was not as likely to be spending as much time at the Theater as in the past. And that meant Mason was working on saving his marriage.

That thought alone saddened her. Yet Belle was not one to dwell on regret or recrimination. Mason had made his choice. It was time for her to move on. Oh, the game would continue, and they would make more money, but it would be as business partners, nothing more. Besides, there was an archaeologist inside who had traveled the world and knew what it meant to live life to the fullest. And they were to have another picnic together next Tuesday. She would again ride on his marvelous machine and enjoy the speed and wind.

Resolved, Belle brightened and flirted a bit more with her coterie of followers. She cast one last look down the street, an act of dismissiveness. At that moment, Mason and Elizabeth stepped out of the Grand Hotel and onto the boardwalk. Elizabeth had her arms wrapped around one of his strong arms, an intimate closeness that did not go unnoticed. He was wearing the Stetson that Elizabeth bought him. That tidbit too did not go unnoticed.

The husband and wife paused and saw Belle up the next block outside the Theater. To Belle's surprise, Elizabeth waved. It was an expression of smug possession, an in-your-face assertion that the man next to her was hers. Belle waved back, a gesture more an automatic response than heartfelt. She looked at Mason who seemed suddenly uncomfortable.

Suppressing an urge to walk down and slip an arm around his and ask when he was coming by for a drink, Belle instead turned to her admirers and motioned for one of them to open the door. She wanted to be sure Elizabeth saw the response. She may have Mason, but Belle had far many more admirers than that shriveled woman would ever have.

Rubbing his tired eyes, Henry yawned and stretched. His first thought was that he wasn't sure how much longer he could do this, partying Saturday night and staying out to the wee hours of a Sunday morning. He had gotten maybe three hours of sleep before Caleb roused him to give him back de la Fuente's journal. He chuckled at the thought. It was as though Caleb couldn't wait to get a buyer for the book.

That was yesterday. This morning Caleb had again awoken him, but this time was different. Though tired, he immediately brightened at the realization that the old coot was going into town. Suddenly, he didn't feel so fatigued.

"You awake, Henry?" Caleb called out, standing just outside the tent.

"I'm awake, I'm awake," he called back from the comfort of his cot.

"Mind lookin' after my things while I'm gone?"

"Be happy to. Just give me a minute to wake up and fix some coffee."

"No bother. I'm fixin' to set out here in a minute or two. Much obliged."

"You have a good time. Tell the Marshal I said 'Hello.'"

Henry got up and by the time he had fixed his coffee, he was watching Caleb head off towards Tombstone. While he drank his coffee, he raised the scanning cone of the IAS and positioned it to scan in a 180° arc in the direction Caleb was to return. He then sat down to a leisurely breakfast so that by the time he finished, Caleb would be far enough away.

Yet his feigned lethargy was not enough to keep him from going over both notes and strategy. There was little more he could get from the journal. It was now time to find out just what was in Caleb's cave.

Finishing the last of his coffee, he collected the Cell Detector and headed across the wash, making sure the IAS was still scanning. Placing the machine on the dirt floor, Henry walked back to the entrance and peeked out, checking once again that the IAS was sweeping the landscape. He had increased the alert volume so that there would be no chance of his not knowing someone was coming. Satisfied, he returned to stand before the pile of stones. Bending down to get a closer look, he could tell that the dirt was not the result of the haphazard of time. It was apparent that Caleb had moved the stones and did his best to cover his actions.

Flicking on the power toggle switch, the CED immediately erupted into loud and rapid clicking. Smiling, he pointed the rod at the pile of stones causing the clicking tempo to increase further. Rolling up his sleeves, Henry got to work, carefully noting where each stone was placed prior to removal. Meticulously placing each stone in an orderly line, he would then replace them accordingly. By the time he had removed all the stones, another hour had passed. Yet he was rewarded with a gaping hole of a small tunnel. Lifting the Cell Detector, he flipped another toggle switch on the top, and the wand emitted a dull glow of light, enough for him to see ahead as he determined where the tunnel led.

On his hands and knees, he crawled the few paces into the other cave. When he saw there was room to stand, he pushed himself up and held the wand aloft. In the faint glow of the wand, he saw the two corpses of the conquistadors and the pile of gold in between them. Flipping the sound toggle to stop the incessant clicking, the room was quickly engulfed in silence.

Catching his breath, he felt his euphoria bubbling over. "Señor de la Fuente and Miguel, I presume," he smiled, giving them a mock bow. Walking over to the corpses, Henry sat on his haunches next to one and studied the remains. The exsiccated skin had shriveled to tightness upon the skull and hands, reminding him of the Egyptian mummy he had studied in Cairo. The drab brown gambeson the man still wore was well preserved. Protruding from the edges, the Jacqueta de Mala, a sleeveless chainmail vest, hinted that one of them, most likely de la Fuente, had some access to wealth prior to his arrival in the New World. Looking for obvious signs for cause of death, he could find none. There were no arrows protruding from the chest, no broken bones he could see, or discolored fabric from blood loss. Even the helmet seemed to be in good order. Perhaps his diary would reveal what had happened.

Yet Henry's attention quickly shifted to the large pile of treasure. Fighting the urge to jab both hands into the pile, he lifted out a bowl and studied it, feeling the weight in his hands, knowing it was solid gold. Admiring the workmanship, he silently calculated the value both in terms of archaeological and precious metal value. Gazing joyously at the treasure, he knew he could wrangle far more from various museums and university archaeological departments around the world than he would by melting it down to ingots.

Carefully returning the bowl to its place, he sifted through the various objects, noting that, in addition to the exquisite turquoise, there were fire agate, deep red opals, and rich purple amethyst all worked into necklaces and pendants.

Knowing he was running out of time, Henry stood up and held the wand high, sweeping around the room to determine if there was anything else. As nothing else was revealed, he returned to the treasure between the two dead men. Pulling out his pocket watch, he calculated that he didn't have enough time to remove the gold and replace the stones before Caleb returned. Despite the urge to take a small specimen, he rationalized that he didn't want to alert Caleb that his treasure had been compromised. Casting one last look around the cave, he grinned with success. In just a short while, all this would be his.

A consistent gentle knocking emerged and broke into Belle's dreaming. Her eyes still closed, she lay comfortably beneath the cover as she slowly awoke and realized it was not part of her dream. Opening her tired eyes, she flipped the cover off and pushed herself to standing.

"I'm coming," she said, wrapping the shawl around her. Casting a quick glimpse in the mirror, she smoothed her hair, and went to open the door.

"Good day, Miss Belle," the head waiter from the Cosmopolitan politely said. "Mister Mitchell sends his compliments and hopes you enjoy this meal provided by the Cosmopolitan Hotel."

Yawning, she stepped to the side and gave a tired flip of the hand towards the table. "Just put it there, thank you."

Recognizing she was still half asleep, the head waiter quickly placed the plates on the table, leaving the covers on. He then quickly ushered the other waiters out. "Just leave everything outside your door," he told her. "We'll take care of it."

"Thank you," she replied, closing the door. Instead of seeing what was to eat, she headed back to flop on the bed and was soon asleep.

Not quite two hours later, she awoke again, remembering Henry had sent lunch again. Pushing herself up, she scooted to the edge of the bed. She was still tired, and the thought that she had another night at the Bird Cage was, at the moment, not very appealing. Standing, she meandered over to the table and pulled the lids off the plates. The eggs benedict did not look quite so tempting, and the toast was dry and cold. Even the coffee was cold. The veal, though probably palatable, was likewise unappetizing.

Her first thought was to simply put everything outside the door, but when the waiters from the Cosmopolitan came, they would see she hadn't eaten anything, which they would in turn tell Henry. That would be bad form on her part.

Scraping all the contents onto one plate, she went to the door, quietly opened it and poked her head out. The hallway was typically quiet for a Monday afternoon. Making her way to lone water closet at the end of the hall, she closed the door behind her and emptied the food on the plate down the privy.

Once back in her room, she placed the empty plates outside her door. Satisfied she had maintained her decorum, she thought about Henry and his gallant behavior. Twice he had sent her a delicious meal, a sort of breakfast in bed. And the picnic was a most enjoyable time. He had behaved the proper gentleman. She found herself thinking quite favorably about him. But she didn't want to overplay her hand. She knew the girls were quite impressed with him, both as a handsome gentleman, and as a, um, well-endowed man. She smirked at the allusion. She had been taught not to be vulgar and to use proper language, to give correct pause before she spoke so that her words had appropriate meaning. But here she was working as a madam, living amongst the very dregs of humanity her parents so disapproved of. Yet for all their commonness and sometimes vulgar behavior, she liked the miners and cowboys and working girls, for they were genuine. The men all treated her with respect and deference. They were protective of her girls and would defend anyone of them should a girl be in trouble.

As she washed and prepared herself for the day, she remembered the scene when her parents discovered she had jettisoned her plans to be a teacher and instead was about to embark on a career as a Pinkerton detective. Her father had been apoplectic while her mother simply stood grim faced, staring out the window. Her father had turned to her mother and fumed, "This is all your fault. You encouraged her to be headstrong, and now look what you've done."

"*My* fault," her mother had tartly replied. "Be thankful she has a head on her shoulders. If you had your way, she'd be married off to some vapid Vanderbilt boy to spend the rest of her life at tea parties and socials, bored to death because her life had been reduced to being nothing more than a trophy, something to display at some party. Instead, she has an opportunity to explore life. Something more than I ever had the chance to do."

Her father, realizing her mother was beginning to get angry quickly sought to diffuse the tension. "Now, now, Helen. Let's not lose our temper. Perhaps I spoke in haste. You have to look at this from my perspective, especially after all the money we spent sending her to college and giving up a promising career in education. Why she could be on the way to being the headmistress of an all-girls boarding school. This is probably just a phase, something to do for a little while."

Her mother had turned her back to him, but caught her daughter's eye, and winked. Her mother understood. Though she had subordinated herself to the role she was expected to play, she was not going to subject her daughter to the same fate.

And now here she was in Tombstone, an undercover detective working as a madam. She grinned imagining the shock on her parent's faces, especially her father, if they ever found out. Just as quickly, Henry came to mind and how well he would fit into her parent's world. She found him a unique puzzle, for he adapted himself to his environment yet never lost who he was. The man wasn't afraid to get his hands dirty. In fact, he seemed the kind of man who could roll up his sleeves and dig in the dirt while discoursing about the latest fashions in Paris or Charles Dickens' literary style in *Great Expectations*. He was confident, outgoing, refined, and wealthy, the kind of man most women would fight to have. She admitted that she was, indeed, attracted to him.

And then Mason came to mind… steady, calm, and dependable… and married. What was it about that man that so distracted her? Where Henry had a sort of dashing elegance that he flaunted, Mason had the face and body of a Greek god, a gift that he was quite unaware of. She giggled at the comparison and the elevation to the pantheon of divinity. Yet it was true. When he first began to visit the Theater, the women immediately descended upon him. It had amused her for it obviously embarrassed him. Thinking it a kindness to rescue him, she had finally interposed herself between the flock and the poor man. A noble gesture at first, it turned into one of preoccupation. She anticipated his visits, primping each day for his presence and finding herself put out when he didn't show. She knew he had responsibilities as a lawman, but she felt the same nevertheless. It was then she hit upon the scheme of using the Bird Cage as a rendezvous for capturing wanted criminals. He had immediately supported the idea and the two of them became partners.

The partnership had been most fruitful, for not only were her bank accounts dramatically improving, she was gaining the respect and admiration of the Pinkerton home office for the number of criminals brought to justice. And it gave her an excuse to spend more time with Mason.

He was now a regular at the Theater and the girls knew enough to leave him alone. Though she heard their occasional petty sniping, she brushed it off as jealousy. Besides, they couldn't be too vocal for they knew Belle could summarily dismiss them without cause. But those were very few, for most of the girls knew she was going to take care of them. They came to regard Mason as Belle's "property" though it didn't prevent the occasional offer, which he always courteously declined.

Which brought her back to her original thought – why was she so preoccupied with him? Henry, a virile and attractive man, was practically throwing himself at her. And there was that little problem that Mason was married… and had chosen to remain true to his words of 'for better or for worse.' Between the two, Henry had the distinct advantage for he was single, and Mason' status was not likely to change as long as Elizabeth lived.

Elizabeth. How could Mason stand being married to that shrew? Small wonder why he spent all his time at the Theater instead of home. Yet it wasn't like he didn't have options. Why he didn't divorce her was beyond Belle's understanding. Had she been married to a man like that, she would have jettisoned his sorry ass a long time ago.

She smirked, putting her hand to her mouth. Did she just say 'ass?' How improper of her. Apparently living in Tombstone was beginning to have some effect on her... a good effect.

Staring at herself in the vanity's mirror, she smiled a lopsided grin and finished coiling her thick blond hair into a bun at the back of her head. It took no effort to realize life was wonderful so far. She was a Pinkerton Detective, had her own fortune amassing in the bank and working as a madam in Tombstone, a city of amazing wealth. She had the attention of two extremely handsome men and was the envy of every woman in town, even the proper ladies who cast those secret lustful glances at the Marshal.

Another year or two of this, and she could move on to another adventure. She'd have enough money saved to invest in a more stable, legitimate business. All she had to do was relax and enjoy the ride.

Henry had time for only a short nap by the time Caleb returned. He emerged from his tent when he heard the IAS begin its loud sporadic beeping each time it swept over the approaching Caleb. Flipping back the tent opening, he stepped out into the later afternoon sunlit day. In a little while, he would be having dinner with his across-the-wash friend. Waiting until Caleb was close enough to give him a friendly wave, he went over to the IAS and shut it down.

"Be over in a minute, once I get my supplies put up," Caleb called out.

"Take your time," he replied, lowering the arm and cone of the IAS before languidly walking back to his kitchen area.

Henry had finished cooking by the time Caleb arrived with his usual fare of beans and beef. "I thought we'd have my famous pasta a la Henry," he announced. "I know you've had a good meal in town, but I thought another good meal couldn't hurt."

Remembering the last time Henry fixed the dish, Caleb was only too willing to partake again. "Much obliged," he said, setting his bland dinner to the side.

Henry played the charming host as he dished up the pasta, asking how Caleb's time in town was with the prospector chatting more than his usual. When Henry had cleaned his plate, he leaned back and let out a satisfying burp. Then, as if remembering something, he jumped up and retrieved a small box. Resuming his seat, Henry winked at him. In a great show of extravagance, he announced, "And now for the pièce de résistance." With a flourish, he produced a bottle of Tennessee whiskey.

"We celebratin' somethin'?" Caleb asked, watching Henry place two tall shot glasses on the table.

"That we are, my good man. I found several more shards with writing on them," he answered, prying the cork from the bottle. Pointing to the shot glasses he said, "I borrowed these the last time I was at the Bird Cage." He poured equal amounts into the glasses, almost to the brim. Lifting his high into the air, he proposed, "To a prosperous find."

"To what you've found," Caleb returned the toast.

"Would you like to see what I've found?" Henry eagerly asked watching Caleb still chowing on his food.

"After I finish eatin'," Caleb perfunctorily agreed out of politeness. After all, the man had shared his meal with him. Still, he had sat through some of Henry's other finds and dreaded a repeat performance.

Henry patiently waited until Caleb wiped the last of the sauce on his plate with a piece of bread. With the meal finally finished, Henry corked the whiskey bottle and got up to retrieve his finds along with two bottles of bourbon. One of the bottles was about one-quarter full, which he set before Caleb. Henry smiled at him with good-natured camaraderie. "You go ahead and finish that one while I open this other bottle." Seating himself, he carefully arranged his pottery before turning his attention to the unopened bottle in hand. Deftly uncorking the bottle, he poured himself a full shot glass. Noticing there was still room for more in Caleb's glass, he encouraged, "Now don't be shy, my good man. Drink up."

Needing no encouragement, Caleb topped his glass.

His sleek smile barely hiding his contained confidence, Henry lifted the glass in toast. "Once again… To a prosperous find and many more."

"I'll drink to that," Caleb nodded then downed the contents in one strong swallow. The liquor burned but tasted strong and full.

Henry refilled Caleb's glass, again from the partially filled bottle. "One more for good measure," he jovially announced, filling his again from the new bottle. Lifting the shot glass, he looked calmly at Caleb and said, "May we always find what we're looking for."

Caleb simply nodded his agreement and again upended his glass and gulped the contents.

"And one more just to say we can," Henry laughed, filling their respective glasses from their respective bottles.

Caleb noticed his was almost empty. "We drink any more an' I'll have ta start drinkin' from yers." Feeling quite content, he lifted the glass in one last salute. Downing the bourbon, he held the glass in his hands and smacked his lips. It had been a great day, now topped off with a fine meal and excellent liquor. It was but a few seconds after he placed the glass on the table that the world suddenly grew black.

Henry remained seated, impassively watching as Caleb's head banged onto the table and his body convulsed, before spasmodically falling off the stool and onto the ground. After a while, Caleb's body stopped its reckless jerking and settled to stillness.

With nonchalant disinterest, Henry sat and studied the man, wondering how such a coarse and common man expected to spend the treasure he had found. All the wealth in the world can't change what one is. A pig in pearls is still a pig. It was only right that the prospector should give up any claim to what he found. Only a man of class and breeding, like Henry, should be allowed to savor the benefits of such a find. A vulgar man like Caleb would only squander it. What a waste that would be. A man like Caleb had no appreciation for the exquisite talent and artistry that went into each piece. He would probably melt them down and lose far more in profit that what he would gain. Such ignorance. Henry was actually doing the man a favor by removing the treasure from him.

Picking up what had been Caleb's bottle of bourbon, Henry strode down to the small stream in the wash and poured the remainder of the contents into the moving water. Crouching down, he dipped the bottle in and out of the water several times, sloshing the insides clean. He looked up at the evening sky then back up at his camp where the lanterns surrounding the dining table flickered light over the body of Caleb, who looked like he had fallen asleep on the ground.

Standing up, Henry grinned with barely contained satisfaction. So far it had been too easy. Inhaling deeply, he controlled his euphoria. In a short time, he would be incredibly rich. Turning, he leisurely strolled back up to the camp site, placing the bottle with the other empties in a small crate that he would take to one of the Tombstone bars to use.

Standing above the prone prospector, Henry rubbed his chin abruptly realizing Caleb was a larger man than he had thought. Looking up again as daylight dwindled into darkness, Henry pulled out his pocket watch. It would be dark in less than half an hour. Best get done what he could with the dwindling daylight.

Grabbing a limp arm, Henry struggled to hoist up the dead man, finally managing to get his weight just right. With an audible "Oomph," he lifted him up in a fireman's carry. Slowly making his way down the hill and across the wash, he amusedly thought he should have killed him before dinner. He would have been lighter, but then a condemned man deserves a last meal.

The way up to Caleb's cave was a struggle and Henry slipped a few times before arriving at the entrance. For now, he decided to put Caleb off to the side and out of the way.

Placing him against a wall, he stepped back. "There now, don't you look comfortable."

Sunset had already passed, and night was quickly descending when he made his way back across the wash. Henry spent the next half hour setting up the IAS and collecting numerous kerosene lanterns that he placed along a line running from Caleb's cave to his. Satisfied that all was ready, he flipped the switch, and the IAS began its rotation.

Carrying several more lanterns and one small crate, Henry arrived at Caleb's claim and commenced to methodically tearing down the wall. As he dismantled the wall, he calculated the number of trips it would take to remove all the gold, one crate at a time. He had already dismissed the idea of using his MATE as it would leave telltale evidence. Unfortunately, there was no better alternative than to use the established path between the two claims.

He was calculating and estimating the total distance the number of trips would prove to be when he removed the last stone. Crawling through the small tunnel, he quickly emerged and headed straight for the gold. Ignoring the other exanimate occupants, he hefted two pendants of gold on the top and immediately felt the nape hairs rise. Tossing them back on the pile he whirled around, jerking the lantern high. Yet nothing was there, and he shook his head in consternation. He was too much a man of science to be spooked by superstition and ghosts. Besides, he chuckled, de la Fuente and companion were in no condition to stop him. Reclaiming the two pendants, he placed them in the crate along with several other items and began his monotonous and repetitive journey, carrying one empty crate to Caleb's cave and returning with one full one.

It was close to midnight by the time Henry made his last run, catalogued the pieces and organized them in neat piles next to the numerous boxes. He was tired, but knew he had some final details to attend to as he listed the final three necklaces and pendants. Trudging back across the wash, he labored his way back up to Caleb's cave. Grabbing the deceased by his arms, he jerked him into the tunnel. Backing in, he managed by pulls and tugs to slide the corpse into the smaller cave.

Pausing when he was finally inside, he stood and wiped his forehead. Casting one final glance around the room, he tugged Caleb around the two corpses and propped him against the wall so that it seemed he was staring at the two conquistadors.

"There," he smiled, brushing the dirt from his hands. "You all can now keep each other company."

Satisfied, he returned through the tunnel and systematically and carefully replaced the stones, adjusting each as necessary. The final ritual was the dusting, and he grabbed handfuls of floor dirt, methodically spreading the dry dirt as though he were dusting flour for baking.

Collecting the remaining lanterns, he joyfully made his way back to his claim, picking up the lanterns along the path. He was ready for sleep as he was dead tired. Smirking at the metaphor, he decided he would leave the IAS running overnight. Just a few hours of sleep were all he needed. When morning came, he would tidy everything up and begin repackaging the gold to ship home, along with the traveling artifacts he kept as evidence of his digs.

Henry let out a snort. In all the years, no one had ever challenged him on the fact that the Hohokam pottery shard with the wavy red painted lines he found here in Tombstone looked amazingly like the one he "found" up near Tucson, and the one he "found" near Presidio de San Bernardino. One of these days he was going to have to add more ancient artifacts to his supplies.

It was then he thought he should probably double check Caleb's cave one more time. Heaving a sigh at the thought of yet another trip, he got up from the desk and trudged across the wash, thinking he was going to be a very happy man to finally leave this place. He had grown tired of Arizona, well except for Belle perhaps, but even she was not enough to keep him here.

Standing in Caleb's cave, he held the lantern high, surveying the room with contentment. All seemed in order. Wondering if Caleb had anything else of value, he rummaged through the clothing bags and other belongings, finding nothing of value. Carefully replacing everything like he found it, he headed for what he decided was a well-deserved rest. After all, he smirked, he'd put in a long hard day's work.

It was midmorning and Henry was inside his cave arranging the crates containing the gold and artifacts so that the ones with the treasure were on the bottom of the stack. Should anyone snoop around, they would have to go through the crates filled only with dirt and pottery. Standing erect to rest for a moment, he smiled at his brilliance, for the weight of the individual crates appeared to be uniform. The ones with the treasure were no heavier or lighter than the others, which made it even better should prying eyes want to know what each contained.

As he stood there, hands on hips, a shadow passed across the opening. Startled, he hustled to the opening only to see two very small airships descending to his side of the wash. They were about forty feet long and eight feet wide at the center. The rear of the ship had four fins. Just forward of the bottom fin, contained in a louvered box, a small engine spun a single, rear propeller in a slow lazy whirl. A wide shallow tube went from the box to the envelope. Two other brass tubes went out from the engine box and up both sides of the envelope, ending several feet above the top fin. Smoke poured out of the tops of the tubes. Up near the front was the pilot's seat, an open lattice structure with just enough room for a man to squeeze himself into a seated position.

"Hey Mister Mitchell," Nantan called out as his airship settled and hovered a foot off the ground. He climbed out of the pilot's seat and grabbed hold of the front anchor rope while Taboca maneuvered his ship next to Nantan's.

Henry quietly heaved a sigh of relief that the treasure was safely stowed and all seemed quite normal. With calm satisfaction, he reminded himself that he had been wise to likewise cleanup the evidence in Caleb's cave. Striding over to where the two ships hovered, he exclaimed, "How fascinating," he said as if overjoyed to see them.

"We can't stay long, but we wanted to show you our toys," Nantan explained.

"We're headed back to Phoenix to pick up some repair parts," Taboca added. "Should be back in a day or two."

"I'll bring my stun-gun," Nantan offered.

"That would be excellent," Henry nodded happily. "Your ships are marvelous. I've never seen ones so small." Quickly studying the layout, he said, "I assume the engine heats the envelope."

Nantan looked triumphantly over to Taboca. "See. I told you he'd understand."

"And my guess is that the louvers are used to control the amount of air flowing over the engine, thus either heating it for ascent or cooling it to descend. Ingenious."

"Exactly," Nantan proudly answered, "which means we can't stay long, otherwise the engines overheat and we'd have to shut them down."

"Do you have time for a cup of coffee? It's already made."

Nantan looked over to Taboca who shook his head 'yes.' "Just a quick cup."

"Excellent. I'll be right back." Henry spun around and bustled back to his kitchen tent, poured three cups of coffee and returned. Handing the hot cups to the two machinists, he asked, "What are you using for your lifting gas?"

"A combination of hydrogen and thermal," Taboca answered. "The hydrogen is contained in smaller bags along the top. The rest is thermal."

"Brilliant," Henry said, quite impressed.

He spent the next several minutes asking questions about design, comparisons of rigid and non-rigid structures, and propulsion. The machinists sipped their coffee and readily answered his curiosity, quite pleased to share their invention with another inventor who seemed so impressed with their work.

Their coffee finished, Henry collected the empty cups and watched as they climbed back into their respective pilot seats, the airships bobbing slightly with the added weight.

"If it's OK with you, we'll come by in a couple of days," Nantan said. "I'll show you my stun gun."

"I look forward to it," he smiled at them. "Have a good trip." He stood watching them as they ascended, picking up speed in the southeasterly wind. Folding his arms as he stared after them, he thought of how fortuitous it was that the two machinists had paid a visit. They could prove useful should anyone question him about Caleb's absence.

Then he remembered he had a picnic date with Belle, and he brightened. It was going to be a good day indeed.

When the District Court convened, the courtroom was just about packed as more than a few wanted to see U.S. Marshal Sadler taken down a notch when Johnny Ringo failed to show up. Among the muted snickering in the audience, some pointed to the Marshal who sat stoically in the front row, waiting for the judge to take up the case. But there were more whose hope it was that the outlaw would show the same decency that the Marshal had extended to him, though they doubted an outlaw would keep his word. An outlaw was an outlaw after all was said and done.

The judge, a white-haired man whose view of the law was that his interpretations outweighed even those of the Supreme Court, looked up from the docket sheet and announced, "I'll now take up the case of Johnny Ringo and the events leading to the death of one George Hatch, a bounty hunter by occupation, address heretofore unknown." Looking at Mason he said, "Marshal. I understand you posted bond for Johnny Ringo. Are you, at this time, prepared to produce Mister Ringo?"

Mason stood up and looked behind him at the filled courtroom, but there was no Johnny Ringo. He saw the glee on a number of faces. With a sigh of heavy disappointment, he turned to the judge. "No, your Honor," he contritely said. "It seems I am unable to produce him at this time."

"I'm not even a little surprised that you couldn't" the judge said, chastising him. "I allowed you to post his bond based upon what I know of your character, also assuming you knew what you were doing. In this case, you have embarrassed both yourself and the court." He was about to launch into a tirade when he abruptly stopped as the door to the court opened and Johnny Ringo breezed in, Deputy Billy Breckinridge in tow.

"Sorry I'm late, your Honor," Ringo grinned with arrogant confidence. "Had a little trouble getting past the guards. If it hadn't been for Billy here, I'd still be outside." He laughed as he made his way to stand next to a pleased and relieved Mason. Leaning over to him he whispered, "Think I wasn't coming?"

"No," Mason smiled at him. "You gave me your word. That was good enough for me."

The noise in the room bubbled up, and the judge whacked gavel a good several times, calling out, "Order. I want order in this courtroom. You all just be quiet now. Order!"

As the room settled down, the judge looked at Ringo. "Mister Ringo, now that you are here, I wish to hear your side of the events. Come stand over here." He pointed to the defendant's table to his left.

"Certainly, your Honor," he said, giving him a tilt of the head as a bow. He pushed through the waist-high swinging gates and moved to stand behind a chair tucked beneath the table. "I had just come out of the Andy's Club Saloon on Allen Street when I happened to look across the street because I saw a man acting sort of strangely."

"What do you mean by 'strangely?' the judge asked.

"He was moving as if no one else was around, like he was real focused on something. I watched him for a moment and then when he drew his pistol, I looked to where he was focused and saw Marshal Sadler come out of the Grand Hotel looking like he might be heading to get a drink at the Bird Cage."

A number of titters erupted along with quite a number of disapproving frowns. "Order," the judge again called out.

Looking directly at the audience, he leaned forward and pointed the gavel at them. "This is a court of law. If you can't conduct yourselves like grown men and women, I'll clear this court." Turning to Ringo he said, "Proceed."

"Well," Johnny continued. "The Marshal had his back to the man, and I thought to myself that this coward was going to shoot the Marshal in the back. And I was right, because I was able to plug him just as he got off a shot at the Marshal."

The judge looked over to Mason who held up the Stetson with the hole in it. Motioning him forward, the judge studied the hat and the hole for a few moments. Motioning him back to his place at the front bench, he asked, "Is this your hat?"

"Yes, your Honor."

"Where were you when this happened?"

"Like Ringo said, I was coming out of the Grand Hotel. I'd had a late lunch there. I was standing outside when I felt my hat go off my head. At the same time, I heard two gun shots close to each other. When I looked back, Ringo was walking over to the man."

"What interaction had you with the deceased before this?"

"It was when I arrested Frank Blackwood. Mister Hatch, the deceased, was a bounty hunter determined to relieve me of my prisoner. I was forced to shoot him. Apparently he didn't like the fact that I refused to give up my prisoner, nor the fact that I shot him."

The judge looked up at the audience. "Anyone else got anything to say or add to this inquiry?" Silence reigned for a bit and when no one offered a counter view, he banged his gavel and announced, "Case dismissed."

Standing outside, Ringo watched as many in the audience slipped out of the courtroom. A number of them congratulated Mason, while a few were grim-faced and said nothing, simply ignoring the Marshal. Johnny noticed only two or three of the good citizens of Tombstone said anything to him.

Johnny looked at Mason. "Looks like I won't be going to jail. Much obliged, Marshal."

"It is I who am obliged to you, Johnny. You saved my life. I won't forget that."

"I'm counting on it," he grinned. "I'll pay you back soon."

"I know you're good for it, Johnny," he smiled. "Now do us both a favor and stay out of trouble."

"Now that I can't promise," he grinned. "But you know I've got your back if you ever need me."

"I'm counting on it," Mason replied, giving him a friendly pat on the shoulder.

Henry stood back and carefully scrutinized the stack of crates inside the cave. All were neatly positioned and firmly placed against the wall. He looked down at his ledger, the entries written in Latin. Unless an intruder was a classics scholar, few would know what was written. Yet another measure of security should someone come while he was absent.

Chuckling, he was beginning to understand why Caleb had grown so paranoid. With the amount of wealth in the cave, he was a millionaire several times over. Yet now was the time to take subtle security measures.

Walking outside, he crossed over to the MATE to check the water level in the tender. He then spent the next twenty minutes collecting dried mesquite branches to add to the stack of wood in the trailer before firing up the boiler. For short distances, he preferred using wood as it didn't take as long for the engine to start up or cool down, and there was plenty of dead wood out here. While the pressure was building, he cranked down the IAS. When the steam was liberally pouring out the MATE's funnels, he checked the pressure gauges and hopped aboard. Backing it up to the IAS, he leaped off to hitch the two together before backing the IAS in front of the mouth to the cave, effectively blocking access. Anyone wanting to enter the cave would either have to climb under or over the IAS, making it extremely difficult to remove anything from the inside without moving the heavy machine first. Satisfied, he took one last look around, unhooked the trailer and headed off to his rendezvous with the lovely Belle Dubois.

Perched atop his machine as it chugged towards Tombstone, Henry basked in the day and his future. Things were working out better than he had planned. The two machinists stopping by was a windfall. They would prove useful in providing any necessary alibis. Secondly, their visit would cause him to delay reporting Caleb's absence by at least a day. Depending on how well the picnic went with Belle, he might be able to start shipping out the treasure by tomorrow, before he had the opportunity to tell of Caleb's disappearance. By the time they discovered the bodies in the cave, he would be long gone.

Leaning heavily against the back cushion of the chair, her arms draped over the armrests, Belle sat in her room pondering what had happened, why she felt so addled. What should have been an enjoyable time turned out to be rather frustrating. It wasn't as though Henry wasn't the perfect gentleman, well... almost perfect gentleman. There were a few times he wanted to proceed farther than she was ready. But he had willingly yielded to her rebuffs, and nothing happened to warrant her not wanting to see him again.

In fact, the day was perfect. He had picked an idyllic spot along the San Pedro for the picnic, under the shade of wide spreading cottonwoods. It was obvious he had taken time to prepare the place, because a blanket was spread on the ground and the wine was already cooling in the river when they arrived. There were two folding chairs to sit on close to the river. He had even arranged a small fire pit for coffee. The man had thought about everything. So why had the afternoon been a struggle?

Despite her best efforts, she couldn't get Mason out of her mind. In her head, she replayed the scene of seeing him and Elizabeth coming out of the Grand Hotel, after enjoying a fine dinner... together. He was wearing the Stetson Elizabeth bought him. The fact that she had bought him one just like the one Belle gave him bothered her. She felt exposed, as though she had revealed too much, overstepped propriety.

Yet she wondered whether that was what was really bothering her. The more she thought about it, the more she understood that she cared for Mason more than she realized. And while Henry chatted away in his charming and gallant manner, she paid but scant attention as she sorted out her feelings.

By the end of the afternoon, she knew she had fallen in love with the Marshal, that she had fallen in love with a married man.

That realization both irritated and frustrated her. She chastised herself for the sheer foolishness of what was probably a school-girl crush. What made her think that he was even interested? And what if he was? He'd already made it clear he would never do anything to destroy his marriage. What was the point of her wild infatuation?

Yet despite her efforts to find Henry a suitable substitute, she couldn't help but compare him to Mason. The more she compared, the less appealing Henry was. That thought itself aggravated her as an absurd exercise.

It was obvious she was getting too involved with some of the personalities associated with her work. Perhaps it was time to notify the Home Office that she needed a change, go someplace where she could get back to the thrill of chasing outlaws, instead of being stuck in some bordello. She wondered if San Antonio might be fun.

"San Antonio?" Henry had repeated when she had absentmindedly given voice to her thoughts.

"What?"

"You said 'San Antonio.'

"I did?" She blinked, wondering if she had revealed anything else.

"Yes, you did. What about San Antonio?" He looked at her with feigned nonchalance, yet he could tell she had not been listening to him.

"Have you been there?" she asked.

"Yes. Several times."

"I've only been there twice. I was trying to think of where this place here along the San Pedro reminded me, and then I remembered San Antonio, though there are a few more trees along the river there."   Hoping she had lied convincingly, she smiled at him.

The rest of the afternoon was uneventful other than rebuffing the desires to go beyond a kiss. When at last he had dropped her off at her boarding house, she had allowed him a deep kiss and promised another date, perhaps a play at the Shieffelin Hall.

Now that she sat slumped in her chair, she debated what she wanted her future to look like. From the financial perspective, Tombstone was proving to be very lucrative. Her arrangement with Mason had netted her quite a tidy sum, and her bank deposits reflected her increasing wealth. If she stayed, she could continue to amass more assets, perhaps in time even invest in some venture. Yet all the money in the world could not buy her happiness and she wanted something more.

She wanted Mason.

Gritting her teeth, she reminded herself that he was not part of the equation. Forget him. Move on with your life. Who knew how long he'd be around? Being a Marshal had its downside, like someone wanting to shoot you in the back.

Standing up, she walked over to the window and drew back the curtain to gaze upon the busy street. Admitting she liked it here, despite the wind, dust and lack of trees, she decided Tombstone wasn't so bad after all. She was a sought-after woman, had a steady income, and expended little effort in her job. Truth was, this was the easiest gig she'd ever had. Now was not the time to change horses.

Who knew what the future held for this booming town. The silver was pouring out of the mines in a never-ending parade of mule teams hauling ore to the stamping mills. The wealth flowing through the town was obvious and she wanted to be a part of it. If she was patient, Tombstone would make her rich.

Henry chewed on his lower lip as he motored home, the treads of his MATE churning effortlessly, spewing out flotsam of desert behind. His picnic with Belle had not been the success he had wanted. While she was willing to continue seeing him, it meant he was likely spending his money on a venture of no return.

And then there was that little part of her calling him 'Mason' several times when the ambiance turned romantic and intimate. He had overlooked it the first time, not wanting to spoil the moment. It was after the second time that he decided to cut his losses.

He was no fool. It was obvious she had a thing for the Marshal. They probably had a little affair happening on the side. He sniffed in disdain at the Marshal pretending to be so upstanding in his marriage. The man was no different than any other.

For some reason, the thought that the Marshal might have more than one weak spot gave him satisfaction. Just how he would exploit that was another matter. For now, he needed to get home and ensure his treasure was secure.

As the camp site came into view, everything appeared in order. Bringing the MATE to a stop, he left the engine steaming and hurried over to his cave, squeezed past the IAS and stood surveying the interior. He was pleased to realize the IAS did an excellent job of blocking sunlight. He would either have to move it or light a lantern to inspect his possessions. The easiest and fastest solution being the best, he grabbed a lantern, struck a match and lit the kerosene damp wick.

Lifting the lamp high, he slowly and methodically studied and counted the stacked crates, ensuring everything was just as he left it. Satisfied all was in order, he went about shutting down the MATE and settling down for the evening. He was about to prepare his dinner when the urge to give Caleb's cave a last look caused him to stop preparations and hustle determinedly across the wash and peer into the silent cave while there was still daylight.

Standing in the mouth of Caleb's cave, Henry paused long, gazing at the meager possessions of the man who now reposed in eternal rest with the two long dead conquistadors in the other cave. While his eyes lingered on the separate items, his mind was rehearsing what he was going to say to the Marshal on the morrow.

With a contented chortle, he turned around, strolled down the hill, skipped lightheartedly across the small stream flowing in the middle of wash, and ambled up towards his camp. Though only mildly disappointed he'd be dining and drinking alone this evening, he reminded himself that it would only be a matter of days before he left this desolate dump behind him. Once the treasure was back east, he would then have the joy of taking his time and unloading a few pieces at a time, saving some of the more significant ones for the European collectors.

Uncorking the bourbon, he poured himself a healthy dose, relishing the full-bodied taste. A trip to Europe would be just the thing, especially after all the time he had spent in the desolate desert of the American southwest. His mind rambling in pleasant thoughts of Paris and Berlin, he looked back to Caleb's cave and lifted his glass in toast. "Thank you, my friend. You've made me a very wealthy man. I couldn't have done it without you." He snorted a laugh. "Here's to life and happiness."

He downed the bourbon and clinked the glass on the table, pouring himself another round. Lifting it again, he continued his salute, all the while staring out over the wash to Caleb's silent claim. "Though the bourbon is good, I prefer French champagne. I'll think of you when I'm in Paris." Thinking about what he had just said, he smirked and added, "Then again, maybe not."

Belle stood against the bar doing her best not to appear bored. It was past midnight, and the dancing and music were as raucous as ever, she was surrounded by her devoted coterie of admirers... and Mason had still not shown up. In fact, it had been at least four days since he had stood at the bar and nursed his whiskey. She knew why but didn't want to accept it. How could he go back to that woman? What

171

could she possibly offer him that would make him want to stay with her?

The thought nagged at her and festered. She had seen them together out in public twice already, walking to dinner again at the Grand and then late one evening prior simply out for a nighttime stroll. Elizabeth appeared to be trying to get her life together and that fact more than irritated Belle. It frustrated her and interfered with her work. Her obsession with the married Mason was becoming more than a distraction and others were noticing. She had better get herself together before she compromised her cover.

Perhaps what bothered Belle the most was when she realized her feelings for Mason were more than mere friendship. She berated herself for violating her own principle of never getting involved with a married man. Nothing good ever becomes of it. And here she was, mooning over Mason.

Belle told herself to let him go, but that was easier said than done. Truth was, she missed him. That he was devoting his time to that worthless wife who was going to backslide at any moment now was beyond her. Why bother? It would only be a matter of time before he was back here nursing his whiskey again.

That thought should have eased her mind, but it didn't. She knew there was always the chance that Elizabeth might succeed, and then where would Belle be? Had Mason been a different sort of man, a husband like all the others, one who would cut his losses when the facts told him it was time to leave, Belle could be patient. She would wait for a man like that. But Mason wasn't that kind of man.

With a sigh of sour resignation, she told herself it was time to forget Mason. Elizabeth could have him. It was time to move on.

Chapter 8

Mason was looping the reins around the hitching post outside the jailhouse when he heard a voice calling him. Looking up, he saw Charlie Parsons, the telegraph operator hustling towards him, waving a telegram at him.

"Hey Marshal," Charlie grinned, officiously walking up. "Got yourself an answer about that Mitchell feller." Handing him the telegram, he waited until Mason scanned the contents. When it looked like he was finished, he winked at him and said, "It says that feller ain't who he claims to be."

"What it says is that there is no one by the name of Henry Mitchell who is presently teaching at the college," Mason studiously replied. "Doesn't mean he's not an archaeologist."

"Suit yerself," he snorted, "but I'd keep an eye on him if I was you."

"And why is that?"

"'Why that telegram there. Why'd you ask fer information if ya didn't suspect something?"

"I asked for information because I like to know what's going on in town," he replied folding the telegram and stuffing it in his shirt pocket. "Appreciate you bringing it here. I'd like you to keep this to yourself for the time being," he warned. "He seems harmless enough, spends enough money here and folks like him. I don't want anyone getting the wrong idea."

"Wrong idea about what? That he ain't what he says he is?"

"That's enough, Charlie. Just do like I asked you. As of now, he's an honest citizen and there's no cause to suspect otherwise. I don't want anyone getting too curious, especially him, if you get my drift."

Charlie blinked for a moment then nodded confidentially. "No problem, Marshal. You can depend on me." With a friendly nod, Charlie loped back up the street to the telegraph office.

Watching him walk away, Mason wasn't so sure Charlie knowing his business was such a good idea. The man had the habit of dropping hints of gossip gleaned from the daily telegraph messages. The juicier ones tended to spread like a Tombstone fire.

Still, the information puzzled him. Why would Henry claim employment at a university when one could so easily verify the truth? Pushing the door open to the jail, he saw David Neagle, Chief of Police, sitting behind the desk. He looked up when Mason walked in.

"Afternoon, Dave," Mason greeted him.

"Afternoon, Mason. What can I do you for?" he smiled politely. David was a short and wiry man who tolerated no gruff from anyone.

"Well," he said, pulling up a chair to sit. "I've got two things. First is to see what outstanding warrants you have, and second is to talk to you about a fellow who goes by the name of Henry Mitchell, the one with the strange locomotive that comes into town every Saturday."

"Him? What's he done?"

"Nothing that I know of," he casually replied. "Just like to keep tabs on folks in these parts."

"That's my job," Neagle stiffly pointed out.

"Now Dave, I'm not trying to interfere," he said. "Your jurisdiction is Tombstone. Mine is all over. I figure the way he comes in and out of town makes it both our business."

"I suppose?" he said, raising an eyebrow. "What's your point?"

"Just have an odd feeling about him, that's all." Mason pushed back the Stetson a bit off his forehead. He thought about telling him of Henry's artifacts and the just arrived telegram but decided he would wait a bit more. Then he remembered Charlie was likely to slip the word. "Henry Mitchell claims to work for Brown University."

"So?"

"Got a telegram here that says one Henry Mitchell doesn't teach there." Mason scratched his cheek. "Now the

174

problem here is that they didn't answer my original telegram. I asked if he worked there. But this does make me curious. And then there's the question of his artifacts." Mason explained Ben's observations.

"You're taking the word of the town drunk over a respected archaeologist?" David scoffed. "I'm surprised at you."

"I understand," Mason acknowledged. "I may be way off the mark, but I've got to go with my hunch. I'd consider it a favor if you'd have your boys keep an ear open, but back off and let me work him." For some reason, Mason felt Henry had more going on than he was telling, and he didn't want him getting skittish.

"I can do that, Mason," he said, smirking. Pulling out the stack of warrants, he slid them across the desk. "Nice work on Frank Blackwood. There's a few more in there with some good bounties on them."

Picking up the pile, Mason studied a few of the more violent criminals. "I doubt we'll see some of these," he off-handedly said, placing several papers on the desk. Sifting through the remaining warrants, he scrutinized three as though committing the faces and bounty amounts to memory. Satisfied, he neatly stacked the papers and handed all but three of them back to David. "Appreciate it.," he said standing up. "Mind if I take these three with me for a bit? I'll return them later today."

"Any time," he replied, pulling the left top drawer open and stuffing the stack in.

Once outside, Mason moseyed just around the corner and up one block to Allen Street where the Bird Cage Theater lay wedged between Hattich's Tailor Shop on one side and the Palace Lunch Room on the other. Though both respectable businesses, they rather enjoyed the additional trade brought in by the Theater. With the Theater open every hour of the day, every day of the year, the Palace Lunch Room especially reaped the benefits of being the closest dining concession to hungry miners who didn't want to travel far between food and fun.

Though it was early afternoon, Mason wondered if Belle would be at work. Pushing the door open, he was pleased when he saw her at the cherry wood bar in the foyer, talking to Billy Hutchinson, reviewing some entries in the ledger. Upon walking up, he heard her say,

"Let me deal with her Billy. Tess has been a good worker. You can't just let her go because she's getting on in years."

"That's just it, Belle," Billy shrugged as if to say it was out of his hands. "She's getting less business than the others. Now I got nothing against her, but face it. They want the younger ones. She's gonna have to move on. Now I can tell her if you want –"

"No," she said, holding up a hand to stop him. "I'll do it. That's what I get paid for. I'll handle it."

"Fine," he nodded, relieved he wouldn't have to deal with the distraught woman. "You do that. Then find someone to take her place, a younger one." Looking up, he noticed Mason. "Hullo Marshal."

"Billy, Miss Dubois," he replied, tipping his Stetson to her.

Belle coolly regarded him, especially when her eyes lit upon the Stetson. "Hello Mason." Closing the ledger, she turned to Billy. "I'll take care of it."

Understanding the discussion was finished, Billy grinned at them both and moved on to check the alcohol inventory.

"What can I get you, Marshal," the bartender asked.

"Do you ever sleep, Jack?" Mason asked, amused that the man always seemed to be on duty.

"I've a cot right under the bar here," he said, straight-faced.

"I believe it. I'll take a whiskey."

"Coming up."

"Give him the good stuff," Belle interjected.

"Always do," Jack replied. "I like a man who knows his whiskey."

While Jack uncorked the bottle, Belle turned her attention to her guest. "So what brings you here to our little house of ill repute? What's the occasion?"

176

Frowning at the chill in her voice, Mason said, "I've three more warrants for us, all told around $2500. I'll get to them in a minute."

Jack placed the whiskey in front of him, and a sangaree to Belle.

Accepting the drink, Mason lifted it up in toast to her. Taking a satisfying sip, he savored the taste a moment then lowered the glass to the bar top. "How well do you know Henry Mitchell?"

"Why?" she stiffly replied.

Noting the reaction, he said, "I know you and he have spent some time together."

"That's really none of your business," she coldly replied, setting her drink firmly down on the bar top.

Puzzled at her brusqueness, he furrowed his brows and said, "Actually it is my business. And it should be your business too." He pulled out the telegram and handed it to her. "I asked the University if he worked there and that was their reply."

Reading it quickly, she handed it back to him. "All it says is that he doesn't teach there."

"That's correct. You would think that if he was the respected archaeologist he says he is, the University would be proud to let the world know." He then once more relayed Ben's comments.

"He's the town drunk," she sniffed. "You'd take his word over any sober person?"

"Ben's not always drunk," he countered. "And often enough he's on the mark."

"You mean like the time he said a group of wild monkeys carried him out of the bar?"

Mason studied her for a moment before asking, "Are you OK?"

"What do you mean?" she guardedly replied.

"You don't seem yourself today."

"I'm fine," she impassively replied.

Recognizing he was going to get nowhere, he decided to change topics. Handing her the three warrants, he said,

"These three have come through here on occasion. Should be easy."

Belle looked at the warrants and associated pictures. "Saw Lennie Hopkins two days ago in here," she said pointing to one of the pictures. "He wasn't using that name though."

"What about the others?"

"Can't say. They look familiar. I'll have to ask the girls. Leave these with me for a while. I'll see they get back to the jailhouse."

"What about Henry Mitchell?"

"What about him? What's he done that you want to waste your time on him?"

"Just a hunch," he shrugged.

"That's it?" she said, cocking an eyebrow. "There are killers loose, cattle being rustled, stages being robbed, and you want to investigate a respected archaeologist because you have a 'hunch?'"

Her terse response surprised him, and he pondered his words before he said something he'd regret later on. "I see you have nothing further to add concerning Mister Mitchell." Quickly finishing his drink, he nodded his thanks to Jack and touched his hat in respect to Belle.

When he was almost to the door, she called out with a hint of sarcasm, "Nice hat."

Mason stopped and turned around, giving her a look of mild puzzlement. "It ought to be. You gave it to me." Without waiting for a reply, he walked out through the doors.

Belle stood numbly blinking at the closed door for a few moments before she turned back to the bar, only to see Jack giving her a look that said she was a fool.

"What?" she asked.

"You didn't know?" Jack said, wiping the bar top with a damp rag.

"Know what?"

"I heard tell that the Marshal went back to the Callisher's General Store and exchanged the Stetson his wife bought him for boxes of ammunition. Can you imagine a wife not knowing her own husband's hat size?" Jack kept wiping.

"Wonder what he told his wife what he supposedly did with the hat you gave him? Seems she's none the wiser though."

Belle thought herself the biggest fool ever. How could she be so blind? He hadn't been to the Bird Cage because he was merely going through the motions of giving Elizabeth the chance to change. Then she remembered how she had just treated him. She was about to rush after him to explain her actions when a pretty woman in her early thirties caught her attention.

"Billy said you wanted to see me," she said, smiling at her.

"Not yet," Belle impatiently replied then caught herself. She would see Mason again and explain. Gazing maternally at the woman, she said, "Let's go for a walk, Tess."

Deciding to take a look at the progress of the Cochise County Courthouse, Mason was halfway down Toughnut Street when he heard Henry's MATE off in the distance. Looking off towards the road to Charleston, he saw the archaeologist perched atop his strange vehicle, the smoke pouring out behind it. He watched as it approached, the speed constant and fast. Henry wore goggles and his hat was jammed on his head. It seemed he was in a great hurry as he motored up 1st Street. Though he lost sight of him, he could hear him traveling Allen Street heading towards the Bird Cage.

The sound of the MATE lowered a bit, and Mason figured that Henry was paying a visit to Belle. The thought concerned him, and he frowned wondering why Bell had been so defensive about the archaeologist. His thoughts were interrupted when the MATE fired up again, and he turned to see Henry heading up Toughnut towards him.

Henry pulled back on the brake levers stopping the MATE when he saw Mason. Disengaging the forward mechanism, he climbed down.

"I'm glad I found you, Marshal," he said, his face a frown of concern. "It may be nothing, but I haven't seen Caleb since the day before yesterday. He had come back from town and we had dinner together like we usually do.

We shared a nightcap and he went off to his claim and I to mine for the evening's repose. I confess that I didn't pay attention yesterday as I was distracted by the prospect of another picnic with the lovely Belle." He smiled to himself when he saw a flicker of jealousy pass across the Marshal's face.

"Obviously I arrived home later yesterday than I normally do and thus the normal evening repast that Caleb and I share was not to be. I thought nothing of it and went about my night in study and research. However, when I awoke this morning, it seemed unusually quiet over on his claim. Invariably when I prepare my coffee in the mornings, I can hear him banging away. Sometimes he'll stop his arduous labor and come over to share a cup. But this morning was dead silence." He almost laughed at the choice of words.

"Did you check in the cave?" Mason asked.

"Well yes," came the reply as though the answer was obvious. "When I noticed that there seemed to be no activity there, I gathered my coffee, pouring him a cup and walked to see if perhaps he was still sleeping, which would be highly unlikely, unless he was sick, and the man is never sick. I've never seen someone –"

"What did you see," Mason impatiently interrupted, "when you entered the cave?"

"Well, nothing," he replied. "At first, respecting a person's property, I stood outside the cave and called to him. When I received no answer, I approached and stood in the opening. As I had mentioned, it was unusually quiet. I called again, yet still received no reply. Thinking perhaps he had gone off to respond to nature's call, I sat at the mouth of the cave and waited. After a sufficiently long enough period of waiting, I traipsed over to his accustomed spot, but he was not there. So I returned to the cave and stepped into his domain, yet nothing looked out of the ordinary, at least that my untrained eye could see."

"What about his tunnel, the small one at the back of the cave?"

"I didn't go in there," he quickly answered, holding up his hands. "I have little knowledge of mining skills and if something is amiss in there, I'd prefer those whose knowledge far exceeds mine to conduct that part of the investigation."

Mason sifted what Henry had just told him. He was right in that this was not like Caleb. The man was much to set in his ways. Routine was a source of comfort. "You say the last time you saw him was two nights ago?"

"That's correct. That was his day to come into town. He had lunch with you. He came home, unloaded his things and we had dinner together. Everything just like always. He seemed in good spirits. We talked about the trip into town and he chatted on about his lunch with you. In fact, now that I think about it, he did seem more chatty than usual. He does so enjoy his meals with you, Marshal," he unctuously complimented.

When Henry mentioned the lunch conversation, Mason's guard and ears perked up. "Chatty? What do you mean?"

"Oh," he chuckled. "You know Caleb. Getting him to talk is a feat in itself. Invariably I'm the one who does the talking because the man barely says two words. That's what happens when one lives alone for so long. Your voice gets rusty from disuse."

"So he was chatty?" Mason said, both impatient and frustrated the man couldn't keep to the topic and reason he was here.

"Yes," Henry replied, pretending to remember what had been discussed. So far, his acting was superb, a performance worthy of the stage. "Quite honestly, I can remember nothing of any great import. I did find it curious that he rambled on about what he would do after he struck it rich." He sniffed in disdain. "Not meaning to speak ill of the man, but he can't even afford a mule to carry his small amount of ore to the stamping mills. At this pace, he'll be buried in Boot Hill and barely afford the coffin. But I let him chatter on about all the glorious things he would buy and do once he got rich. I suppose dreaming does help a man keep his focus. And what does it hurt to let him dream. After all, it's not like it's going to happen any time soon." He gave his best benevolent smile, thinking that not only was it not going to happen any time soon, it wasn't going to happen at all.

"And you're sure he's not somewhere around the claim?"

"I wouldn't have driven all the way here if I thought he was still there," Henry replied, frowning at him.

"Of course," Mason answered. He mulled the news, torn between the desire to immediately look for Caleb as a Federal Marshal, or telling one of the town constabulary of the concern, knowing that word would eventually leak out. Johnny Behan was still away, and David Neagle was the authority in town. David was a good man, but he had his hands full. Though Mason liked Caleb, had he not known about the man's discovery, he could simply chalk it up to another robbery and let the Tombstone lawmen handle it. But if something had happened to Caleb and word got out that gold had been found, all hell would break loose. He would need to handle this himself.

"I'll come out in the morning," Mason said. "Perhaps he'll show back up between now and then."

"If there is anything I can do, Marshal," Henry solemnly said, "I'll help in any way I can. Caleb's a good man and I enjoyed his company."

"Appreciate it," Mason said. "Do me the favor and make sure no one touches anything. Set up that intruder machine you have if you need to."

"Absolutely. I'll guard his cave with my life," he melodramatically answered.

"Let's hope it doesn't come to that," he half-smiled. "You finished in town here?"

"Got some laundry to drop off, but I can be on the road in less than half an hour."

"Then I'll leave you to it," Mason said, stepping back.

"You can depend on me Marshal." Henry confidently stated as he stepped onto the iron tread and pulled himself up. Cranking up the engine, he let it run a few moments, inwardly glowing with the performance he had just delivered. The way he manipulated the Marshal into believing his story was intoxicating. It was small wonder why actors and actresses so enjoyed their craft. Releasing the brake, he shifted it into gear and the MATE lunged forward. "See you tomorrow," he called out.

Henry traveled down the street before stopping outside of Wuhan Mei's store and hopped down. With a lighthearted stride, he pushed through the door. Wuhan Mei smiled as he entered.

"Good afternoon, Miss Mei," he cheerfully greeted her. "You look wonderful today, as usual."

Bowing at the compliment, she responded, "It is good to see you Mister Mitchell. How may I help you?"

"I've come to inquire about Missus Sadler's bill," he said, looking quickly around the store.

Pulling out her ledger, she flipped a few pages and ran a finger down the side of a page. Stopping, she read the entries and said, "It is not yet time. Another week perhaps, maybe more. She has not asked for it for several days."

"That's what I thought," he nodded sagaciously. "I would consider it a favor if you would make a delivery as soon as possible, this afternoon perhaps, something strong and special." Henry placed a stack of silver dollars on the counter. "I know this is an inconvenience, but hopefully this will cover any additional expenses."

Wuhan Mei nodded in solicitous understanding. "It will be as you wish."

Giving her a respectful bow, he retraced his steps and leaped aboard the MATE. Releasing the brakes, he started his journey back to his claim. He couldn't help smiling. So far, all his planning was being executed perfectly.

Mason stood in the doorway, his shoulders sagging. The windows to the room were open, and the curtains ruffled in the breeze that blew in over the ledges and swirled past him. The only light in the room was from the fading sunlight.

Looking forward to some time spent in conversation with his wife, he had come back to the boarding house to take Elizabeth to dinner. Instead, he found her sprawled across the bed, the bottle of laudanum uncorked on the nightstand. Elizabeth's road to recovery hadn't even lasted a week.

He remained rooted in the open doorway, staring at her, trying to decide whether he was more disappointed in her for her lapse or himself for believing she would actually change. He contemplated the past several days of the new and improved Elizabeth. Though her pallor was still like one who lived in darkness, she was beginning to put on weight. While he liked the change, it did little to affect the dullness in his heart. Still, he was attentive and caring, believing she at least deserved that. Who knew, perhaps her steady improvement might rekindle the emotions that had once been there. But now, seeing her draped across the bed in drug induced oblivion, the dullness returned. Mason wondered if anything was ever going to be different.

Closing the door behind him, he crossed to the nightstand to pick up the laudanum bottle, puzzled as to how she came by it for he had searched the room and cleared it of any and all traces of the destructive drug days ago. Gazing at the bottle, he studied the exterior vainly looking for any telltale signs of who might be responsible. But the sides were clean, merely translucent glass, a receptacle to hold her elixir.

He was half-tempted to pour the remaining contents out the window, but it would be an exercise in futility. She would find more, and nothing would change. He corked the bottle and placed it on the nightstand.

He stood at the edge of the bed in momentary indecision. His growling stomach reminded him that he needed to eat. His resentment grew for he knew his meal would be taken alone, like so many others. After being out in public with Elizabeth, he would now have to make excuses as to why she wasn't with him, making up some foolish story that everyone knew was not true. And the clucking of tongues would begin again, and he resented the overt pity in their condescending attitudes.

With a sigh, he lifted his emaciated wife and slipped off her clothing. Pulling back the covers, he placed her in the bed, tucking a cover over her just under her arm pits. He stepped back to stare at her. Her frail body beneath the clean sheets reminded him of an open coffin just before the burial. Leaving the windows open, he adjusted the Stetson that Belle had given him and walked out to find something to eat.

A while later, he stood on the boardwalk outside Walsh's restaurant. The meal had been good, and no one had bothered him as to the whereabouts of Elizabeth. Deciding it had been too long between whiskeys at the Bird Cage, he headed down Allen Street.

Surrounded by her coterie of admirers, Belle was by the Polyphon Music Box choosing a musical disc from the lower cabinet when Mason walked in. He watched her for a moment as she blithely chatted with the men around her, impressed with how she offered attention to each man in a way that made him feel he was important to her. He wondered if that was how she felt about him.

As he approached the bar, Jack already had a whiskey poured and on the countertop. "You look like a man who could use a drink," the bartender observed.

"Thanks Jack," Mason replied, lifting the glass in salute. Downing half the contents, he felt the liquor warming him, relaxing him. Looking in the mirror behind the bar, he continued watching Belle, studying her smile, her laugh, her mannerisms. Despite his best efforts, he felt himself captivated. But then he remembered the last visit here and her brusque responses to his questions concerning Henry Mitchell. It then dawned on him that perhaps she and Henry were more involved than he thought, and that bothered him more than he wanted to admit. Was it because he didn't trust Henry? Or was it because he was jealous?

That he might be jealous bothered him even more. If he was going to be an effective lawman, he would have to get rid of distractions. Elizabeth alone was enough of a problem and he didn't need anymore. Maybe coming here tonight wasn't such a good idea after all. Thinking he probably should find somewhere else to drink, he finished his whiskey and placed two bits on the counter. Before he had a chance to turn and leave, he felt a hand on his arm.

"It's good to see you, Mason," Belle said, locking his gaze with hers.

"Evening, Miss Dubois," he politely replied, touching the brim of his Stetson.

"Are you leaving?" she frowned at him.

"I was thinking about it."

"But you just got here," she said, more of a complaint than a statement.

"Yes, I know," he answered. Realizing he really had nowhere else he had to be, he added, "But I suppose I could stay a bit longer."

"Good," she firmly responded. Getting the bartender's attention she told him, "Give him another, Jack."

Nodding in response, Jack took Mason's glass and refilled it, then went about making Belle a sangaree.

"I believe the last time you were here you had asked me about Henry Mitchell," she said. "And I don't think I gave you the answers you were looking for. So let's try again. Go ahead. Ask away."

"Are you sure?" he asked, raising an eyebrow.

"Yes," she reassured him. "I was a bit of an ass the last time. Sorry."

Mason gave her a smile of forgiveness. "What do you know about him?"

"He's a good-looking man, dresses sharp –"

"You can skip that part," he said, his eyes half-lidded.

"OK," she smiled playfully at him. "It's obvious he's educated. His manners tell me he either had a privileged upbringing, or went to a preparatory school somewhere, most likely the east as he claims as he has the occasional eastern accent. Whether he is an archaeologist or not, he talks a good story. That said, he's quite gifted in the sciences as his various inventions show. It's also obvious that he has wealth, especially with the money he spends here every Saturday. It may be earned or inherited. He doesn't talk about family, preferring instead to wow the girls with tales of Europe. Oh, there is one other thing."

"What's that?"

Looking around to see if anyone was in earshot, she lowered her voice. "He knows I'm not French."

"Really?"

"He speaks it fluently.   Puts me to shame.   Speaks several other languages as well."

"Spanish?"

"Yes, I believe so. Why?"

Mason paused then leaned in closer. "I think you and I need to go somewhere private."

Smiling, Belle tenderly touched his arm. "What will Elizabeth say?"

"Pardon?" He frowned at her then realized what he had just proposed. "I... I, um, I didn't mean it like that," he reddened.

"Not interested?" she replied, pretending to be hurt.

"Of course I am, I mean no," he fumbled, flustered. "Stop that. You know what I mean. We need to talk."

"Oh," she said as though suddenly understanding, though impishly smiling at him. Looking at the bartender, she said, "Jack. Mason and I are going to the back for a while. Hold the fort 'til I get back."

"Will do, Belle," he calmly answered.

"Come on then, Marshal Mason Sadler," she purred. "Let's adjourn to the stage." She led him into the main room, past the gaming tables and benches filled with miners and cowboys waiting for the next show, and up the stairs to the stage where the main curtain was drawn. Once behind the heavy curtains they walked over to a small table behind the sets.

"We have about twenty minutes before the next act goes on," she said, nodding at the actors, actresses, singers and stage manager flitting around backstage. "So," she smiled, sitting down. "You sound so mysterious."

Flipping the chair around, he spread-eagled it and sat opposite her, folding his arms across the top rail of the chair. "I suppose I do," he began. "What I am about to tell you might sound a little crazy, but I believe it's true. It concerns Caleb, the prospector with the claim opposite Henry."

"That old coot you go to lunch with every time he comes town?"

"Yes, him. That old coot is not as crazy as everyone thinks." He then relayed the tale about the fortune in gold and the two dead bodies. The more he told, the wider Belle's eyes grew. By the time he finished, she was leaning forward on her elbows, absorbing every word he said.

"So there was another cave inside of his cave," she said, "and the mouth was covered with rocks to make it look like nothing was there?"

"And that's where he found the gold."

She sat back, stunned. "And so many folks told him he was crazy for claiming a cave that had seen so much use already. How is it possible that no one had ever seen that before?"

"Who knows?" he shrugged. "The problem we have is that Caleb is now missing."

"How do you know that?

"Henry came into town today to tell me. I'm going out tomorrow to have a look."

Frowning, Belle paused for a moment then said, "You think Henry had something to do with him being missing?"

"I don't know," he answered, shaking his head. "Part of me says he wouldn't come here to tell me Caleb was missing if he had anything to do with it."

"He could also be doing that to throw off suspicion," she replied.

"That's what the other part of me thinks," he nodded agreement. "Problem is, I don't have anything specific to cause me to doubt him except for Ben's tale and the telegram." He took his hat off and placed it on the table.

Belle smiled when she looked at the Stetson she had given him, but her smile was more for the handsome man who wore it. "Maybe I was hasty when I said Ben wasn't the best of sources."

"I thought the same thing until he showed me the differences. He's not the fool everyone thinks he is."

"So what do we do?"

"Like I said, I'm going out for a look tomorrow morning. That will give me a better idea."

"What do you want me to do?" she asked.

"I think you need to get closer to Henry. Find out what you can."

"How close?" she teased.

Mason pursed his lips then quietly replied, "Whatever it takes to get the job done."

Deciding not to tease him further, Belle said, "How do you know Caleb was telling you the truth?"

Mason shrugged. "I asked myself the same question. But from what I know of the man, he wasn't given to tall tales. Too much the practical sort, if you know what I mean. Still, I knew something had happened by the way he was acting this last time we had lunch. That was when he told me about his, um, discovery."

Placing a hand on top of his, she said, "If it's true and word gets out, there won't be enough law in these parts to handle the craziness that's bound to happen."

Her touch felt electric, and he reveled in the sensation. Part of him said he ought to feel guilty for feeling like this, but that part was pushed aside as he convinced himself that he had done nothing wrong. Besides, she was a partner in law enforcement, a friend. What more could happen?

"I'll know more tomorrow," he said, leaving his hand where it was.

For a brief moment, neither said a word. Their eyes focused on each other, a subtle understanding passed between them. Belle was the first to break the spell.

"I'd better get back," she said, squeezing his hand and standing.

"Of course," he said, also standing, suddenly feeling exposed. 'Think I'll head out through the basement. See what's going on down there."

"See you tomorrow?" she asked, smiling prettily at him.

"Wouldn't miss it," he immediately answered, then silently chastised himself for the way he said it.

"Me either," she said. In one quick movement, she stood on her tiptoes and kissed him on the cheek. Stepping back, she winked at him and silkily glided away.

Watching her leave, Mason's heart fluttered, and he blinked at the thrill. By the time he collected himself, she was already past the curtains, down the stairs and at the bar sipping her sangaree.

Chapter 9

The beeping from the IAS alerted Henry that someone was coming. From the vantage of his position behind the desk, he saw a lone rider and knew it was the Marshal. Henry was tired, for he had spent a frantic afternoon and evening yesterday after he returned from town taking extra cautionary measures in case the Marshal became too inquisitive. He had unpacked all the treasure, consolidated it, and sequestered it in sacks of various sizes among the work boxes containing his tools, oil cans, parts, and dirty rags. Attaching the trailer to the MATE, he loaded a number of crates to give the appearance of work. He figured that once the Marshal left, he would repack all the crates, load them into the trailer, and head out up to Benson to start shipping the treasure back east. He could then return and 'assist' the Marshal in his investigation.

For good measure, he had made one last visit to Caleb's cave while it was still daylight, carefully ensuring all looked ordinary. Satisfied everything was in its proper place, he had contentedly crossed back to his own claim, and settled down to devour Diaco de la Fuente's journal once again.

Thus comfortably assured all was as he planned and with the morning sunlight spreading gloriously across the sky, he poured himself another cup of coffee and turned off the IAS. As the beeping died, he called out, "Some coffee, Marshal?"

"Don't mind if I do," Mason answered, reining in his mount and stepping down. "Anything?" he asked, ticking his head towards Caleb's claim.

"I haven't been over there this morning, if that's what you mean," Henry said. "Haven't seen or heard any activity. Thought about going over there but thought better about it in case I disturbed some evidence or something."

Accepting the coffee, Mason took a sip and looked around. "Looks like you're packing up. You moving on?"

"Just getting some artifacts ready to ship back east," he said, "though truthfully there's not a whole lot more here I can find to keep me here."

"Where you headed?"

Sipping his coffee, he shrugged, "Thought about going up towards Oracle. Heard some scuttle about jars and bowls they've dug up on some claims. But I'll stay as long as you need me," he quickly added.

"Ladies at the Bird Cage will be mighty unhappy," he said as observation. "And I'd guess Miss Dubois will be a might disappointed too."

"Ah, Miss Dubois," Henry smiled. "A woman of rare pulchritude. I have every intention of devoting more time and attention to her. I say, the picnics have been most enjoyable, if you know what I mean," he winked, "speaking as one man to another."

"Actually, I don't know what you mean," Mason calmly replied, "but she did say she too enjoyed the time with you."

"Did she really?" Henry perked up, puzzled that Mason seemed so nonchalant. Yet he knew that all was not well in the Marshal's home, especially after Henry's last gift to Elizabeth. It was just a matter of time before the woman succumbed to her weaknesses. And he needed Elizabeth to distract the Marshal's focus, at least until Henry had a chance to get away.

Finishing his coffee, Mason gave the cup back to Henry. "Well, that will all just have to wait a bit. Let's go see what's up in Caleb's claim."

It was as they entered the cave that Henry sputtered, "What the hell?"

For there on the ground, arrayed in a geometric pattern like waves from a pebble dropped into still water, the stones from the wall spread out from the now gaping wide-open hole in the wall to where Caleb and company reposed.

"This wasn't here yesterday," he explained, his voice registering his shock. "I swear it. I came here when I got back to see if he was here, and he wasn't. But it didn't look like this. This is impossible. I've had the IAS on ever since I got back. There's no way anyone could've gotten in here without me knowing it."

Mason noticed the honest shock to the man. Looking at the pattern, he said, "It's obvious someone had to have spent some time doing this. You sure this wasn't here yesterday?"

"Of course I'm sure. I'm a scientist, my good man. I notice things like this," he indignantly replied, though apprehensive. His mind worked feverishly working through the various explanations for the bodies inside.

"Did you come back here to Caleb's cave after you came back from town?"

"Of course," he replied without thinking, then quickly added, "I thought there was a possibility he might have come back while I was gone.

Slowly nodding at Henry's response, Mason wondered just how much the man knew. "Might as well see what's inside there," he said, gazing directly at the small opening. Briefly looking around for a kerosene lamp, he found one among Caleb's supplies, lit it, and headed for the small opening. Crawling through the small tunnel, he emerged into the cave.

Henry nervously remained rooted where he was, doing his best to appear innocent, waiting for the inevitable. A few moments later, Mason emerged, pushing the lamp before him. Turning down the flame, he stood up and brushed the dirt off the knees of his pants. Impervious to Henry's agitation, he began studying the rest of the main cave.

"W… well?" Henry stammered. "What's in there?"

"Nothing," he shrugged.

"Nothing," he numbly blinked. "Nothing? Are you sure?"

Mason gave him a curious glance. "Yes, I'm sure. Have a look for yourself." He pointed to the lamp on the ground by the entrance.

Without a second thought, Henry turned up the lamp and crawled through the tunnel. Once inside, he stood up and held the lamp aloft, casting flickering light upon an empty cave. His mouth slacked open as he worked through possible explanations, but nothing made any sense. Taking one last walk around the room, he studied the floor, but the overlapping of his and Mason's footprints had disturbed and obliterated any possible pattern or sign.

Scooting back out, he stood up to see Mason slowly walking around the interior of the main cave. "I don't get it," Henry said, staring at the stones on the floor. "Why go through all the trouble to do this?" It was then, in the sunlight that slipped into the cave, that he saw it, artfully placed within the pattern... letters formed from darker colored stones. The first was an 'E', then 'N' followed by 'R.' He quickly spelled out E-N-R-I-Q-U-E.

His mouth suddenly dry, he tried to swallow. Looking up, he saw Mason watching him.

"Yes," Mason calmly said. "I saw it too, though I find it curious that whoever did this spelled 'Henry' using the Spanish equivalent."

"It's a common name," he defensively replied, "both in English and Spanish."

"So it is," Mason smiled. Casting one last look around the cave, he said, "I don't see anything here of use. Mind if I have a look over at your place?"

"Why?" Henry sputtered, quickly chastising himself for his defensive response. "Sorry. I'm a bit unsettled. Help yourself. I don't see how this could have happened between the time I came back yesterday and your arrival today. I had the IAS scanning ever since I returned. There has to be a logical explanation," he answered, forcing himself to relax.

"I'll take some more of that coffee, if you have any left," Mason said. "I'll be over in a minute. I just want to take one last look around."

"Take your time," he amiably replied, doing his best to appear the gracious host.

While Henry brewed up another pot of coffee, Mason stood at the entrance of the cave, slowly taking in the contents. Retrieving the lamp, he turned up the flame and crossed over to the rear gaping hole where Caleb had been mining his silver. Crawling in, he held the lamp with one hand as he waked forward, hunched over. The path went in for a good forty feet before making a bend to the right. Just after the bend was where Caleb was digging. Mason paused and held the lamp closer to the dug-out portion of the wall that went in almost eight paces and as tall as a man could stand. But other than the debris on the floor, there was nothing else in that portion of the tunnel.

Mason retraced his steps and pushed further back into the cave that quickly reduced in size so that he was forced to proceed on hands and knees. A few minutes later, the tunnel split, the left side being far too narrow for a man to squeeze through, the right side sloping down and constricting to no more than a spread hand wide. He was at the end and knew nothing more was beyond. Backing out, he turned around once he had space and headed back to the opening and into the wide space of the main cave.

Stretching, he thought to himself that he was glad he was a Marshal, a job that allowed him to be outside in the openness of the western prairies. Being stuck underground as a miner would be just as bad as living in San Francisco.

Adjusting his Stetson, he walked out of Caleb's cave, down the wash and back to where the crates were stacked inside Henry's small cave. "Do all these have something in them?"

"Not all. You're welcome to take a look. Just be careful with any that have an artifact in them." He smiled to himself; thankful he had decided to transfer his treasure elsewhere. By the time the Marshal was finished with the crates, he'd be too bored to linger here any longer.

Methodically taking his time, Mason lifted each crate. Those obviously empty, he set to the side. Those that had some weight to them, he pried open and examined the contents. It was almost two hours later by the time he was finished. He made a mental note that fifteen of the sixty-eight crates were empty. Deciding he'd had enough, he finished the last of the coffee.

"Do you still have that book Caleb gave you?" Mason abruptly asked.

"Book?" Henry squeaked, suddenly off balance. "What book?"

195

"The book that Caleb gave you, written by that conquistador, de la Fuente," Mason replied, studying the man who was doing his very best to hide his sudden nervousness. Henry's reaction was what Mason had wanted, for it showed the archaeologist was far more involved than he pretended.

"Oh, um… yes, that book," he sputtered, silently cursing himself to be caught off-guard like that. "Let me get it for you." As he pretended to search for it, he wondered how the Marshal knew about the book? Did that imbecile Caleb actually reveal what he had discovered to the Marshal? Suddenly Henry realized that if the Marshal knew about the book, he knew about the gold. A mixture of dread and urgency washed over him. He would have to accelerate his plans. He no longer had the luxury of waiting. Still, he comforted himself, there was nothing in the cave and nothing that could be pinned on him.

"Here we are," he said, making a grand display of discovery as he pulled open the top drawer to his desk. Handing it to Mason, he said, "Please be careful with this. It's very old and valuable."

Mason opened the book and silently read the first few lines. "Valuable?" he said cocking an eyebrow.

"In terms of archaeology," Henry explained. "I haven't finished analyzing it, and there's no specific provenance to it."

"Provenance?"

"The place where it was found," he said, frustrated that he had to explain when what he really needed was to think. "Caleb said that some miner up in Colorado gave it to him, but I question that. More analysis of the document could shed light on the identity of the author and thus the activities which he wrote about."

"I see. Well, I'll just keep this for a little while, as evidence." He saw a pained look flit across Henry's face, followed by a forced calm.

"It's written in Spanish."

"Yes, I can see that."

"You can read Spanish?" Henry queried against hope.

"Yes."

Immediately deflated, Henry put up a good front and said, "Well then. Let me know what you come up with."

"You can count on it," Mason evenly replied. "I'll be heading back now. I'd like for you to stick around for a bit longer, if you don't mind. I may still need your help."

"Of course, Marshall. Anything I can do to help," he politely replied, forcing a smile. "I'd like to ship those back," he said, pointing to the crates on the trailer. "Any problem with that?"

"I don't see a problem," he answered, knowing he would have to keep a watchful eye on the man. Thanking him for the coffee, he mounted his horse and headed back to Tombstone.

Watching him ride away, Henry was beside himself. When they found nothing in Caleb's cave, the Marshal had examined each of Henry's crates. Any fool would know the man was looking for the treasure. Damn. Fortunately, Henry could now repack the treasure in the empty crates, and no one would be the wiser.

Looking over to Caleb's claim, he grimaced at the mystery of missing bodies. Something was dreadfully wrong. Had someone seen him hauling the treasure over to his claim? And why was his name written in the stones, even if it was in Spanish? And why Spanish? Was this a subtle message, a warning that someone knew he had stolen the gold, murdered Caleb, and was now going to blackmail him? And where the hell were the bodies. They couldn't just up and walk away. Someone had to have moved them.

Determining to find out the truth, he turned on the IAS and set the volume on as loud as possible. As the machine's cone swept the area, it emitted the appropriate beeps as he crossed the wash and walked up to Caleb's cave. When he was inside the cave, the sounds ceased. Carefully making his way to the mouth, he remembered Caleb's elaborate stone wall he had built to lurk behind once he was outside, part of his routine to ensure he was not being watched. Scrunching down to follow the wall, he realized it went both left and right.

Choosing to go left, he bent over and scuttled along the path until it abruptly ended ten paces later. Turning around, he retraced his steps and went past the mouth to the cave, following the path as it curled around and dipped out of the range of the IAS. To his dismay, the path was completely hidden and led away from the claim down towards the wash. Whoever took the bodies could have easily dragged them out this way without being noticed.

He followed the path a bit more when it ended at a small circular wall, the place Caleb had used as his latrine. Beyond that, one could see across the open desert all the way to the Huachuca Mountains. With a sigh, Henry retraced his steps until he once again stood in front of the cave. When he appeared at the mouth, the IAS emitted a satisfying beep.

Folding his arms, Henry remained rooted in thought as he sorted out the possibilities. Whoever took the bodies had sent him a warning. Not only did he have the bodies, he knew Henry's culpability. The question now was – what should he do? If he left, he'd have the law on him. If he stayed, the odds of being discovered increased.

It was then he noticed that the IAS was strangely silent. Looking up, he saw it still slowly sweeping in a 180° arc, yet each time it passed where he stood, it offered no sound. Sighing with frustration, he started down the path towards his claim when he was surprised to hear the IAS beep. Abruptly stopping, he stared at the cone as it swept away from him, paused at the end then returned to pass over him without a sound.

Puzzled, he remained where he was letting the cone complete its sweep then repeating it several times. Each pass produced the same result – no sound came forth. Determined to discover what was wrong with the machine, he again started walking. This time the IAS beeped each time it passed over him.

The epiphany smote him with aggravated clarity. The machine only worked when something was moving. That meant one could fool the machine simply by standing still each time the cone passed.

Uttering a soft "damn," he trudged back to stand behind his desk. Vacantly staring at the spread-out notes on the desk, he decided the smartest thing he could do was repack the treasure and start shipping it piecemeal. Fairbank wasn't that far away, and he could get there in no time on the MATE. He would send the most valuable items first, the solid gold medallions and pendants. They contained the most gold. Then he'd send the finely crafted pieces, the necklaces, rings and other jewelry. They had the greatest value by weight.

He grimly smiled with smug satisfaction. He already had potential buyers, discerning individuals who appreciated the rarities of man's wealth, no matter how collected. 'No questions asked' was his motto and it was both respected and appreciated. Many of his clients were overseas, which made the disposal of this particular hoard that much easier. All he had to do was get it safely on its way back East – then he could relax and deal with events here. Whoever it was who took the bodies would be hard pressed to pin the blame on him.

Casting one last look at Caleb's claim, he mused that he had somehow gotten used to the man's company and would probably miss the conversation, no matter how banal and limited it was… for a little while. But then, the man was common, a member of that great unwashed who propped up the labors of the intelligentsia. Besides, the man's absence was a small price to pay for the future.

Slowly surveying the surrounding area, despite the active presence of the IAS, he then retrieved the treasure from the secreted locations. Hauling the goods into the privacy of his cave, he set about repacking the various items according to value.

It was while he was packing that he remembered the book that the Marshal now possessed, and he knew it was just a matter of a day or two before the Marshal translated the book and knew everything Henry did. That thought gave impetus to his motivation. Pausing to check the time, he saw the day was already passing away. It wouldn't be until tomorrow before he could get his treasure away from here.

The more he packed, the more frustrated he became thinking that Caleb had blabbed about the treasure to someone. Damn that Caleb. You couldn't trust anyone anymore.

Henry bolted awake with what sounded like the hammering of something heavy against metal. Flinging the covers off while simultaneously reaching beneath his cot for the 12-gauge coach gun, he leaped up and jammed his feet into his shoes. Gingerly approaching the cave opening, he searched the area outside. The noise was coming from where the MATE was parked.

Raising the gun to firing position, he stealthily worked his way around to get close enough so that the brilliant moonlight gave view to the cause. His surprise rapidly morphed to anger as he saw the hazy form of one individual hammering at the MATE with a large stone, attempting to knock off any protruding parts, while two others were in the trailer lifting the neatly packed crates high above their heads and throwing them on the ground causing them to shatter open, spilling the contents.

"Hold it right there," he hotly exclaimed, the gun pointed threateningly at them. There was something familiar about them, but in the moonlight, it was hard to determine; it was as if he recognized them but couldn't remember where.

The three men abruptly stopped, mid-action, their heads twisting awkwardly to stare at him. After a few moments of motionless pause, they resumed their banging and crate throwing, unaffected by either his presence or threats.

"I said stop!" When his words had no effect, he pointed the barrels at the man banging on the MATE. "Stop, or I'll shoot."

Without even acknowledging the threat, the man shifted position to get a better angle on one protruding part then resumed a fierce and deliberate banging.

"This is your last chance," Henry coldly stated. When the man didn't hesitate in his damage, Henry fired both barrels, exploding the man's head from his shoulders. As the man's body slumped to the ground, Henry rapidly flicked the release lever opening the gun, jerked the empty cartridges out and jammed two more shells in and cocked it closed.

The shots caused the two in the trailer to stop their crate-tossing and stiffly clamber off the trailer. However, instead of surrendering or attacking, they spasmodically fled away up the wash, their gait stiff legged and jerky.

His adrenaline still up, Henry had half an urge to follow them but decided against it. Instead, he clambered up onto the MATE, his shotgun at the ready, waiting to see if they would return. After almost half an hour, he felt himself getting tired and his eyes burned from lack of sleep and the strain of keeping watch. Deciding they probably would not come back, knowing he was expecting them, he climbed down to see the extent of the damage and the results of his killing the man. Returning back to the cave, he grabbed a kerosene lamp, lit it and held it aloft with his left hand, his right hand firmly holding the coach gun.

When he returned to where the dead man lay, he sucked in his breath. Lowering the lamp to give greater clarity, he felt the nape hairs raise when he saw the headless and desiccated body of what looked to be one of the conquistadors from Caleb's cave. Disbelieving the sight, he prodded the corpse with his foot, surprised at the light resistance of a body long drained of life fluids.

Lifting the lamp high, he scanned the surroundings, more to reassure himself that no one else was there. But his mind remained on the corpse. The likelihood that this long dead creature was responsible for damaging his machine was beyond credible. Someone was obviously using the dead men to scare him, to intimidate him. They were after the treasure.

He abruptly remembered the shattered crates and his treasure. Within the light of the lamp, he turned around and saw the broken crates on the ground and the spilled contents reflecting the lamp's glow. Placing the lamp of the edge of the trailer, he quickly hustled back to the cave and retrieved several more lamps, setting them strategically around the trailer while he scooped up the valuables and deposited them inside the cave.

When he was satisfied he had collected as much as he could see in the dim lights, he extinguished all the lamps. Ensuring he had plenty of ammunition, he climbed up into the MATE's driver's seat and settled down to wait for the dawn, his senses on edge.

By the time dawn's tendrils fingered over the hills, Henry was exhausted. The adrenaline burst had long since subsided and the long hours of straining to hear anything unusual had numbed him to dull fatigue. Climbing down from the machine, he decided the first thing he needed was coffee, something to perk him up while he sorted out what to do.

With the water heating, Henry returned to the trailer, carefully scrutinizing every parcel of dirt, looking for any treasure he may have missed. Discovering a few more necklaces and pendants, he commended himself that he had inventoried all the items. Though it would take time, he would be able to determine if anything was missing.

He then turned his attention to the MATE. Though scratched and dented, the damage was not as severe as he had worried. A number of smokebox clamps were broken as was the equalizing reservoir below the driver's seat. He would have to jerry-rig something for the reservoir until he could either fix it himself or get a replacement part. He liked neither option as it meant he'd have to nurse the MATE's speed and duration of use. More importantly, it also meant he might have to delay shipping back his treasure.

Heading back to the tent, he passed by the headless corpse. In the daylight, it looked pitiful, the taut skin stretched to brittle tightness over protruding bones. Henry looked around for the head but figured there couldn't be much left after the coach gun took it off the shoulders.

Staring at the corpse, he realized he would need to do something with it. He couldn't bury it as that would take time and it would be obvious that someone or something was buried, and merely piling stones over the corpse was a dead give-away.

He smirked at the choice of words. Still, he would have to do something with it so that no one ever knew it existed. Pondering his possibilities, Henry walked back to where the water was now boiling. Filling the top of his two chambered coffee pot with grounds, he poured in the steaming water. Waiting for the water to pass through the grounds, he separated the two chambers and poured the hot brew into a mug. Taking a sip, he sighed with pleasure. The coffee was strong, just the way he liked it.

Standing in the mouth of the cave, now in the morning's light, he took measure of what he needed to do. The first two priorities were to get rid of the corpse and account for the gold. Taking another sip, he set the mug down and went back to the corpse.

Bending down, he lifted the cadaver and carried it back to the cave, propping it against the stack of crates. "You can sit here for a while, until I determine what to do with you," he said as though talking to a recalcitrant child.

For the next hour, Henry compared the contents of the broken crates with the ledger. Once satisfied he had everything, he packed the loose treasure in other empty boxes, adding sand and pieces of pottery on top should anyone question the contents. He then carefully marked the contents against the entries in the ledger. It was when he realized he still had some empty boxes that he knew what he would do with the corpse.

Hoisting the corpse up, he carried it back to the trailer. Lowering the tailgate, he tossed the dead man up into the trailer. Folding his arms, he stroked his chin as he thought aloud. "Now... I have two options here. Taking a stone and crushing your brittle bones would make the packing easier, but it is messier. I do have a good wood saw and could simply cut through your bones. It would be tidier, but it might take longer. What to do, what to do?" Looking pointedly at the headless skeleton, he asked, "Any suggestions? No? Well then, I suppose I'll just have to decide."

Climbing up into the trailer, he methodically pulled what clothing he could away from the body. Some fabric had molded to the skin and he left it attached. Deciding to try the saw first, he went back to his supplies and pulled out the sturdy sharp-toothed blade. With wicked determination, he returned to the corpse. Grabbing ahold of a booted foot, he jerked it out from the edge and began sawing between the ankle and foot bones, easily cutting through the dried leather. Once through, he studied the leather and foot for a moment wondering if he should have cut it smaller, but then decided it would still fit in one of the crates.

Laying it to the side, he repeated the process with the other foot. He continued up the shin bones, apportioning off like measurements to keep the pieces uniform. The legs and arms seemed the easiest to cut and those were reduced to crate-sized pieces quickly enough. It was when he came to the pelvis and ribs that he decided a large stone would be quicker.

It was when he had crushed the last rib that he remembered the scattered head. It dawned on him that parts of the skull might still be scattered around. Stacking the last pieces on the pile of bones, he began a careful search of the ground. His first find was part of the jaw, then a few large pieces of skull. The rest was scattered among the stones and rocks, too small to be significant.

Yet there was one thing that puzzled him, something he had pondered the entire night. Why didn't they just steal the treasure instead of throwing it over the side? It made no sense. What bothered him more was that his IAS had not alerted him to their presence, which meant anyone could make off with his treasure at any time. That thought alone more than terrified him.

And then there was the corpse itself, now reduced to bit-sized pieces. Why bother hauling the dead man here? What was the purpose? His mind ached with the illogic of it all. Yet the fact remained that someone knew about the gold and was trying to prevent him from leaving. Only one person knew about the treasure, and that was Caleb... and now the Marshal. Why would that idiot prospector tell someone, especially the Marshal? That hardly made sense, but then the man wasn't necessarily playing with a full deck. He might have told someone he trusted, someone he knew he could depend on, someone who would help him.

The image of Marshal Mason Sadler emerged. Caleb had more than once mentioned how much he admired and respected the Marshal, how he was a man who was a genuine friend. Suddenly the nuances began to clear. Caleb obviously told the Marshal. Then, when Henry had told him Caleb was missing, he must have come out and discovered the bodies and that the gold was missing.

It all made sense, Henry grimly smiled to himself. The last time the man was here, it was obvious he was searching for the gold. He knew Henry had it but couldn't outright accuse him of it. When he couldn't find it, he went to the Caleb's cave. Now why would he do that?

Henry looked quickly around then headed over across the wash. By the time he was mid-way, his IAS picked up his movement and began its beeping, much to his annoyance. Now the damned thing decided to work!

Standing in the mouth of the cave, he rapidly scanned the interior before looking at the arranged stones in the dirt outside the small opening. Moving to get a better look, he jittered to a stop when he read the added word O-R-O just below E-N-R-I-Q-U-E. Grimly chuckling in understanding, Henry knew the Marshal had added the Spanish word for gold. The man was playing a game. Damaging the MATE prevented him from leaving. Breaking the boxes to find out where the gold was, was all part of the plan to intimidate him.

The man was clever, Henry mused. But two could play at this little cat and mouse game

It was already past dinner time when Mason saw him stagger out, or rather pushed out through the saloon doors. Shaking his head in disappointment, he walked over to the still inebriated miner who weaved unsteadily on the boardwalk as though unsure how he suddenly came to be outside.

"Time for you to go home, Ben."

Turning at the sound, Ben squinted in the sunlight, focusing on the voice before recognition swept through him. "Hullo, Marshal. What brings you here?" he frowned.

"Just out for a walk, Mason patiently answered. "Why don't you go on back to your cabin and sleep this off?"

"I ain't tired yet. Say," he slurred. "How about spottin' me drink? I'll sell ya another genuine ancient Indian bowl. Made some just the other day," he giggled.

"How about a cup of coffee instead?" he suggested.

"Coffee?" Ben retorted with contempt. "Why would I want coffee? The very idea! A man asks for whiskey and this fella wants t'give him coffee." Ben stared hard at him then blinked as though seeing him for the first time. "Say, I forgot to tell you I saw that fella you have lunch with. You know," he slurred, "that one fella's got the claim next to that archaeologist fella."

"What fellow?"

"That miner fella, Caleb."

Mason's ears perked up. "You saw Caleb? When? Where?"

"Don't rightly 'member," he slowly replied. "T'other night, I think. Or was it last night? Last night it must'a been. Ended up down around the Three Brothers somehow. Next thing I know I wake up and it's darker than a mine with no candles and I'm cold and somebody let the dang fire go out. Say, Marshal, you sure you can't spot me a drink. This talkin' is makin' me mighty thirsty."

"You finish your story, and we'll see about a drink," Mason calmly replied.

Knowing the Marshal wasn't going to budge, Ben licked his lips to emphasize his thirst and continued. "Well, like I said. I wake up and it's cold. I'm shiverin' tryin' t'find some bit o' coals when I look up and there he is standin' not more'n three paces away. I knew it was him 'cause he'd spotted me a couple o' drinks a few times and even bought me a lunch once. A right decent fella."

"Then what happened?" Mason asked, urging Ben to stay on track.

"Well, I sees him and I says, 'Hey Caleb. Whatchu doin' out here? Why ain't you back on your claim diggin' or sleepin' or somethin'? Well he just looks at me and says not a word, not one word. I'm thinkin' mebbe I was havin' a dream, but I knew it weren't no dream 'cause I was shiverin' too much to be dreamin' and besides, I still had some o' the bottle left and it burn just fine goin' down, so I knew I wasn't dreamin'. So I says again, 'Hey Caleb. How about spottin' me drink. This here bottle's done gone empty.'" Pausing, he looked forlorn and used up. "Say Marshal, I'm feelin' right tired. How 'bout we set a spell and I could sure use a drink."

Pointing to the bench behind him, he said, "You sit down there. I'll get us a beer."

"Beer?" he objected then, seeing Mason's determined face, reconsidered. "Beer would be good."

Mason returned with two glasses of the frothy brew, handing one to him. Briskly nodding his thanks, Ben drained half the glass before smacking his lips and sighing with contentment.

"You were saying you saw Caleb standing just outside the fire pit," Mason prodded.

"Yup. He weren't no more'n three paces away. So I says, 'Hell, if ya ain't gonna talk, at least ya could do is find me some sticks to get this fire goin'.' Well him and that other fella –"

"There was someone else with him?"

"Yup, a weird sort o' duck if ya ask me. Skinny fella, with a face like a man's been dead a long time. Dressed in some sort o' costume with a funny metal helmet on." He patted the air above his head for demonstration. "Well, those two goes off and collect up some dead wood and purty soon I got us a fire goin. But I'll be damned if as soon as I got that fire goin', they was scared to death of it. Wouldn't come more'n five paces away. Well, by now I was getting' warmer, with the fire and all, and starts to wantin' to talk. A man cain't set by a fire with a bottle and friends and not want to talk. But they said nary a word. I even offered them a drink, but they refused. Well I was startin' to get a little put out, 'cause it's impolite to refuse another man's offer of the bottle. So I pushes myself to standin', and by the time I gets up, they was gone, like they was never there." He swilled back the rest of his beer, loudly smacked his lips and burped.

"Did you see them again, after that, in the morning perhaps?"

"Nope," he summarily replied. "By the time I was awake this mornin', it was already lunchtime. So I high-tailed it back here."

Mason pondered the story, wondering how much of his fabrication might be true. "You sure it was Caleb?"

"Course I'm sure. I ain't got no cause to lie to you."

"How'd you come to be down Three Brothers way?"

Ben scrunched his face in concentration. "That's the dang funny thing about it. I cain't 'member how I got there nor who else was there. I had my minin' candle with me, but my pick was back in the cabin." Looking at Mason's still full glass, he said, "Say Marshal, if you ain't gonna drink that, I can help you."

Chuckling, Mason handed him the glass then stood up. "Go on home when you're finished, Ben."

"Much obliged, Marshal," he happily replied, lifting the glass in toast.

"Home?" he repeated, standing over him.

"Sure, sure," he mumbled. "I'll go home."

"See that you do," Mason said with finality.

Mason left Ben enjoying the remains of his beer and headed down the boardwalk towards the Bird Cage. It was the middle of the afternoon, but he could use a drink right about now. Ben's tale about seeing the miner near the campfire troubled him as did the little detail about the stranger with him. The fact that he related seeing a man matching Caleb's tale of the dead men was just too coincidental. Just how much of Ben's tale was myth was always frustrating, for there was always a kernel of truth in the tale. The problem was, which part was the kernel? And if Caleb was alive, why was he going to such extremes to stay hidden? If his life was in danger, why hadn't he sought out Mason? One thought lasted as he pushed open the door to the Theater – where was all that treasure?

And then there was de la Fuente's journal. Mason had begun reading it on the way back into town. Pointing his steed in the right direction, he could take his time as the horse slowly meandered the trails and road back home.

Even with a cursory reading, Mason understood why Henry had been so loath to let go of the book. It was obvious that de la Fuente had obtained a chest full of treasure, the same treasure Caleb had found along with the two conquistadors. What puzzled him though was Ben's story. Had he actually seen Caleb? And the man he described with Caleb seemed too much like the one Caleb had told him about. This was all too absurd... yet too coincidental. Shaking his head and sighing in frustration, Mason stood outside the Theater, pausing to let others come and go.

Belle saw him as he entered and beckoned him to the bar. Leaning in to confidentially whisper, she said, "Word has it that Lester Corbett is supposed to be gambling here tonight."

Mason nodded in understanding. "I better get some shut-eye if I'm going to be of any use then. Thanks Jack," he said as the bartender placed a whiskey in front of him.

"What did you find out?" she asked.

"Nothing," he grimly said, taking a sip.

"Nothing?" she frowned at him.

"Well... maybe something. Caleb wasn't there, just as Mister Mitchell said. But the entrance to the smaller cave was opened, all the stones placed in a neat pattern. Obviously someone had taken his time. I crawled in to take a look, but there was nothing inside it. It was obvious that someone had been in there because the ground was messed up. When I told Mitchell there was nothing inside, he was more than shocked, something along the lines of someone expecting different results. He then went in to look for himself. While he was in the cave, I noticed something strange about the way the stones were arranged and when the sunlight hit them just right, it was easy to make out the word 'Enrique.'"

"Enrique? Isn't that Spanish for Henry?" she said, more of a statement than a question.

"Exactly," he replied, lips pursed. "I have more than a hunch he's mixed up in this. I just can't figure out how. If he had something to do with Caleb's disappearance, why bother telling me about it?"

"Make you believe he's innocent," she answered.

"We've already been through that," he mused aloud, "but it just seems too pat, too contrived, even for him. I just wish I had something more specific." Then he remembered Ben's tale and related it.

"Almost sounds like the monkeys and the bar," she chuckled.

"I know. The problem is that there's enough in his story that causes me to wonder just what he did see. You're going to have to get to Mitchell, quickly. If I can't pin anything on him or anyone else, I've got no cause to hold him here."

"I'll do my best," she smiled, batting her eyes.

Gazing at her, he chuckled to himself that she at even less than her best would be impossible to resist, which meant he needed to leave before he made a fool of himself. Tossing down the rest of his whiskey, he touched the brim of his Stetson. "See you later."

Standing outside as night enveloped the sky, Mason decided against going up 6th Street choosing to avoid the whore cribs and soliciting women on the east side of the street. Though he understood their reason for being there, it was still painful to see sometimes, especially the women who were past their prime, barely scraping by in a town where wealth flowed like the San Pedro.

Turning north on 5th Street he left behind the noise and bustle of the saloons and night life on Allen Street. The street grew quieter as he walked past the businesses and homes of the more respectable citizens. It was almost quiet by the time he turned left onto Stafford Street to head home to Pascholy's Boarding House.

He had already passed Turnverein Hall and was coming up on the construction site of Saint Paul's Episcopal Church. Crafted from hand formed and sun-dried adobe bricks, it was nearing completion. Reverend Endicott Peabody had already put the word out that the first church service was going to be held next month. Mason was pleased that religion was finally going to have a permanent place in Tombstone, not that many of the miners would be attending. They spent their Sundays either working in the mines or playing in brothels and saloons.

As he walked on, his thoughts were already drifting to Caleb, the treasure and Henry when he thought he saw movement at the front doors of the Church. Slowing down, he noticed a door open slightly then close but not completely. The action was repeated several times but with slow and deliberate movements. Taking note that the wind was not strong enough to cause the door to move like that, he headed straight for the Church.

By the time he got to the doors, they were closed. Testing the handle, he found it loose and opened the door. Stepping inside, he paused and listened. A scuffling noise sounded on the side working its way towards the altar.

"Whoever is in here, you need to come out now," Mason boldly commanded. The noise stopped and he held his breath, listening. When no further noise or voice responded, he added, "I'm U.S. Marshal Mason Sadler. I'm going to stand by the door here and I want you to come out. Now."

There was a long pause followed by a slow scuffle towards him. Holding the door open, Mason stepped outside into the bright moon filled night wanting to make full use of the light to see who the mischief maker was. What approached him caused him to stumble backwards as a stiff legged man jerked his way towards him.

"Caleb?" Mason blurted as the prospector lurched to a halt two paces away, still inside the sanctuary, though bathed in the moonlight. Another figure hovered behind him.

Yet Caleb didn't look the same. "My god, what's happened to you?" Mason sputtered as he took in the maggot infested cadaver that now wavered as it stood before him. The smell of rotting flesh enveloped him, and he involuntarily stepped back, scrunching his face in disgust.

Instead of answering, Caleb simply stared at him, his head twitching as thought trying to decide what to say. After

211

a few moments, he stepped back and allowed the man behind him to fill the space.

Mason's mouth gaped wide then shut tightly as he stared at the skull of a man with a conquistador morion on its head, the dry skin stretched tight upon the face. Holding up a boney finger, the man pointed to Caleb then made a choking motion to his own throat.

Mason stutter stepped back and looked rapidly around to see if anyone else was around. The man waved at him to stop. He again repeated the gesture.

"Can you speak?" Mason asked, his voice almost as dry as the man's skin.

Instead of answering, the man continued the pointing and choking motions.

Catching his breath, Mason's mind raced with the impossibility of it all. He had heard the stories just like everyone else. They involved Indians, or settlers, or individuals long dead that came back to warn the living, fanciful inventions that would make Ben's tales seem plausible. But this here, now, just wasn't real. It couldn't be real. Yet here he was... and there they were – two supposedly dead men standing before him. They were dead... right? As his mind darted in different directions his logical part took over. Perhaps all the stories that he had so summarily dismissed might have some truth to them, like Ben's tall tales. Then he reasoned that he was in a church and if something weird like this was going to happen, here would be the logical place, even if it didn't have a cemetery yet. Staring at the man with the morion that was now too large on its head, he remembered the journal from Caleb's claim.

"*Está usted Diaco de la Fuente?*"

Abruptly stopping, the man jerked his head up and down.

"Can you speak? *Puedes hablar?*"

The man twisted his head 'no,' the body moving slightly with the head.

"*Entiendes Inglés?*"

De la Fuente held up his hand pressing his fore finger close to his thumb indicating 'a little.''

"I suppose that will have to do, because my Spanish is not that good."

De la Fuente pointed to Caleb again and made the same choking motion.

"He's dead?" Mason ventured the obvious. "*Muerto*?"

Diaco slowly nodded 'yes.'

Without thinking about it, Mason asked, "Did Henry Mitchell kill him? Enrique. *Enrique lo mató*?"

Diaco's agitated body settled as if relaxing. He nodded 'yes.'

Mason stood silently working through the absurdity of the present moment. Here he was, talking to a dead man about another man's murder, the very man who was now standing behind him. He grimly chuckled imagining how well that would play out in court.

"Does Henry have the gold?" he asked. "*Enrique tiene el oro*?"

Diaco again nodded 'yes.'

"Where's the other one of you?" Mason said, remembering Caleb's tale had two conquistadors in the cave. "*Dónde está tu amigo*?" When Diaco made the choking motion, Mason frowned at him. "He was already dead."

Diaco continued the choking motion, then pointed to his head. Placing a hand on either side he jerked them away like he was pulling his hair out. He repeated it several times, but Mason could make no sense of it.

"*No lo entiendo*. I don't understand." Realizing the question was too difficult to act out especially in terms of 'yes' or 'no' questions, he changed his approach. "Do you know where the gold is? *Sabes dónde está el oro*?"

De la Fuente nodded.

"Is it with Henry now? *Es con Enrique ahora*?"

Again de la Fuente nodded.

Mason pursed his lips pondering where Henry might have hidden the treasure. He had searched all the crates and found nothing. He knew there were other locations the treasure could have been hidden and he regretted he hadn't taken the time to conduct a more thorough search. Yet he had no probable cause, other than his suspicions. At least now he had something more to go on… didn't he? After all, he wryly mused, who would doubt the word of a dead man?

"OK," he said. The whole ridiculousness of this encounter along with the strain of thinking in Spanish suddenly tired him, and he wanted to clear out of here before someone came along and asked him what he was doing. "I'll take care of it. Um… *Voy a cuidar de él.*"

De la Fuente nodded and stepped back into the sanctuary, motioning for Mason to close the door. Standing outside the nearly completed church in the bright moon filled night, the sounds of the town seemingly quieter than normal for a midweek evening, Mason suddenly felt foolish, wondering if what had just happened was all in his imagination, a conjuration of his desire to find Henry guilty.

Frowning, he deliberated a few moments more before shaking his head and moving on towards home. He was halfway down the block when he turned around just in time to see two figures emerge from the church. With stiff and awkward gait, they crossed the street and disappeared into the barren hills to the north.

When he could no longer see them, Mason turned and slowly walked on. When he entered his room at the boardinghouse, Elizabeth was asleep. A single kerosene lamp flickered its low flame on the dresser table. With the windows closed, the room was stuffy. Though his body told him he was tired, his mind was far too engaged to let him rest.

After opening the window, he cast a glance at his wife. Her breathing was shallow as one in deep sleep. On the nightstand next to the bed was the bottle of laudanum. Picking it up, he noticed it was corked this time. Though he could not see how much remained, he knew it was less than this afternoon.

Putting the bottle back on the nightstand, he crossed the room, took off his hat and placed it on the wall peg. Sitting in the lattice-back chair by the door, he leaned forward, resting his arms on his thighs. He wanted to sleep, but the thought of lying in bed next to the drugged Elizabeth was suddenly distasteful. For some reason, the room smelled of death and the vision of the swarming maggots on Caleb's body made his skin crawl. Caleb's decaying body morphed into Elizabeth causing Mason to bolt upright to standing.

At that moment, the morbid epiphany came. Elizabeth was slowly killing herself, and there was nothing he could do about it. No matter how much he wanted to, he could not save her. It was too late. Even sending her back to San Francisco would change nothing.

Mason gazed down at his wife vainly trying to come to grips with how he felt. Obviously he was sad, but it was more melancholy than heartbreak. He knew that he should feel something more, but try as he might, it was no longer there. Memories of happier times in San Francisco only increased his melancholy.

Yet deep down, Mason was a practical man and knew that he couldn't change what was. Thoughts of what might have been had no reality, no place in living each day. It was time to move on.

Retrieving his Stetson, he set it on his head, adjusting it to comfort. He would do the right thing and care for her, regardless of how long it took. Turning the doorknob, he opened the door, pausing to look back. Uttering a silent prayer, he prayed that when she did die, she would not return to haunt him.

Standing at the bar in the Bird Cage, the raucous energy of dancing and loud music filling the theater, Belle gazed intently at the Marshal. "I thought you were going to get some sleep."

"Just couldn't seem to get settled," he replied, taking a careful sip of hot coffee. "Appreciate the coffee."

"Anytime," she smiled. "I usually have some ready and hot throughout the night. I can only drink so many sangarees." Looking behind her at the dancers, she said, "Corbett's downstairs waiting to play Faro. How do you want to do this?"

"Send one of the girls down to him. Say that I'm waiting for him outside the back door, that if he doesn't come out in five minutes, I'm coming in." Seeing her puzzled face, he explained, "I'll be out front."

Smiling, she caught the attention of a young flirtatious and leggy redhead.

"Yes Belle?" she said as she approached, giving Mason a fetching smile.

"I need you to do something for me," Belle said, chuckling at the overt ogling the girl was giving Mason. "Pay attention Mollie."

"Yes, Mam."

Belle explained her mission and moments later, Molly was downstairs sidling up next to a cowboy who was engrossed in watching the Faro game.

"Lester Corbett?" she whispered in his ear.

Startled, Lester was more than pleasantly surprised to see who diverted his attention. "Yes?"

"Miss Dubois said for me to tell you that the Marshal is on his way outside heading to the back door. He's gonna bust in here in less than five minutes. Miss Dubois said you ought to know."

Grinning at the news, Lester said, "Tell her I'm much obliged."

Mollie leaned in closer to whisper, "She doesn't like the law messing with the Theater."

Nodding in understanding, Lester quietly extracted himself from the group of men watching and waiting for their opportunity to play. Making his way upstairs, he paused at the edge of the dance floor, scrutinizing the activity. No one seemed to pay him any attention for they were all engrossed in either dancing or drinking.

Confident that he was going to slip away unnoticed, Lester casually weaved his way around the edge of the hall and out to the main bar area, passing close to the Polyphon music box where Belle was surrounded by her usual group of admirers.

Opening the door, he stepped outside. Looking quickly around, he saw nothing more than the usual customers going in and out of the Theater. A few men were resting on the benches outside. Pausing to take a deep satisfying breath of night air, he saw one man get up, a tall man, who moved so quickly that he didn't have time to react. By the time his mind told his body to flee, Lester felt the iron grip of the Marshal's hand around his arm and the hard barrel of a .45 in his side.

"Hello Lester," Mason calmly said.

"I thought you was supposed t'be by the backdoor," he indignantly said.

"I was, but when I saw Miss Dubois send one of the girls downstairs, I had a hunch she was letting you know I was here."

A single shot split the night, followed by another. Mason felt Lester suddenly get very heavy as he slumped to the boardwalk. The men already on the boardwalk dove for cover as Mason twisted around to see a figure across the street, a gun in his hand pointing at them.

Using the limp Lester as a shield, Mason trained his pistol of the man. "Drop it." When the man hesitated, he firmly commanded, "I said drop it."

After a few tense moments, the man lowered the pistol and tossed it on the ground.

"Come out to where I can see you," Mason ordered.

The man moved, but with each step, he appeared to lessen in stature. By the time he reached the middle of the street, he was nothing more than a boy.

Holstering his pistol, Mason lowered the now dead Lester to the boardwalk. Walking out to confront the boy, he said, "What's your name son?" The boy looked to be no older than ten years of age.

"Charlie."

"You got a last name Charlie?"

"Nash."

"Why'd you shoot him Charlie?"

"He killed my Pap," he matter-of-factly replied.

Mason nodded in understanding. Caught in the act of rustling a few head of cattle, Lester Corbett had gunned down the boy's father.

"How old are you, son?"

"Twelve."

"Where's your mother?"

"Home."

Then Mason remembered the boy's family had a ranch just north of Fronteras. That was almost 50 miles away. "How'd you get here?"

"Walked."

"Walked?" he said, astonished. "How long it take you?"

"'bout a week."

"What did you do for food?"

"Had some to begin with then headed to the river. Lot's o' food in there."

Mason slowly shook his head, considerably impressed. The boy had lived off the land. His father had taught him well. "You weren't afraid? At night?"

"Pap said the only difference tween day and night was ya couldn't see too good in the dark."

"So," Mason said, amused at the boy's confidence. "You're not afraid of ghosts?"

"Pap said it ain't the dead ya gotta worry about. It's them folks what's livin' causin' problems."

Though the bit of wisdom had some truth to it, after tonight's encounter with Caleb and de la Fuente, Mason wasn't so sure about that.

"Where'd you learn to shoot like that?"

"My Pap taught me," he answered, his voice bereft of emotion. "Said a man who cain't shoot ain't worth a bucket o' piss."

"What's going on here?" Constable Harry Solen said, hustling up the street. Off to his right, a small crowd had gathered around the dead Lester Corbett. Looking at the bystanders gawking at the dead cowboy, he said, "Don't just stand there. Some of you men get him up and take him to the undertaker."

"Hello Harry," Mason said as Harry walked up.

"Hullo Mason. What happened?"

"This is Charlie Nash," he said, indicating the boy with him. "His father is George Nash. That there on the boardwalk is, or rather *was*, Lester Corbett. Charlie came here to settle the score with Lester."

218

"Now son," Harry fussed at him. "You can't take the law into your own hands."

"He killed my Pap," the boy firmly replied.

"The constable's right, Charlie," Mason said in a fatherly tone. "You can't take the law into your own hands. That's why we have lawmen."

'You bein' lawmen didn't stop my Pap from gettin' killed," he stubbornly answered.

"That's true." Mason smiled at the boy's reply. "Good people get hurt every day. But that's why we have the law, to get rid of evil men so ranchers like your Pap can raise cattle and prosper."

"This is all very fascinating," Harry harrumphed, glaring at Charlie, "but the fact remains that you just killed a man."

"That he did, Harry," Mason interrupted, "though the warrant for Lester Corbett says dead or alive. Now I'm not one to quibble, but it looks like Lester is more or less dead and we have one less problem on our hands."

Frowning, Harry thought a moment then relaxed. "I suppose your right, though he's lucky he didn't hit anyone else."

"Yeah," Mason stared hard at him, "especially me."

"I ain't that bad o' shot," Charlie huffed.

Suppressing a grin, Harry looked at Mason and asked, "You claiming the bounty?"

Mason paused as though thinking, glancing at the boy from the corners of his eyes. "The way I see it, I had help from Charlie here, so he deserves at least half. But when I look at what happened, I really didn't have possession of the outlaw when Charlie killed him. So it seems to me the boy ought to get the entire bounty."

Impressed, Harry nodded in understanding. The money would help the family keep the ranch. "Come by tomorrow son and I'll get your reward for you."

"Reward?" he blinked in surprise.

"Yes," Mason paternally said. "There was a thousand-dollar reward for him."

Charlie's mouth slacked open. "A thousand dollars?"

219

Mason looked over to Harry. "He's going to need someone to escort him home. I'm sure his mother's worried about him."

"She knows where I am," Charlie replied.

"I'm sure she does," Mason kindly said, "but she's a mother and that's what they do. I'm surprised she let you come here."

"Weren't up to her," he stubbornly answered, though still awed by the amount of the reward. "I'm the man o' the house now,"

"Well the man of the house needs to get home to take care of it," Harry firmly stated. Looking at Mason, he said, "I'll take him with me. He can sleep in one of the cells tonight."

"You takin' me to jail?" Charlie sputtered, eyes wide.

"No son," Harry soothed. "I'm giving you a place to sleep for the night. The door stays open. You're free to come and go as you please. Then in the morning I'll send someone to take you home."

"I can get there by myself," he said, folding his arms.

"Don't be a damn fool boy," Harry replied, irritated with the boy's obstinacy.

"Charlie," Mason explained, lowering his voice. "If or when word gets out that you got the bounty for killing Lester Corbett, there will be plenty of men wanting to take it from you."

"I can take care of myself."

"I'm sure you can," Mason agreed, "but there are some folks who will hide in the night and shoot you in the back." The implication was not lost on the boy.

"I didn't shoot him in the back."

"I didn't say you did," Mason replied, beginning to grow tired of dealing with the boy's stubbornness. "Listen to the Constable. Your Pap taught you a lot of good and smart things. Seems a shame not to listen."

Charlie mulled a bit than said, "OK." Looking at Mason he said, "Don't seem right me takin' the whole reward. You brung 'im out."

"The way I figure it," Mason sagely answered, "is that you did all the tracking and pretty much most of the work. I wouldn't feel right taking any of the reward."

"Much obliged," Charlie nodded. He started to walk off with Harry then stopped. "Say Mister," he said to Harry. "I got somethin' to say to the Marshal."

Harry waited, but when the boy simply looked at him, he rolled his eyes and said, "That's fine. I'll be over there." He pointed to benches in front of the Theater.

As he walked away, Charlie got closer to Mason. "Couple o' days ago, I was comin' outta the river north of Millville, workin' my way through the hills on the north side of the road that goes tween Charleston and Tombstone when I saw three men. It were dark so I couldn't get a real good look at 'em. But there was somethin' about 'em that give me the creeps."

"Like what?" he asked, suddenly interested.

"Well, they was all walkin' funny." He mimicked a jerky stiff legged walk. "All three o' 'em was doin' it. One of 'em was wearin' something' on his head that was real shiny. I followed 'em fer a little bit to see which way they was goin', but they was too interested in somethin' than was makin' a weird noise somewhere I couldn't see. I wasn't gonna stick around and find out, but I figured you oughta know about it."

"Thank you," he answered, giving him a quizzical look. "Why couldn't you say that in front of him?"

"I didn't want him hearin'. You helped me and I figured if they was outlaws, then I'm returnin' the favor."

Mason chuckled. "You got a good head on your shoulders Charlie. It's time now for you to get on back home and run that ranch, make your Pap proud."

"I will Marshal. They were in them hills not far from here," he added, trying to be helpful.

"Yes. I got it. Thank you. You go on now. The constable will take care of you." He watched Charlie amble over to Harry. The boy seemed quite unaffected by his killing Lester. Yet Mason couldn't help but feel impressed that the boy had spent the past week living on his own, tracking his father's killer. The boy was a survivor.

His gaze wandered to the front of the Theater and he saw Belle standing just outside the doors, watching him. Touching the brim of his Stetson, he acknowledged her presence. Her arms folded in front of her, she sashayed over to him.

"Looks like we lost our reward," she teased, looking over to where Charlie stood next to Harry. "Though I understand it will be put to better use."

"He's a fine young man," Mason observed.

"Heard he's a good shot too."

"Thankfully so."

"How about we go back to our normal routine of using the back door. Seems a whole lot safer," she said, smiling at him.

"A lot safer," Mason agreed, realizing had the boy been less of a shot, Mason might have been the one being hauled off to the undertaker.

Chapter 10

Henry rubbed his bleary eyes. The night had been restless. What little sleep he did get was probably no more than an hour at any one time. He would doze and then startle awake believing he had heard something, but each time nothing was there. With the morning sun chasing the evening's shadows away, he climbed down from the MATE, slowly stretched, and trudged off to the main tent to begin his morning ritual of preparing coffee.

Behind him the IAS continued its silent surveillance. Henry had even gone so far as to use Caleb's rocks-in-a-can method for those areas the IAS didn't pick up. Convinced the intruders would return, he had spent an uncomfortable night in the rigid seat of the MATE. Now with the morning daylight, he wondered if Mason and his partners were purposely wearing him down, the old 'attack one night and then wait several days to attack again.' By then the enemy is too tired to fight well.

While the water heated, Henry racked his brain as to where best to hide the treasure. It was obvious that the Marshal knew it was here, he just didn't know where. He had thought of returning it back to the original cave with the thought that the lawman would not think to look there, but he couldn't chance it. Anyone could stumble into the cave and discover the gold. What he needed was a secure place, a place no one would look.

A shadow passed over head and he looked up to see an airship pass. By the looks of the gondola, it was a transport ship. His immediate thought that it was a bit early for an airship transformed into one of glee when an epiphany hit him. The machinists had the tools and materials to repair most any machine. In fact, they could get him another equalizing reservoir and he could simply replace the damaged one. Why not use them to repair the MATE?

Then a stronger revelation burst. He would use Wuhan Mei to assist him. She was dependable and knew how to keep her mouth shut. He would store the treasure in Hoptown while the machinists fixed the MATE. The MATE was still operable, though he would have to carefully nurse the pressure and speed. Still, with the treasure gone from here, he could relax.

More than elated at the brilliance of the idea, he smirked to think that he would use the Marshal's friends to fix the vehicle that would take the treasure out of Tombstone. The irony was perfect.

Mason yawned as he wrapped the reins around the hitching post in front of Walsh's restaurant. He was tired and he knew why. He had stayed too long at the Bird Cage last night. But then, what was there to go home to? She would still be passed out, and the thought of staying in a room that smelled of death still weighed heavily on him. He wondered if his fear was because of Caleb and de la Fuente. He still couldn't get the rotting smell from his senses. His unease caused him to end up falling asleep in one of the jail cells.

Harry had nudged him awake when his shift was finished, telling him he was foolish for giving up a comfortable bed for a jail cot. Offering little explanation, Mason had gone back to the room to clean up, but Elizabeth wasn't there. He had hurriedly washed his face and shaved, hoping that Elizabeth would stay away long enough for him to finish. He hadn't given much thought to why she might be absent when Belle came to mind. Not that he wanted to compare, but the difference between the two women was glaring. Belle was beautiful, vivacious, and smart, all the things his wife had once been. With the way Elizabeth now looked, she probably wouldn't even get business if she could get employed at one of the rundown cribs at the back of whore's row. And anything she did make would be spent on laudanum. Eventually, she'd probably be found dead somewhere, either from an overdose or murdered, a nameless victim of life's vagaries.

That thought lingered while he toweled his face dry. He stopped and looked at himself in the mirror, the towel still at his face. What was happening to him? Here he was, rushing through his morning routine in the hopes that he wouldn't have to deal with Elizabeth. Had his life come to this, scurrying around trying not to be seen by his wife? If he was so set on avoiding her, why did he bother to stay married to her? Why not just divorce her and send her back home?

With a soft sigh, he finished drying his face. He had no answer. He was married, for better or for worse. The wedding vows they exchanged said 'to love and to honor until death do us part.' Was the rest of his life going to be like this? How much worse was it going to get before any sane man would say that's enough?

Looking about the room, the sunlight beaming in through the window, he was thankful that at least the smell was gone. He opened the window and pulled the curtains back, letting the breeze in. He then opened the door to have the wind flap the curtains and push through the room and into the hallway.

As he strapped his holster and gun on, the wind felt good and lifted his spirits. Adjusting his Stetson he looked once more into the room, liking the brightness. That was the way it should be.

Once outside, he stretched, glancing down Safford Street towards the church. It seemed different in the daylight, less intimidating. The workers were already on site putting in the windows. Had he really talked to two dead men last night? Yet the vision of the prospector's maggot infested body caused him to grimace. The feeling quickly passed as Mason thought about the man who had so recently been planning his lavish future was now dead, a casualty in the war for riches. Though he never considered Caleb a close friend, he liked the man. That he disliked Henry made it easier to believe the tale. Still, he would need a whole lot more than a dead man's word to bring Henry to justice.

Heading down 2nd Street, he turned the corner by Wuhan Mei's Shop onto Allen Street. She was standing out front talking with two Chinese men. Upon seeing her, he touched the brim of his Stetson.

"Morning, Miss Mei," he greeted her.

"Good morning, Marshal," she smiled, and continued smiling until he passed then returned to the business at hand.

Mason had half an urge to stop and ask her about Elizabeth, but he knew he would receive the same answer, offered with the same ingratiating smile. She didn't know where Missus Sadler was, but if she saw her, she would tell her that her husband was looking for her. Mason knew better. Elizabeth was probably in one of the opium dens.

As Mason continued walking, he pondered whether he should get her and take her back to the room. That's what a responsible husband would do. But a responsible husband wouldn't have brought her here in the first place. A responsible husband would have stayed in San Francisco, working for her father in some oppressive office where the light and life of outdoors only came in through the windows. A responsible husband would be dead by now, his skin pale from the lack of sunlight.

Had he been wrong to bring her here? He had worked through that question so many times that it no longer had any meaning. They were here, now, and that was what mattered. With Elizabeth's social grace, she could have been the belle of Tombstone. Instead, she made her choice to live among the common people she had so abhorred in San Francisco. The irony was not lost on him.

Awakening to his surroundings, he breathed deeply the morning's breeze, glad to be alive and outside where a man could see sky and mountains. The streets were already busy with the day's affairs. Miners passed each other as they either went to start their work or, having finished their stint in the numerous tunnels below the town, were heading off to one of the many saloons. Stores were already doing a brisk business. The Wells Fargo coach was just leaving for its first trip to Benson. His stomach grumbling reminded him that he had not eaten yet today. A strong cup of coffee and some breakfast would help him push past this lethargy. The door to the Elite restaurant opened just as he stepped onto the boardwalk. Two machinists stood in the doorway.

"Good morning, Marshal," Teboca cheerfully greeted him, Nantan at his side.

"Good morning," he smiled. "Haven't seen you in a while. How was your night at the Bird Cage? Any problems?"

"Um," Nantan smirked. "Not really. There were a couple of cowboys who weren't happy, but Miss Belle set them straight."

Nantan leaned forward and lowered his voice. "She even managed to find us some *willing* dance partners."

"We weren't interested in doing the other thing," Taboca said. "Twenty-five dollars to rent a crib is rather expensive. Besides, I never could understand why I should pay for something I could get for free."

"That's what he gets for being married," Nantan grinned. "I, on the other hand, am not, though in this instance I agree with him. Too expensive for too brief a time."

"I agree," Mason nodded. "By the way, I wanted to thank you for your assistance with Dan Lowry. That was quite a throw. He was dizzy for almost an hour after that."

"Any time, Marshal," he smiled with pride. "Are you a fan of baseball?"

"Can't say that I am yet. Watched part of the game last month at the Boston Mill. While it looked interesting, I don't really understand it. And it's a little slow for my tastes."

"That's because you haven't really experienced professional baseball," Nantan said. "The San Pedro Boys are a pretty good team, but they're amateurs. You need to see a game between two professional teams."

"Like the one you're putting together?"

"Yeah," he grinned. "Exactly."

"He'll have to tell you all about it another time," Teboca interjected. "We've got to get back to Bisbee. One of the cargo airships has a burnt-out motor. Some fool let the pressure valve rust shut and ruptured the compression tank."

At the mention of airships, Mason eyes brightened. "About a week or so ago, I saw two small airships passing over head here. It was very late at night, and I was surprised by their size. They were quite small."

Taboca grinned knowingly at Nantan. "That was us."

"We designed and built them ourselves," Nantan proudly added.

"Almost seemed too small to support a man's weight, plus the weight of an engine," Mason observed.

"It's all in the design and amount of heat you can generate," Nantan explained.

"I'm sure it is," Mason chuckled when an idea emerged. "I wonder if you and your airships might be able to help me."

"Sure, Marshal," Taboca replied. "What do you have in mind?"

Mason pondered a moment, debating just how much to tell them. His real reason for wanting their help was to see what Henry was up to. Coming in undetected would give him an advantage. "I'm looking for a man out south of the Three Brothers Hills. If you two could take those ships of yours up, it would help my search."

"No problem, Marshal," Nantan readily agreed. "When do you want to go?"

"Do you have time today?"

Taboca looked at Nantan, giving him a "Bisbee-can-wait" shrug. "Sure. Now?"

His stomach growling again, Mason said, "Give me a few minutes to grab a quick bite. Where can I meet you?"

"Our ships are at the Tombstone Driving Park. Mister Doling let us put up on the other side of the stables."

"I'll see you there shortly then."

In less than an hour, Mason had wolfed down three cups of coffee, steak and eggs and was already on Contention Road a mile out from Watervale. Try as he might, he could see no airships. It wasn't until he approached the far side of the stables that he heard the sounds of engines and saw the two machinists standing by their small airships tethered to a bottom fence rail. Seeing him, they gave him a cheerful wave of recognition. Dismounting, Mason gazed around the stables then at the airships.

"Since we don't know what this person looks like, Taboca and I thought that it would be best if you were in one of the ships," Nantan said, pointing to what appeared to be his ship.

"Me?" Mason sputtered. "I don't know anything about these things."

"It's really quite easy," Taboca said, pointing to the control board and two levels in the pilot's position. "All you have to do is remember a few basics. The ship can only go forward, left, right, up, and down. The two levers on the side of the pilot's seat here are for steering. Pull the left lever and push the right, you go left. Pull the right and push the left, you go to go right. The two levels up on the control board are just like a carpenter uses. You use those to help keep the ship balanced and level."

"How does it stay up?"

Pointing to the tube from the engine compartment to the envelope, he said, "The heat from the engine goes into the envelope and heats the air-gas mixture. Because the back end gets heated first, it tends to stay the warmest. Occasionally you'll feel the rear end rise up on you, sort of like a bucking horse, though not quite as strong. When that happens, just open the vents and it'll settle. Keeping the ship level is a combination of opening and closing the vents."

As he explained further, Mason became intrigued. He had rarely been up in an airship, preferring the safety of his horse to get from one place to another. Yet the adventure tempted him. By the time Taboca finished explaining about the release valves and fuel line, Mason had overcome his initial misgivings.

"Alright," he nodded. "I agree. Which one of you is staying?"

"You'll be using my ship," Nantan said.

"Thank you. You can use my mount to work the ground below us. She's a good horse but can get spooked on occasion. You'll just need to treat her a little gentler."

"Marshal," Nantan replied. "I may be a machinist, but I am born Chiricahua. I know how to ride."

"Of course," Mason sheepishly answered. "Head back to Tombstone and take the road out of town towards Charleston. When your about two miles out, there's a trail that heads west that will curve around and eventually follow a wash heading southwest towards the San Pedro. We're heading towards the last hill –"

"I'll see the airships," Nantan interrupted, smiling. "I'll know where to go. Just what am I looking for?"

"A friend is missing, and who knows what has happened to him. I'm looking for anything that might give me an idea of what happened."

"I understand. Here. You'll need these," he said handing him a set of glasses with colored lenses.

"I can see quite well without glasses," Mason said, staring dubiously at the colored lenses.

"It gets quite bright up there," Taboca informed him, pointing to the clear sky. "You'll need to leave your hat here, otherwise it will get blown off. The glasses help protect your eyes."

Begrudgingly accepting the wire-framed glasses, he reluctantly took off his Stetson and placed it on the fence post. "This better be here when I get back."

"Hey Marshal. You gonna fly in one of them contraptions?" a voice called out.

Looking up, he saw John Doling ambling towards them. "There's a first time for everything," Mason replied with a lopsided grin.

"Stop into the saloon when you get back and I'll treat you to a cold beer, all of you. Got some ice in just this morning."

"Thanks. I'll do that," Mason answered, noticing the pleasure the two machinists displayed at the invitation. "Say John, you're from out east, aren't you?"

"Originally from Maine, but this is home now."

"You know anything about Brown University?" Mason asked, putting on the shaded glasses.

"Not really," he shrugged. "Supposed to be a good school, I guess. Why?"

"The fellow who has the claim southwest of the Three Brothers is an archaeologist, goes by the name of Henry Mitchell."

"Him?" John laughed. "The one with that strange steam engine with the conveyor belts around the wheels?"

"Yes," he replied, observing the perked interest of the two machinists. "Why do you laugh?"

"The man's a gambler, a good one. Not afraid to put down some money. Knows a winner when he sees one."

"Horses?"

"Of course. Why else come here?"

"He come here often?"

"Often enough to make money. If it wasn't for that crazy locomotive of his, I probably wouldn't know him from all the others who come here to bet on the horses, except he's a consistent winner."

"His steam engine is very impressive." Taboca said.

"Have you seen his other inventions," Nantan asked, his respect obvious.

"I've seen that beeping thing if that's what you mean," Mason answered.

"That's his IAS, his intruder alert system. It's quite clever. He also has some other incredible inventions too," he fairly gushed.

"Well, we'll be headed down that way," Mason answered, hiding his irritation at their admiration for a man who was most likely a murderer. "You'll probably get a chance to visit with him again."

Nantan helped Mason into the pilot's seat, giving him a quick refresher on the instructions Taboca had provided. After a few jerks and starts, Mason managed to get the airship aloft and was soon heading over the undulating desert. He was surprised at the quiet, like being out in the desert at night, far away from the mining, the stamp mills, and the noise of humanity. He was reminded of the last time he had traveled in an airship. It was a passenger ship out of San Francisco heading to Phoenix then to Bisbee. Elizabeth was with him. The memory was not a good one for it brought back the row their leaving San Francisco had caused with his father-in-law, not to mention the tension with Elizabeth. The few times she did speak to him during the trip, it was to castigate him for the fool's journey they were embarking upon.

The airship trip was downright pleasant compared to what happened after the stagecoach dropped them off in Tombstone. Standing in the hot dusty street, their baggage on the ground surrounding them, she had stared malevolently at him and said, "You're going to hell for bringing me here." She promptly sat down on a trunk and refused to move until a buckboard nearly ran her over.

It never got any better after that. Elizabeth politely ignored or refused the invitations of the Tombstone gentry as beneath her attention. After a while, the invitations dried up. But it mattered little, for by then she had discovered laudanum.

Shaking his head, Mason adjusted the goggles and returned to the purpose at hand. Looking around to get his bearings, he gazed down just as they were passing over Walnut Gulch. In the distance to his left, Tombstone rose up like a russet brown oasis, an assortment of adobe and wood buildings stuck together for comfort surrounded by the innumerable mines. After the fire in June of last year took out a chunk of the east part of town, most folks chose to rebuild in adobe.

He shook his head at the memory. The crazy fools from the Arcade Saloon started it all simply wanting to know how much of a bad batch of liquor they had left. Some folks say smoking is a vice. Well they found out how much of a vice it was when the fool smoking the cigar got a little too close to that liquor. It all happened so fast that few folks even had time to save anything. That fire took out everything between Fifth and Seventh streets and from Fremont on down to Toughnut street. Miraculously no one was killed, though George Parsons was lucky to be alive after he was buried by some falling timber. He was dragged out in time suffering only a mashed nose that Doc Goodfellow did his best to repair. Now each time Mason saw George, he couldn't help but remember the fire.

But six months later, one would be hard pressed to find any evidence of a fire. Emerging like the phoenix from its ashes, Tombstone had been rebuilt, a testament to the town's determination. It would take a lot more than a fire to kill Tombstone.

To his right, the verdant green of the San Pedro River snaked its way north and south. Large sections of trees were cut away for the mills at Charleston and Millville. To his right, he could see the Boston Mill at Emery City. From the corner of his eyes, a swirl of smoke caught his attention and he turned to watch a locomotive hauling six passenger cars slow down as it approached Fairbank. Off in the far distance ahead, the Huachuca Mountains filled the vista.

"These things don't turn very quickly," Taboca called out, "So you need to start maneuvering well before you get to where you want to go."

"One more thing," Mason blithely called back. "I forget. How do we get down?"

"Open the vents and power down the engine."

Nodding in understanding, Mason pointed to the series of hills ahead. "We're going to the far end of these hills, then work our way back towards Tombstone."

Mason focused his attention on the terrain below, studying the contours and vegetation. Yet far quicker than he had anticipated, they were approaching Henry's claim. As they slowly arced around the hill, down below he saw Henry loading small crates onto a trailer attached to his odd locomotive. Close by, the machine Henry used to detect movement was sweeping the vicinity. So engrossed with his work, Henry did not hear or see them approach.

Catching Taboca's attention, Mason held his finger to his lips indicating silence then jerked his thumb downwards indicating he wanted to land. Nodding in understanding, Taboca pointed to the other side of the hill, behind Henry and his sweeping intruder detector.

Smiling at the man's cleverness, he followed Taboca to where the hill blocked their descent. Once down, Taboca leaped out of his seat and shut off the engine before assisting Mason with the same procedure. He then wrapped the front tether line around a large rock and placed several more rocks on top.

"There's enough heat in the envelope for now to keep it filled for a while, but the longer we stay here the envelope will begin to settle and the longer it will be before we can take off again. Fortunately, the sun can help." He went back to the engine box and opened up a thin compartment on the bottom, sliding out a wide folding mirror. Walking to the other side of the ship, he positioned the mirror to reflect the sun's light and heat onto the envelope.

"You want to be real careful not to walk in front of the mirror," he warned him. "It can get quite hot."

Following Taboca's example, Mason set up his mirror and the two then scrambled over the hill to spy on Henry. Covertly clambering the last one hundred paces, they made sure their shadows did not give them away. When they were just a short distance away, they settled down to watch.

Henry was methodically loading and stacking crates into the trailer, logging each crate on a ledger. Satisfied with the entry, he recounted the number of crates then disappeared to retrieve another, repeating the process until he had the trailer about half full. Recounting one last time, he placed the ledger in the trailer and went around to start the engine.

Recognizing he was preparing to leave, Mason decided to announce his presence and stood up, motioning Taboca to likewise stand. Nonchalantly approaching down the side of the hill, they were almost upon Henry when he startled.

"My god," he exclaimed above the engine's noise. "You just about scared me to death. When did you get here and how come my IAS didn't see you?"

"How about turning that off?" Mason said, pointing to the MATE.

Henry obliged then looked at Taboca then Mason. "I am glad to see you, Marshal," he gushed, walking over to him. "And thank god you have the machinist here." He then frowned. "How did you get past my IAS?" Quickly looking around he frowned. "Where are your horses?"

"We came by airship," Mason casually responded.

"Airship?" Henry looked up at the neighboring hills. "Where is it?"

"There's two of them actually, small ones," he explained, thumbing over his shoulder.

"What happened?" Taboca said, looking at the scratches and dents on the MATE.

"Terrible news," he said in exasperation. "I was attacked last night."

Mason immediately perked up. "Attacked? Where?"

"Why, my good man, at my campsite right here, naturally. I awoke during the night to loud banging and discovered three men rampaging through my things. Why look here," he complained, pointing to the damaged equalizing reservoir. "I'm lucky they didn't completely break this or I'd be stuck out there forever."

"You said it was three men?"

"Yes," Henry replied, musing to himself *as if you didn't know*. "I managed to shoot one."

"You shot one of them?"

"I did," he confidently said, admiring the Marshal's genuine look of surprise. Oh the man was a born actor.

"Kill him?"

"Not that I could tell. There was no trace of him when I checked this morning, and I couldn't find any blood on anything. It was most peculiar."

Mason scrutinized the archaeologist. "Apparently you're not hurt."

"Unscathed as it were," he grandly declared. "But still, it was obvious they were looking for something, for all my artifact crates that I had packed in the trailer were hurled over the side to shatter in the ground below." He carefully watched the Marshal's reaction. The man was simply superb in pretending he didn't know all this. The surprise and concern he displayed were just perfect.

Frowning, Mason sorted out the news. Why would someone ransack the campsite? Did someone else know about the gold? He studied the archaeologist, doubt beginning to creep in. The man was making up the story. Most likely he did the damage himself to the machine. In fact, the broken crates, the supposed attack by three individuals and the supposedly shot man who left no blood were all made up to divert Mason's attention from the truth. He was being sent down a rabbit hole.

Uncomfortable under the Marshal's scrutiny, Henry turned to Taboca. "I truly am glad you are here. As you can see, the equalizer reservoir is damaged, and I would have to modify it to make it work until I could get a replacement. I had hoped to catch you before you returned to Bisbee to see if you could assist. And to my good fortune, you show up at just the right time.

"I don't have any tools with me," Taboca said, bending down to examine the reservoir. "Looks like someone damaged one of the pressure heads."

Henry blinked with surprise. "You know about them?"

"I'm a machinist," he coolly replied. "Except for the wheel and belt configuration, this is just like any other locomotive, though on a smaller scale."

"Can you help me?"

"Yes," he said, standing up. Remembering the man's generosity at the Bird Cage, he offered, "I won't be able to get to it today, but I can come back tomorrow. I'll bring a replacement with me."

"That would be marvelous," Henry said, pleased that his largess was paying off.

"It's the least I can do," Taboca smiled, "especially after your generosity the other night."

"It was my pleasure," Henry replied, waving his hand to brush the appreciation aside. "After the pleasure of your last visit, how could I, as an inventor, not demonstrate my appreciation to two inventors such as you and your friend."

"Nantan's my cousin."

"Your cousin then," he politely nodded. Looking at Mason, he motioned to the numerous crates in the trailer. "I was going to attempt to ship these back to the university, but it would be wiser to wait until the MATE is repaired."

"Mind if I take a look?" Mason asked.

Henry stared blankly at him. "You checked these the last time you were here," he pointed out.

"Just one more time," Mason calmly replied, "while you two talk about your inventions and other things.

236

"Fine," Henry flatly stated. "How about checking the ones still in the cave? These in the trailer are already nailed shut and ready to ship."

"I'll just do a few," he lightly said. "Shouldn't be but a minute or two. Mind if I borrow your claw hammer?"

His lips pursed, Henry retrieved the hammer and handed it to Mason. "Please be careful. There are valuable artifacts in there."

Climbing onto the trailer, Mason lifted the top crate and felt the weight. "This is heavy."

"Of course it is, my good man," Henry replied, one eyebrow raised in attitude. "The artifacts are packed in sand."

"Sand?" Mason said, placing the crate back in place. "Why sand?"

Sensing an opportunity to delay the Marshal's inquisitiveness, Henry explained, "When a specimen is discovered and damaged or broken, archaeologists will use sand to protect the pieces when shipped. This protects the pieces from bumping against each other, preventing further breakage. This is especially important when the pieces are reassembled at the university. If shards rub or break, it makes it that much more difficult to put the piece back together correctly. Why any –"

"I get it," Mason interrupted. Looking at the crates, he guessed that if the treasure was in there, it would be mixed with the artifacts. His thoughts were interrupted when Taboca spoke up.

"What are you looking for, Marshal?"

"Just inquisitive," he replied, knowing he could not reveal the real reason. Jamming the claw under the lid, he carefully pulled back, the nails groaning as they loosened. Repeating the process on each of the edges, he removed the top and peered in. Just as Henry said, it was filled with sand. Digging his finger in, he felt hardness, but whether it was from pottery or gold was hard to tell. Using two fingers, he dug a bit more in order to grab hold of the hard object. As he pulled it up, he saw that it was a broken piece of pottery and pushed it back down. With as many crates as the archaeologist had, Mason knew it would take him far too long to determine where Henry had hidden the gold.

Hammering the top back in place, he hopped down and gave the hammer back to Henry. "Looks like you have quite a bit of pottery to send back," he said, brushing his hands.

"That I do," Henry replied, relieved the Marshal had given up the search.

The IAS began beeping and the three looked up to see Nantan cantering in. Waving cheerily, he dismounted and walked over to them, leading the horse behind him.

"Is there a reason I'm the recipient of so much attention?" Henry stonily asked.

"It's more to do with the missing prospector than you," Mason replied. "Hello Nantan. Got here just in time. See anything?"

"Nothing unusual, Marshall," he shrugged. "Hello Mister Mitchell. Thanks for the fun the other night. That was very kind of you."

"Don't mention it," he airily replied.

Nantan grinned at his cousin while thumbing at the Marshal. "How'd he do?"

"Quite well."

"See? I told you it would be just like that."

"What are you two talking about?" Mason asked.

"Our airships," Taboca answered. "Nantan has the idea of making air travel affordable to anyone. With smaller airships, people won't have to take a large passenger ship. They can travel at their will."

"Airships for the common man," Henry said, thinking the idea brilliant. "A top-notch idea. However, I can foresee problems with that many ships in the air at one time."

"That's just it," Nantan excitedly replied. "We assign airspace to individual ships. In other words, they're not allowed to fly higher than a certain altitude. Bigger airships have to fly higher. Each type of ship would have restricted flying space."

"I see you've thought this all out," Henry said in admiration. "How much do you propose to sell these machines for?"

"Before you answer that," Mason interrupted, he glanced over across the wash and already knowing the answer, asked, "Caleb come back yet?"

"Not that I've seen," Henry solemnly replied. "Hasn't been any activity over there and I haven't gone over there since the last time you were here. I figured it was best to leave things alone."

"Very wise. Think I'll have another look while you three visit." Giving them a patronizing smile, Mason crossed the wash and climbed up the trail to Caleb's cave. Standing in the entrance, everything looked just as the last time. Yet he sensed something was different. Looking around, his gaze fell upon the pattern of stones. For some reason they didn't look quite like the last time. Positioning himself to overlook the array, he saw that the stones had indeed been moved. Though the spiral pattern was the same, there was a new word below E-N-R-I-Q-U-E that spelled O-R-O.

Gold.

Mason let out a sigh of exasperation. If he hadn't had the experience last night with Caleb and de la Fuente, he would think this was all some sort of perverse joke, that he wasn't getting enough sleep, or some other rational explanation. But he couldn't deny what he had seen with his own eyes. And then there was Ben's story and the boy's story.

But he still had no proof that Henry was responsible for the prospector's disappearance. And it was obvious that Caleb was gone for he certainly wouldn't have left all his things behind. Casting a frustrated glance at the man's belongings that now had a light layer of dust on them, Mason pondered his options. What he needed was to get Henry alone, away from everyone else, when he had the treasure with him. That would be a start. But he still had nothing that would hold up in any court. But he would have to get to Henry before he shipped the treasure back east. The most logical shipping point was Fairbank, and with the MATE, it would be hard not to be noticed. Telegraph would be the fastest way of getting the word to him, short of someone spying on him every minute of the day. But that meant he'd

239

have to get Charlie Parsons involved, and Mason wasn't so sure that was a good idea.

Mason walked back to the entrance and gazed out across the wash to see Henry and the two machinists in animated conversation. Henry was showing them a machine. What puzzled him was who else knew about the gold? And why did they destroy the crates? It made no sense. His first thought was that Henry did it himself, but why take the chance of being discovered? And why damage your own equipment if you want to get the treasure out of here as fast as you can?

Someone else must know about the treasure. But then, why not just simply take it? Eliminate Henry and make off with the gold?

Frowning, he puzzled through the problem. There was nothing he could do at the moment. Henry wasn't going anywhere. It was time Belle used her charm to distract him. His eyes brightened. That was it. While Belle was entertaining him, he would come here and find that damned treasure.

Walking out and down the path, he crossed the small stream and headed back up to where Taboca was talking to a Henry who seemed a bit put out.

"Of course I have permits," he crisply answered.

"I'm not meaning to cause irritation, Mister Mitchell," Taboca apologized. "It's just that I have to let them know."

"Them?" Mason said, walking up.

"The machinists guild," Henry sourly explained. "Once they get their hands on it, it will be nonstop interference."

"I'm sorry Mister Mitchell," Taboca said. "But my hands are tied."

"You can't simply look the other way?" he irritably said.

"You know we can't do that, Mister Mitchell," he replied. "If word got out that Nantan and I had not reported these machines to the guild, we would be removed from the guild and never allowed to work as a machinist again."

"Oh," he grumpily replied, "I suppose I understand. You want to see all my permits?"

"Yes please."

"Fine," he stiffly said. "Please don't touch anything."
Moping over to the field desk, he opened the drawer and
pulled out a satchel. Returning to stand before the Marshal
and the machinist, he made a great show of effort by
unclasping the buckle and withdrawing a folder. He handed
it to the machinist. "There all there. Please leave them in the
order I have them."

"Of course," Taboca solicitously answered. Flipping
through the papers, he nodded in satisfaction and handed the
folder back to Henry. "Everything seems to be in order,
except for the transfer of machinist' rights. It says there that
you've retained those rights. Unfortunately, that doesn't
apply here in the Arizona Territory."

"Are you telling me that I can't operate the very
machines I invented?" he demanded.

"Um," Nantan hesitantly interjected, "you can operate
them, you just can't repair them."

"What?" he sputtered. "I invented these things and I
can't repair them? That's absurd! You don't know my
machines like I do."

"I agree with you, for the most part," Taboca said then
pointed to the MATE. "That is not all that complicated.
You've merely changed rails for independent motorized
belts. Ingenious, but not impossible."

Affronted, Henry pointed to the IAS. "What about my
intruder alert system? Can you fix the signal cone if it goes
out?"

"Um... That might take a bit more effort," he admitted.

"And what about my Residual Cell Emanation
Detector?"

"The what?"

"That," Henry hotly stated, pointing to the glass case
near the field table. "It's used to detect life form cells."

"Uh..." Taboca's confident assurance evaporated.

Glaring at Mason, Henry said, "Can they do this?"

"I'm afraid so," he shrugged in reply.

"This... this is absurd! Are you going to let them get
away with this?" he challenged Mason.

Mason tilted his head as he focused his attention on him. "Get away with what? The machinists are legally entitled to do what they've been chartered to do, with the full backing of the government. You don't have machinists in the east?"

"Well, yes, of course we do," he blustered. "It's just that they know us men of science are very particular about our work. They're very understanding and leave us to our inventions."

"Well we don't work like that out here, in the uncivilized west," Mason said.

"That's not what I meant," Henry protested.

"I'm sure it isn't," he all too readily agreed, though unconvincingly. "Still, I'm sure those back east can wait another few days before all this treasure gets shipped back." Henry blanched and swallowed hard, a reaction Mason could not help but notice.

Seeking to alleviate the man's anger, Taboca said, "I'm sorry Mister Mitchell –"

"That's Doctor Mitchell," he bristled. "I have a P-H-D."

"Of course," he soothingly said, "Doctor Mitchell. But that is the way things are done out here. I'm surprised you haven't encountered this before. The Marshal here tells me you're an archaeologist studying ancient Indians. Naturally with all the time you've spent in the Territory and Mexico with your various machines, you've had to have had some contact with machinists."

"No I haven't," he flatly answered. "I spend all my time down here while you spend all your time up there." He pointed skyward.

"That is true," Taboca admitted. "We do tend to spend most of our time aloft or in the hanger. Tell you what. We can come back tomorrow, fix the pressure head and you can get your shipment off to the university before we tell the guild you're here."

"Now that's more like it," Henry brightened. "I knew there was something about you two I liked."

Grinning, Taboca turned to Mason. "If there's nothing else here, Marshal, we probably ought to be getting back, especially if we're going to come back tomorrow."

Redirecting his attention to Henry he added, "And I would consider it a favor if you would explain your Residual Cell Emanation Detector to me. It sounds quite fascinating."

His ego stroked, Henry replied, "Of course. I would be delighted to."

"You two go on ahead. I'll take my horse," Mason affably said. "And thanks for the ride. I enjoyed it."

"Anytime, Marshal," Nantan grinned.

Waiting until the two machinists were out of earshot, Mason turned to Henry and said, "Didn't want to bring this up in front of them, especially with the way they favor you, but I got a telegram the other day that said you weren't a teacher at that university."

"You mean 'professor,'" Henry stiffly said.

"Alright, professor then."

"That's because I'm on sabbatical," he self-righteously replied.

"Sabbatical?"

"I'm on a paid leave of absence. I don't teach when I do research for the university."

"Ah," Mason nodded thoughtfully. "Yes, that certainly explains it."

"Why were you checking up on me?" Henry asked, indignation edging his tone.

"Always like to know who lives and plays here, especially the big spenders. That was right nice of you to treat Nantan and Taboca like you did."

"Purely selfish motives, I can assure you," he half-smiled. "As you saw, they were very accommodating to my needs."

Smiling in understanding, Mason gave one last glance about the place, wishing he could see what was inside those crates that was worth so many men's lives. Instead, he thanked Henry for his time and mounted his horse.

Watching Mason slowly amble away, Henry bit his lower lip as he pondered what to do. That the man was checking up on him reinforced his belief that the man knew about the gold. And this time, the Marshall had nearly

243

caught him. Thank god he opened the one crate that only had shards in it. What were the chances of that happening, he silently chuckled. He would have to get the treasure out of here before the machinists came back on the morrow. It was times like these that he wished he had a junior partner, someone to do the errands. But that meant he would have to share, and that was something he was quite unwilling to do.

He remained patiently standing and watching. The Marshal was far enough away that the IAS had already stopped beeping. Finally, two small airships ascended from behind the hill. Impressed by the size, he remarked that he should have asked more questions about the design so he could build one of his own. A ship that size would come in very handy.

Waiting until the airships were far enough away to not notice him, he stoked the boiler of the MATE. As the temperature increased in the boiler, Henry loaded the last of the treasure crates into the back of the trailer. For good measure, he had added a couple of crates packed with his artifacts. With the treasure safely stored with Wuhan Mei, he could take his time in sequestering it out and away from Tombstone. Casting one last look around, he climbed up to the pilot's seat and released the brakes. Chugging forward, he slowly guided the MATE to the well-worn path into town.

Coming out towards the main mule train road between Tombstone and Charleston he noticed movement to his right. Turning to look, he saw two men standing not quite hidden in a small wash among the flowering ocotillo, cholla, and mesquite. He sucked in his breath when he immediately recognized Caleb and Diaco de la Fuente. They made eye contact and their heads turned stiffly, following Henry as he passed.

A shout to his front caused him to turn his head to see a muleskinner with his team attached to several ore wagons heading towards him. The man recognized Henry and gave him a wave. Raising his hand in a perfunctory wave, Henry snapped his head back to the right. However, Caleb and Diaco were nowhere to be seen.

Henry's first inclination was to detour over to where he had seen them, but he reasoned that that was what they wanted him to do. Yet the fact that the Marshal was still on his tail gave urgency to Henry's trip to town. Fortunately, he would be coming into town on the Hoptown side.

After more than an hour, Henry's MATE limped into Tombstone and parked just outside Wuhan Mei's Shop. The noise from the machine caused her to emerge.

"Ah, Mister Mitchell," she smiled at him as he clambered down to the street. "You have a very wonderful machine."

"Thank you, Miss Mei." By now, a number of children and passersby stopped to gawk. "I wonder if I might have a word with you, in private."

"Certainly," she obsequiously bowed, motioning to go inside.

"Um," he hesitated. "I have some important items in the crates in the trailer attached to my machine."

Immediately understanding, she spoke rapidly in Chinese to the bystanders and in only moments, the street was cleared except for one man who stood next to the MATE with all the authority of a professional guard.

"No one bother you now," she smiled. "Please," she again motioned to go inside.

Standing inside the shop, he explained, "I need a place to store my crates… a safe place away from prying eyes."

"I understand," she smiled and nodded. "You want that nobody touch. I have just the place for you. Very safe. How many boxes do you have?"

"Thirty eight."

"How long?"

"Two weeks at most."

"OK." Silently calculating for a moment, she then said, "I charge you two hundred."

"Agreed."

The arrangement completed, Wuhan Mei arranged to have the crates unloaded while Henry watched. Once the trailer was empty, Henry went back into the store and handed her two $100 Bank Notes.

"Thank you," he said, relieved.

"You are welcome," she smiled back. Despite her curiosity to know what was so valuable in the crates, she knew she could make far more money keeping others' secrets.

Belle and Mason stood outside the Bride Cage in the cool of the midnight air. The stage performances had just ended, and the band was winding up the music for dancing. They were not alone as other patrons had stepped outside for the coolness, smoking cigarettes and chatting with friends. They cast friendly glances at the Marshal and the Madam and returned to their conversations.

"Is there some place quiet we could go?" Mason asked.

Belle's first impulse was to tease him, but thought better of it and said, "Just let me tell Jack I'll be gone for a few minutes." She disappeared through the doors, returning a few moments later.

"Let's take a walk," he offered.

They turned right at the corner and headed down 6th Street and then turned right again on Toughnut slowly walking past the miner's cabin and on towards the new courthouse construction site. Mason hadn't said a word until they crossed 5th Street.

"You remember asking me that question about the dead coming back to life?" he quietly said.

"You didn't believe it," she replied. "Even the two machinists had doubts. Well one did. The younger one seemed to think it was possible."

There was a long pause before Mason said, "Well, now I do too."

Belle abruptly stopped, causing him to likewise stop. Looking up at him, she studied his face wanting to make sure he wasn't teasing her. Deciding he was serious, she asked, "So what caused this change of heart?"

Mason then revealed the experience at the church. "Part of me wonders if I dreamed it all, but I know what I saw."

"And you're sure it was him?" Belle asked, wondering if the strain of the job and Elizabeth were too much for him.

Mason looked down at her. He could tell by her tone that she doubted what he said. "Why would I make this up?" he stonily asked.

"Maybe you did dream it," she soothed.

"Do you believe Annie?" he challenged.

Pausing to choose her words, she replied, "I think Annie means well, but I wouldn't consider her a reliable source."

"And did I dream that I returned home and found Elizabeth sprawled on the bed in one of her drugged stupors?" he tersely demanded. "Was I still dreaming when I left the room and came to the Bird Cage, and you told me Lester Corbett was downstairs playing Faro? Was I still dreaming when that boy shot and killed Lester Corbett right out of my hands?"

Belle could feel the frustration and tenseness in his voice. Reaching up she compassionately squeezed his arm. "I'm sorry Mason. I didn't mean it like that. You hear the stories and you never pay any attention to them. Then when someone you know and trust tells you the same story, it's hard to accept it as true." She left her hand on his arm.

Taking a deep breath, Mason relaxed. "I understand. Think of how I feel. I never did give credence to the tales, and now I've experienced one. You're the only one I could tell, the only one I knew I could trust."

Warming to his confidence, she asked, "What are you going to do?"

"I don't know," he shrugged. "Like I said, they can't talk and though they understand speech, they can only really answer 'yes' or 'no' questions."

"Can they write?"

"Never thought to ask. It's not like I had pen and paper with me."

"Sorry," she sheepishly replied. "Still, why do you think they wanted to talk with you?"

"As far as I can figure," he said, adjusting his Stetson, "is that Caleb trusts me. He wants me to bring his killer to justice."

"He knows who killed him?" Belle asked, her voice hushed.

"Yes," Mason slowly replied, turning to her. "Henry killed him."

"Henry?" she startled. "I don't believe it. Why would Henry kill a poor prospector? I thought he liked the man."

"He wasn't a poor prospector," he quietly answered. They were approaching the City Hall site and he looked around to see if anyone was around or within earshot. Lowering his voice, he said, "Henry's not quite the lily-white man he portrays himself to be."

"I suppose you may be right, though this all sounds pretty far-fetched," she said, frowning in thought.

"Yes, it does," he readily agreed. "Still, I can't argue with what I saw with my own eyes."

They stopped in front of the half-completed building, silhouetted against the moonlit night. Belle slipped an arm around his, placing one hand on top of the other, feeling his thick and muscular arm beneath the shirt sleeve fabric. Though relishing the physical contact, she kept her mind focused on the tale.

"How do you know Henry killed him?" she challenged.

"Because I asked."

"But why? It doesn't make sense. Henry has enough money of his own. Why kill a poor prospector?"

"How much money is enough?" Mason rhetorically asked. "For some folks, more is never enough." Mason sighed. "Of course there is that little problem that the word of a dead man isn't exactly something that would hold up in court."

"You said there were two of them?"

"Yes," he frowned. "And that's the confusing part. Caleb told me he saw two corpses in the cave with the gold. I assume both were conquistadors. Yet when they appeared to me, it was Caleb and de la Fuente. When I asked about the other, all I got was that he was dead, as if I didn't know that already."

"You're sure the other one with Caleb was de la Fuente?"

"Yes, I asked. But it's all so crazy on the face of it. Caleb supposedly finds a wealth of gold in his cave. Somehow Henry finds out and kills him for it. Where he has it hidden, I don't know, but I'm guessing, if it exists, he's going to be shipping it out very soon. Then back from the dead, Caleb and de la Fuente accost me to tell me Henry's killed Caleb and has the gold. When I went to the cave, there was nothing there to implicate Henry. No dead bodies, no gold. All I see is 'Enrique' and 'Oro' written in the stones outside the cave entrance."

"Pardon?"

Mason explained about the stone pattern arranged neatly outside the gold cave. "The first time I was in the cave only the word 'Enrique' was there. The second time the word 'oro' was spelled out beneath 'Enrique.'"

"'Henry' and 'gold' written out in Spanish," she mused. "I assume Caleb didn't know Spanish."

"Not a word."

Belle shook her head. "So de la Fuente arranged the words?"

"Unless you have a better suggestion, that's what I'm going on."

Belle was silent for a while then said, "It all seems so improbable, especially Henry murdering a man in cold blood, just to steal his money. It doesn't seem like something he would do."

"You may be right," he sighed. "But I can't simply wish away what I know I saw. Yet I can't just simply assume my visitors from the dead are telling me the truth. I need proof."

"Ah," she smiled knowingly. "Perhaps I can help."

"I was hoping you'd say that," he smiled at her. "Will you be seeing him again soon?"

"Yes. In fact, we're supposed to go on a picnic tomorrow."

"He may be a little late," he said, explaining the damaged machine.

"Someone attacked his camp?" she said, obviously surprised.

"That's what he claimed. It's all too strange, too convenient. The machine suffered some damage. He claimed he shot one of the attackers, but there's no blood or sign of anyone having been there, let alone being hurt. My first thought was that he did it himself to distract attention. But that doesn't make sense because if he does have the gold, he'll want to get it out as quickly as possible. Damaging his machine doesn't fit."

"So someone else knows about the gold?"

"Either that or we assume the Caleb and de la Fuente are involved."

"You really think that?" she skeptically asked.

"I don't know what to think," he replied. "None of this makes any sense, but I need to look at all options, no matter how crazy they seem."

Giving him a confident smile, she said, "Let's see what I can find out tomorrow."

Chapter 11

While Taboca repaired the damaged equalizing reservoir, Nantan stood next to Henry as the archaeologist admired the machinist's creation, an oddly shaped sawed-off coach gun. The barrels were three times the diameter of a normal barrel, and a small box shaped container was positioned just behind the trigger housing.

"This is something like the one I made back home," Nantan explained. "I didn't know when we were going back to Phoenix, so I made this while we were here to show you."

"He even has the copyright registered in the Library of Congress," Taboca proudly interjected without looking up from his work.

"My good man," Henry coldly remarked, "not everyone is out to steal the ideas and inventions of gifted individuals such as your cousin."

"That's not what I meant, Mister Mitchell," Taboca apologetically replied, pausing and looking over at him. "It's just that he's the first one in our family to have a registered copyright." It was said with pride.

"Ah yes," Henry nodded. "My apologies. In our business, one has to be wary when other's express too keen an interest in our creations, eh?" He gave him a paternal smile. "But, to your ingenious invention," he said turning his attention to Nantan. "Why are the barrels so demonstrably larger than usual?"

"That's because of the wire inside the cartridges," Nantan responded. Demonstrating with his hands, he elaborated, "The cartridges are larger so that I can insert the wire inside. The wire is looped around the inside of each cartridge and anchored to the base, which is further connected to the battery below the trigger housing. You have to be careful when you loop the wire not to cross the loops, or the electrode projectiles won't go very far."

"And this, obviously, is the battery housing," Henry said holding up the gun and pointing to the box by his right hand.

"Yes. Ammonium Chloride and paste to solidify the contents."

"How far will this shoot?"

"That one there will go out to about fifty to sixty feet."

"All finished, Mister Mitchell," Taboca announced.

"I say," Henry grinned amicably at him. "That was quick. How may I recompense you for such service?"

"Nothing," Taboca shrugged. "It's the least I could do."

"How about another evening at the Bird Cage?"

Nantan's eyes blinked wide with pleasure, but he waited for Taboca to answer for them. "You don't have to do that, Mister Mitchell," the older cousin said.

"I know I don't," Henry magnanimously answered. "But it gives me pleasure, no matter how transitory, to offer the enjoyment of the, um, finer, pleasures of life for other inventors like yourselves. Now I won't hear a word to the contrary." He handed the gun back to Nantan and walked over to his desk beneath the canvass awning. Taking paper and fountain pen, he bent over and wrote a note to Belle. Standing, he waved the paper in the air to dry the ink.

"Here," he said, walking back and handing the note to Nantan. "Miss Belle and I are good friends, and I know she will take even better care of you this time."

"Thanks, Mister Mitchell," Nantan gushed, his thrill obvious.

"Yes, thank you," Taboca chimed in.

"I say," Henry said, giving Nantan an inquisitive glance. "Would you consider allowing me a day or two to study this marvelous device?" He pointed to the stun gun. "I promise to safeguard its secrecy," he added when he saw the machinist hesitate.

Nantan looked over to his cousin who gave him a 'why-not' shrug, before adding, "You already own the copyright, and I'm sure we can trust Mister Mitchell."

"Quite right," Henry readily agreed.

Nantan thought for a moment then mimed Taboca's shrug. "Sure. Take your time." He handed the weapon to Henry.

"I promise to take good care of it," he said with a jovial smile.

Folding the note and stuffing it in his pocket, Nantan looked over to Taboca. "I guess we're about done here then. We ought to head on back to Bisbee so we can get finished in time to come back to Tombstone."

Taboca gave him a sly smile of understanding then turned to the evening's benefactor. "Thanks again Mister Mitchell."

"Anytime." He casually watched as they collected up their tools and headed to the two airships tethered just beyond the campsite. In moments, the two machinists were airborne, heading west towards Bisbee. When they were far enough away, he ambled back to his desk. Clearing it off, he lay the stun gun on top and sat down to examine it. In the back of his mind was the question of whether he could replicate it quickly enough. Now that the MATE was fixed, there was no reason to delay his leaving, and this little toy would be a nice addition to his collection.

Smiling, he pulled out his pocket watch. He needed to get ready for his picnic with Belle. But first things first, he would need to secure this delightful weapon. Standing up, he headed to the MATE and opened up the toolbox just under the pilot's seat. Pulling out several pieces of burlap, he carefully wrapped the gun and placed it in the toolbox before closing the hasp and locking it.

Turning around, he slowly surveyed his campsite. His gaze then traveled across the wash to Caleb's claim. With a contented sigh, he acknowledged that he was ready to move on. He was ready to get back to civilization. Yet there was something about Tombstone and the environs that held a strange fascination. There was an aboriginal beauty to the land, and the people were rugged and self-reliant. Still, the length of time he had spent in the Arizona Territory had certainly been long enough that had anyone suspecting him of the Toronto art dealer's death would have made himself known by now. After he disposed of this latest treasure, he would retire to Europe, perhaps France, knowing it would be much harder to extradite him.

He snorted a laugh. In order to extradite, they had to prove he was guilty. And he was much too clever for that.

Lazily seated in a cushioned folding chair, Belle gazed out across the San Pedro. Henry had selected a lovely spot. The river was wide, but shallow. A sand bar hugged the edge of the water where a number of tall cottonwood trees provided shade and where Henry had set up a folding table with chairs. A second bottle of wine was already chilling in the river. The man thought of everything.

The table between them, they both had turned their chairs to face the river. The meal and the warmth of the day had them both settled in contented amicability, simply looking out over the river, catching sight of the occasional kingfisher.

Giving him a warm smile, she was finding it hard to understand why Mason so mistrusted the man. His whole argument was based on the town drunk and a telegram that said he wasn't teaching there. His explanation that the man might be on some sort of sabbatical simply undercut the validity of the concern.

And then the fabulous story of the dead men. A large part of her thought he was making fun of her questions about the dead coming back to life. And just when she would believe it, he would tell her it was all a joke. Yet, that wasn't like him. That was something she had never seen in him, especially with her. And he had been so serious when he relayed the tale. He believed he actually saw the old prospector and some long dead conquistador who supposedly told him that Henry had killed Caleb and stolen the treasure.

Yet everything about this whole affair seemed just too incredible, too impossible. For all his supposed villainy, Henry appeared quite the normal man. Well, maybe not by Tombstone standards, but he added a bit of charm and refinement to the baseness of the town. And the man was an inventor.

She reveled in the experience, perched once again atop the MATE and riding along in the marvelous machine for today's picnic. Why would someone with his brains and status need to kill someone, especially someone like that old prospector? It made no sense. She had given thought to the likelihood of Henry's guilt, and despite her Pinkerton training, she could come up with no logical reason to assume he was a murderer – gold or no gold. The man was obviously wealthy. Did he really kill for a pile of gold that no one had actually seen? And how did she know Mason wasn't making this all up, that the stress was finally getting to him? He did look awfully haggard last night. Then again, if she had to deal with Elizabeth, she'd probably be crazy by now too. Was she being swayed because of how she felt about Mason? Was she doubting because of Henry's suave manners?

In order to satisfy Mason, and herself, she had subtly probed to find any inconsistencies in his stories when they had arrived at the river.

"Mason told me that someone attacked your camp the other night," she said, sipping her wine. "I'm surprised you weren't hurt."

"I see news spreads quickly," he smiled at her.

"It's not that big a town," she pointed out. "What did they want?"

"That's just it," he frowned. "After all this time of nothing more exciting than finding a piece of shard or reviewing my findings, I awoke to the sound of banging, only to discover someone was trying to damage my MATE. Not only that, there were two of them in the trailer picking up my precious collection of artifacts and hurling them overboard as though trying to shatter the contents. I grabbed my coach gun and yelled for them to stop, but they simply ignored me. It was most odd."

"You weren't afraid?"

"I didn't even give it a thought," he shrugged. "I was too concerned with what they were doing."

"Why would someone want to break your crates with the artifacts?" she asked, glancing at him.

"I asked myself the same question," he said, as though giving great thought to the reason. "I can find nothing logical about damaging my possessions unless they were looking for something. It is not unknown that I have pecuniary resources available to me. Perhaps they were looking for money."

Belle nodded. That seemed logical. It was common knowledge that Henry was a big spender. She was surprised he hadn't been robbed long before now. "Why didn't they just tell you to give them the money?"

"That's the puzzling part. They all but ignored me, as though I was in the way. It wasn't until I had commanded them to stop three times before I shot one of them."

"You shot one?" she said, jerking her head around to look at him.

"Well," he shrugged again. "At least I thought I did, but when I went to check in the morning, there was no sign that anyone had been wounded. And I know I'm a much better shot than that. Why I've hunted with some of the finest families in Europe. I know I hit him. But you'd be hard pressed to prove it."

"No body? No drag marks showing them dragging him away?"

"None," he replied, marking the way the question was asked. With half-lidded eyes, he abruptly realized there was more behind her questions than simple curiosity. With her closeness to the Marshal, it was all too obvious she was working with him. Then the true epiphany hit. This was another of their hustles. He knew of their arrangement at the Bird Cage. Several of the girls had commented on how the Marshal seemed to always show up when wanted outlaws were in the Theater. He had watched the two of them execute their game the last time he was in the Theater. He was up in one of the cages. Belle and the Marshal were engrossed in conversation. Belle called one of the girls who ambled off around the dance floor while the Marshal left. A few moments later, a cowboy burst from the downstairs and practically ran through the dancers to the waiting Marshal outside.

It was a brilliant hustle, one he admired for it was all done legally. And now here she was, probing to find out where he had hidden the gold. He smugly chuckled to himself. They could search the claim and all his equipment and possessions and never find a thing. But what that meant was they were on to him. He would need to clear out of Tombstone very soon. But first he would need to find out where they hid the bodies of Caleb and de la Fuente and permanently dispose of them. No body, no crime. But then… was that really necessary? If the Marshal had the bodies, it meant he couldn't prove anything. That was why he and Belle were going to such extremes. The Marshal knew he had no evidence, so might as well get the gold instead… Henry smiled to himself for it was what he would do given the same circumstances.

"How did you get your machine fixed so quickly?" she asked, interrupting his musings.

"Those two machinists," he answered. "Nantan and Taboca. They came by this morning. Fortunately, the damage was not too severe." He then remembered Nantan's more than passing interest in the cave and the crates and wondered if the two machinists were part of the scam.

"What do you do once you collect all your artifacts?" she had innocently asked as he held the wine bottle up, checking to see how much remained.

"I send them back to the university to await my return," he explained. "There I catalogue and record them, reserving the best pieces for the university. The others I arrange to send to other institutions."

"Do you actually teach for the university, or do you spend all your time looking for artifacts?"

Giving her a curious look, he answered, "I rarely teach. Why do you ask?"

"If it were me, given the choice between being in a classroom or out here like you, I'd much rather be out here looking for artifacts and things. The thought of being stuck in a classroom day-in and day-out is not my idea of something I'd be happy doing. The fact that they pay you to be out here is marvelous." She smiled prettily at him. "It sounds like the perfect occupation."

"It is," he smiled back at her. Focusing his gaze at her, he said, "There's been something I've been curious to ask you."

"Yes?" she guardedly replied.

Pausing, he said, "What is your real name?"

Chuckling, she answered, "Katherine."

"Katherine," he repeated. "It's a pretty name, fitting for one such as yourself."

"That was very gallant," she complimented.

"But it's true," he urbanely said. "So why did you decide to assume the French persona?"

"Purely business," she calmly replied. "For some reason, being French adds to the mystic and aura of the working girl, though I have never been one," she hastily added.

"I never thought you were," he placated. "Seems to me there's more money being a madam than as a working girl."

"Quite true. And I do so appreciate you keeping my little secret."

"It's the least I can do," he smiled serenely at her. "More wine?"

"That would be wonderful," she smiled back at him, raising her glass.

Henry filled her glass and watched as she sipped. She was a delightful creature, one who understood the importance of money and position. She was the kind who would start off as a madam but rise to great heights. As long as her beauty held out, she would be a mover and shaker. Pity he would now have to put a stop to all that.

Hands jammed on his hips, Mason stood taking in Henry's various machines as well as the camp itself. He had to give him credit, the man was neat and organized... too organized. Everything was arranged as though expecting someone to come by while he and Belle were having their picnic. The man was clever.

Recognizing he had been expected, Mason did a cursory search. It was when he noticed the orderly stacks of crates seemed different that he paused and counted. He counted twice to make sure, the results being the same both times. Thirty-eight crates were missing.

Pushing his Stetson back off his forehead, he marveled at the man's brilliance. The whole story of the attack was pure fantasy, concocted to give him an alibi, for it was Henry himself who damaged his own machine, just enough to look like malice but not enough to disable. Taboca had confirmed the damage wasn't all that bad. Then Henry tossed a number of crates off the trailer to give the impression someone was looking for something.

Mason pursed his lips, irritated with himself for not looking further at the number of broken crates the last time he and Taboca were here. It didn't matter now. Henry could explain away why there were thirty-eight crates missing.

The question was – where had Henry hidden them? They were obviously not here at his claim. Turning around, he gazed across the wash to Caleb's claim. He doubted Henry would place them there, but he'd be a fool not to check.

Trudging down the hill, he jumped the small stream that seemed larger than usual. They must be pumping more water out of the mines, he mused. Climbing up to Caleb's cave, he paused in the opening and turned to look across the wash. He wasn't sure what he was looking for, perhaps something out of place.

After scanning Henry's site with no results, he heaved a sigh, turned around and walked into Caleb's cave. As he expected, everything was as before, layered in the sand that time and the wind blew in. Even the words 'Enrique' and 'Oro' were still there. Lighting a lamp, he crawled into the small cave, reemerging moments later.

Walking to the entrance, he rubbed his chin in thought. Henry had taken the gold somewhere safe. Abruptly, Mason knew where the gold was. But that created another problem, for Wuhan Mei would never reveal the location no matter how severe the threats. It would be bad for business.

Having gallantly escorted Belle back to her boarding house, Henry now stood at the doorway to her room. "Miss Belle," he urbanely said. "Might I have the opportunity of dining with you this coming Friday afternoon? I will arrange an experience you will not likely forget."

"That would be lovely," she replied without hesitation. "Where?"

"With your consent, right here. I will have it catered by the finest establishment in Tombstone. It will be an evening of intellectual discourse augmented with gastronomical delight. After dinner, I will escort you to that fine establishment called the Bird Cage Theater."

Momentarily taken aback by his audacity, Belle reasoned she could take care of herself should the need arise. Besides, it was only dinner and having such a charming host would be fun. "Yes," she smiled at him. "That would be acceptable."

"Until then," he suavely said, taking her hand, bowing and kissing the back of her hand. *"Au revoir, ma belle petite."*

"Et toi aussi. I will see you tomorrow evening?"

"Mai oui. I wouldn't miss it.

Belle stood in the doorway for a moment, watching him elegantly walk away. The man had charm. In fact, the man had manners and decorum. She was enjoying herself and Mason's doubts caused her to wonder whether the Marshal wasn't more than a little jealous. Henry had provided nothing to substantiate Mason's accusation that the man was cold-blooded killer. She was about to go close the door when she saw Charlie Parsons climbing the last few steps to the hallway.

Seeing her, he smiled broadly and waved a telegram at her. "Howdy Miss Belle. Got a telegram for you."

"Hello Charlie," she smiled patiently at him. "What's it say?"

"It's from your mother," he answered handing it to her. "Says that Henry Mitchell fella works where he says he does but he's not there now." He sheepishly looked at her. "I had to look up what that 'sabbatical' meant."

"Thank you, Charlie." Belle took the telegram and read, *Henry Mitchell employed at Brown. On sabbatical.* Folding the telegram, she knew Mason was not going to like the news. "How much do I owe you?"

"Oh," he goofily smiled, "you don't owe me a thing. The person at the other end already paid for it."

"Well, it was very nice of you to bring this to me. You come by the Theater and I'll buy you a drink."

"Aw, Miss Belle," he blushed. "The Missus don't take kindly to me gallivanting around at places she don't approve of." He leaned in and whispered, "But I'll take you up on that offer as soon as I can." Placing his finger against his nose, he added, "What she don't know won't hurt her."

"Of course not," she sweetly replied.

"Guess I'd better get going. Got a telegram for the Marshal about that same Mitchell fella."

"Oh?" Belle's ears perked up. "Anything you can share with me?" she said, her voice sultry as she touched his arm.

"Don't reckon why not," he self-consciously replied. "This here one says that that Mitchell fella is on sabbatical in Japan. Makes one wonder if they aren't a tad confused, seeing as Mister Mitchell is alive and well right here in Tombstone."

Belle blinked at the revelation, her confidence suddenly rocked. "Thank you, Charlie," she distractedly said.

"Anytime, Miss Belle." Giving her a respectful nod, he ambled back down the hallway.

As Belle stood in the doorway, Mason's misgivings began to take on new meaning.

Her body twitching with drug induced desperation, Elizabeth yanked open the drawers to her dresser, frantic in her efforts to find a bottle, any bottle, that might contain any amount of laudanum. Finding only empty bottles, she tossed them haphazardly on the floor. Her anxiety grew as her hopeless search yielded no boon. "Money," she breathlessly said to herself. "I need money."

Her search turned to rummaging through clothing, pockets, and jewelry boxes. A knock on the door pierced her awareness and Elizabeth's head jerked around at the sound. She cowered for a moment as though caught in some indiscretion. When the knocking continued, she hesitantly approached and opened the door. A well-dressed man stood in the doorway, holding a small package.

"Good evening, Miss Elizabeth," Henry politely, yet suavely said. "I do apologize for this inappropriate visit, but I thought I ought to come by to see that your medicinal needs had been met. I do hope I am not disturbing you."

Instead of answering, Elizabeth thrust her head out into the hallway, rapidly looking left and right. Seeing no one, she stood up and silently motioned him inside.

Walking in, Henry took note of the room's disarray, with satisfaction. "It appears you have lost something. May I assist you in finding whatever it is?"

"Do you have any money," she abruptly announced. "I can pay you back."

"That won't be necessary," he soothingly said. "I believe I have just what you were looking for." He handed her the package.

Blankly staring at the small brown-paper wrapped parcel tied neatly with twine, she awkwardly blinked as if struggling to understand what it was.

"Here," he gently said. "Let me help you." Untying the twine, he unwrapped the paper, tucking it under his arm while he opened the top of the box. Elizabeth's eyes gleamed wide when she saw the bottle of laudanum. Withdrawing the bottle, he pried the cork free and handed the bottle to her. "Bottoms up," he smiled.

"Thank you," she abstractedly replied, upending the bottle to gulp down the elixir.

"That doesn't look like enough," he studiously observed. "Perhaps you should take a little more, take the edge off, if you know what I mean." He winked in shared confidence.

Needing no urging, she took a long draught, a drop of the elixir slipping out the corner of her lips. In just moments, she felt the panic sluffing rapidly away, replaced by overwhelming contentment. She held the bottle out for Henry to take. Suddenly she felt sleepy. Her hand released the bottle, which Henry was quick to catch. Ignoring him, she pulled off her nightshirt revealing her nakedness.

Henry studied the woman, who at one time must have been quite a beauty, for bits of her elegance still showed. But now, her skin hung on her spare frame as though tired of living. There was little attractive in her present state, and he doubted she'd get any business were she a whore in any of the dirty cribs on the edge of town. The woman was used up.

He watched her slide into bed, pulling up the thin sheet. It wasn't long before her eyes closed, and she was breathing the pattern of one chasing dreams.

Henry sat on the edge of the bed, impassively staring at her. Reaching a hand up, he gently touched the once fair skin, using a forefinger to trace the eyebrows and cheekbones then lingering on her lips. Leaning forward, he kissed her, feeling no response in return, not that he had expected one.

Standing up, he went around the bed to retrieve what was probably Mason's pillow. Returning to her side, he tilted his head to study her once more before pressing the pillow over her face. She didn't struggle and even if she had, her feeble efforts would have been no match for Henry's strength.

When he knew she was dead, he lifted the pillow, fluffed it, and returned it to its place. Lifting the laudanum bottle up to the flickering light of the lamp, he saw it was almost half empty. Satisfied, he placed it on the nightstand by the bed, carefully leaving the cork off to the side. Retrieving the small box, he scooped up the wrapping paper and twine. Methodically rewrapping the box, he took one last look around the room. Satisfied all was as it should be, he went to the door and paused, listening for any noise in the hallway. Hearing none, he opened the door and stepped into the dimly lit corridor. Silently closing the door, he made his way to the top of the stairs before quietly rehearsing his lines for the desk clerk who saw him go upstairs.

Once downstairs, he went over to the middle-aged man behind the counter who had looked up when he heard Henry descending. "I was hoping to see the Marshal. I knocked on the door but received no answer. I waited a bit hoping he might return."

"The Marshal?" the clerk loftily replied as if Henry should know better. "He doesn't spend a lot of time here. Prefers the company of another, if you know what I mean."

"Really?" he replied, feigning more than curiosity.

Looking quickly around at the empty foyer, the man leaned forward and lowered his voice. "I'm surprised you hadn't heard. Seems to be pretty common knowledge, if you know what I mean."

"I don't get into town much," he explained. "I'm an archaeologist, so I spend most of my time exploring."

"Ah," the man nodded in recognition. "You're that fella with that locomotive contraption."

"That I am," he proudly answered.

"Is that for the Marshal?" the clerk asked, looking at the package in Henry's hands.

"No," he smiled coyly. "It's for a friend."

"Ah," he smiled back in understanding. "Should I tell the Marshal you were here?"

"That's not necessary, my good man. I surmise with your gift of reasoning, you probably know where he is right at this moment."

Flattered, the man bobbed his head. "Probably at the Bird Cage. He and that French Madam are downright more than friendly."

"Is that so? Well then," he said, touching a finger to his forehead in salute. "You've been most helpful."

Once outside, Henry strode off towards the Episcopal Church pausing long enough in the darkness to rummage around in the construction debris to find the bottle of perfume he had sequestered earlier. Unwrapping the empty box, he placed the bottle inside then carefully rewrapped the paper and looped the string around the edges before tying it in a neat bow.

Casting one more glance around ensuring he was still alone, he smiled at his cleverness – the same box for two gifts to two women. He chuckled pondering which one would enjoy it more, then realized Elizabeth's pleasure had already ended... quite permanently.

Just as he had hoped, Mason and Belle were at the bar when Henry walked into the Theater. Seeing him, Belle gave him a warm smile. Mason turned around to see who had caught her attention. Discovering it was Henry, he gave him a polite nod.

"Evening Miss Dubois, Marshal," he suavely said as he walked up.

"Hello Henry," Belle brightly said. "Is that a present for one of the girls?" she asked, eyeing the wrapped box.

"Actually, it is something I neglected to give you at our last enjoyable soiree by the river. It was such a perfect day, and your company was so distracting, I simply forgot I had it with me." He presented the gift with a bow and great flourish.

"Ah," she beamed. "How *très charmant. Qu'est-ce que c'est?* What is it?"

"You'll have to open it to find out," he bemusedly replied before turning to the man behind the bar. "Jack, my good man, a whiskey please."

"Right away Mister Mitchell," the bartender cordially answered, reaching for a bottle containing the expensive whiskey.

While Belle untied the string, Henry addressed Mason. "So Marshal, any progress on the whereabouts of our wayward prospector?"

"Nothing yet," he replied, though watching the excited Belle pulling the paper away from the box and opening it. Inside was a small cobalt blue vase with an engraved silver cap. Gently prying the cap open, she twisted the stopper and placed the open bottle near her nose, inhaling the delicate bouquet of roses.

"This is wonderful," she gushed. "Here, smell this," she said lifting it up to Mason to smell, laughing as he stiffened and pulled his head back. "It won't bite," she smirked, still holding it up.

Awkwardly bending forward, Mason inhaled the aroma of roses, reminding him of the perfume Elizabeth used to wear, before she no longer cared about her appearance. "Very nice," he half-heartedly offered.

"Wherever did you get this?" she asked, obviously pleased with what was probably an expensive gift.

"I have a friend back east, Gloucester area."

"Gloucester?" she brightened. "Have you been there?"

"Often," he replied with assurance. "Lovely area."

"Have you been to the beach at Brace Cove? As a little girl I used to –" she caught herself when she realized what she as saying. "Um, you'll have to tell me all about it sometime."

Giving her a smile that said he would keep her secret safe, he said, "I would like that. As I was saying, my friend in Gloucester has an exquisite shop of the finest and latest perfumes from the continent. When I discovered you were from Paris, I immediately asked him for something that would suit you. I hope I have come close."

"Close?" she exclaimed. "This is marvelous. I shall have to use it only for special occasions."

Watching the interaction, Mason felt like an outsider. Hiding his frustration, he couldn't help but notice that Belle was obviously attracted to the man and he couldn't understand why, especially with everything he had shared with her about Henry. That she discovered nothing useful from her last picnic didn't mean the man wasn't guilty. Yet Henry went about his daily activities as one who had no cares in the world. He certainly didn't act like a man guilty of murder. And that frustrated Mason even more, for he was sure the archaeologist was hiding more than a single murder.

Belle once again inhaled the bouquet of the perfume. "It reminds me of the delicate fragrances of Japan." She shot a subtle glance at Mason.

"An excellent observation," Henry expansively replied. "My Gloucester friend specializes in fragrances from the orient."

"Have you been to Japan," Mason asked, trying not to appear too interested in his answer.

"Many times," he confidently replied. "Oriental medieval art is the most desired art amongst the European upper crust, though, truth be told, it's a little extravagant for my tastes."

Belle gave Mason an 'I-told-you-so' look that did not go unnoticed.

Henry turned to Mason, "I say, Marshal, I can't help but think that something evil has happened to poor Caleb. I have a theory, if you're interested."

Mason stared at the man, a mixture of admiration and astonishment at the man's cool audacity. "I'd like to hear it," he said.

"Well," he replied, pausing for effect. "I think it has something to do with that journal Caleb had."

"What journal?" Belle inquired.

"Caleb had the journal of a man named Diaco de la Fuente," Henry explained. "According to the journal, de la Fuente claimed to be part of Coronado's expedition to Kansas. Coronado was searching for the seven cities of Cibola, looking for gold."

"Really?" Belle asked, her interest piqued. "Did he find any?"

"Unfortunately, no. In fact, poor Coronado died a broken man, bankrupt and penniless in Mexico City, a mere forty-four years old when he left this world."

"How sad," she commented.

"Why do you think it has to do with the journal?" Mason interjected, hiding his annoyance at the almost intimate interaction between Belle and the archaeologist.

"Have you read it yet?"

"You have it?" Belle asked, surprised.

"Yes –"

"Here," Henry suavely interrupted. "Let me assist the poor marshal here. Caleb had the journal and gave it to me to read as he was not conversant in Spanish. I gave it to the marshal as a possible piece of evidence when Caleb disappeared."

267

"Did you read it" she asked Henry.

"Naturally. But I considered the claims made within the work to be somewhat suspect."

"Why?"

"Well," he began, relishing the alluring Belle's interest and the Marshal's obvious discomfit. "First, Caleb said a friend gave him the book when he was in Leadville, Colorado. Coronado was never in Colorado. Secondly, why would a prospector have a journal in his possession, one that he most likely couldn't read then simply give it away?"

"Maybe he didn't know what he had," Belle offered.

"A most reasonable assumption, my dear Belle, but it still begs the question of why was it in Colorado? That is the way of archaeology. There are many forgeries being passed around these days and it takes careful analysis to separate fact from fiction. Yet even more troubling is the claim that de la Fuente had found gold, when the entire Coronado expedition found none. Remember, Coronado went bankrupt as a result of his expedition. If he or anyone had discovered gold, I doubt Coronado would not have made use of it." Turning to direct his attention to Mason, he pointedly asked, "Wouldn't you agree, Marshal?"

"Sounds plausible," he replied, impressed with Henry's adroit sidestep manoeuver of absolving himself of any culpability.

"However," Henry sagely continued, "there are many who are fooled by forgeries into conducting rash acts."

Mason stared at him, marveling the man who was pawning off contemporary Indian pottery as ancient could hold a straight face.

"Thus, my hypothesis of the attack on me the other night was as result of thinking the journal contained valuable information. That's why they were destroying my crates, for whoever it was believed I still had the journal." He gazed confidently at both of them, as though his explanation was both rational and logical.

"And how does Caleb fit into your theory?" Mason wondered.

"Well, my good man," he loftily replied. "That's just it now, isn't it? Some person or persons discovered the existence of the journal, most likely while in Leadville, and followed Caleb here. He was most likely accosted, perhaps even kidnapped, to hand over the work. When they discovered he gave me the journal, they came after me."

"An interesting theory," Mason offered, his doubt obvious.

"One you would do well to consider," Henry sharply responded.

"I'll keep that in mind." Finishing his whiskey, he touched the brim of his Stetson to Belle then gave a polite nod to Henry. "You two have a good evening." Once outside, Mason adjusted his Stetson and pondered the man and his effect on Belle. He couldn't tell whether he was bothered most by Henry's deceit, her inability to see through the man's fraud, or the intimacy between them. Regardless, he would bring Henry to justice, even if he had to compromise Belle to do it.

"I do hope I didn't offend the good marshal," Henry said, after Mason had walked out. "I wasn't implying he wasn't doing his job."

"He's fine," Belle reassured him. "I'm sure he appreciated your insight."

"I do hope so. He's a fine man and it's truly unfortunate he is burdened with a wife who requires so much attention."

"You know about her?" Belle slyly asked.

"Who doesn't?" he said, rolling his eyes. "It's a testament to his devotion to her that he puts up with her foibles. But it does beg the question of just how long can it go on? He is a U.S. Marshall after all. But," he smiled, "that's another matter and not my concern. Besides, I shan't be here much longer."

"You're leaving?" Belle's eyes widened in surprise.

"I'm afraid so," he sighed. "I've done about all I can here. I had contemplated leaving earlier when Caleb's disappearance precluded my departure."

269

"You didn't tell me this before," she said, hiding her disappointment for she had come to anticipate his presence in the Theater almost as much as Mason's, not to mention the enjoyment of the picnics… and riding on the MATE.

"I'd been putting it off. The university wants me to return and sort through the items I've sent back." He leaned in and chuckled, "They're complaining that there are too many boxes stacking up, and I better get back there and clean them up."

"When will you be leaving?"

"Another week or so. I'm not in any hurry to leave. Besides," he charmingly said, taking her hand and kissing it. "I have good reason to remain. I've promised a certain lovely creature that I would dazzle her with a feast fit for the gods. And how could I live with myself if I disappointed her?"

Mason headed back home along Safford Street, slowing down as he approached the Episcopal Church. After his encounter two nights ago, he had come to view the Church a bit differently, especially in the dark. It wasn't a particularly imposing building, not like the proposed courthouse, yet it held a macabre fascination now that he had seen and talked with the dead. He slowed down even more when he saw the church door open, and a boney arm thrust out with a skeletal hand motioning him to come to the church.

Though it was past midnight, he cast a rapid look around at the surrounding moonlight terrain and shadowed buildings. Increasing his pace, he arrived at the door though choosing to remain outside. Just inside the door, de la Fuente and Caleb stood waiting for him.

"Yes?" Mason said, surprised that he didn't find this interaction unnerving.

It was Caleb who communicated this time. His body still beset with maggots, he pointed to Mason then to himself and then clasped his two decaying hands together.

"Friends. Yes," Mason assured him. "We are friends."

Nodding, Caleb continued. Pretending he was carrying a box, he marched in place a few steps then splayed his hands wide as though asking a question.

"The gold," Mason guessed. "You don't know where the gold is."

Caleb nodded briskly.

"Henry doesn't have it right now. He's hidden it. I think he has hidden it with Wuhan Mei."

Caleb and de la Fuente turned to each other, then to Mason and shrugged.

"Wuhan Mei owns a store in Hoptown. She keeps things for people sometimes and promises to keep them safe. We'll have to wait until Henry goes back to collect the gold. He'll probably want to do it soon so he can ship it back east. You two will need to keep out of sight. We don't want Henry to know about you."

Both Caleb and de la Fuente nodded in understanding. Caleb then pantomimed again, by pretending to hold a crate.

"The gold?" Mason said.

Caleb nodded. He then placed the imaginary box on the ground, picked it up and placed it two feet to the left then stood up and splayed his hands with a shrug.

"I already said I don't know where the gold is," Mason frowned.

Caleb shook his head in response, and repeated the gesture, complete with a shrug.

"I don't understand," Mason said.

The prospector paused for a moment in thought, then stepped outside and waved his hand at the surrounding buildings.

"Tombstone?" Mason ventured.

Nodding, Caleb picked up the pretend crate and set it back down then waved again at the surrounding town.

"The gold is in Tombstone," Mason said.

Caleb nodded. He pointed to the imaginary crate and then to the distance towards Benson, followed by a shrug and hands spread wide. He repeated the gestures several times while Mason struggled to understand.

"Are you asking which way he will take the gold?"

271

Caleb abruptly stopped and bobbed his head.

"That's a good question," Mason answered. "He's going to have to take it to a train depot to send back east, unless I can stop him before he gets the chance." Looking intently at Caleb, he said, "Don't worry, my friend. We'll get the gold back and we will make Henry pay for what he did to you."

Clasping his hands together again, Caleb gave Mason a bow of thanks.

"When you do get the gold back," Mason cautioned, "hide it good this time." Taking a step back, he did a quick scan of the area and walked off, leaving the two dead men to wait a bit before they faded into the night.

Mason didn't look back this time, choosing to mull the interaction instead. Though still somewhat repulsed at Caleb's appearance, he was more surprised at his own casual attitude to the whole affair, as though talking to the dead was just an ordinary everyday event. Yet what drew his attention most was Henry Mitchell. What bothered him was Belle's blindness to the man's obvious guilt. Why couldn't she see it? Maybe it was time for Caleb and de la Fuente to pay her a visit. He was still deep in thought when he entered the large foyer of Pascholy's Boarding House. He was surprised to see someone still up.

"Evening Louis," Mason said to the man behind the counter. "It's late. Surprised you're awake."

"Eh, I'm still working on the ledgers," he answered, exhaling a large breath of frustration. "I'm not balanced and I'm a stickler for wanting to know where it's off."

"You're a good man, Louis" Mason complimented. "The banks could use a man like you." He started up the wide stairs when Louis interrupted his progress.

"That archaeologist fella was here looking for you earlier. Said he knocked and no one answered. Waited a bit and decided to go look for you. Don't know what he wanted, but he had a package in his hands. Said it was for a friend."

"I saw him," Mason replied, sourly remembering the gift of French perfume Henry gave Belle this evening. "Thanks." Grabbing the smooth mahogany handrail, he suddenly felt tired as he trudged up the remaining stairs. Something was going to have to give. He couldn't continue on like this. It had gotten to where he hated coming home. He was going to have to do something with Elizabeth. He had been so strong willed in bringing her here; why couldn't he bring himself to force her to change, to seek medical help?

Standing before the door, he felt an abrupt calmness wash over him. He would send her away. She would get cleaned up and her health restored. In the meantime, he could focus on his job without the distraction of a needy wife. He would put his foot down and there was nothing she could do or say about it. He had made up his mind and that was the end of it.

At peace for the first time in a long while, Mason inserted the key to unlock the door.

Wuhan Mei startled awake to the sounds of destruction coming from down below in the store. Pushing herself up out of bed, she quickly wrapped a cloak around her plump body and opened the drawer of the night table to pull out a pistol. Quickly lighting a lamp, she cautiously made her way to the edge of the stairs. Pausing at the top, she called out, "Huang Fu? Are you there?"

The cacophony abruptly stopped followed by the sound of the front door opening and closing.

Her nerves tense, Wuhan Mei slowly edged her way down the stairs, the lamp held high and her pistol ready. It wasn't until she was at the bottom that she knew not only were the intruders gone, so was her nighttime watchman.

Her lips pursed in anger, she lit several other lamps before taking stock of the damage. Clothing racks had been knocked over as well as the display figures in the front windows. Some shelves had likewise been pushed over, but for the most part, there was little damage that couldn't be fixed or cleaned up.

Walking to the front door, she studied the lock which seemed to still work just fine. Her pistol still in hand, she opened the door and stepped out onto the boardwalk. All seemed quiet, as usual for so early in the morning. Shaking her head, she huffed with more than mild irritation at the absent Huang Fu. It was as she was about to go back into the store that the man in question poked his head out from behind the side of the store.

"Miss Mei?" his hoarse voice called.

"Huang Fu?" she snarled. "Why do I pay you good money to have this happen to my store? What are you doing outside instead of inside where you belong?"

"Are they gone?" he nervously asked.

"You mean the ones who destroyed my store while you fled like a scared rabbit?"

"But Miss Mei," he quivered as he approached. "You should have seen them."

"Now why would I want to do that?" she snapped. "Why would I want to watch as someone destroys my livelihood?"

"But Miss Mei,' he warned, his voice tremoring with fear. "They were *jiāng shī*. I saw them."

"Have you been drinking?" she retorted. "This is America. There are no *jiāng shī*, no walking dead."

"But I saw them with my own eyes," he whined. "There were two of them. One was covered in maggots."

"Bah!" she dismissively retorted. "Get inside and clean this mess up while I see if anything is missing."

It was when she walked back to the counter that she noticed a bag of flour had been opened and the contents spilled out on the countertop in one smooth layer. Someone had used a finger and written 'H-e-n-r-y.'

Wuhan Mei furrowed her brows in puzzlement as she sorted out what it meant to whom it referred. Then she remembered Mister Mitchell, the archaeologist, that his first name was Henry, and that she was hiding thirty-eight crates for him.

Whoever it was that came here tonight was sending her a message, and it certainly wasn't any *jiāng shī*. *Jiāng shī* she could handle. Someone coming in here trying to ruin her business was another matter. She would have to let Mister Mitchell know that he would have to move his things. After that, she would find out who did this to her store and once she was finished with them, they'd wish they were dead.

A single kerosene lamp gave light to the room where Mason sat at the edge of the bed, Elizabeth's hand in his. In glaring contrast to the warmth of his touch, hers was cold, the chill of death having suffused her wan body.

Though he had expected tragic consequences with her decent into the addiction of temporary euphoria, he always believed she would live, especially now that he had decided to be firm and send her off to some sanitarium somewhere where she would recover.

As he sat and stared at the lifeless body, his mind lumbered with overlapping thoughts. He searched his heart for affection, but what he felt staring at her was a great sadness, a sadness one feels when fate has so cruelly interposed itself by taking the life of one who could have had a future. That she no longer looked like the vibrant woman he had married reinforced the harshness of fate. Yet she had chosen her path.

Then he thought of her parents, especially her father when informed of his daughter's death. His anger, grief, and vengeance would be boundless. He would blame Mason alone for her death. He would demand that her body be sent back to San Francisco, but that would mean Mason would have to travel back to the city at a time when he had pressing matters like Caleb's murder. Besides, he had no desire to go back to San Francisco, no matter the reason. He would bury Elizabeth here. If her father wanted her in San Francisco, he could come get her.

Yet Mason knew the man's vehemence would pour out like flood waters, destroying everything in its path, especially him. He would have to prepare as though for a violent storm. But that would have to wait for now. For now, he would need to get ahold of Doc Goodfellow and have him come determine the cause of death, though that would be the easiest part. Then he'd need to get the undertaker and purchase a plot at Boot Hill cemetery.

He shook his head at the thought of walking behind the hearse for even the short distance from the boarding house to Boot Hill. The thought of the town's folk offering their pity bothered him. He didn't want or need their pity. He knew many of them for the gossips they were.

With a sigh, he released Elizabeth's hand and stood up. Opening the door, he cast one last look at his wife before closing the door behind him.

Chapter 12

Mason stood by the grave, his Stetson in his hands. The small crowd who had followed the hearse to the cemetery at Boot Hill were already headed back into town leaving him to silently mourn alone. The parson had offered a heartfelt graveside service, but Mason paid scant attention, his thoughts wandering to the time before Tombstone, when he was courting Elizabeth, when she was the object of every young bachelor of the affluent families in San Francisco. Her father had been against the marriage from the beginning. After all, Mason was not from that Brahmin society and could never measure up to the standards of gentry. What possessed Elizabeth to choose him was truly beyond him, for he was rough around the edges, more comfortable in the rugged outdoors than behind a desk in some office.

The obsessive pursuit of money held no fascination for him. All he needed was enough to live on and that was plenty for him. The fact that he was gaining a solid and steady income with Belle meant that he had more than enough for the time when he decided to take off the badge and settle down. Hopefully that would be quite some time from now.

Looking out beyond the cemetery, he saw the Dragoon Mountains in the far distance out across the level chaparral. Breathing deeply, he savored the sparseness of the land, a rugged place where a man could breathe and get lost in the beautiful emptiness. It was invigorating; it was life itself, something neither Elizabeth nor her father could understand. Living in San Francisco was like being in prison, chained to the rest of the city's teeming masses as they swarmed, shoulder to shoulder, going about their daily grind. And then there was the other part of San Francisco, the part where Elizabeth lived, where the privileged caste viewed their place as above the common man, where the rules were different, where pedigree was everything.

The more he thought about it, the more Mason knew his life had just got complicated. Elizabeth's father would not rest until he had exacted a brutal revenge for his daughter's death. It didn't matter to him what form it took, as long as Mason suffered unmercifully. From the moment her father received the telegram, Mason's life was measured in ticks of the clock, until he was dead, or her father was. His life was now one of looking over his shoulder.

With a sigh, he cast one last look at the grave before turning to retrace his steps home. Looking up, he saw Nantan and Taboca standing reverently at the entrance to Boot Hill.

"We just heard about the death of your wife," Taboca said as Mason approached. "We're very sorry."

"If there's anything we can do," Nantan offered.

"Thank you," Mason quietly replied. Then thinking of Elizabeth's father, he added, "I just might take you up on that."

"Anything, Marshal," Nantan eagerly reiterated. "We're at your service, any way we can help."

'Thank you." Mason said, noticing the round object Nantan held in his hands. It was a small brass globe with a series of spikes embedded into it. The globe itself was about six inches in diameter. "What do you have there?"

"Oh, sorry," Nantan apologetically said, realizing he had forgotten what was in his hands. "It's a bomb," he matter-of-factly explained then quickly added, "but it's not primed," when he saw Mason's eyebrow leap up.

"Sorry Marshal," Taboca said. "We wanted to show our respects and didn't have time to put it in a safe place. We thought it better to bring it with us."

"I understand," Mason patiently replied. His melancholy temporarily interrupted, he asked, "How does it work?"

"Well," Nantan began as they walked the road back to town. "I designed it to be dropped from an airship. The casing is a thin layer of brass, though any other metal could be used, but it has to be able to support the numerous plungers." He held up the bomb and pointed to one of the flat-headed spikes. "They're all actually detonators. Inside is an explosive. Right now I'm using gunpowder, but I figure TNT would work as well. When dropped from the airship, the bomb doesn't drop straight down unless the airship is stationary. Otherwise it drops on a trajectory. With this design, it won't matter if the airship is moving or the bomb is dropped in a curved trajectory. When it hits the ground, at least one detonator is forced into the explosive and ignites, causing the bomb to explode. That's why I put detonators all around so that when it hits, it will have to land on at least one detonator."

Reaching out his hand, Mason tested the heft of the bomb, surprised that it was not as heavy as it looked. "How big a radius does it impact?"

"Depending on the explosive and what else you add to the insides, anywhere from thirty to one hundred feet," Nantan answered.

"Suppose it hits in the sand or in a river?"

"There's always a chance there won't be enough force to push the detonator," Nantan responded. "So far, my tests have resulted in only one dud. I figure if I can get the detonators more sensitive, the bomb will work better. But I have to balance that against the bomb's stability. If the detonators are too loose, anyone bumping it might set it off."

"Very ingenious," he complimented.

"He's looking to sell the idea to the military," Taboca added.

"Seems a good place to start," Mason agreed. They were almost to the edge of town when he saw her standing under the boardwalk's awning at the edge of the street. Both Taboca and Nantan saw her too.

"If there's anything we can do for you, Marshal, anything at all. Just call on us and we'll come right away," Taboca said, nudging Nantan away so that Mason and Belle could talk in private.

"Thank you," he said, wondering how soon he might have to take them up on the offer. But his attention shifted to the lovely Belle who stood patiently waiting for him. As

Taboca and Nantan split off to wend their way into town, Mason walked up the stand before Belle.

"I figured you needed some time alone," she said. "And I didn't want the townsfolk to interrupt your thoughts with their petty gossip if I was there."

"You know it wouldn't have mattered to me," he replied.

"But it matters to me," she countered. "Are you doing OK?"

"Surprisingly so, yes. Thank you for being here."

"Where else would I be?" she answered. "I heard you're moving out of your rooms at the boarding house. What are you going to do?"

"I'm just moving out of the room I shared with Elizabeth. I need a fresh start. I was even thinking of buying a homestead somewhere close by, maybe along the San Pedro."

"Really?" she said, surprised. "You like it here that much?"

"Yes I do," he honestly replied. "This town's growing, but not like the cities back in California that cram themselves on top of each other. This town will grow, but it will come to a point where it will slow down and then probably stop. By then, order will be established, schools and churches will provide stability, and it will be a Garden of Eden in the desert."

"Sounds romantic," she chuckled, "a quaint hometown right here."

Mason gazed down at the stunning beauty before him, his heart quickening at her presence. He knew he should feel guilty – Elizabeth was hardly buried and here he was already captivated by another. Abruptly he realized that if his life was in danger, so was Belle's. His first impulse was to cut off all contact with her, to protect her. But he reminded himself that it was no secret that the two of them spent time together. Once Elizabeth's father discovered their connection, Belle would suffer just as much.

"Come," he said. "Let's you and I talk. I have a feeling things are going to get complicated real soon."

"I'm sure there's nothing we can't handle," she cooed, slipping an arm around his as they walked along Safford Street. She hugged his strong arm, wondering if that home he wanted might include room for her.

Liking her touch, he casually asked, "You meeting with Henry Mitchell this afternoon?"

"Yes," she replied, "another one of his picnics."

They walked a few paces in silence before Mason said, "You be real careful. I've a feeling he's going to do something crazy real soon."

Belle stopped him and turned to face him. "I'm a big girl," she reminded him though smiling. "I can take care of myself."

"I don't doubt it," he huskily replied. "I just don't want anything to happen to you."

Standing on her tiptoes, Belle placed a gentle hand on one side of his face and tenderly kissed him on the opposite cheek. "It won't," she confidently said.

Ignoring the glances and overt looks of disapproval, they walked arm in arm to the Bird Cage Theater.

Belle reveled in the pure thrill of the moment, in the early afternoon with the wind in her hair and the speed of the MATE churning effortlessly towards Henry's camp. Her hands on the twin steering levers, she marveled at the ease of control. When Henry offered to let her drive the MATE, she was like a little girl with anticipation. Doing her best to contain her excitement, she let Henry play the role of suitor. Yet at the back of her mind, she wondered how much of him was real.

The meal itself was everything Henry had promised. The food was the best she'd had since coming to Tombstone and Henry had been so polite and proper that she let her guard down more than once.

"Henry," she said between nibbles of a succulent steak in au jus. "Have you ever actually *been* to Japan?"

"Several times," he answered, giving her a barely noticeable look of curiosity. "Why do you ask?"

"Well," she said, "you talk of your travels in Europe. I just wondered if you ever got to the far East."

"My travels take me around the world, even to the dark continent of Africa."

"How do you find time to teach and travel so much?"

"Well," he said, pouring more wine. "Truth is I really don't teach much. The university likes what I bring back so they give me quite a bit of freedom."

"So do you take sabbaticals or does that apply to you with as much traveling as you do?" She sipped her wine, studying him.

"Oh," he shrugged. "I don't take sabbaticals. Those are for the older professors who need a break from the classroom."

"So let's pretend," she coyly said. "If you were stuck in the classroom and were suddenly given the opportunity to go anywhere in the world for a sabbatical, where would you go?"

"Where would I go?" he frowned, trying to ascertain the direction of her inquiry. There was something odd about the way she asked it.

"Yes," she smiled sincerely at him. "You've been around the world and have seen so many places, which one is your favorite? Where would you like to go?"

Henry studied her for a moment before answering. Though the question seemed innocent enough, something nagged at him. "I prefer Europe over any other continent, France especially, both Paris and the Mediterranean coast. Though I must confess that I'm also very partial to the island of Crete."

"Not Japan?" she sweetly inquired.

"Heavens no," he said, waving a hand in dismissal. "While a beautiful country, I prefer my own kind." He smiled charmingly at her. He now knew why the question bothered him. It was obvious she knew his game, which meant she was working with or for the Marshal. And if that was the case, then it was also obvious that she knew he was not who he claimed to be. Henry knew his namesake was in Japan and had hoped the man's absence would be long enough for him to finish here. Now that the Marshal was on to him, he would have to make good his immediate escape. Yet he had anticipated such a possibility that he might be compromised. It was now time to leave Tombstone.

"I have the perfect after dinner activity," he said, casting sly eyes at her.

"And what might that be?" she half-smirked.

"Not what you think," he jovially replied. "I was thinking of a late afternoon ride on the MATE." Leaning forward, he whispered, "And I'll even let you drive."

Thus it was with barely contained excitement that she finished her late lunch and climbed up on the machine. To her great pleasure, as they had roared out of the city, she saw Mason heading towards the jailhouse. When he looked up, she gave him a confident wave and received a grim stony stare in return.

They headed southwest towards Henry's camp and arrived in less than forty-five minutes. Hopping down from the pilot's seat, he reached up to help her down.

"This calls for a celebration," he cheerfully announced. "You're the first person I've ever let touch my machine." Abruptly realizing the innuendo, he snorted a laugh then coughed to cover his mirth. "Um, I have an exquisite twenty-year-old sherry that I've been saving for a special occasion, and I think today is as good as any. Please make yourself comfortable"

Still riding the crest of euphoria, Belle happily plopped down in one of the padded field chairs next to the table Henry used for dining. Looking across the wash, she asked, "Is that the miner's place?"

"Yes," Henry said, looking over his shoulder. "It is such an odd thing that he disappeared like he did," he remarked, peeling the foil wrapper off the top of the bottle. "I can't help but think something evil had happened to him, which is strange for the man had nothing worth being robbed for. All I can think is that he perhaps got involved in some game of chance that did not turn out well for him." Gripping the cork top, he twisted it out of the bottle and placed it on the tabletop. "Pity I don't have the appropriate sherry glasses, so we'll just have to make do with these." He grinned as he held up the two large shot glasses he purloined from the Bird Cage.

"So he still hasn't returned?" She continued staring at the cave, wondering what the inside was like where Caleb had supposedly found the gold. Now that she was here, her curiosity blossomed

"No," he said, pouring the amber colored elixir into the glasses, "and I doubt he will." Handing her a glass, he lifted his in toast. "To you, madam, the aptly named Belle, for you are indeed beautiful."

"Thank you," she said, accepting the compliment. The sherry was smooth and sweet. "This is delicious."

"It's a cream sherry from Jerez de la Frontera." As she turned her attention back to Caleb's cave, he sat down on a chair on the opposite side of the table. Marking her, he pretended to take a sip then let his arm drop to pour some of the contents onto the ground below his chair.

"So what's it like in his cave?" she asked, finishing the rest of her sherry.

"Rather Spartan," he answered, refilling her glass. "The man was barely getting by. Though he said the silver vein was good quality, he mined far too little to be of value. All his earnings went into his daily sustenance."

"This is very good," she giggled, holding up the shot glass. "I can feel it already. I didn't think sherry was this strong." Her words became slurred, and she began slouching in the chair.

Henry waited and watched as her body settled even more into the chair, as though all strength and energy were sluffing off. Soon her eyes were closed and the hand holding her shot glass flopped to the side, releasing the glass to fall onto the ground, spilling the remaining sherry.

Henry gazed down at the lovely woman sagging in the chair, her body in the relaxed repose of drug induced lethargy. He then looked up and slowly surveyed the surrounding area. He smiled at the ease of getting her back here. The MATE was useful in many ways. The problem was now what to do with her? He hadn't anticipated her involvement, but she was too close to the Marshal to simply leave here. Knowing the Marshal, he'd be on the lookout for her return.

Henry looked at what remained of his camp. He would take the Cell detector with him but would leave the IAS here. He only had to dismantle certain parts of it to make it not only inoperable, but almost impossible to replicate.

Looking down at the lovely Belle, he decided that he'd take her with him. If necessary, she would be a bargaining chip. If he got away clean, he would drop her off somewhere remote enough to give him plenty of time.

Henry chuckled at the situation. He had wanted to enjoy Belle and now here she was, her arms spread wide, powerless to do anything. If he wanted, he could take advantage of her, and she could do nothing to stop him.

Part of him wanted to do just that, but it seemed far too crude and animalistic. He was, after all, a man of refinement. To take advantage of a powerless woman placed him on the same level as the dregs of society so prevalent in Tombstone. He would not deflower her in such a condition. Where was the challenge in that?

Looking back down at her, he smiled that his chivalry didn't mean he couldn't peek at the merchandise. Dropping to his knees, he studied the exquisite beauty of her face. Casting one last furtive glance around, he proceeded to undo her blouse, his hands methodically releasing each button. Waiting until the last button was undone, he was surprised to see that she wore no corset, instead choosing a simple thin strapped silk slip that did little to hide the ample breasts beneath it. He was more than impressed with her beauty, remarking that she did not need the tucks and pulls of corsets and bodices to make her body beautiful. She jettisoned the pads and frills of the latest full-bodied skirts, choosing instead a simple ankle length skirt one would use for travelling.

He was about to pull down the top of the slip when she uttered a soft moan. Concerned that he had not used enough of the drug and it might be wearing off, he sighed in disappointment. However, that did not stop him from briskly pulling her slip open and taking a lingering peek. Smiling with approval, he suppressed the urge to do more and hurriedly refastened the buttons and stood up.

"Now's not the time to get distracted, Henry," he quietly said to himself. Pulling out his pocket watch, he clicked it open. They had been here long enough. It was time to get out of Tombstone.

Henry was both quick and methodical. Lowering the IAS, he dismantled the cone and interior rod, tossing both into the trailer attached to the MATE. He then raised the support arm as high as it would go. Returning to his desk, he assembled all his notes and papers, casting a wistful glance at the beautifully crafted desk, but then shrugged knowing he'd get another. Placing his papers along with de la Fuente's journal in a briefcase he placed it in the toolbox under the pilot's seat on top of the stun gun.

Satisfied, he returned to stand in front of Belle watching her as her slow breathing expanded her chest. Ruefully wishing he had had time to enjoy the pleasures of her body, he let out a soft disappointed sigh. Grabbing ahold of her arm, he hoisted her up, thankful she was far lighter than Caleb had been. Positioning her over his shoulder, he clambered back over to the MATE and to the trailer behind, gently placing her on the bed. Climbing onto the trailer, he slid her body forward to a corner before tying both her hands and ankles with a thick rope. Standing up, he looked at his handiwork remarking that she wasn't going to be happy when she finally woke up. Then again, maybe she liked being tied up. Barking a laugh, he draped the tent canvas over her. Jumping down, he fired up the boiler, carefully scanning the surrounding area while the pressure built.

When ready, he cast one last look at the camp spot wistfully wishing he had the opportunity to consummate his liaison with Belle right here, out in the wild of the Arizona Territory. Now that would have been a worthy memory. With a shrug, he engaged the engine and maneuvered it close to the IAS until they touched. Pressing the throttle in one burst of a push, he toppled the IAS into the wash.

With a happy nod of relief, he engaged the engine and sped off towards Tombstone. It was time to collect his treasure and disappear.

Wuhan Mei looked up as Henry entered the shop. "Good. You are here," she bristled, walking over to him. "You need to take your boxes and go."

Henry stood just inside the door staring at the disarray. "What happened?"

"Somebody came here last night and left me a message," she replied, still simmering. "It said that I can no longer keep your boxes."

Frowning, Henry was perplexed. Who else knew he had the gold stored here? "Do you know who did this?" he asked.

An older man with a receding hairline who was sweeping near the front windows stopped. Gazing directly at Henry, his eyes wide, he said, "It was *jiāng shī*, two of them. I saw them myself."

"*Jiāng shī*?" Henry said.

Wuhan Mei huffed in irritation, her fists jammed onto the ample hips. "*Jiāng shī*, walking dead. Bah! I told you already, no walking dead in America."

"But Miss Mei," he whined. "I saw them."

Her lips pursed, Wuhan Mei shook her head in frustration. Jerking her head to look at Henry, she said, "Someone knows you have merchandise here. You take it with you, now. I can't do business like this." She jerked her hands wide, encompassing the wrecked store.

"That's why I'm here, Miss Mei," Henry reassured her. "Go ahead and load me up and I'll be on my way and out of your hair."

"Out of my hair?" she repeated, furrowing her brow as she sorted out the meaning.

"I won't be a bother anymore," he explained.

"Yes, yes. That's good." Twisting around she confronted her helper. "Huang Fu. Get Mister Mitchell's merchandise. Get someone to help you."

"Yes, Miss Mei," he said bowing.

To Henry's satisfaction, the crates were rapidly loaded and he was heading up 2nd Street towards Safford. Things were going well and if all went according to plan, the town would be too preoccupied, especially the Marshal, to notice him slipping away to the north.

Mason stood at the bar in the front lobby of the Bird Cage distractedly sipping a whiskey, wondering why Belle wasn't there. He had finished moving out of Pascholy's Boarding house and had yet to unpack his things over at the Aztec House. There was plenty of time for that. While Joseph Pascholy wasn't pleased to see him leave, he understood. There were just too many demons there right now. Besides, Mason still hadn't telegraphed Elizabeth's father of her death. He knew what was going to happen, and right now, he could only deal with one catastrophe at a time. He needed to bring Henry Mitchell to justice first, then he could devote his attention to saving his own life.

Frowning, he asked the bartender, "Shouldn't Belle be here by now?"

Jack paused wiping the counter and looked up at the tall clock by the Polyphon Music Box. Mimicking Mason's frown, he replied, "That's odd. She's never late."

"Maybe I ought to swing by her place and see if she's OK," Mason said. He was about to down the rest of his drink when the door to the Theater opened and an austere man dressed like an accountant disdainfully entered searching briefly around the front room when his eyes lit on Mason.

Crisply walking over, he stood at attention next to him and addressed him. "Mason Sadler?"

Turning his head to look at the man, he said, "Yes?"

Standing full height, he said, "My name is Harold Tiebot, and I am here on behalf of your father-in-law, Mister Reginald Worthington. I attempted to find Missus Sadler but was unsuccessful. I was then directed that I might find you here. I have a response to the telegram Missus Sadler sent to her father. I was directed that this response be shared with the two of you. Is Missus Sadler available?"

Mason's shoulders slumped. With a pained sigh, said, "No, she's not available."

"She's not?" he blinked in surprised at the response. "And why not?" he stiffly asked.

"Because," he slowly answered, "she's not." He turned to give his attention to his drink, draining the last bit in the glass.

"Mister Sadler," Harold Tiebot condescendingly began, "I've spent the past four days traveling to get here. First in an airship, which I detest as it confirms my fear of heights. Second, in a horrid stagecoach filled to overflowing with unwashed bodies. It is imperative that I see Missus Sadler."

Slowly twisting to face him, Mason rested one elbow on the bar counter. "And what's so important that you need to see Missus Sadler?"

The man cautiously looked around then lowered his voice. "Mister Worthington has acquiesced to his daughter's request and has sent me to deliver the sum of $10,000 to be deposited into her bank here."

His lips tightening, Mason stared hard at him. "We don't want his money. So you can just turn around and go back home."

"But, but," he sputtered. "You can't do that. Mister Worthington specifically sent this money to his daughter."

"I heard you the first time. Now I'm telling you again. I don't want his money." Looking in the mirror at the clock against the opposite wall behind him, he said, "I suggest you get back on that stage and hightail it out of here while you still can. That stage won't be but another twenty minutes before it leaves. This town gets pretty wild in about an hour and there's no telling what might happen to a man like you. Ain't that right, Jack?"

"That's right, Marshal," he calmly replied, still wiping the countertop. "You better listen to the Marshal, mister." He paused and looked the man up and down. "Why you look right purty all dressed up fancy like that. There's gotta be at least a dozen cowboys would love to have them duds you're wearin'."

The man's eyes burst wide with fear. At that moment the doors to the Theater burst open and five cowboys came in hooting and hollering, clamoring for whiskey and fine women. They paused long enough to give the man a once over causing him to clutch his briefcase to his chest and scramble out in jittery fright. The cowboys gave him a passing notice before heading to the bar and gaming tables.

"How was that, Marshal?" Jack said. "Did I sound hick enough?"

"You were perfect," he said, giving him a half-smile, though tempered with the thought that news of Elizabeth's death couldn't wait much longer. "Think I'll go check on our madam."

Mason was hardly out the door when Harold Tiebot confronted him. "I just found out. Is it true?" he asked, aghast.

"Is what true?" Mason replied, knowing the next question the man would ask.

"Is she dead?"

"Is who dead?"

"You know who I mean," he indignantly stated. "Is Elizabeth dead?"

Mason paused with a sigh. "Yes. She died two days ago."

"How? What happened?" Harold Tiebot said in a rush.

His lips pursed, Mason bent forward so only Harold could hear. "She died of a drug overdose."

Harold stutter-stepped backwards, almost off the boardwalk. "This is most distressing," he fretted. "Mister Worthington will be most displeased." Jerking his head up to stare at Mason, he said, "You have my condolences. When I inform Mister Worthington of the state of his daughter, it will not go well for you. I am sorry." Spinning around on his heels, he briskly headed off to catch the stage back home.

Mason watched him strut away knowing he was right. But that still gave him at least a week before his father-in-law would retaliate. Until then, he had more pressing matters, the first being the whereabouts of Belle.

In the late afternoon, Henry stood near the privy in the back of the Tivoli Gardens, a small can of kerosene, a fuse and matches in his hands. Casting one rapid glance around, he entered the privy and placed the can near the wall, inserting the fuse cord into the opening, letting the remainder dangle over the side and onto the floor. Striking the match, he lit the fuse, ensuring it began burning before calmly blowing out the match and tossing it down the privy hole.

Closing the door behind him, he adjusted his clothing, doing his best to appear normal. Casting one last look around, he was pleased that he saw no one as he made his way past John Slaughter's Butcher Shop then across the vacant lot between the auctioneer's house and Spangenburg's Gun Shop. Pausing briefly before crossing 4th Street, he looked straight across to the vacant lot between the furniture store and the New Orleans Saloon. He had already scouted his escape route and knew that the vacant lot continued on to the OK Corral Stables where he would turn right into the very same place where the Earps and Clantons had their date with destiny. By then, the fire would be raging and he'd emerge onto Fremont Street far enough away to be noticed.

Watching for the occasional horse and wagon, Henry crossed the street. By the time he approached the Stables he heard a faint explosion almost immediately followed by the commotion and panicked cries of "Fire! Fire!" and then the alarms from the mines joined in.

Picking up his pace, Henry hustled on up to where the MATE was parked on Safford Street. In one smooth motion, he leaped onto the MATE and increased the boiler pressure. Looking back over his shoulder, he could see the smoke beginning to billow as the canvas roof of the gardens and dry wooden framework erupted into flames, which were quickly spreading.

Smirking with satisfaction, he looked down to the attached trailer. The crates with the gold were evenly arranged around the tarp covering the lovely madam of the Bird Cage Theater who was motionless beneath the canvas. The drug induced sleep would be wearing off soon, and he needed to be as far away as possible before she awoke. He engaged the engine, and the iron belts of the MATE began their circular grinding as it lurched forward.

Belle felt heavy, thick and uncomfortable. Even opening her eyes required too much effort. As the sounds around her invaded her thoughts, her awareness grew that she was not at home in her bed. She fidgeted to get comfortable but for some reason she couldn't move her legs or arms. Opening her eyes to darkness, she felt the heaviness of the canvas on top of her. It was then she realized that she was lying on her side with her hands tied behind her back. Her feet were likewise tied together.

Forcing herself to relax, she thought back to the last thing she remembered – when she was alone with Henry at his campsite. She then heard an engine increase in volume, and knew she was still with him. Moving her feet, she felt firmness all around her. Deciding she needed to see her surroundings to determine where she was and what was going on, she curled her knees up to her chest and pinched a bit of the canvass between her feet. Uncurling her legs, she was able to slide some of the canvas off.

She repeated the action and by the time the canvas was off her face, she felt the bumps and swaying of movement. Looking up, she could see the late afternoon sky. Evening was not far off. Surely someone would see that she was not at work and know something was wrong.

But what angered her more was the realization that Henry had kidnapped her.

Contorting and struggling, she managed to push herself up against the corner sides of the trailer. Twisting her head, she could see Henry up above in the pilot's seat, his gaze firmly ahead. Turning back to look behind them, Tombstone was beginning to dwindle. At that moment, she also saw the billowing smoke and heard the faint cries of 'Fire!'

From the corner of his eyes, Mason had caught movement off to his right when he saw Henry crossing 4th Street. The man seemed in a hurry to get somewhere. Though more than curious why Henry was in town and where he was going in such a hurry, it was when he was about to open the front door to Inez Martin's boarding house that the fire alarms exploded.

Jerking around, his first impulse was to rush to help, yet something didn't feel right, and he swung back around and pushed through the door. The man behind the counter looked up as he entered.

"What's going on out there?" the man asked, his face contorted in indecision.

"Fire," Mason shot back. "Arthur, you need to alert everyone." Taking the steps two at a time, he called back over his shoulder, "Is Belle Dubois upstairs?"

"I don't know. She was with that archaeologist fella," he answered back, slamming his ledger closed. Tucking it under his arm, he hurried after the Marshal.

Mason was halfway down the hall when he saw the plates stacked outside Belle's door. Striding up to her room, he tried the doorknob, finding it locked. "You have a key to this?" he snapped as Arthur came up the final steps.

"It's downstairs."

"Get it," he demanded. It wasn't as request.

Arthur spun around midstride and bounded back down the stairs, returning mere moments later handing Mason the keys while he pounded on the doors lining the hallway.

Rapidly selecting the key to her room, Mason unlocked and flung it open to find an empty room. Scowling, he whirled around and stormed out, flinging the set of keys to Arthur who was urging the few residents not at work to gather their valuables and get outside.

Mason raced down the stairs, out the door and up 3rd Street, threading through the groups of men who were dashing to assist with the fire. He arrived at the corner of 3rd and Safford just in time to see Henry in the distance chugging rapidly away towards the north. For a brief moment, he thought he saw someone in the trailer behind the MATE.

Turning around, he saw the smoke swelling in thick black and grey clouds and heard the cacophony of men and women in panic. He paused for only a moment in indecision before running back to the OK Corral to saddle up his horse, frustrated that Henry was getting father away with each passing minute. He was putting the bridle on when Jimmy Coyle rushed in.

"Where you going?" Jimmy demanded. "We need all the help we can get. The Occidental's already in flames."

"Can't Jimmy," Mason tersely replied. "Belle's just been kidnapped by a murderer and he's heading north with her."

"What? Who?" he asked, frowning in surprise.

"Dammit Jimmy, I don't have time to explain," he snapped as he leaped up into the saddle.

"OK Mason," he said, recognizing the urgency in the Marshal's voice. "You need help?"

"Don't have time to wait," he said as he urged his steed forward. "Stay here and save our city."

Mason sped on and was soon on Contention Road heading towards Watervale. Henry was nowhere in sight. Silently cursing the delay in pursuit, he reasoned the MATE would not be hard to track, especially as it left a chewed-up trail behind it. But that still didn't assuage his irritation. Yet within his anger was a cold determination that Henry would suffer dearly if he harmed Belle.

As he approached the Tombstone Driving Park, he saw Taboca and Nantan standing outside the saloon talking to John Doling. Veering off from the chase, he galloped up to where they were standing.

"Hey Marshal," John Doling grinned. "Looks like you're in quite a rush."

"The city's on fire again," he rapidly replied. "See what you can do to help." Jerking his head to focus his attention on the two machinists, he said, "I need your help."

"Of course, Marshal," Taboca readily answered.

"You have your airships here?"

"Yes. We were just getting ready to go out and test some of Nantan's bombs."

Mason thought quickly. "Good. They'll come in handy." He then hastily explained why he as there and whom he was chasing.

"Mister Mitchell?" Taboca repeated, disappointed.

"He's not who you think he is. He's a very dangerous man."

"He still has my stun gun," Nantan blurted.

Mason cast a cold glance at him. "Stun gun? He has your stun gun?"

"Well I didn't know," he defensively replied.

Relaxing slightly, Mason nodded. "Of course you didn't. The man's a talented inventor. But he's also a gifted liar, and a killer. How soon can you get those things in the air?"

"Only take a few minutes," Taboca answered.

"When you get aloft, I want you to use those bombs of yours to force him to the Dragoon Mountains to the northeast there." He pointed to the hills in the distance. "It's rugged terrain and the MATE will be difficult to maneuver. And be careful, Belle's in the trailer."

"We will, Marshal," Taboca acknowledged, nudging Nantan to get going. As the two machinists ran behind the stables to their ships, Mason turned his horse to resume the chase. The two airships rose quickly and were soon ahead of him. With the distance increasing between them, he focused his attention on the direction of Henry's MATE. Slowing his mount down to a jog, he knew he couldn't keep up the pace he wanted if he still wished to have a horse to ride back. Besides, with Taboca and Nantan up in the air, they would be able to keep track of Henry's route of escape.

Henry motored along the highway towards Benson, quite pleased with himself. He was making good time, the gold was secure in the trailer, along with Belle, and it was merely a matter of just a few hours until he arrived at the train station to ship his goods back east. It would be well past dark by then, which meant he could drop Belle off somewhere out of the way. He would have to make a brief detour and deposit her someplace where it would take a long time for her to alert anyone.

Pursing his lips in thought, he pondered the wisdom of kidnapping her. Was he that afraid of the Marshal? What did he hope to gain with her here? Wasn't she just additional baggage, a burden? He had thought to use her as leverage, a bargaining chip should the Marshal suddenly get too close. Yet, the truth was, he found himself smitten, and that irritated him. He had been so careful all these years not to get entangled, and here he was escaping north with a beautiful woman he had just kidnapped. He snorting a laugh thinking the whole absurd affair reminded him of a pirate capturing some lovely wench and carting her off on his ship.

Yet Belle was more than a prize. The woman had talent and was ambitious. Maybe if he broached the topic in the right way... after all, she wanted to be rich, and teaming with him would make her far wealthier than pretending to be a madam. Chuckling to himself, he grinned that kidnapping her was probably not the best argument to join him. Likewise, it meant taking the time to convince her, and right now time was of the essence.

A flash and loud bang exploded to his front left, causing him to jerk the MATE to the right, off the road and into the chaparral. His heart thudding, he snapped his head left and right searching for a cause or explanation.

Another explosion, closer this time, caused him again to jerk the controls and steer the MATE to the right. Feverously searching the surroundings, he turned his focus behind him, yet could see nothing. A third explosion a mere one hundred feet behind him got his attention and he flipped around, pushing the speed of his machine to its limit.

As Henry propelled the MATE faster, he quickly realized he was heading away from Benson towards the Dragoon Mountains. Another explosion behind him convinced him that someone somewhere was directing him to the mountains.

It was when the MATE bounced up over a small embankment and his head jerked back that he saw the two small airships above him. Immediately knowing it was Taboca and Nantan, he was furious that the two machinists were interfering with him. He silently cursed that all the bonhomie he had built up was all for nothing. He saw an object dropped from one of the ships seeming to head straight for him. Keeping his course the same in order to evade at the right moment, the object's descent began to trail behind him landing in an explosion fifty yards to his rear.

His face scrunched in anger and indignation while his mind raced as to why they were doing this. Still, at the same time, his analytical process wondered at the bombs they were dropping and how they were constructed. Yet he had little time to relish the idea as he recognized he was being forced into the mountains. He grimly chuckled thinking the fools thought the MATE couldn't handle the terrain. He would show them. By the time night spread across the sky, he would be safe within the security of the Dragoons. They would have to call off their scouting and he would escape out the other side. In fact, now that he was discovered, he might turn south to Mexico instead.

While he briskly scanned the terrain up ahead, an odd shape followed by a brief glare of light caught his attention off to the side. Snapping his head to the right, he was taken aback when he saw two men not far from his speeding path standing next to a spreading ocotillo. One of them was wearing a helmet that looked much too familiar. Staring in disbelief, he recognized the desiccated body of de la Fuente. Standing next to him was the rotting corpse of Caleb. Their heads turned to follow him as he sped by.

His immediate thought was of Marshal Sadler. It was too apparent that the man had this all planned out, even though he was in Tombstone when the fire started. How he knew Henry was heading north was a puzzle. He must have had more than the two machinists helping him. Henry cast a quick glance to the trailer behind him to see Belle out from under the canvas, wedged tightly against the corner. Her hands and legs still tied, she was staring up at the airships.

As the MATE bounced over the undulating prairie, Henry focused on what lay ahead. Once night fell, the airships would lose their ability to track him. Further, they would have to return sometime to refuel, while he could simply use the available deadwood strewn throughout the terrain to feed the engine. Though he had lights on the front, he would wait to use them until he was sure the airships were gone.

Smiling, he knew what he would do. Once the airships departed, he would head south to Mexico.

As Mason rode over the sagebrush plain, his quarry in the far distance, he was pleased that Taboca and Nantan were able to turn him. He hoped, despite Henry's extensive travels in the Territory, that the man knew little of the Dragoon Mountains, a rugged maze of granite peaks, gaping crevices, and abrupt precipices, the place where Cochise once had his stronghold. Mason knew Henry was hoping to lose the advantage of the airships by pushing his machine into the mountainous terrain that would make it difficult for them to maneuver while providing him with some overhead cover if he could get deeper into the mountains, especially with night coming.

Mason remembered the last time he had been in the Dragoons. It was the only time he had lost the trail of an outlaw, a two-bit cattle rustler just coming back from Mexico. The man had managed to lose himself in the labyrinth of vertical granite spires and towering rock faces. Balanced rocks and boulders, some the size of a miner's cabin, were scattered across the steep hillsides making him wary as he pursued his quarry, for they looked too precarious in balance making him wonder what little effort it would take for some to come crashing down.

And then there were the wooded canyons, thick with evergreen oaks and sycamores. If Henry managed to get himself hidden in one of the canyons, he would be harder to find, even with the airships. Still, Henry would have to emerge at some point, though with the edible plants in the mountains, the archaeologist could survive for quite some time.

The question though was why would Henry want to stay in the mountains? Most likely, he would get into the low foothills, wait until dark and when it was safe, head back out and south to Mexico.

Mason looked up at the sky, praying that daylight would last long enough to force Henry deeper into the mountains, making it more difficult for him to extract himself.

Gazing up at the airships then at the approaching Dragoon Mountains, Belle understood what the two machinists were doing. That Taboca and Nantan were aloft told her that Mason was not far behind. The problem was what could she do to help? Trussed up like she was, it was difficult to do anything. She had already tried slipping her hands from behind and underneath her but there was simply too much dress in the way. She would have to wait until the opportune moment and get free. Until then, she would need to be as sweet as possible.

But it still didn't stop her from chastising herself. She should have listened to Mason when he first expressed his doubts. She should have done a better job in vetting Henry. She was too caught up in the moment, the attention, the game. Now here she was, tied and bound like some amateur agent. She could only imagine what her superiors would say. She should have paid better attention, she should have... she should have... She looked up at Henry, a handsome man in the game of his life, trying to escape with what must be an unimaginable fortune. She admitted what she should have done was quite irrelevant at the moment. In addition to suffering the jolting ride in a metal trailer, she needed to come up with a plan to stop this man.

By the time Henry entered the mountains, night was settling across the land. One airship still followed him, lower now to track better. He couldn't see where the other one was. The fact that one airship remained more than irritated him for it pushed him deeper into the rugged terrain, forcing him to slow his speed and carefully choose his path. The maze of teetering boulders, steep hillsides and increasing presence of sycamores, oaks, and underbrush began to blend into a uniform shapeless mass.

After a short while of picking his way, he knew he could go no further without lights. Deciding that even if the airships saw him, when he found a spot to park and turned off the lights, they would have a difficult time at best trying to find him again.

Reaching forward, he engaged the dynamo switch just below the pilot board. Yet nothing happened. Flipping the switch several times with the same result, he snarled as he brought the machine to a halt.

"Are we stopping for dinner?" Belle cheerily called out.

"Not quite," he replied, ignoring her. Reaching under the switch, he found the main lead wire hanging loose. With a not so soft "Damn," he fiddled with the wire, attaching it as best he could to the remaining lead from the switch. Crossing his fingers, he flipped the switch on, and a burst of bright eye-searing light shot out from the carbon arc lamp in the front, brilliantly illuminating everything in its path.

Henry slowly coaxed the machine forward when an idea hit him. Stopping the machine again, he went forward to the carbon arc lamp in front, heat already emanating from the iron casing. The lamp was designed to swivel side-to-side as well as rotate upwards. Releasing the anchor straps, he grabbed the top handle and swung the intense beam skyward. It took only a few sweeps before he found the airship hovering just a few hundred feet above them. He zeroed in on the pilot housing, following the ship wherever it moved until it began to drift away.

"That should occupy him for a while," he observed, twisting the light to the front and securing the anchor straps. He walked back to where Belle was still awkwardly sitting in the front of the trailer. "Comfy?" he smiled at her.

"Not really," she replied. "I don't suppose you could see you way to tying my hands in the front. That way I could get a little more comfortable during our little escapade."

"Hmmm," he pretended to think, "not yet. We've a little ways to go still and then I'll see to your comfort."

"How charming," Belle deadpanned.

An hour later, after slowly and carefully threading his way in, Henry came to a spot beneath several tall oaks. It had sufficient space around it so that he could turn the MATE and trailer in a complete circle and leave by the same way he came in.

"Here we are," he announced, shutting down the engine. As the engine slowly died, so did the carbon arc light. Before they were engulfed in total darkness, Henry hustled back to the trailer and pulled out two Rochester lamps, quickly lighting them. The dim light of the lamps was a stark contrast to the magnitude of the arc light.

"I say," he observed, holding one lamp up and pretending to look in the trailer. "Not having planned for such a detour, I'm afraid our evening meal will be rather sparse. I do, however, have some fine Tennessee whiskey."

Belle shivered a bit, "How about a fire?"

"And alert your friends to where we are?" he chuckled. "I think not."

"Then I'll take that glass of whiskey."

"I thought you didn't like whiskey?"

"A girl takes what she can get," she shrugged.

Henry sniffed a laugh. "Whiskey it is then."

"How about untying my hands?" She twisted her body to allow him access to her bound wrists.

Henry paused a moment before answering. "If I untie you, do you promise not to do anything stupid?"

"Like run away?" She shook her head. "Where would I run to? I know we're in the Dragoons, but that doesn't help much, especially at night. Besides, there are nasty things in the dark. A fire would keep us warm and keep them away."

"Sound reasoning," Henry agreed, opening a larger crate and withdrawing a bottle of whiskey, "but a fire does advertise where we are." Rummaging a few moments, he found two tin cups.

"You've blinded the one airship pilot and he's probably trying not to crash into anything. I don't know where the other airship is, maybe back to get more fuel. Either way, they haven't a clue where we are anymore."

"That's possible," he nodded in admiration. She was a smart one, very logical. He was surprised at how calm she was. "There's still your marshal friend."

"He's probably still putting out the fire in town," she unconvincingly said.

"I doubt it," he grinned. "Those two machinists in their airships didn't' decide to follow me on their own. I have no doubt your marshal is close, too close for my comfort." Henry poured a healthy dose of whiskey into each cup then corked the bottle. "You still haven't answered my first question. If I untie your hands, do you promise not to do anything stupid?"

"I promise," she readily agreed.

Reaching over the trailer side, he untied her wrists then handed her a cup of whiskey.

Rubbing here sore wrists, Belle accepted the drink. "When you promised me another ride on the MATE, this wasn't quite how I envisioned it." She took a sip, felt the liquor burn down her throat and coughed. Frowning at the cup in her hand, she said, "And some wonder why I prefer sangaree."

"You just don't appreciate fine whiskey," he said with an air of superiority.

"On that you and I agree." She placed the cup down on one of the crates. "There is one small question that has been puzzling me."

"Oh?"

"Why am I here?"

Henry slowly shook his head with amusement. "Now Katherine. Do you really expect me to believe that you have no clue as to why you are here?"

"Actually, yes." She picked up the whiskey and inhaled the strong bouquet, debating whether to take another sip. Deciding the temporary warmth it provided was better than being cold, she took a swallow and grimaced. Tugging at the canvas tarp that had covered her during the trip here, she pulled it up around her shoulders.

"You really have no clue?" he asked, his doubt obvious.

"Oh, I know about the gold and poor Caleb," she replied thinking that there was no sense pretending she didn't know his game. "Did Caleb have to die?"

"The unfortunate consequences in the quest for wealth. Consider him collateral damage," he nonchalantly shrugged.

"I suppose. Still, why bring me along? I'm only in the way."

"True, true," he agreed, nodding, savoring his whiskey. "But then there is that pesky marshal friend of yours. His obsession with justice can be a bit annoying. Had he left well enough alone, I could have been long gone by now. And let's be honest, shall we? There is no one who would miss Caleb."

"Except Caleb," she pointed out.

"Ah yes, well there is that part, isn't there," he chuckled.

"So I'm to be some sort of bargaining chip, just in case?" She took another sip, deciding the whiskey wasn't so bad after all.

"That's exactly it."

Silence settled for a while, interrupted by the occasional coyote howl in the distance. Henry climbed into the trailer and sat opposite Belle. Uncorking the whiskey bottle, he poured another large helping and offered to do the same to her.

"Not yet, thanks," she said. Glancing at the crates surrounding her, she asked, "So how much gold is in here?"

"Enough to live on for the rest of our lives," he triumphantly answered.

"Our lives?" she said, noticing his choice of words.

"Come now, Katherine," he smiled knowingly. "We're both cut from the same cloth. My game is finding treasure and selling it. Yours is pretending to be a madam. While yours is interesting, it will never match the sheer profits of my enterprise, even with the little game you and the Marshal have going."

"But I don't have to kill anyone to do it," she countered.

"Puh-lease," he half-sneered. "Tell that to Lester Corbett. So you didn't pull the trigger. But your game with the Marshal still resulted in a man shot dead. And what about the bounty hunter, or the many others who get shot because they interfered with your game? Don't pretend you're any different from me. There are more men dead as a result of your little arrangement with the Marshal than what few I have dealt with."

Belle blinked at the accusation. She could bring up the fact that all the men killed or hurt were criminals, like Henry. But that probably wasn't the best approach to use at the moment. "When you put it like that, you may have a point."

"Exactly," he self-righteously agreed.

"So where do I fit in?"

Henry studied her over the rim of his cup. Even after being dragged here against her will, knocked about in the trailer as they made their way into the mountains, she seemed unaffected by it all, beautifully unaffected. Belle was that rare woman who could be knee deep in mud and still be magnificent.

"I had pondered inviting you into my, um, business affairs. Think about it. What a team we would make. We would live in lavish luxury. Your earnings as a madam would be but a pittance to what we would earn."

"Really?" she said, seeming to appear interested. "And just how do you see me fitting in?"

Henry's heart leapt as he noticed her choice of words. Not 'how *would* you see me,' but 'how *do* you see me fitting in.' She was obviously interested. All he had to do now was sell her on the role.

"We would be equal partners," he offered. "Between the two of us, there's nothing we couldn't do."

"Not meaning to rain on you parade," she countered, "but you're the inventor, the scientist and the researcher. I have none of those skills. Why include me in your ventures?"

"I say, that's just it," he said, slapping his thigh. "You have the boldness, the audacity, not to mention the distracting beauty, to pull off any hustle we might need. I can get us to where we need to go. You can be the face of the business, the one who works the contacts, develops the clientele."

Belle held out her cup. "I'll take a little more now."
While Henry refilled her cup, she said, "We'd be equal
partners?"

"Yes."

She sat back, holding the cup in both hands, pretending
to ponder the offer. "How do I know I can trust you?"

"Have I ever done anything to harm you?" he said.

"You mean besides kidnapping me?"

"Well, that was unfortunate, but necessary at the time,"
he explained.

"I suppose I can understand," she said. "The gold here,
how do you plan on getting rid of it?"

"I already have buyers in Europe," he grinned.

"Europe?" she brightened. "We'd have to go to
Europe?"

"Yes," he enthusiastically replied.

"Europe," she sighed in happy memory, nestling back
into the corner of the trailer. "It would be wonderful to be in
Europe again."

"You could take accommodations in my villa until you
found a place of your own," he offered.

"You have a villa in Europe?" she exclaimed. "Where?"

"A little town in the Bourgogne region called Joigny."

"How marvelous," she gushed.

"You would like it there," he said.

"I'm sure I will," she coyly replied.

Henry blinked several times before calming himself to
rationality. "So you agree?"

"I'm leaning very favorably to answer 'yes.' But I need
to look at it from all perspectives. If I throw in with you, I'm
immediately suspect in Caleb's death."

"That will pass," he countered. "No one will miss the
old coot."

"That may be, but we've got to go about this just right.
I've still got a nice bank account in Tombstone. You're
asking me to leave it all behind."

Henry tugged down a crate and pushed it towards her,
using his feet. "There. That's yours. You can have it."

Belle set her cup down. She paused in her reach for the crate to look at him. "Mind if I untie my legs?"

"I'll do it," he gallantly offered, leaning forward to unwrap the rope securing her ankles.

"Thank you." She grabbed the crate and tugged it towards her. "It's heavy," she said.

"That's because it's full of gold."

"And that's nice, but it doesn't help me with needing money now. I'd still have to wait until we get to Europe to exchange it."

"I have plenty of money," he said.

"No offense, but I've never been beholden to anyone for anything and I'm not going to start now."

"So what do you suggest?" he asked, his impatience beginning to grow.

"Like I said, I have a sizeable bank account here." She took another sip of her whiskey thinking she was beginning to like the strong flavor.

"We can't afford to go back," he flatly stated.

"We can't," she agreed, "but I can."

"What are you saying?" he guardedly demanded.

"What I'm saying is that you haven't planned this very well. You kidnap me knowing that Mason was sure to follow. That wasn't very smart," she said as though lecturing him.

Sitting straight up, he cocked his head to stare at her. He knew he should be insulted, but her calm analytical demeanor caught him off guard. "So what do you suggest?"

Tucking her legs underneath her, she arranged her dress to cover her feet. "We know that Mason is tracking us. It's not like it's all that difficult. Though this is a marvelous machine, it does leave an obvious trail. What we need is for him to direct his attention to rescuing me so that you have time to escape. You'll obviously have to go to Mexico because everyone will be looking for you north of the border. Can you work your way through Mexico without getting into trouble?"

Henry was momentarily mute as he marveled at the woman's detached analysis.

"Henry," she said, interrupting his reverie. "Are you listening?"

"Yes, my dear, I am." He smiled with a wary confidence. Her demeanor said she was on board with him, but it seemed much too easy. "Why the sudden change? And what about the Marshal? It's obvious your interest is more than just friendship."

"Then you misread my intentions. He's a rather good-looking man," she said, inwardly smiling at his reaction, "who was in a bad marriage. I saw him as a challenge, especially with his holier-than-thou refusal to wander away from his marriage vows, like so many other men do, especially those upright city leaders in Tombstone," she sneered. "Unfortunately," she shrugged, "now that his wife is dead, he's no longer a challenge."

"And the sudden change?" he asked, pleased with her answer.

"It's not as sudden as you think," she said, beginning to feel the effects of the whiskey. She looked down at her empty cup then back at him. "Is there any more of this stuff?"

Smirking, he held up the bottle, still half-full. ""You were saying?" he said as he poured a large dose into her cup. He smiled suavely thinking that if she passed out drunk, it would save him the trouble of watching her and he could get some sleep.

"I was saying that my change of heart was not as sudden as you think. I was beginning to get bored with the madam performance. Though I was making good money, it wasn't good enough. When Mason told me about you and the gold, I figured here was an opportunity to quit this place. Why do you think I so readily accepted your invitations to picnics?" She eyed him over the rim of her cup.

"Not because I was an attractive catch?" he asked, fishing for a compliment while thinking back to the timing of the picnics and his discovery of the gold.

"Your good looks certainly made it a whole lot more appealing," she smiled. "And there was the way you tossed money around in the Bird Cage like you had far too much of it. I knew you had something going on and I just needed to find out what it was."

Henry sat back, his mouth slacking open when it dawned on him that she was hustling him as much as he was hustling her. That realization simply reinforced his admiration of the woman. She would be a superb partner.

With a wide yawn, Belle set her cup down. "I'm getting sleepy." Wrapping herself within the canvas, she curled up and settled down, resting her head on her arm. She was soon breathing the shallow breaths of deep sleep.

Henry shook his head, marveling at this most unusual woman. Yet there was nagging doubt in the back of his mind. Her answers, though seeming genuine, were too facile, almost as though they had been rehearsed. He wanted to trust her but couldn't afford to let his guard down. She was an opportunist, one who would jump to the winning side just in time. And that made her dangerous, even if they successfully escaped to Europe.

Folding his arms and crossing his stretched-out legs, Henry settled back against the stacked crates. He knew what he had to do and bringing her with him did not fit into his plans.

When the carbon arc light burst upon the airship, Taboca immediately scrunched his eyes shut, but the intensity of the light penetrated his tightly closed eyelids so that when the brightness finally shifted away and he hesitantly opened his eyes, he could see nothing. Reaching forward to the control panel, he felt along the top until he came to the engine throttle. Pulling back on the toggle, he powered up the engine to increase altitude for he knew he was too low among the sharp peaks of the mountains.

He felt himself rising and began slowly counting to thirty figuring that thirty seconds of lift ought to get him above the peaks. There still remained three significant problems. First, he still couldn't see. Second, once he leveled off at altitude, he would have the problems of drift and direction. He was flying blind. If he drifted with the wind currents, who knew where he'd end up once his sight finally returned. With that in mind, he adjusted the rear rudder, putting the airship into a tight circular loop. That would at least slow down the drift a bit.

But that left one more problem. He was running out of fuel. Unless his sight returned very soon, he was going to crash.

Reins in his hands, Mason tugged up the collar of his shirt against the chill night air as he carefully led his horse along the trail that the MATE had left. Even in the dark, the trail was relatively easy to follow, especially after he saw that burst of light sent skyward illuminating one of the airships. He had looked up, wondering if it was Taboca or Nantan piloting the airship. He could tell by the intensity of the light that whoever it was, was going to be night-blinded for a while. But that beam of light was still well far off in the distance and he knew that his quarry was hours away.

Silently thanking the two machinists for forcing Henry into the mountains, he pondered how he was going to rescue Belle. Henry was both dangerous and unpredictable. Listening to the night noises, Mason strained to hear the sounds of the MATE or any of Henry's other machines. For all Mason knew, Henry had that intruder machine set up and working, which would alert him that the Marshal was approaching. That meant he would have to circle around, but by the time he got into position, Henry could simply retrace his path and escape the same way he came in.

He knew Henry was hunkered down for the night, hidden as best he could, undoubtedly waiting for him to show up. Looking up at the star-filled night, Mason debated how much longer he should follow the tracks, knowing that Henry was expecting him. Henry was no fool and would use the night to his advantage. If Mason continued much longer, he would most likely stumble upon the MATE, and that would be bad for everyone except Henry.

Deciding he would let Henry have the sleepless night, Mason moved off the trail several paces where a few sycamores provided overhead cover. Securing the reins to a tree, he loosened the saddle girth.

"Let's see what they got to eat around here," he said, gently scratching the horse's cheek and forehead.

Slowly probing the area, he found some sagebrush and desert ferns, grabbing handfuls and placing them on the ground for his horse to graze on. Untying the bedroll, he wrapped it around his shoulders and sat down on the opposite side of the tree. Settling against the tree, he tilted his Stetson over his face and closed his eyes.

Though tired, he knew he would get little sleep for his mind would not let him rest. Rescuing Belle and bringing Henry to justice were just the beginning of his problems. Despite his best efforts to concentrate on the immediate troubles, his mind replayed memories of his life with Elizabeth. Yet each memory seemed to end up in his father-in-law's office and his bitter altercation with the pig-headed man. Mason didn't' know what form his father-in-law would take in retribution for his only child's death, but he knew it would be a life for a life.

Henry felt the trailer move and his eyes blinked wide. A low-lit lamp in hand, Belle was trying her best to quietly climb over the side. Tilting his head back down and shallow breathing as though still asleep, he felt the increased brightness though his eyelids as she held the lamp towards him. When the light shifted, he opened his eyes to see her tip-toeing back down the trail, the Rochester lamp held to her side. When she was about fifty feet away, she turned to check on him. Satisfied she had been successful, she increased her pace.

Rope in hand, Henry leaped out of the trailer and stealthily followed her. As the path bent away from the where the MATE was parked, her pace quickened, and he could hear her faintly calling "Mason?" "Mason?" When she received no response, she picked up the pace even more, hiking up her dress.

Realizing he had to act if he didn't want her to escape, Henry charged and dove at her, tackling her and sending the Rochester lamp spinning into the ground. Though momentarily startled, she fought like a wildcat, but Henry's strength overpowered her. Roughly turning her over onto her belly, he yanked her arms behind her and tied her wrists together, tight. Leaving her on her stomach, he jumped up and began stamping out the small fire that had burst when the lamp spilled its contents on the dry brush.

Distracted, he nearly didn't see Belle pushing herself to her feet and hurrying off down the trail. His lips pursed, he kicked dirt onto the still simmering twigs and brush, and gave chase, tripping her so that she landed hard on her shoulder.

"The gods damn you woman," he snapped. Jerking her up, he slung her up over his shoulder as he hurried back to squelch the fire that had renewed its consuming power. Flinging her down on the ground, he ripped off her skirt.

"How dare you," she indignantly berated him.

Ignoring her, he used her skirt to slap and smother the low spreading flames. It took nearly half-an-hour before the flames had diminished to where he could catch his breath. He continued stepping and smothering the fire, casting an occasional sharp stare at his captive who sat glumly between the fire and the trail to the MATE.

When he was satisfied that the fire was sufficiently out, he stood towering over Belle. "That was stupid," he coldly announced.

"I didn't want to wake you," she sourly retorted. "I was merely trying to ascertain where Mason might be."

"Of course you were," he mocked. Reaching down he grabbed hold of her shoulders and yanked her to standing. "Looks like I revert back to my original plan. Besides," he said, pushing her forward, "I doubt I ever could have trusted you. It's better this way."

"For who," she shot back. Glancing at the dress draped over his arm, she said, "You owe me for a new dress."

"It's your own fault for being stupid. You could have set the whole mountain on fire."

"You shouldn't have tackled me," she shot back.

311

"And you shouldn't have lied to me and tried to escape," he huffed.

Henry jabbed a hand under her arm and forcibly propelled Belle forward.   Struggling to keep up, she exclaimed, "You're hurting me."

"And I'll do a much more if you don't behave," he coldly replied.

"What? You going to shoot me?" she sneered.

"If I have to," came the detached response.

His answer abruptly shut her up as she immediately realized if it came to her being in the way of his escape, she was expendable.

Back at the trailer, he lowered the tailgate, hoisted her up and dumped her in.   While she struggled to sit up, he snatched another length of rope and yanked an ankle back. Wrapping a loop around the ankle, he easily avoided the kick with her other foot, catching it and tightly securing both ankles together.

"That hurts," she complained.

"Too bad. You should have thought of the consequences when you decided to run off."   Grabbing ahold of her shoulders, he scooted her up to the far corner of the trailer and draped the canvass over her. "At least you'll be warm."

"How am I supposed to sleep all trussed up like this?" She stared evilly at him.

"Do your best," he flippantly replied, climbing down. Hands on his hips, he thought about the fire and the probability that the Marshal saw it. Damn. Looking back over his shoulder, he reasoned that she wasn't going to make more trouble tonight. He could leave her there while he moved back down the trail to keep watch. Going to the locker beneath the MATE's pilot's seat he unlocked it to retrieve a pistol. Reaching in, he was pleasantly surprised to remember he still had Nantan's stun gun. Taking out both pistol and stun gun, Henry stuffed the pistol in his belt and headed down the trail.

He had barely gotten settled when he heard her. She was singing… loudly. Remarking that she had a reasonably good voice, it still didn't abrogate the fact that she was giving away his position. With an angry growl, he boosted himself up and stalked back.

"Shut up!" he snarled.

Ignoring him, she kept singing.

Leaping onto the trailer, he backhanded her across the face. "Any more stunts like that and I'll shoot you here and now," he said, his voice frigid.

Belle tasted the blood in her mouth and defiantly spit it out. Staring daggers at him, she started singing again though not as loudly.

Henry cocked the pistol and jammed the cold steel barrel against her forehead. It caused the singing too stop only for a moment.

Her eyes closed against the inevitable, Belle softly started singing a hymn she had learned in church. She was half-way through the first verse when she felt the pressure from the pistol against her forehead dissipate. Hesitantly opening one eye, she felt the trailer shift and saw Henry leaping down. Laughing at calling his bluff, she sang even louder until she felt him yank the canvass off her. It was when she felt the cool boiler water dumped over her head that she sputtered in shock. Gasping a deep breath, she began shivering uncontrollably.

"I've another bucket ready for when you decide to start again," he said, amused at her shocked reaction. "In fact, that was so much fun, I think I'll do it again."

"No! Please don't," she begged to no avail as he doused her with the other bucket.

"Don't forget," he cheerfully reminded her. "I have a boiler full of water just in case." Without waiting for a reply, he collected the stun gun and headed back to his original spot, leaving her to shiver in the cold night air, her teeth chattering.

Taboca's night vision was finally beginning to return when he heard Nantan calling to him.

"What are you doing?" his cousin asked. "And why are you so high up and so far away from where I left you?

You're over the San Pedro. I've spent the past hour looking for you."

"He's got a carbon arc light and he blinded me," Taboca called back. "I had to get higher."

"You OK?"

"I am now." Taboca could see few lights in Tombstone in the distance off to his left. It was a stark contrast to the first time he and Nantan flew over the city. There was an acrid smell of smoke in the wind.

"They still in the mountains?" Nantan asked.

"As far as I know," he shrugged. "Have you been back to the city?"

"No. I just got some more fuel and came back looking for you, but Mister Doling said it was pretty bad."

Nodding, Taboca announced, "We might as well go back and start again in the morning."

"That's fine with me. It's cold up here."

Swinging the two airships in a slow arc, they headed towards the Tombstone Driving Park.

Chapter 13

Dawn had yet to spill over the ridges and hills of the Dragoon Mountains by the time Mason had cinched up the saddle and was slowly and deliberately riding along the trail left by Henry's MATE. His senses on edge, he scanned the surrounding hazy boulders and hills just beginning to take shape in the growing light. As he rocked to the slow rhythm of his horse, he puzzled at one of the sounds of the past evening. Though very faint, he could have sworn he had heard a woman singing.

Unsure of just how far Henry might have gotten into the mountains, he slowed his pace down even more then dismounted and proceeded on foot, holding the reins in one hand, and a pistol in the other. But now, the long shadows of morning were starting to recede. Brilliantly illuminated crests were offset by the deep shadows of the opposite ridges that still blocked the sun. Just before he rounded a bend in the trail, he heard them and looked up.

The two machinists were back, following the trail as best they could. He saw a hand wave and returned a wave in kind followed by a finger to his lips telling them to be cautious. He was pleased they were back, for it gave him a little bit of an advantage as it would keep Henry busy while Mason snuck up.

Looking down, Nantan saw the Marshal leading his mount. Waving to get Taboca's attention, he pointed down to the trail. As they both looked down, Mason gazed up. Nantan waved and saw the Marshal give a brisk wave back, quickly turning his focus on what lay ahead.

Turning his attention to his cousin, Nantan hand motioned Taboca to swing wide while he continued following the trail. Nodding in understanding, Taboca pushed and pulled the rudder levers, and the small airship split away.

While Taboca positioned himself to come at the trail at an oblique angle, Nantan lowered the airship to where it was almost skimming the hilltops. It was low enough to offer a good view, but not too low to be dangerous. After about ten minutes of ups and downs monitoring the trail, he noticed that it seemed to end in a large swath of trees in a wide barranca. Slowing down, he powered up when he heard what sounded like escaping gas immediately followed by the echo of two gunshots reverberating in the canyon below.

Uttering a soft, "Damn," Nantan struggled to maintain speed and direction, knowing he was going to have to bailout soon. He quickly searched the rugged terrain looking for some spot, any spot, flat enough to land.

Up above, Taboca had heard the shot and saw Nantan's predicament. Realizing that he too was susceptible, he powered up and rose higher in the sky, all the time watching where Nantan would land. He watched as his cousin increased the heat to the envelope, desperately trying to stay aloft. But the envelope was beginning to buckle and despite his efforts, Nantan was going to crash.

Nantan feverishly searched for a place to set down, but the growth was too thick, and he knew the envelope would likely be shredded before he hit the ground. Suddenly the barren course of a dry riverbed edged in sharp mesquite and spreading oaks appeared in front of him. Fighting the stiffening elevator flaps he maneuvered his airship directly over the widest part, doing his best to turn the ship to face into the wind.

As the ship settled, Nantan prepared to extract himself from the pilot housing. He had no desire to be caught beneath the envelope. He had heard the stories of pilots suffocating when they were unable to free themselves from the weight of the envelope.

The ship was still ten feet above the ground when Nantan pulled himself out of the pilot housing, grabbed hold of the landing skid and swung himself below the ship. No sooner had he swung out that he felt his feet touch the ground.

Releasing the skid, he jumped to the side and out of the way as the airship settled and folded over the engine and pilot housing.

Nantan continued scrambling out of the way, leaping behind a grouping of large rocks just as the heat from the engine ignited the remaining gas, spewing the envelope, engine, and support structure in one large explosion.

Higher up, Taboca saw Nantan fleeing up the side of the riverbed in time before the airship disintegrated.

Mason had just rounded a large outcropping, noticing the increase in overgrowth when he heard the shot and saw Nantan feverishly fighting with his airship. Abruptly halting, he took two strides backwards beside his horse. No sooner had he pulled out his Winchester from the saddle holster when he heard another shot. He instinctively rolled to the side just in time as his horse suddenly reared and toppled over almost landing on him. Scooting behind the animal, he leveled his rifle towards the direction of the shot intensely scanning the brush and rocks. Feeling the animal's still warm body, he knew it was dead. Then he saw the two wires leading from the horse's neck back across the trail and into the thick scrub and trees and knew what had happened. Scowling, Mason glared across the gap to the other side of the trail. He could see the MATE not too far off, tucked under several trees. That Henry had tried to shoot him was bad enough. That he had killed his horse was beyond the pale. The man was going to pay dearly for it.

Hunkered down behind the dead steed, Mason scanned the area, his rifle at the ready. He was about to crawl to the side when movement to his front caused him to stop. Pushing out from where the wires led into the thick scrub, Belle staggered out, her hands tied behind her. Right behind her, Henry firmly grasped her neck.

"That's far enough," Henry coldly commanded, brandishing his pistol to make the point.

His Winchester centered on the man's head, Mason calmly stood up and aimed at Henry who now pointed the pistol to her head. "Hello Belle. I see you have everything

317

under control." She was missing her skirt and stood there in bloomers and riding vest. Yet she looked like a drowned rat in her wet clothes, her hair drooping and her make-up running down her face. Though shivering, she smiled at him.

"I was just about to make him surrender when you arrived," she casually replied.

"How sweet," Henry interjected with a sneer, "the two lovers with all their bravado. Don't think I don't know your little game."

"And what game would that be?" Mason asked, holding his rifle rock steady.

"Please don't insult me," he said, rolling his eyes. "Even a blind man could see the way you two act around each other. You pretending you're married, pretending to be so self-righteous, while you spend all you time with her. And her, pretending she's not in love with you. When I saw the hustle she had going, I thought she might make a good partner. After all, the woman knows how to manipulate men. But when she called me 'Mason' –"

"I did?" Belle said, twisting her head slightly to look back at him.

"Yes."

"When?"

"The picnics. Does it matter?" he irritably answered.

"Oops," Belle smirked, looking back at Mason. Again twisting her head to look at her captor, she said, "Is that what this is all about?"

"Don't be a damned fool, woman," Henry retorted. "We all know what this is about – gold. I have it, and you want it."

"That's where you're wrong," Mason coolly replied. "We're here because you killed a man, a good man." There was movement in the bushes about ten yards directly behind Henry, and Mason hid his surprise when he recognized Caleb and de la Fuente.

"The man was common, a worthless product of ill-matched parents. The world will not mourn his passing." Henry quipped.

"What gives you the right to determine who lives or dies?" he said, gazing directly at Henry, but watching as the two dead men emerged from hiding and slowly approached, their spasmodic steps pausing as Caleb bent awkwardly down and with two hands, picked up a large stone.

"An odd question for a U.S. Marshal to ask. You do that all the time, determining who lives and who dies."

"It's not the same, Mister Mitchell," Mason evenly replied, "if that is your real name."

"Ah," he nodded with approval. "I see you've been doing your own brand of research. Good for you. But, what my real name is really of little importance in all of this. And all this jabber is getting us nowhere. You see that I have your precious lover. You know I am not afraid to kill. I will kill her if you don't cooperate."

Mason, slowly shook his head, sniffing in disdain. "And here I thought you were a man of science. There is really only one result for you at the moment. You kill her; I kill you. You don't kill her; I still kill you. You're only option to stay alive is to drop your weapon and give yourself up."

Momentarily taken aback, Henry frowned in indecision, but quickly recovered. "You'd actually let me kill her," he said, testing for the Marshal's bluff, "the woman you love."

"If she dies, it's because of you, not me," Mason said.

Henry gazed directly at him. "Seems like you just have bad luck with women," he mocked. "Poor Elizabeth couldn't handle you running around on her and look what happened."

"Elizabeth chose her own destiny," he said.

"You mean like coming to Tombstone?" he taunted.

"That's right," he answered, hoping Caleb and de la Fuente would hurry up as he wasn't so sure he could keep the man distracted for much longer. "She made her choice. Besides, what's that to you?"

"The way I look at it, you owe me," Henry objected.

"How you figure that?"

"Who do you think provided her with all that fun?"

Mason shrugged dismissively. "Looks like you wasted your money."

"I thought so too," he jeered. "That's why I had to put a stop to it."

"Really? How?"

"Let's just say it's hard to breathe with a pillow over your face."

Mason muffled his surprise at the revelation. Yet he felt no anger by her death at his hands, and that surprised him. "So now you're responsible for two murders."

"The way I figure it, I did you a favor. You didn't love her, and I did your dirty work for you."

"Well now, since you put it like that," Mason half-smiled, "I guess you did do me a kind of favor." He watched as de la Fuente hung back as Caleb slowly approached, raising the stone in his hands. "Though your method was not the way I would have handled it." Pausing for just a moment, he said, "But now that we're here, I do have to ask who you are, why you're doing all this."

"Does it matter?"

"Let's just say that my curiosity is getting the better of me. And the way I figure it, unless you drop your weapon, only one of us is leaving this place alive, and I doubt it will be you."

Momentarily taken aback, Henry's bravado quickly returned. "I guess we'll just have to see about that, won't we? But to satisfy your curiosity my name actually is Henry Mitchell, but not the Henry Mitchell of Brown University."

"Are you an archaeologist?"

"Of sorts," he evasively answered.

"Apparently you're not very good at it," Mason observed. "Ben saw through your fake artifacts."

"Ben?"

"The town drunk," Belle interjected.

Henry cocked an eyebrow. "The town drunk knows Indian artifacts?"

"Yes," Mason acknowledged. "And it was he who pointed out your flaws as an archaeologist."

"That's a matter of opinion," Henry retorted. "I'm good enough at it to have found this gold."

"Caleb found the gold," Mason evenly replied. "You merely took it from him."

"Now you're quibbling," Henry nonchalantly replied.

"So what do you do with all your treasure?" Mason asked. "You'd have to get rid of it somehow."

"Buyers are easy to find, especially in Europe," he confidently explained. "Right now they're very big on the American West. This little pile of treasure will bring me quite a handsome return. I might not have to work again for some time."

Mason aimed the rifle at the man's forehead. "The way I see it, you won't be working again at all."

Henry was about to retort when his world went black.

As awareness coalesced, the pain in Henry's head throbbed in excruciating rhythm to his heartbeat. Struggling to open his eyes, the brightness of the afternoon sun caused him to squint. Clarity finally came, but all he could see was sky, and O god his head hurt.

Wanting to feel the back of his head where the pain seemed to be centered, he tried moving his right hand, but it wouldn't budge. He repeated the effort, but something was tugging at it, refusing to release it.

Slowly twisting his head, he looked over to see his wrist secured by a leather strap to a stake firmly entrenched in the ground. Frowning, he swiveled his head to the left and saw the same condition for his left hand. Lifting his head as best he could, despite the pain, he saw his legs were likewise staked. He was splayed out on the ground like Da Vinci's Vitruvian Man. A shadow spread across his face, and he looked up to see the Marshal standing over him.

"Comfortable?" Mason casually asked.

"Wha... what happened," he groggily asked.

"I had some help from some friends, both of whom you know." He stepped back and Caleb's maggot eaten body blocked the sunlight, his eyeless skull staring down at him. Just off his shoulder, de la Fuente's desiccated face mirrored the prospector.

Recognition came slowly, but once he realized who it was, he tried to shake his head in disbelief. "Impossible."

"Apparently not," Mason chuckled.

"He's awake?" Belle asked, standing next to Mason. She had wiped her face clean of makeup, looking quite fresh despite her still damp clothes.

"For the moment," Mason answered.

Henry continued staring between Caleb and de la Fuente, muttering "Impossible. You're both dead. I know you're dead. I killed you. This is impossible."

"You keep saying that," Mason pointed out, "yet here they stand, literally back from the dead. I'm sure there's scientific explanation for it, but that's something for the three of you to talk about. Looks like you'll probably have plenty of time."

"Wha.. what do you mean?" he frowned, the pain not diminishing. "What happened?"

Mason thumbed at Caleb and explained, "Like I said. I had some help. While you and I were having such a wonderful conversation, Caleb struck you from behind."

"Impossible." Henry winced at both the pain and the revelation.

"There you go again. You can see them with your own eyes, yet you refuse to believe what you see. I know," he said as if suddenly an inspiration. "You need to more proof. Perhaps touching one of them will help. Caleb?"

On cue, Caleb stiffly lowered himself to his knees and leaned directly over Henry, bringing his half-eaten face within inches of the man's horrified face. Henry twisted away, despite the pain, wrinkling his face in disgust. "O god, take him away. Get him out of here."

Caleb reached a boney hand and grasped Henry's chin, forcibly twisting his head to look at him. A maggot dropped from the eye socket onto Henry's face and he cried out, "Get it off me! Get it off me!" With a boney finger, Caleb flicked the maggot away and then jerkily stood up.

Breathing heavily, lucidity settled within, and Henry looked up at the two dead men. "OK, OK, I suppose it's possible." Looking directly at Mason, he took a deep breath to settle himself. "Well Marshal, looks like you've won this time. Why am I staked out like this?"

Mason bent forward and said, "Remember when you said I determine who lives and dies? Well, looks like there might be some truth to that." Pointing to de la Fuente he said, "You stole his gold and then you killed Caleb to take it for yourself. The way I figure it, they have a right to justice. But since no court would accept their complaints, I'm rendering verdict in the judge's place."

"What?!" he sputtered. "You can't do that. You're law-bound to take me back, to face trial."

"You've already faced trial," Mason indifferently replied. "I called these two witnesses and you've been found guilty. The evidence is also in the trailer attached to your machine. It was an open and shut case."

"What about my statement?" he objected, almost pleading. "Don't I get a say?"

"You did already. You admitted to killing both Caleb and my wife. You're a smart man. How would you adjudicate this?"

"I wouldn't," he quickly replied. "I'd take me back to get a fair trial."

"You had a fair trial," Belle interjected.

Jerking his head to look at Belle, he pleaded, "Are you going to let him get away with this?"

Frowning as though puzzling out some difficult problem, she tilted her head and pursed her lips. "Hmmm. Let me think for a moment. All finished. Yes. I am going to let him get away with this. Remember, you were going to kill me?"

"But I was only bluffing," he implored. "I wouldn't have hurt you. You know that."

"Oh sure," she shook her head in feigned surprise. "Now you say that."

"But you have to believe me," he begged.

"Too late," she sweetly smiled. "We'll miss you at the Bird Cage." She then turned her back to him to where Mason was holding conversation with Caleb and de la Fuente.

"We'll help you unload the trailer," Mason said. "I suggest you consolidate the gold in as few crates as possible.

Once we're finished, we'll take the machine and leave. He's yours," he said, nodding at the prone man behind him. Looking at de la Fuente he said, "*Entiendes Usted*? Do you understand?"

Diaco de la Fuente nodded and pointed at Henry then at himself.

"Yes. *Sí*. He is yours. *Él es tuyo*."

De la Fuente placed both hands on his chest and bowed in thanks.

"You can't leave me here," Henry called out.

Ignoring him, Mason and Belle walked with Caleb and de la Fuente to the trailer still attached to the MATE. While the prospector and the conquistador awkwardly climbed up on the trailer, Mason searched for something to open the crates, finally finding a claw hammer amongst the tools on the MATE.

For the next hour, Mason opened the crates while the other three dumped the contents out, retrieving the gold items from the sand and placing them in a neat pile in one corner of the trailer. Occasionally, Belle would pause to look at a trinket, a necklace, a ring or some other jewelry item. Mason noticed that whenever she did that, the other two would pause ever so slightly and surreptitiously watch her. Oblivious to their stares, Belle would admire it for a bit, then place the item in the growing pile.

Finally, they reduced the thirty-eight crates of sand and gold to fifteen of just gold, which they carefully arranged and neatly stacked on the ground. Pausing, to look at the results, de la Fuente picked up a crate and motioned for Mason to take it.

"No thanks," Mason said, waving him away. "Only a fool would think this would make life easier. You keep it. Hide it somewhere no one will ever look."

Tilting his head in confusion, de la Fuente tried again.

"No, *gracias*. *No lo quiero*. I don't want it."

With a bemused shrug, de la Fuente made the same gesture to Belle.

"*Pero no, muchas gracias*. *Es suyo*. It's yours."

324

De la Fuente looked at each of them in turn, shrugged and returned the crate to the stack.

Turning to Belle, Mason ticked his head towards the MATE and said, "Do you know how to drive that thing?"

"I think so," she said, brushing her hands. "I watched him when we were driving the few times in the past, though I did miss a lot on this last trip."

"You can't do this," Henry called out. "What kind of lawman are you? You'll have to live with this. This will be on your conscience."

"Now that's true," Mason agreed. "I will have to live with this. But then, I've had to live with worse." Turning to Belle, he said, "How about we leave these three alone to get reacquainted."

"Good idea," she smiled, slipping an arm around his. They were next to the MATE when they turned around to see Caleb and de la Fuente squatting on either side of the splayed Henry, taking turns poking him. He squirmed with each poke, loudly wailing for Mason to come back, begging the Marshal not to leave him here.

Ignoring him, they climbed aboard. Belle looked at the control panel then at Mason who was settling in next to her. "We'll need wood to fuel the boiler."

Giving her a bemused smile, he climbed back down and started collecting deadwood while she worked on stoking the low embers in the fire box. Mason made several trips, depositing armloads of dry mesquite and dead limbs. By the last run, Belle had pressure building and was in position.

"Just pile that there," she directed, pointing to the tinder box.

Climbing up to sit next to her, he gave her a warm appraising smile. "You look good," he impishly grinned.

Smirking, she bumped her shoulder against him. "I've looked better. Let's see if I remember how to work this thing."

Thankful that Henry had positioned the MATE for an easy escape, Belle pushed the Johnson bar forward and opened the cylinder cocks. Releasing the engine brakes, she opened the throttle and the MATE lurched forward.

325

Slowly motoring around the central grouping of trees, she headed towards the trail when she caught Caleb waving at her and lumbering towards her. Applying the brakes, she brought the MATE to halt.

Caleb walked over to Mason's side and beckoned him to bend down. As Mason leaned over, Caleb held out a closed fist. Mason reached down and Caleb placed something in his hand. Mason opened his hand and saw a stunning gold ring set with a large flawless amethyst. Caleb pointed to Mason then to Belle then clasped both his hands to his heart.

"I understand," Mason smiled. "Yes. Thank you."

Giving him what passed for a smile, Caleb jerkily walked away to join de la Fuente in tormenting Henry whose plaintive cries begging for help increased in urgency.

"What was that about?" she asked with more than passing curiosity.

"Something between him and me," he mysteriously replied.

Henry's wailings interrupted her questioning. "What do you think will happen to him?" Belle wondered.

"Not something I care to think about," Mason shrugged. "Knowing those two, he'll get what he deserves." He saw movement beyond them and Nantan emerged from a clump of scrub brush. Wide-eyed, he gave Caleb and de la Fuente wide berth, hustling over to Mason and Belle.

"Isn't that Mister Mitchell on the ground?" he nervously asked.

"Yup," Mason nonchalantly replied.

Nantan looked back and forth between the two sitting in the Pilot's seat, both quite unaffected by what was happening behind them.

"Want a ride?" Belle cheerfully asked.

With an unconvincing, "Sure," he positioned himself in the trailer, staring at the two dead men poking and tormenting the archaeologist. "Who are they?"

"Friends of Mister Mitchell," Mason offhandedly replied.

"Are they –"

"Dead?" he said. "Yes. Didn't you once say that you believed someone could come back from the dead?"

"In *theory*, yes," he answered, captivated by the scene. Forcing himself to drag his gaze away, he noticed Mason's mount off to the side. "Isn't that your horse?"

"Yes."

Nantan was about to ask what happened when he saw the twin wires leading from the dead animal to the thick scrub across the trail. "Sorry. He had my stun gun," he said by way of apology and explanation. "I probably should get it." Without waiting for a reply, he leaped out of the trailer and followed the wires into the scrub, returning moments later with the weapon.

As he walked back to the trailer, his head and eyes swiveled until he was walking backwards, unable to break his macabre fascination with the two dead men tormenting Henry. Caleb was picking maggots off his decaying flesh and dangling them over the staked-out man. With each release of the squiggling worms, Henry cried out in abject panic.

Seeing the machinist, Henry wailed, "Nantan! Don't let them leave me here!"

Jerking his gaze away as though stung, Nantan tossed the stun gun in the trailer and hustled back aboard. Wedging himself into a corner so he could keep an eye on what was happening, he called over his shoulder, "Let's get out of here."

"Hold on to your hats," Belle announced, releasing the brakes.

When Henry saw the MATE sluggishly move forward, his pleas became more frantic. As the MATE gathered speed, his distress turned to anger and he lashed out with venom, but his words were quickly lost in the distance.

Belle expertly navigated back the way they had come and soon enough they were out of the Dragoon Mountains and onto the level prairie. Mason studied Belle out the corner of his eye. Her hands on the steering mechanisms controlling the mechanical beast, she could barely contain her enthusiasm.   He was about to say something when she snapped her head to him, her eyes bright with excitement.

"Can I keep this?" she gushed.

Bursting a laugh, he nodded. "Don't see why not. He won't be using it anymore." Glancing back at Nantan who continued staring back at the mountains, he said, "You may have to clear it with the machinists first."

Nodding happily, she turned her attention back to driving. When her stomach grumbled, she looked over at Mason. "I'm starving. Take a girl to dinner?"

"I'd be delighted to," he said,

"You won't be embarrassed to be seen with a madam?" she teased.

"I would be proud to be seen with you," he soberly answered.

"That's what I hoped you'd say." There was a pause before she leaned heavily into him. Gazing directly into his eyes, she said, "You're mine now. Understand?" It wasn't a request.

Locking her gaze with his, he said, "That's what I hoped you'd say."

Breaking out into a broad smile, she snuggled tighter against him, thinking this was just about the best two days she'd had in a long time.

Mason wrapped an arm around her then looked back at Nantan who was wedged into the near corner of the trailer. In the distance above them, Taboca followed in his airship. Inhaling a contented sigh, he was thankful for the two machinists. They had put themselves in danger to help him. He would not forget their loyalty. Feeling Belle beside him, he mused that his life just got better. Abruptly his father-in-law came to mind, or was that now *former* father-in-law. Whichever, he would deal with him when the time came. Right now, it was enough to get back to Tombstone and see how bad the fire was.

Casting an affectionate gaze at her, he abruptly frowned when he pictured them living together and the immediate problem of their union. One of them was going to have to learn how to cook and it sure wasn't going to be him.

Studying her, he quietly chuckled knowing that if it came to a test of wills, she wasn't going to cook either. Leaning back to look out over the chugging engine towards the town, he mused that Tombstone had plenty of restaurants and eating out wasn't such a bad option after all. Besides, when Reginald Worthington initiated his revenge for Elizabeth's death, they wouldn't have time to worry about what or where to eat.

But Worthington could wait. For now, he just wanted to get back to Tombstone, check out the fire damage then spend the rest of the day and night in the arms of this incredible woman. His future had certainly improved.

The adventure continues in *An Ounce of Lead*

Thank you for choosing to read this story! If you enjoyed
this book, please leave an Amazon Review.
Thanks for reading!
-pdmac

WEBSITE
www.pdmac-author.com

FACEBOOK
www.facebook.com/pdmacauthor/

OTHER BOOKS

Teen & Young Adult Coming of Age Fantasy:
The Wyvern Chronicles

The Sixth Kingdom
A Spy in the Court
Raising the Dead
Wizard King

Bridge Quest: A GameLit Adventure Series

Bridge Quest
Orc's Bane
Lord of Innis Torr

Steampunk Western: Tombstone Trilogy

Fool's Gold
An Ounce of Lead
The Devil's Disciple (Coming Soon)

Viking Time Travel Romance

Beyond Her Touch

A Dystopian Novel

Rebirth of Angels

A Time Travel Novella

Ctrl Z: The Do Over Stone

Poetry
a young man no more

CO-AUTHORED BOOKS

Dragons of Isentol

Throne of Deceit
Rune Marked
Empire of Serpents